BARBARA DELINSKY

Friends & Lovers

HQN™

ISBN-13: 978-0-373-77494-4

FRIENDS & LOVERS

Copyright © 2010 by Harlequin Books S.A.

The publisher acknowledges the copyright holder of the individual works as follows:

HAVING FAITH
Copyright © 1990 by Barbara Delinsky

THE DREAM
Copyright © 1990 by Barbara Delinsky

Recycling programs
for this product may
not exist in your area.

www.HQNBooks.com

Printed in U.S.A.

CONTENTS

HAVING FAITH

CHAPTER ONE

"JUST WAIT." Laura Leindecker's voice was soft and riddled with pain. "You'll see. He comes across as being honest and charming, and that's what people think he is. That's what I thought he was. For twenty-four years, that's what I thought." She swallowed hard in a bid for strength. "But I know better now. He's not what he seems. He cheats and he lies."

Ignoring the headache that was part and parcel of late afternoon on a hell of a day, Faith Barry came forward, bracing her elbows on her desk. "Did he come right out and confess to having an affair?"

Laura swallowed again. "He had no choice. I found the note. It was right there in the pocket of his trench coat. I'm sure he meant for me to find it. He was the one who asked me to take the coat to the dry cleaner, and he knew I'd check the pockets."

"How did he know that?"

"Because I always do it. Bruce is a tightwad, still he leaves money in his pockets." She frowned. "I think he does it to test me. He's always telling me that I don't really work. But what does he expect," she asked, growing beseechful, "when he has me doing this, that and the other for him all day long? It takes time to see to his custodial needs. But that's my job. So I check his pockets." She paused. "Only there wasn't any money this time." Her voice shook. "Just the note."

Faith nodded, which, aside from injecting an occasional question, was pretty much what she'd been doing for the past fifteen minutes. Laura Leindecker's story wasn't a new one. Faith heard similar ones often, and though the details might differ, the anger, the hurt, the sense of betrayal were the same.

Faith hurt for her. She knew that her questioning didn't help. Still, it was a necessary means to an end. "Can you tell me what the note said?" she asked gently.

Laura looked at the carpeted floor while she gathered her wits. Keeping her lids lowered against humiliation, she said, "'Better than ever. Next week, same time, same place.'" Her eyes rose, filled with hurt. "It was written on notepaper from the Four Seasons. That's our favorite hotel. We've eaten at the restaurant there a dozen times in as many months, and I'm not exaggerating. And he had the gall to take her there."

"To the restaurant?" Faith asked. "Do you think he'd risk that kind of exposure?" She knew of Bruce Leindecker. Most Bostonians did. He'd made his name in real estate, and while he was far from a mega-mogul, his face was well-known.

"I wouldn't put *anything* past him," Laura cried in a moment's lapse of composure. "No decent human being would risk that kind of exposure, but then no decent human being would cheat on a woman who's been faithful and loving and giving and patient and understanding and solicitous for twenty-four years!"

Faith had to marvel at Laura if, indeed, she'd been all those things for so long. Faith had been married for eight years, and in that time she'd only managed to stay faithful. Somehow, all the rest had gone down the tubes—but mutually so. The divorce had been amicable.

"Do you have children?" she asked. She thought she remembered reading about some, but she wasn't sure.

"Two," Laura told her and let out a defeated breath. "They trusted him, too, though it's a miracle. I can't begin to count the number of times over the years when he was to be at a football game or a dance recital and then didn't arrive until the janitors were closing up." She paled when a new thought hit. "I wonder how many of those times he was with a paramour. There were so many opportunities. So many late nights. So many business trips."

"Did you ever suspect anything?"

"No. I told you. I trusted him. I was a fool." She pressed a finger over her lip. When that was ineffective in stanching her tears, she took a handkerchief from her purse, pressed it to her nose, then dabbed at the corners of her eyes.

Faith remembered the first time she'd had a client break down in her office. She'd wanted to put her arms around the woman and tell her everything was going to be all right, except it wasn't true. That particular woman was on welfare, had two preschoolers and chronic asthma, and didn't know how to balance a checkbook, let alone fill out a job application.

Laura Leindecker's situation was different. She was older, for one thing, early fifties, perhaps, and the children were probably grown. She was also more formal, very pretty, elegant in an understated way. She seemed in good health, but Faith knew looks could be deceiving. One thing was sure, though. She wasn't on welfare.

Still, she was in pain. Rich or poor, it didn't matter. Infidelity hurt. Betrayal hurt. The pending dissolution of something that had stood for nearly a quarter century hurt.

Faith waited until Laura was in control again. Quietly

she said, "I know that this is all very difficult for you, Mrs. Leindecker, but if I'm to represent you, I'll have to know more. When you confronted your husband with the note, when he admitted to having the affair, how did he react?"

Laura brooded on that for a minute. "He was charming."

"Charming…how?"

"He acted totally humbled. He apologized. He said he'd made a mistake. He almost cried." She shot a teary glance skyward. "Bruce has never cried in his life. Calm, even-tempered, in control—that's Bruce."

"Perhaps if he nearly cried, it's a sign he was truly sorry."

"No. It was an act."

"Maybe he's only now realizing the ramifications of what he's done."

"No doubt," Laura agreed a bit facetiously. "He's wondering where he's going to sleep tonight. I told him I'd call the police if he tried coming home."

Faith was uneasy with threats, particularly ones that would be impossible to enforce. Unless Laura could show that her husband posed a physical danger to her, the police wouldn't do a thing—except report the call in the local newspaper the next week. Once a domestic quarrel went public like that, things were harder to resolve.

"Where were you when you told him this?"

"In his office. When I found that note, I dropped everything and raced right in there. I've never been so angry in my entire life."

Faith could believe that, since Laura struck her as being a relatively sedate soul. But humiliation and hurt often found an outlet in anger.

"He kept telling me to quiet down," Laura went on.

"He didn't want anyone in the office to think something was wrong." Her gentle voice went higher. "This is a man who has a weekly tryst with a woman who isn't his wife at a hotel where any number of people can recognize him, and he's worried about being embarrassed at work?" And higher. "Well, what about me? Do you think I'll be able to show my face ever again in that hotel and not be mortified?"

"You will," Faith assured her in a calming tone. "Given who and what your husband is, he was probably discreet."

"At the Four Seasons?"

"There are ways. A room can be taken by the woman. The man arrives after her. No one has to know what floor he goes to or what business he's on. It's simple."

"It's disgusting."

"Yes, but it's done all the time, and with no one the wiser save a wife who finds a note in her husband's coat. Do you have any idea who the woman is?"

"He refused to tell me."

"Do you know how long it's been going on?"

"He wouldn't tell me that, either. He's protecting her. He's afraid I'll go after her in a divorce suit."

"You don't need to go after anyone. Not in this state. The fight won't be about the divorce, just the settlement."

"And I want a big one," Laura said in a show of bravado. "I sacrificed the best years of my life for that man. He was a nobody when I met him. I stood by him through the early years. I was patient. I gave him support. I saw that his needs were filled—" She stopped, looking stricken. Then she grew defensive. "Yes, I *did* fill his needs. It's not my fault that he had to further prove his virility. He should have known better. This is going to cost him."

"It's going to cost you, too, Mrs. Leindecker," Faith felt compelled to point out, albeit gently, "and I'm not only talking about my fee. I'm talking about the emotional pain involved in divorce. You may feel that nothing can be worse than finding a note in your husband's coat pocket, but that's not so. If you decide to file for divorce, things could be harder than you imagine. You'll be alone for the first time in twenty-four years. Have you thought about that? Is it what you want?" She let the question sink in for a minute. "And beyond the emotional, there's the physical settlement. If your husband agrees to your demands, that's fine. If he doesn't, the trouble's just begun."

Laura eyed her warily. "You're trying to talk me out of this. Why?"

"Because that's my job."

"I thought your job was to represent me. You have the reputation of being a tough lawyer who fights hard for her clients. I'm willing to pay you to fight hard for me. Why won't you?"

"I will, if that's what you truly want. But as a lawyer, I have a moral obligation to try to salvage the marriage before we end it." She couldn't stress the point enough. "As an officer of the court in this state, I have an *ethical* obligation to do that. No-fault divorce doesn't mean that the marital gates should swing open and shut with the flick of a finger." She paused. "Some people come to me after years of marital counseling and months of discussing divorce. You and your husband haven't done either of those things—at least, not to my knowledge. Have you ever had marital counseling?"

"No."

"Have you ever considered divorce before?"

"No. I told you. I trusted him. I was completely taken in."

Faith looked down at her hands, laced and unlaced them, then sat back in her seat. "You had a shock this morning when you found that note. Sometimes a shock like that starts certain wheels moving. They pick up speed and propel you toward something that, if you were to stop and really think about it, you might not want."

Laura clutched the lip of her purse. "I want a divorce."

"You haven't even slept on the thought."

"I want a divorce."

"Are you sure that there isn't the slightest chance of a reconciliation?"

"Yes, I'm sure. I can't trust Bruce anymore. I want a divorce. Will you represent me?"

Faith recognized stubbornness when she saw it, but she had a stubborn streak of her own. "I'll represent you, but only if you go home and think really hard about what you want to do. Today's Friday. If by next Tuesday you still feel that there's no hope for the marriage, I'll help you get your divorce." When she saw Laura pull a checkbook from her purse, she held up a hand. "Wait until Tuesday. If the divorce is what you want, I'll take a retainer then."

"I thought you'd want the money now," Laura said in surprise. "Aren't you afraid that after taking up your time today, I may turn around and go to another lawyer?"

Faith smiled. It was a tired smile, subdued by her headache, not in the least bit smug. But it held pride. "You may, and that's your choice. I think, though, that I offer something unique. I'm a woman and I'm tough. I also happen to get along with most every judge I've faced, and that's what's different here. I'm not strident, like some of my colleagues. I'm not militant. I'm a professional, and a professional gets results. So if results are what you want, you'll be back."

LAURA LEINDECKER LEFT shortly after that, which was none too soon for Faith who immediately went off in search of a painkiller. Her secretary didn't have any, but she'd half expected that, since Loni was as close to a flower child as a 1990's woman could be. She was sweet and extremely capable, and Faith found a nostalgic charm in her dedication to all things natural and pure, but she had no painkillers.

Nor did Monica, the colleague with whom Faith shared the suite of offices and Loni.

So Faith returned to her desk, determined to beat the headache with sheer willpower, and set about answering the phone calls she'd deliberately left for the end of the day. Several of them were difficult and required adjunctive calls, such as the one to the client suing for custody of her eleven-year-old son, whom she'd just learned was picked up for shoplifting in the local five-and-dime, or the one to the client who had shown up in a hospital the night before with injuries from a beating given her by the husband who, by order of the court, had been forbidden to approach her.

Sheer willpower didn't have much of a chance against emotional situations like those, and by the time Faith hung up the phone, her headache was no better. So she closed her eyes, put her head in her hands and concentrated on relaxing. But it had been a hard week, and her tension reflected that. She was grateful it was Friday. Though she had plenty of work to do over the weekend, the pace of weekend work was different.

Buoyed by that thought, she reached for a small recorder to dictate several letters. Loni had left for the day, which was fine for the letters since they didn't have to be typed until Monday. It wasn't so fine for the phone. Before Faith had a chance to turn the line over to the answering service, she received back-to-back calls that were both tedious and time-consuming. By the time she finally hung up the phone, she'd just about had it.

That was when the buzzer rang in the outer office. Someone was at the front door of the suite, locked now that Loni was gone. For a minute, Faith considered ignoring it. She considered curling up in a ball in the corner of the sofa, burying her aching head under her arms and shirking every legal responsibility she had. Last time the buzzer had rung after hours, though, it had been a seventeen-year-old girl who had seen Faith on television and wanted help in stopping her parents from making her abort the baby she carried.

Rubbing her temple, Faith left her office. She was barely into the reception area when she felt a wave of warmth. The face beyond the glass door was a familiar one, not a client, but a friend.

She opened the door and smiled up at the tall, dark-haired man who stood there. "Sawyer," she said, almost in a sigh. She slipped her arms around his waist and gave him a hug. "How are you?"

"Better now, sexy lady," he drawled, squeezing her tightly. Then he held her back. "Am I interrupting anything?"

"Work. Always work."

"You work too hard."

"Look who's talking," she scolded, but she was delighted he was there. Taking his hand, she drew him into the office. "I haven't seen you in months. How can that be, Sawyer? We work in the same profession. We work in the same specialty. We even work in the same building. Why don't we ever bump into each other?"

"Good question," he decided. "I think you're avoiding me."

"Me? But you're my best friend!" When he arched a

brow, she amended that to, "My best boy friend." When his mouth quirked, she said, "Male friend. My best male friend. I wouldn't have made it through law school without you. Or made it through those early days at Matsker and Lynn. Or had the courage to leave there and go out on my own."

"The feeling's mutual, Faith. You know that." He gave her a quick once-over in appreciation of the fact that she looked professional but individual. Both qualities applied to her practice, as well. "I'm proud of you," he said with a grin. "I'm really proud of you. You've done well for yourself."

As she held his gaze, her own grew melancholy. "I suppose."

"What do you mean, you suppose? Look at your practice."

"That's what I've been doing. All week long."

"And you have a headache," he said, suddenly seeing it in her eyes as he'd done countless other times when she'd been under strain. "And," he went on, "you don't have anything to take for it. Why don't you ever buy aspirin?"

"I do. It's at home."

"But you don't need it there. You need it here." Taking her shoulder, he ushered her to the sofa and pushed her down. "Stay put. I'll be right back." Before she could protest, he was out the door and jogging down the hall to the stairs.

She had to smile. Sawyer wasn't an elevator person any more than she was, which was, in fact, how they had originally met. Uptight but eager first-year students, they had literally bumped into each in a stairwell at the law library. Once they'd picked up the scattered books, papers and themselves, they'd started to talk. Though

Faith had been black-and-blue for a week from the encounter, the friend she'd found in Sawyer had been worth the discoloration.

She took elevators more now, particularly after hours or when she faced a climb of four or more flights in high heels. Sawyer's office was six floors up. But he was a man, a tall, broad-shouldered man who wasn't worried about rape. Nor was he wearing high heels.

Chuckling at that thought, she put her head back, closed her eyes and sat quietly. In a matter of minutes, Sawyer was back with the pills in his hand. He took a cup of water from the bubbler and waited while she swallowed the aspirin. Then he leaned against Loni's desk with his long legs crossed at the ankles.

"It really *is* pretty amazing," he remarked.

"What is?"

"That we don't run into each other more. I miss seeing you. How've you been?"

She nodded and smiled. "Not bad. Busy. That's good, I guess."

"It is good. How are things at home?"

"Quiet," she said in a voice that was just that. "Lonely sometimes, but it's better this way. More honest. Jack and I went in different directions. For too long we pretended something was left, but it wasn't." She rested her head against the sofa back, but her eyes were fixed intently on Sawyer. "You know what I mean, don't you."

Sawyer knew. And he knew Faith knew he knew, because she'd known his wife. Joanna had needed something else, too. They were married soon after he returned from Vietnam, and for two years she nursed him back to health physically and emotionally. She was good at her job. He had recovered, gone through law school and entered a profession in which he thrived. Joanna hadn't known what

to do with the strong and independent man he became.
In the end, she found someone who needed her more.

"She married him," he told Faith.

"The fellow with MS?"

He nodded. "She'll devote her life to him. I admire
her for that."

"Do you talk with her often?"

"Nah. She's busy. I'm busy. She knows she can come to
me if she ever runs into trouble. I owe her a lot. I think I'll
always feel that way. But we weren't very good at being
husband and wife, and after a while, the constant trying
was a strain."

Faith thought about the irony of two divorce lawyers
being divorced. "Makes you wonder, doesn't it? Did we
go into this field because we knew firsthand the pitfalls of
marriage? Or did we see the pitfalls of marriage *because*
we went into this field?"

"Had to be the first," Sawyer decided without pause.
"We were both having doubts about our marriages even
back when we were in law school."

"Not really doubts. Frustrations, and they weren't all
that bad. It's just that we talked about them, you and I.
Some people don't. Some people suffer year after year
in silence. Just this afternoon I met with a woman who
wants to end a twenty-four-year marriage. She was telling me that—"

He held up a hand. "Shh. Don't say it."

"There's not much to say, just that she never thought
to—"

"Careful, Faith. That woman is one of the reasons I'm
here."

Faith frowned. "Laura Leindecker?"

"Bruce Leindecker. I'm representing him in the
divorce."

"You're representing Bruce Leindecker?" Faith repeated. Slowly she sat up. As understanding dawned, she broke into a cautious smile. "You and I—" her finger went back and forth "—are going to be working together?"

"Yup."

She dropped her hand to her lap, and her smile widened. "After all this time. I don't believe it." In the next instant, the smile vanished. "Can we do it? Don't we know each other too well?" But she answered herself in the next breath. "No. There are no grounds for conflict of interest as long as neither of us compromises his client by saying too much. Right?"

"Right," Sawyer said. He folded his arms across his chest.

"Good thing you stopped me a minute ago."

"Uh-huh."

But she was confused. "Who told you I was defending Mrs. Leindecker?"

"Mr. Leindecker."

"How did he know? It's been barely two hours since the woman walked out of here, and we don't even have a formal agreement."

"She seems to think you do. The minute she left you, she called her husband to gloat."

Faith squirmed a little inside. "Gloat—was that his term or yours?"

"Does it matter?"

"Yes. Because it's wrong. Laura Leindecker was angry and hurt. Even if she was the type—which I don't think she is—I doubt she was up for gloating."

"You underestimate the woman," Sawyer said like a man.

"Have you ever met her?"

"No, but her husband knows her well. It sounds like gloating is among the mildest of her faults."

"Sawyer, that man cheated on her," Faith argued, immediately taking the side of her client, which was the rule of thumb in discussions between lawyers. "She's been a loyal wife for twenty-four years and—"

"She has a martyr complex. She's prim and proper and not very flexible when it comes to her husband's business demands. Don't let her con you into believing that she's an angel, Faith. No man turns his back on an angel."

Faith's jaw dropped. "I don't believe this. Are you saying that he was *justified* in philandering?"

"No. All I'm saying is that there are two sides to every story."

"Precisely. That's why we'll take this case before a judge and, if need be, a jury."

"Or settle out of court."

"Or not handle it at all." Her voice mellowed. "Look what just happened. We have to be careful, Sawyer. When we're together we talk. It would be all too easy to discuss things we shouldn't." She chewed on her cheek for a minute, then rose from the sofa and walked to the far side of the room. "This isn't the way I imagined it. I always wanted to work on the *same* side as you. I thought maybe we'd represent codefendants in some kind of civil suit." Turning, she started back toward him. "I don't want to fight you."

He arched a brow. "You can always tell Mrs. Leindecker that you won't represent her."

"But she has a right to representation."

"Let someone else do it."

She stopped talking. "You'd like that, wouldn't you? And your client would like it. He's scared. That was why he called you so quickly. He's scared, because he knows

I fight hard." She rather liked that thought. She didn't like the next, though. "Is that why you stopped in here, Sawyer? Did you come to try to talk me off this case?"

"Absolutely not," Sawyer said, coming to his feet. "I want to work with you, even if we are on opposite sides of the case. I've heard you're good. I want to see how good. But if working against me will inhibit you—"

"Why should it?"

"Because we're friends."

"Will our friendship inhibit *you?*"

"Of course not," he said crossly. "A client is a client. Every one deserves the best I can give."

"Should I be different? More partial? More emotional? Should I be making any less of a commitment to my clients than you make to yours?"

"Take it easy, Faith. You're making something out of nothing."

"No," she said, but more thoughtfully. "I know you, Sawyer. Remember the hours we used to spend talking? Remember the times we discussed sexual stereotypes? Remember the times you confessed that you believed women were too emotional for certain types of jobs?"

"I was talking about the presidency of the country, and I still feel that way."

"And I still think you're wrong."

"Fine. Good. I respect that."

She came closer. "I also think your opinions go beyond the presidency. You think women are too emotional, period."

"Not true. Just too emotional for certain jobs."

"Like the presidency."

"I've already said that."

"Or Chairman of the Board of General Motors?"

"What woman is interested in cars? Chairman of the Board of General Foods, now there's a possibility…."

"Sawyer, that's awful!" she cried. She was standing directly before him, hands on hips, chin set. "Talk about stereotypes. You don't have to be interested in cars to be involved with General Motors. You have to be interested in big business and in profits, and if you try to tell me that women aren't economically savvy, I'll scream."

He did his best not to grin. "Calm down, Faith. You're getting too emotional."

"Too emotional?" she echoed, but she saw the humor of the situation. And she couldn't be angry at Sawyer. He was too nice a guy. "Why is it that when a man raises his voice he's being emphatic, but when a woman does it she's being emotional? Answer me that, Sawyer Bell."

"It's all in the voice. A man's voice—raised—is forceful. A woman's is shrill."

"Is that how you see it in the courtroom?"

"Sometimes."

"And it turns off the judge?"

"Or the jury, or both."

"But we lady lawyers are winning cases. How do you explain that?"

His eyes twinkled. "You lady lawyers who are winning cases have learned to be less emotional and more emphatic."

"That's a compliment, I take it?"

"Definitely."

"Do you see those few female execs of Fortune 500 companies as being more emphatic and less emotional?"

"No doubt."

"But they couldn't be President of the U.S. of A."

"Not yet. They may have come a long way, but they still have a long way to go."

"And women like Margaret Thatcher, Indira Gandhi and Golda Meir?"

He grinned. "They weren't trying to rule countries dominated by male chauvinist pigs."

Faith laughed. She'd forgotten how much fun talking with Sawyer was. As parochial as his views of women were, he knew it, even ridiculed it. In that sense he was probably one of the most liberal men she'd ever met.

Slipping an arm around her shoulder, he drew her to his side. "You laugh, Faith. I like that."

"How can I help it? You're irresistible!"

"So are you." His grin gave way to a look of open-eyed hope. "Come with me tonight. There's a tribute for Dewey O'Day at Parker's. It's going to be boring as hell, but I knew the guy. He gave me good coverage when he was with the *Herald,* so I really have to go. Come with me."

She made a face. "Boring as hell, huh? That's not a great selling point."

"Me. You'll be with me. You'll be helping me survive."

"Sawyer, I hate those things."

"So do I, but I have to go." He cupped her shoulders. "If you go too, we'll have fun. It won't last more than an hour or two."

"Or three. I know these things. They drag on forever."

"We'll sneak out before the speeches begin. In the meantime, there'll be food and booze."

"I don't drink."

"Neither do I, so we'll each have one and we won't be bored at all."

"That sounds totally irresponsible."

"So?"

"What about the case?"

"What case?"

"The Leindecker case. Maybe we shouldn't be seen together."

"That's crazy. We're friends. And colleagues. There's no reason why we can't spend time together. We won't be discussing clients, will we?"

"No."

"So? What do you say?"

"Oh, Sawyer." She let out a breath. "I have so much work to do."

"On Friday night?"

"Yes, on Friday night."

"Do it tomorrow."

"I have other stuff to do tomorrow."

"So you'll have a little more. Come on, Faith. Live a little."

She looked dubious. "At a tribute to Dewey O'Day?"

"With *me*. We'll have a good time. I promise."

Faith tried to think back to the last time she'd had a good time. It seemed ages ago. "You promise?"

"I promise."

CHAPTER TWO

THE ROOM WAS PACKED. Everyone who was anyone in Boston political circles was there, as well as members of the business and professional communities who had at one point been touched by Dewey O'Day. That was no small number; the man had been the nose of the *Herald* for forty years. Faith suspected as many people were there to butter up his successor as to pay tribute to Dewey himself. Sawyer confirmed it in a low drawl as they meandered through the crowd.

His whisper swelled to a full voice when he extended a hand to an older man who smiled as they approached. "Senator Cooperthorne. How have you been?"

"Fine, Sawyer."

"Do you know Faith Barry? Faith, this is Peter Cooperthorne, State Senator from Winthrop."

Faith offered her hand and a cordial smile. "It's a pleasure, Senator."

"The pleasure is mine. Good taste, Sawyer. She's a fine-looking woman. Is she yours?"

Sawyer shot Faith an amused glance. "Uh, no. She's a friend. Actually, a lawyer. Actually, a very skilled lawyer. I'm surprised you haven't heard of her. She's something of an authority on family law."

But family law wasn't Peter Cooperthorne's thing, as Faith discovered when he quickly launched into a discussion of the city's latest union dispute. Actually it wasn't so much a discussion as a monologue, and a rambling one at that. Sawyer, who did occasionally dabble in labor law, took the first opportunity to excuse himself and guide Faith away.

"Hot air," he side-mouthed to her. "The man doesn't know diddly about labor psychology, but he has an endless supply of hot air."

"He is the consummate politician," she side-mouthed back, then smiled at a familiar face. "Hi, Tommy. How goes it?"

"Great. But I haven't seen you in a while. You don't come visiting anymore."

Faith sent him a dry look, then made the introductions. "Tommy Lonigan, Sawyer Bell. Tommy is with the Probation Department," she explained to Sawyer. "We've had, uh, mutual clients."

Tommy wasn't leaving it at that. "Faith is the best thing to show her face in the Somerville Court House in years."

"I can believe that," Sawyer said. "Nice meeting you." With a light hand at Faith's back, he started her moving again. "Don't know how he'd know about years," he said under his breath. "He looks like he's fresh out of high school."

"UMass. And he's been out for three years." She nodded at another familiar face, but didn't stop. When Sawyer swept two glasses of wine from a passing tray and handed her one, she took it. They walked on.

"Sawyer!" A dapper-looking man stopped them. Sawyer introduced him as a former client; Faith recognized him as one of the city's major philanthropists. "So you're paying tribute to old Dewey, too?"

"Sure," Sawyer said. "He's been fair to me."

The man leaned closer and lowered his voice. "Wish

I could say the same, but he has a chip on his shoulder when it comes to money. He knocks me in his column every chance he gets, and if it isn't me, it's my car or my house or my art collection. As far as I'm concerned, he should have retired twenty years ago."

"If you feel that way," Faith couldn't help but ask, "why are you here?"

"Because I'm a good sport. And because the governor's showing up later and *he* likes old Dewey." He winked at her, clapped Sawyer on the shoulder and moved on.

Faith looked at Sawyer. "At least he was honest. What do you think he wants from the governor?"

"Probably a job for his new son-in-law. From what I hear, the kid's a real dud." He chinked his wineglass to hers. "Cheers."

"Cheers." She took a swallow and let Sawyer guide her on.

They stopped to greet a mutual acquaintance, a TV reporter who covered the State House and who, when he was off duty, covered himself to the exclusion of most other topics of conversation. Faith thought him a self-centered bore, which she promptly told Sawyer when they finally escaped.

"Not only that," Sawyer announced, "but he sleeps with a teddy bear." He took another swallow of wine.

Faith nearly choked on hers. Laughing, she looked up at him. "A teddy bear? How do you know that?"

"He had an affair with one of the lawyers in our office. She saw the bear."

"Now that's interesting," Faith decided. "Not boring at all." But it was the exception to the rule. For another hour, they wound their way through the crowd, and though they were often stopped by fellow lawyers and other acquaintances, they were never tempted to linger in any one circle for long.

Then the speeches began. "Let's leave," Faith whispered. She and Sawyer were at the back of the room, shoulder to shoulder against the wall. They'd had two glasses of wine apiece, and while they weren't quite tipsy, they weren't quite not. "I'm hungry."

"How can you be hungry?" he whispered back. "You ate a full plate of hors d'oeuvres."

"They were puny and, besides, you ate half of them."

"I did?"

"You did. What would you say to some Peking ravioli and a little kung pao shrimp?"

"I'd say, 'Ah so.'"

Faith snickered.

He leaned closer. "Shh. You'll disturb the MC."

"The MC," she whispered back, "is a lousy speaker. His voice doesn't carry. I can't hear a word he's saying. Who told him to be MC anyway?"

"He's the Speaker of the House. He can do what he wants."

"Except speak."

Sawyer snickered.

"Shh. You'll disturb the MC."

"You want to listen? I thought you wanted to leave."

"Can we?" she asked, eyes lighting up.

"Not yet. I want to hear Dewey."

"But he'll be last. I know how these things work. A million of his cronies will stand up—"

"Not a million. Maybe a dozen."

"At least a dozen, and they'll tell all kinds of lies—"

"Not lies. They'll talk about his good points and joke

about his bad points." He paused. "Yeah, they'll lie." He paused again. "Want to go?"

She grinned. "I thought you'd never ask."

Without another word, they worked their way to the door, crossed through the lobby and went out into the night. A cold blast of air might have cleared their heads some, but the weather was mild, as New England autumns could unexpectedly be. So, light-headed and lighthearted they headed down School Street.

"Not Chinese," Sawyer said, as though he'd been debating the merits of kung pao shrimp ever since Faith had mentioned it. "Want to go to Houlihan's?"

"On a Friday night? We'd never get in."

"Sure we would. All it takes is a ten slipped into the right hand."

But Faith didn't want to go to Houlihan's. "I've been there for lunch three times in the last two weeks. How about Seaside?"

"Talk about lines getting in."

"Talk about slipping a ten—won't it work there?"

But Sawyer didn't want to go to Seaside. "I represented the wife of the owner in a scruffy divorce. Her husband's a bastard. On principle I avoid the place."

Faith could understand that. "How about Zachary's?"

"Too far away. I want to walk. How about the Ritz?"

She screwed up her nose. "Too stuffy."

"And Zachary's isn't?"

"How about the Daily Catch? I want to go to the North End. I feel like squid." She caught his eye. "Do you like squid?"

"I have been known," he said, "to be so mesmerized by the taste of the body of the thing that I forget and leave the tentacles dangling down my chin."

Faith sputtered into a laugh. She looped her arm

through his. "You're fun to be with. Jack would never say anything like that. He'd never *do* anything like that."

"So why did you marry him instead of me?"

"Because I didn't know you when I married Jack. Besides, by the time I met you, you were married to Joanna."

Sawyer grunted. "She never laughed. She smiled sometimes, but she never laughed. She wasn't the type." They turned onto Washington Street and he declared, "Squid sounds just fine. I'm in the mood for the North End. Think there's a festival going on?"

"If there is, we may not get into the Daily Catch."

"We'll get in."

"You're slipping tens again?"

"Don't have to. I represented the owner when the city was giving him liquor-license trouble. We won. He loves me."

Faith tried to decide whether she'd heard about that case, but her mind wasn't as sharp as usual. What she did decide was that it didn't matter whether she'd heard about the case or not. "Why is it you have all these illustrious clients? Mine are nowhere near as exciting."

"So why are you on television all the time?"

"Because I'm attractive, articulate and female." She tugged at his arm and drew him down Water Street. "I want to go home and change first. I'll stick out like a sore thumb walking through the North End in a silk dress and heels, and my feet hurt."

Sawyer was feeling thoroughly agreeable. He had no problem with changing clothes first. And she did have a point. The North End was best enjoyed wearing sneakers. "I'm at Rowes Wharf. You're at Union Wharf. If we stop at my place first, yours is right there on the way to the North End."

So it was decided. They talked as they walked, laughing most of the way once Sawyer got started on jokes. He had a knack for telling a story, could put on an Irish brogue, an Arkansas drawl or a Brooklyn bark with equal skill, and his repertoire was endless. Some of the jokes were funnier than others, some dirtier than others. Faith was muzzy enough to laugh at anything.

By the time they reached his condo, they were feeling quite good, which was why Faith didn't refuse him when he uncorked a chardonnay and poured her a glass.

"I don't drink," she reminded him as she took a sip of the wine. "Mmm. This is nice."

"It should be. It was a gift from a friend's wine cellar on the occasion of my settling a malpractice suit for him." He sampled the wine, then arched an approving brow. "Not bad."

"Not bad at all. Go change. I'm hungry."

Setting his glass on a coffee table, he headed down the hall. "Make yourself comfortable. I'll be right back."

Faith wandered across the living room. The decor registered in the back of her mind as being modern enough, pleasant enough, coordinated enough. The object of her interest, though, was the view from the window. The harbor's darkness was broken by the lights of passing boats, by buildings flanking the water, by the airport. She could see plenty of boats and buildings from her place, but she had nowhere near as good a view of the airport. Sipping her wine, she watched a plane take off, another one land, a second take off, a second one land.

She loved traveling. She'd done some when she'd been growing up, when her father had still been paying the bills and she'd still had the time. After that, she'd slacked off. Traveling with Jack hadn't been much fun. He wanted to see all the places she'd already seen, busy places like

London and Paris, where he could plan out a daily program and sightsee from morning to night. She tried to understand that his job wasn't as demanding as hers. He worked in his father's business, and there was nothing particularly riveting about the manufacture of cardboard boxes. Her job, on the other hand, was both busy and challenging. Her idea of paradise was a long stretch of white sandy beach, a frothy fruit punch and a juicy novel.

So, after a while, she hadn't encouraged Jack to make travel arrangements. She'd contented herself with a week each summer in a rented house on Nantucket, plus whatever legal meetings she could spare the time to attend. But she missed the anticipation of going somewhere new, somewhere just to play.

"Like the view?" Sawyer asked, coming up behind her. He'd changed into jeans and a sweatshirt, and was carrying his wine.

"Oh, yeah." She looked him over. "Not bad, Sawyer. You're staying in shape. Still running?"

"Sure am."

"Every morning?"

"Bright and early. Boston's great at six. Just me and the pigeons and the street cleaners and the dozens of yuppies who live around here and think it's cool to run." He chinked his wineglass to hers. "Cheers."

"Cheers," she said and took a drink. "But you're not a yuppie."

He swallowed his wine. "Nope. Know who is, though?"

"Who?"

He grinned smugly. "Wally Ahearn."

Faith couldn't believe that. "Wally Ahearn? No way. Wally Ahearn was so antiestablishment he was nearly outlawed on the law-school campus."

"But he got his degree."

"Yeah, wearing a gauzy something his guru lent him. Wally Ahearn a yuppie? He *runs?*"

Something about the way she said it—and about the image of Wally as they remembered him in the guru's gown—made them both laugh. Sawyer forced himself to sober, but only after he'd taken a healthy drink of wine. "Trust me, Faith," he said in a trustworthy voice. "Wally no longer looks like a walrus."

"Okay, chalk walrus, and if he's a yuppie, he can't look like a hippie, but I can't, I *can't* see him wearing three-piece suits." She frowned. "He's not actually practicing law, is he?"

"Nope."

"I didn't think so. I always imagined he'd go off to the hills and raise honey bees, or something. Somehow a law degree didn't fit him." She raised the glass to her lips.

"He's a proctologist."

Faith's wine went down the wrong way. Putting a hand on her chest, she began to cough. Sawyer slapped her back, stopping only when she'd caught her breath. "Why do you *say* things like that?" she cried.

"Because it's true." When she gave a final cough, he said, "Take a drink. It'll help." She took a drink, then a deep breath, and when she'd finished doing that, he drew her to the sofa. "Sit."

"I can't sit," she said. "I want to go home and change, then get something to eat." But she sat. After a minute, she began to laugh. "A proctologist? That's too much."

Sawyer retrieved the wine bottle from the counter that separated the kitchen from the living room. "Have I ever lied to you?"

"No, Sawyer."

"I'm an honorable man." He refilled her wineglass,

refilled his own and sank down into the chair across from her. "The last of the good guys." Leaning forward, he chinked his glass to hers. "Cheers."

"Cheers," she said, and took a drink. As the wine warmed her senses, she thought for a minute. "You and Larry O'Neill. The saviors of our class. Where's Larry now?"

"Springfield, Illinois. He's doing tax work."

"I can believe that. He has a big family to support. How many kids now?"

"Eight."

"No!"

But Sawyer nodded. "So help me, eight kids."

"He had three when we graduated, and that was nine years ago. He's been busy."

Sawyer laughed. "His wife is the busy one. Do you remember her?"

"Charlene? Of course, I remember Charlene. She was always pregnant. Still is, I guess." She raised her glass. "To Charlene."

"To Charlene," Sawyer said and took a drink. "So how about you, Faith? Do you want kids?"

"Sure I do. I want twelve."

"Twelve!"

"Three sets of twins and two sets of triplets."

"I can't picture it."

"Why not?" she asked, sounding hurt. "Doctors can do anything nowadays. I put in my order, they get out their little test tubes and their little petri dishes, I get my kids."

"Ahhh," he said sagely.

"That's right, ahhh. So how about you?"

"Me? No way. I'm not getting pregnant with one, let alone twins and triplets. Don't want to ruin my figure."

She laughed, and a grin remained long after the sound had died. She sat back in the sofa, feeling more relaxed than she had in months and months. "You're fun, Sawyer. How could I have forgotten that?"

"Out of sight, out of mind."

"But we always had such good times. Remember the lunches we had with Alvin Breen? Or the seminars we went to? Remember the time we served on a panel together in Pittsfield?"

"Do I ever," he said. There was a wry twist to his lips and a playful gleam in his eye. "You were the only woman, and you took advantage of it to the hilt. You wore a bright red dress, bright red shoes, bright red lipstick, bright red nail polish, and you sat there looking like a perfect piece of fluff. Boy, did you fool them. Their mouths dropped open when you began to speak."

Faith sipped her wine, then said with an innocent tip of her head, "It wasn't my fault they thought I was dumb."

"You let them believe it, you shameless hussy."

"They *chose* to believe it. Most men do."

"Doesn't it make you mad?"

"Mad? When I get such satisfaction seeing them with egg on their faces?"

Sawyer threw back his head and laughed. "I love it," he said, then sat forward. "You're remarkable." He chinked his wineglass to hers. "To you."

"To me," she said with a grin and, with a flourish, finished her wine. She was feeling delightfully warm. Any rough edges that were left over from the week had melted away.

Sawyer rose, took the wineglass from her and set it on the table, then grabbed her hand and drew her up. "Let's go. I'm hungry."

"I think I'm a little high."

"Me, too. We need food."

Minutes later, they were heading down Atlantic Avenue in the general direction of Faith's place. "This is fun," he announced. "I haven't done anything spontaneous in a long time."

"Me, neither. My life is predictable. There's work, work and more work."

"Ever get tired of it?"

"Yup. Then the phone rings, I get a new case and I'm revived."

They walked along at a jaunty pace.

"You're not really representing Dorothea Winchell, are you?" Sawyer asked.

"Sure am."

"She's a fraud."

Faith wasn't at all offended. "Uh-uh. She loved the man. She was with him for ten years. Ten years. And in that time, she took a lot of abuse."

"He chose not to leave her anything in his will."

"He had Alzheimer's. Did he choose, or was he unable to choose? Or did his children prevent him from choosing?"

"You'll lose," Sawyer warned, but playfully. That was the kind of mood he was in.

Faith was in a similar mood. "Losing is relative. As his common-law wife, she has a right to a little protection. We won't get all we're asking, but something is better than nothing." She sent a perky look up at him. "And you're a fine one to be talking. You're representing John Donato. Now, if that isn't a lost cause, I don't know what is."

He was undaunted. "It's a *great* cause. Donato puts up a building. Halfway through construction, the city council finds an obscure code that says the building can't be that tall. Donato is expected to lower the building at a million-dollar loss. The city owes him."

"From what I hear," Faith drawled, looking off toward the Aquarium, "Donato obtained his original permit in a slightly, uh, unorthodox manner."

"Y'heard that, did ya?"

"Yup."

"Who'd you hear it from?"

"I'm not telling. Is it true?"

"Now, if I told you that, it'd be a violation of lawyer-client privilege."

"I won't tell anyone," she whispered loudly.

In answer, he wrapped an arm around her waist and pulled her close. Their hips bumped. Laughing, they adjusted their gaits to match, and walked on. To the left, the lights of the Marketplace lent a gaiety to the night. To the right, the Harbor was unusually serene. They felt peaceful, happy, totally at ease with the night and each other, and because of that, they talked about things they might not have normally discussed.

Such as the people they'd dated since their respective divorces.

"Brandi Payne? You actually went out with Brandi Payne?" Faith asked in good-humored disbelief as they turned into Union Wharf.

"Sure did."

"I hear she's a bitch."

"You hear right. She gives new meaning to the term swelled-headed. I suppose you have to give her some credit. She came in as the Channel 4 anchor when the station was trailing the other two, and she's brought it to the top. But full of herself? Whew!"

"What possessed you to go out with her?"

"We have a mutual friend. He had a party. We met. I

asked her out. I wanted to see what the private persona was like, and boy, did I ever. We ran into Alec Soames and Susan Siler at the restaurant. They were in town to do a signing at the Ritz, and they happen to be a stunning couple. Brandi didn't like that much. She wants all eyes on her. The comments she made to Alec and Susan about their book were bad enough, but the fuss she made about what table we were going to have and whether the service was good enough and whether the butternut-squash soup had too much salt were downright embarrassing."

"Poor Alec and Susan."

"Poor Sawyer."

Faith was grinning as she opened the door to her condo. "What I want to know," she said, punching out the code to turn off the alarm, "is whether you took her to bed." When the alarm didn't stop, she frowned, concentrated, punched out the code a second time.

"That's a very personal question."

"You're a very personal friend. Damn, what's wrong with this?" The alarm was still humming, waiting to be disengaged. Slowly and with deliberation this time, she gave separate emphasis to each digit in the code. Still the alarm resisted. "I don't believe it," she cried.

"Are you hitting the right numbers?"

"I'm hitting 4-3-8-3. That's my phone number." She put two fingers to her forehead and closed her eyes. "Alarm code. 8-2-9-2." She had punched in the first two when noise exploded around them. The noise died just as suddenly when she entered the last 2. She grinned up at Sawyer. "There. All better. But you didn't answer my question. Did you sleep with Brandi Payne?"

"No, I did not."

"Why not? She has a great bod."

"By the time we finished dinner, I was so turned off

by the woman herself that I didn't give a damn about her bod." The phone rang. "Good timing," he said and started toward it. Abruptly he stopped. "Uh, it's yours."

Laughing, Faith turned into the kitchen and answered it. "Yes?" She grew serious. "Emergency 24?" She frowned. "My alarm. Oh, my alarm! I'm so sorry. That was a mistake. I confused my phone number with—no, no, there's no need to call the police. The code? Uh, uh, 3-6-5. Yes. Thank you." She hung up the phone and looked at Sawyer, who was leaning against the doorjamb. "They wanted to make sure I was okay. Wasn't that nice? If I hadn't given them the right code, they'd have called the police. It's a very clever system. As you can see, none of my neighbors have come running to the door to see whether it's me or a burglar in here." She thought for a minute. "Maybe I need a dog. You know, something intimidating. A watchdog."

"But you're afraid of dogs."

"How do you know?"

"I was with you once when you were attacked by a poodle. Don't you remember? It was four or five years ago. We'd just come from lunch at Dini's, and there was this adorable little—"

"Adorable, nothing!" Faith cried, remembering the day. "That dog was vicious! It was coming right at me with its teeth bared."

"You *thought* it was coming right at you, but the fact was that it was headed for a schnauzer behind you. And it didn't have its teeth bared. It was grinning." He chuckled. "Boy, were you scared."

"And you laughed. You laughed at me."

"I couldn't help it. It was funny. You're always so serene-looking, even when you're in court, and then this little dog comes along and—"

"I'm going to change," she interrupted. "I'm hungry."

"Good idea. What's this?"

She had taken a bottle from under a cupboard and was putting it in his hands. "Champagne."

"I think I've had enough to drink."

"So have I. But this is special champagne. It was given to me by Dennis and MaryAnn Johnson when we finally found the right baby for them to adopt. The agencies had given them trouble, because Dennis was convicted of marijuana possession eighteen years ago. Not a spot of trouble since, still he has a record. So we went the private route. It took two years, but the baby is perfect." She grinned. "So this is happy champagne. Open it."

Sawyer looked at the bottle. "Happy champagne, huh?" He was certainly happy. "Why not. You go change, while I open it. I'm feeling underdressed."

Faith leaned close, stretched up to his ear and whispered, "Better underdressed than undressed." She came back down, eyeing him quizzically. "I've never seen you undressed. Do you know that, Sawyer? I've never even seen you without a shirt on. Why didn't we ever go to the beach?"

"We were too busy."

"We went to movies. You and Joanna and Jack and me. Why not to the beach?"

"The beach is for vacations. We never vacationed together."

"Why not? It would have been fun."

"Maybe we didn't trust ourselves. Go change, Faith. I'm hungry."

"Mmm. Me, too," she murmured and went off toward her room.

Sawyer managed to uncork the champagne without too much trouble. He had more trouble finding fluted glasses, then laughed when he realized what he'd gone looking for. Faith wouldn't have fluted glasses any more than he would. A few wineglasses, yes. Wineglasses were good to have on hand in case company popped in with a bottle. Fluted glasses were for more sophisticated drinking, and since Jack hadn't imbibed any more than Joanna, there were no fluted glasses here.

So he took two wineglasses, filled them with champagne and ambled into the living room. It was small and didn't have much furniture, but what it did have was in good taste. Faith had that. Joanna didn't, which wasn't to say that he hadn't liked the house they'd shared. It had been an old thing on the outskirts of Cambridge. They'd bought it soon after they married, thinking that renovating it would be good therapy for Sawyer, and it had been that. He'd taken pride in stripping and staining the woodwork, putting in a new floor, updating the kitchen. It had given him a sense of accomplishment. Joanna's satisfaction came through his—and through filling the place with homespun things. Nothing matched. She had no eye for style or design. She created a cozy clutter that, unfortunately, began to grate on Sawyer when he grew to want breathing space.

Faith's place, small though it was, had breathing space. He was amazed that he thought so, since he'd had enough wine to create the illusion of closeness and warmth, but he felt perfectly comfortable here.

He walked around the sofa and perched against its back, which ran parallel to the glass sliders that looked out on the harbor. Actually, he mused, the view was sideways. It took in as much of the city as the harbor. As for details, he couldn't see many. The glass was reflecting the room behind him more strongly than anything else.

"Cheers," he said, and held one of the wineglasses out

toward his reflection in the glass. He was about to take a sip when his reflection was joined by Faith's. She was wearing jeans and a sweatshirt, and without her heels, seemed suddenly more petite. "Come," he told her reflection. "I want to make a toast."

"Another toast," she breathed. Rounding the sofa, she came to his side and took one of the glasses. "Cheers," she said.

"*I* want to make the toast."

She stopped the glass an inch before her mouth. "Okay. You make the toast."

"Cheers," he said and took a drink.

She laughed, declared his toast, "Profound," and sipped the champagne. "Ah," she said when the last of the bubbles had slipped down her throat. "Nice. Did you miss me?"

"Sure did. I was trying to look out your window, but I couldn't."

"Wait," she said. Holding her glass to the side, she went back through the room and turned off the light. "There." She returned to the nook he'd found behind the sofa. "Like it?"

He stood and moved close to the glass. "Oh, yeah. It's different from mine. You can see the city. And the boats in their slips. You even have a patio."

"You have a balcony."

"This is different. Must be the trees. How did you manage to get trees in here?"

"Sanguinetti Landscaping. They specialize in potted things. Nice flowers and shrubs and plants and stuff. I wanted green."

He turned to look at her. She was faintly lit by the reflection of the city lights, and seemed almost ephemeral.

"You're a very wise girl. I don't understand why some man hasn't snapped you up yet."

"I've only been divorced for a year."

"But you're a catch." He returned to the sofa and sat close by her side. "Didn't someone tell me you dated Paul Agnes for a while?"

"Twice. We went out twice."

"Didn't like him?"

She sipped her champagne. "Not enough."

"To go to bed with him?"

"Right. That was pretty much all he wanted. Why was that, Sawyer? Why *is* that? I thought times had changed. I thought AIDS had put the fear of God into singles. But sex has been the one thing that's first and foremost on the minds of the men I've seen since the divorce. Not that I've seen that many. I'm not in a rush to get involved with anyone. I'm busy with work. I rather like being able to come and go as I please. And I'm not lonely, except sometimes a guy will ask me out for dinner or to a show and it sounds like fun. So I go. And it is fun, until we get back here and he wants to come in. If I say no, he's angry. If I say yes, he's into touchy and feely before you can blink an eye, and when I say no to that, he's doubly angry. So I'm damned both ways. It shouldn't have to be like that."

Sawyer, who'd been sampling his champagne, set the stem of the glass on his knee. "Know what your problem is?"

"No, what? Tell me. I want to know."

"You're too pretty."

"There's no such thing."

"There is, and you are. You're a striking woman. It may be the way you dress. Or the way you carry yourself. Or your confidence. You're feminine without trying to be. It's hard for a man to look at you and not think of sex."

"You don't."

He took a larger swallow from his glass. "That's 'cause you're Jack's girl. You've always been off-limits to me, so I look at you other ways. I know how intelligent and creative and honest and fun you are to be with."

She sent him a glowing smile. "You are my favorite man." She slipped an arm around his waist and raised the other, glass in hand. "To you," she declared.

"To me," he echoed.

They both drank deeply of the champagne. Sawyer slipped from her side. "Hold still. Don't move." He half walked, half ran back to the kitchen, scooped up the champagne bottle and was back.

"Maybe we shouldn't," Faith whispered as she watched him refill their glasses. "I'm hungry."

"Me, too, but we haven't finished with the toasts." Setting the bottle on the floor, he sat beside her again and raised his glass. "To Jack and Joanna."

"Why are we toasting them?"

"Because they're not here to toast themselves."

"But why do they have to be toasted?"

"Because they're good sports. They put up with us." He chuckled, then pulled a straight face. "To Jack and Joanna." He chinked his glass to hers.

"To Jack and Joanna," Faith said and took a drink. Since there were two people in the toast—and since Sawyer seemed to be doing it—she took a second drink on the heels of the first. "Sawyer?"

"Umm?"

"Maybe we should fix them up."

"Jack and Joanna? Nah. Wouldn't work. Joanna's too maternal."

"Jack's paternal. It would be great."

"Only if they had a kid, but they'd never make it in the sack."

"That's an awful thing to say, Sawyer!"

He considered that for a minute. "Yes. I'm sorry." He looked at Faith.

She looked at him. "You're not sorry at all."

"No."

They laughed. This time it was Sawyer who slipped an arm around Faith's waist. "I can tell you anything. Do you know how nice that is?" He tugged her close to give her a hug, but somehow they lost hold of their perch on the back of the sofa and half slid, half fell to the floor. That made them laugh harder.

"Ahhh," Sawyer groaned through his laughter. "Are you okay, Faith?"

"I'm down, but not out," she declared with mock pomposity. More humbly, she said, "Something spattered on my sweatshirt. Am I bleeding?"

"That was champagne. Com'ere." He helped rearrange her body so they were tucked snugly against the sofa and each other, facing the world beyond the glass sliders. Taking only a minute to replenish their glasses of any champagne they may have lost in the fall, he picked up where he'd left off.

"You're special. I don't know any other woman I can do this with. I really can tell you anything. Anything."

From time to time, one word slurred into the next, but it was subtle, too subtle for Faith, in her own less-than-sober state, to notice. "Tell me something," she said. She tapped his chest with her finger. "Tell me something you wouldn't tell anyone else."

He lowered his voice to a whisper. "Joanna was a lousy kisser."

"A lousy kisser? But she was a nurse. What about all that mouth-to-mouth—"

They burst into hysterics, leaning over one another in laughter. Sawyer was the first to recover. "Honest to God, I don't know how she ever did that. When it came time to kiss, she didn't open her mouth. I couldn't get her to open her mouth."

"And I'm sure you were persuasive."

"I tried. She didn't like the feel of it. So I stopped trying after a while." He looked down at her face in the darkness. "Was Jack persuasive?"

"No. He was punctual."

"Punctual? What's punctual got to do with kissing?"

"Jack was a systematic lover. Certain things were to be done certain ways at certain times, and that was that. Kisses were a meeting of the mouth. They started out as pecks. After seventy-seven seconds of that, they became smooches, and after two minutes and ten seconds of that, they got wet. They stopped completely when he began to pant."

"Sounds like a dog," Sawyer observed, and they broke up again. This time when they sobered, Faith set her wineglass aside. Levering herself up with a hand on his chest, she faced him.

"Show me," she ordered. "Show me how you kissed her."

Something in the back of Sawyer's hazy mind told him that would be wrong. "I can't. I've forgotten."

"Then show me how you kiss, period. I'll bet you're good. I want to know what a good kiss is like."

"So do I."

She cupped his face with her hands. "Kiss me, Sawyer. Show me how you do it. Please?"

Sawyer looked at her upturned face, so dimly lit as

they sat on the floor behind the sofa. He looked out at the city, where thousands and thousands of people were enjoying each other, and he wanted to enjoy himself, too. He *was* enjoying himself.

But he wanted to kiss Faith.

For a long moment he thought, or tried to think of the reasons why he shouldn't. But he was high. He couldn't come up with a single one.

CHAPTER THREE

"How I kiss," he said softly. He raised both hands and slid them into her hair so that he could frame her head and tip it up. "The first touch isn't much more than a token. It's kind of like a hello."

"Is this what you used to do when you walked in from work?"

"No. That wasn't much more than a peck on the cheek, and sometimes it wasn't even that. I thought you wanted to know what a *kiss* kiss was like."

"I do."

"A sex kiss?" he asked, daring it because the wine had loosened his tongue.

"Mmm."

"Okay. First, there's this." He lowered his head, put his lips on hers and moved them just a little before lifting his head again. "It's a way of me finding out if you want to be kissed. Sometimes Joanna didn't. Sometimes she'd turn her head. No way I could miss that message. You, on the other hand—" he gave a skewed grin "—didn't pull away, so I can guess that you want more."

Faith did. "That little thing was just a teaser."

"That's what it was supposed to be. It's supposed to make you want more."

"The first step in persuasion? Okay. So what do you do next?"

"More of the same." Lowering his head again, he did

just that. One light touch after another, each gentle but enchanting, none lasting long enough to provide any deep satisfaction.

Faith liked the way his lips could be firm but still gentle. She liked the warmth of his breath and the faint smell of wine. She liked the feeling of leisure. "Mmm. This is nice. Jack would have already moved on. He had to keep on schedule. But this is nice."

Sawyer agreed. He continued to dole out those fetching kisses, because they were captivating even him. In between, he talked. "Schedules don't work when it comes to sex." He brushed the upper bow of her mouth. "The thing is that sometimes after that first hello you want it hard and fast." He sampled the corner of her mouth. "Other times you want it slow. Sometimes," he said, pausing to kiss her chin, "you want to widen your focus a little. Sometimes a woman's mouth makes you curious about how other parts of her taste." He slid his mouth up to her cheek, then her eye, kissing each lightly. He came down the gentle slope of her nose in an inevitable return to her mouth. "Sometimes," he whispered, "you even want to taste with your tongue." He did that, tracing the curve of her mouth, then sucking in a shallow breath. "Mmm, Faith. You taste very good."

Faith's eyes were closed. She felt as though she were floating, no doubt, she reasoned, on the champagne bubbles that shimmered inside her. "Jack never told me that," she said. Her words were wispy and seemed to overlap. "He never talked when he touched me. He was letting his body do the speaking, only I could never hear the words. Why was that?"

"Maybe because you were concentrating on what was going to happen next. That's what Joanna always did. She didn't want to linger. Move right along, folks. Come on, keep going. She wanted to get on with it and get done as soon as possible. She wanted to get it over with."

"I didn't want that," Faith protested, then hesitated. "Well, maybe I did. There was nothing inspiring about what was happening. I never enjoyed Jack's kisses. Certainly not the way I'm enjoying yours. Go on, Sawyer. Kiss me more. I liked what you were doing."

So Sawyer kissed her more, still those same first-stage kisses that he was finding so pleasurable. He knew that the wine had put a glowing sheen on his awareness of the world. He also knew that Faith was a friend, not a sex partner, but that didn't stop him from enjoying the scent of her skin and the dewiness of her mouth. Her lips were soft and pliant, just as a woman's should be. She wasn't reticent, as Joanna had been. Nor was she aggressive, as some other women could be. She let him set the pace, and she responded to it. She seemed very much in tune with him. He liked that.

When he caught a soft sigh slipping from her lips, he opened his mouth to catch it. Her sigh became a gasp, and he quickly pulled back. "You don't like that?"

"I do." She laughed. "I do. It surprised me, that's all. Do it again. I'll be ready this time."

She tried to be, still she wasn't prepared for what happened when Sawyer opened his mouth on hers and gave her the kind of kiss he was primed for. The soft hellos and gently foraging smooches gave way to deeper curiosity. But he didn't have to force her mouth open. It moved with his, reacting to his in all the ways that seemed perfectly natural and utterly right. So he kissed her more deeply, then more deeply again. His tongue found hers, went beyond and around it, swept through the inside of her mouth in a journey that took his breath away.

He gasped for air and tried to steady the fine tremor

that shook his arms. "Whew. That's never happened to me before."

"What?" she whispered. She was taking small, short breaths.

"Getting caught up like that."

"You didn't get caught up with Joanna? I always thought men had to get caught up if they were going to be able to complete the sex act."

"Right," he said, "but at different times and levels. Was Jack always ready at the start?"

"Hard, you mean?"

"Hard, I mean."

"Yes. Jack made up his mind that it was time to make love and, bingo, he was hard. I sometimes wondered whether he needed me at all. It could have been anyone under him."

"That's not true. He loved you."

"In his way, but that kind of love had little to do with the sex we had. I'm telling you. It was preprogrammed sex. Nothing like what we're doing now." Her voice dropped to a whisper. "What do we do next?"

Sawyer was still too aware of her taste on his tongue. Taking his hands from her hair, he sat against the sofa back. "Next we take a break."

"Why?"

"Because I need to catch my breath." It was more than that, he knew. It was a tiny voice inside telling him that something was going to get out of hand if he didn't slow down. He was feeling too good. Whether it was the wine or Faith, he didn't know, but his blood was pumping a little too warmly through his veins. And that last, deep, tongue-twisting kiss had done something to his groin. Things were beginning to feel tight down there. He needed a break.

Reaching for his wineglass, he took a swallow.

Faith was sitting up, eyeing him through the darkness.
"You didn't like it," she whispered, and even in spite of
the non-sound of her voice, he caught bits of accusation
and hurt.

He put a hand to her cheek. "I liked it too well." Slipping his hand down, he caught one of hers and flattened
it over his heart. "Feel that? Is that the feel of something
I don't like?"

"Could be," she said, pouting. She'd never pouted
before in her life. She hated people who pouted and would
have hated herself—if she'd known. "People's hearts bang
when they're upset or afraid. Could be that you don't want
to be doing this, but you feel you have to since I asked.
Is that it?"

"No way! If I didn't want to be doing this, I'd get up
off the rug and walk away. Do you see me doing that?"

"Maybe you're too tired."

"I'm not too tired."

"Or drunk. Maybe your legs won't work."

He set the wineglass aside. "They work just fine. And
I am not drunk," he insisted. He tried to put separate
emphasis on each word, but they slurred together. Pulling
her across his lap and into his arms, he declared, "I liked
what I was doing. I'm going to do it again."

But what he did was different. At least, Faith thought
it was. Not that she could remember the fine details of
what he'd done before, since the amount of wine she'd
drunk robbed her of that clarity, but she remembered the
titillation of it. What he did now was even more titillating.
It was bolder, more confident, persuasive in ways that
had nothing to do with clarity and everything to do with
pure sensation. By the time he ended the kiss, she was
grasping his sweatshirt for dear life.

"Is *that* how you kissed Joanna?" she whispered between short gasps.

He didn't know. He hadn't been consciously thinking of Joanna. He hadn't been consciously thinking of much but the fire that licked at his nerve ends.

"Maybe we'd better stop," he whispered back. Her head was cradled in his arm. He looked down at her face to find features whose eagerness shone through the dim night light.

"I don't want to stop. I want you to show me more." She bobbed up. With the sudden movement, she swayed. Steadying herself, she sat on her haunches between his legs. "I want to do something."

"What?"

"Touch you. Jack didn't like being touched. He didn't think it was important. He didn't need it to be aroused. But it might have helped me." She averted her eyes in a moment's reconsideration. "Maybe not. Jack had a nice enough build, but there was nothing spectacular about it. Maybe my touching him wouldn't have done a thing for either of us." She looked back up at Sawyer and whispered, "Let me touch you. Just a little." She relaxed her grip on his sweatshirt and flattened her hands on his shoulders. Slowly she drew them toward his neck, back to the top of his arms, almost timidly down over the musculature of his upper chest. And everywhere her hands went, her eyes followed.

She let out a single, clipped sound, halfway between a sigh and a gasp. "Like this," she whispered. "Just like this. So nice."

Sawyer didn't know whether he was more pleased with the look of awe on her face or the feel of her hands on his chest. "Wait." His voice was sounding hoarse. "I'll make it even better." Before either of them could begin to wonder whether they were going too far, he whipped the sweatshirt over his head.

Faith sat back on her heels, looking at what he'd bared. "Sawyer, you're so big!"

"Is that good or bad?"

"Good! Good! I hadn't realized…" Her voice trailed off when she brought her hands up and touched him. His skin was warm, even hot, but she was truly stunned by how much of him there was. She'd known he was well-toned, but she hadn't known he was so broad in the shoulders. Moving in a slow, dreamy way, her hands took forever to cover him. Part of that was because the hair on his chest slowed her down. It created a friction that she found surprisingly exciting. Where the hair thinned and tapered into a narrow line, she purposely kept her hand slow to fully appreciate the firmness of his skin.

Sawyer had never been so erotically charted. He leveled his shoulders, took in a deep gulp of air that expanded his chest even more. With that oxygen feeding his brain, he grabbed Faith under the arms and drew her forward. His mouth met hers in a kiss that, for the first time, held raw hunger.

It should have frightened Faith off, or at least alerted her to the fact of his arousal. But she was too aroused, herself, to think of anything but enjoying more. Wrapping her arms around his neck, she immersed herself in the kiss. Somewhere in its midst, he began to caress her breasts, but that fact was lost amid the overall headiness of what she felt.

"Hold on for a second, babe," he dragged his mouth from hers to whisper. He tried to ease her away but she made a throaty sound of protest and tightened her grip on him. Reaching back for her wrists, he dragged them forward. "Wait. I want to touch you." He held her gaze while he covered her breasts with his hands. After a second he began to knead her flesh. It was the most wonderful thing Faith had felt yet. Her expression told him so.

"Didn't Jack do this to you?"

She nodded. "But it didn't feel like this."

"What does it feel like?"

"Good. I don't know. Really good. Did Joanna like it when you touched her breasts?"

He shook his head. "It embarrassed her. Does it embarrass you?"

Faith swallowed. She was breathing more quickly again, and he wasn't even kissing her anymore. "No. It makes me hot."

"I want to take off your shirt."

"Maybe you shouldn't. Maybe this is enough." But he chose that minute to rub his thumbs over her nipples, which were distinct even through her bra and sweatshirt. "Mmm, do it." She reached for the hem herself, and while she was pulling the sweatshirt over her head, Sawyer unhooked her bra. By the time she lowered her arms, she was naked from the waist up. For a minute, she sat very still looking up at him. Her expression would have been wary if her features were working right, but they didn't seem to be responding efficiently to the commands of her brain. "Is this right, what we're doing?" she managed to ask. She was feeling warm and tingly and more than a little muzzy.

"Oh, yeah," he professed a bit brashly. "We're the best of friends, Faith. Nothing between us is wrong. Here." He held his wineglass to her lips and gave her a drink, then took one himself. Then he set the glass aside and touched her. "You have very beautiful breasts. They stand there, just waiting for me."

"Joanna's didn't stand there?"

"They sagged."

She sputtered out a laugh. "You're awful!"

"I'm serious," he said, but softly. His eyes didn't stray from her breasts, and as he talked, his hand moved lightly, if a bit unsteadily over her flesh. "I didn't really see them much. She kept them well hidden. I think she was ashamed of her body." Raising his eyes to hers, he said, "You're not. I can feel it in you. You're proud to be a woman. That's really refreshing, Faith. Do you know how refreshing it is?"

For a minute, Faith couldn't say a word. He was brushing his fingers over the tips of her breasts. She fancied there was a wire stretching from that point to another point deep inside her. With each brush of his fingers the wire twisted.

"Faith?"

"Mmm?"

"Are you okay?"

"I think so."

"How does that feel?"

"Incredibly—" Her voice caught. She tried again. "Incredibly nice." But just then, the wire snapped. She came forward and up on her knees, looking for his kiss. He gave it to her with just the force she needed, but even before the kiss was over, the hunger had grown. Hugging him tightly, she cried, "Sawyer?" Her mouth was by his ear, her high-pitched cry urgent.

"What is it, sweetheart?"

"Something's hurting. I'm feeling so empty inside that it's hurting. Help me. Please, help me."

Sawyer was feeling the same hurt. It had managed to surface through the aura of pleasure that was clouding his view of reality. "Shh, it's okay, sweetheart." He held her tightly for a minute, but the feel of her bare back beneath his arms, not to mention the heaven of her breasts against his chest, drove him on. "Okay," he whispered. He took her mouth in a kiss at the same time that he reached for the snap of her jeans. The zipper was quickly down. She scrambled back to push at the denim and her panties. Together they shimmied both from her legs. Then, while he ran his hands over the parts of her body that were newly uncovered, she hurriedly worked at his jeans.

His zipper was more difficult to lower than hers had been. He was fully aroused, and while that hindered her progress, the discovery excited her beyond belief. No sooner was his fly open when she slipped both hands into his briefs and found the heat waiting there.

"Oh my," she murmured. "Oh my."

"'Oh my' is right," he growled. Tumbling her backward onto the carpet, he quickly shucked his pants. He had to be inside her. There wasn't any doubt in his mind that if he didn't make it fast, he'd die of frustration. Her thighs were open. She rose to meet him when he came between them, and when he entered her, she cried out.

It was the heat. He knew because he felt it himself. It was the heat and the moisture and the wine that made her sheathing so perfect. He tried to savor it, tried to move in and out with the proper understanding of how well she fit him, but he didn't have the patience. He was burning from the inside out, and the only way to fight that was to surge hard and deep toward fulfillment.

Faith was with him all the way. She goaded him on with the movement of her hips, her legs, her restless hands. Their bodies grew damp with sweat, and the sweat mingled. They drove each other ever higher. And when he reached the release he sought, the spasms of his body beat against and between her throbbing.

That should have been the end of it. They should have

fallen apart on the floor, done in by drink or exhaustion or sheer bliss. Somehow, it didn't work that way. They did lie there for a minute until they'd caught their breath. But then it was as if they forgot they'd climaxed. Sawyer was still hard inside her, and when he began to move, she gasped in delight.

It took longer this time. Their movements were slower, more drugged, but no less pleasurable. After a time, it was hard to tell where one peak ended and the next began.

FAITH CAME AWAKE very reluctantly the next morning. On the one hand, things were as always. She was in her bed, where she was every morning when the sun rose over the harbor and skipped sideways into her window. On the other hand, things were different.

Her head hurt, for starters. She discovered that when she tried to move it around on the pillow. Her eyes hurt, too. She opened them a slit, immediately realized her mistake and shut them again.

And she was naked. The sheets felt different against bare skin. Moving a hand to her ribs, she confirmed the finding, but that didn't make it any easier to understand. She never slept naked. She was usually too cold for that. Winter or summer, it didn't matter, she always wore something, preferably long-sleeved and ankle length, to bed.

She was warm, though, and for an instant she wondered whether she'd set the electric blanket higher than usual. But she didn't have the electric blanket on. At least she didn't think she did. It was still in storage. And yet she was warm. Gingerly exploring that warmth, she moved her leg. In the process, she discovered two things.

The first was that her muscles hurt. Not just any old muscles, but those in her legs. To be exact, those in her thighs.

The second was that she wasn't alone. Her foot had hit something solid. It was the source of the heat, she knew. She also knew that it had been well over a year since she'd shared a bed with Jack. She hadn't shared a bed with any other person since.

Momentarily ignoring the pounding in her head and the ache around her eyes, she forced herself to look at the side of the double bed that was usually vacant. It wasn't vacant now. A head capped with dark, rumpled hair was in possession of the second pillow. Just below that head was a sinewed neck, below that a pair of broad shoulders, below that a smoothly muscled back that held remnants of a tan.

Unable to take her eyes from that back, Faith took in a quick breath and sat up. She clutched the sheet to her breasts and swallowed once, hard. That was all it took for the events of the night before to slowly begin to filter through the fog that still clouded her brain.

"Sawyer?" she called in a very low, very shaky voice. The second time around, she managed to make it a little louder, but no less shaky. "Sawyer?"

He didn't move. For a split second she wondered whether it wasn't Sawyer after all but a big dummy he'd left as a joke. She'd like that. She'd like the things—pictures, images, flashes of memory—from the night before to have been make-believe.

But no. That was real live flesh, real live Sawyer Bell, real live *naked* Sawyer Bell beside her.

"Sawyer?" she called, this time in a panic. "Sawyer!"

He jerked, then groaned and put a hand on the side of his head.

"Sawyer, get up!" Tugging the top sheet free of the quilt, she scrambled to the side of the bed and wrapped it around her as she stood. When she looked back at Sawyer, he was rolling onto his back. "Get up, Sawyer. Oh please, get up."

He opened his eyes a crack, much as she'd done not so long before. As she'd done, he squeezed them tight again. But Faith wasn't allowing him the leisure she'd had to let memory come calling. "Sawyer." He grunted. "Sawyer!"

He pried his eyes open and focused on her, and for a minute he simply stared, trying without success to make sense out of what he was seeing. Finally he frowned. "Faith?" He knew it had to be her. There wasn't anyone who had quite her face, quite her hair, quite her voice. But he had no idea what she could possibly be doing standing by the side of his bed draped in a sheet.

Then he realized that the setting was wrong. Moving his head by short, pained inches, he saw that he wasn't in his own bedroom at all. His bedroom was done in navies and browns. This one was heavy on whites and hurt his eyes something awful. And the bed was too small. His heel was caught on the bottom edge of the mattress. That never happened with his extra-long king. And he would never, *never* sleep on flowered sheets under a flowered quilt, but unless his eyesight was truly going, that was what he saw above and below his hip. His *naked* hip.

Bolting upright, he winced and caught himself for a minute, then grabbed the quilt from the bed and, though he was plenty warm on his own, wrapped it around him as he hurried to stand on the opposite side of the mattress from Faith. Memory was fast returning, coming in flashes like a strobe tormenting his brain.

"What happened?" he rasped. He hoped she'd tell him that he'd simply had too much to drink, so she'd put him to bed. Somehow, between the look on her face and the images that were flashing in his mind, he doubted that was the case.

"We did it," she whispered in dismay. Then she paused and allowed herself a last-ditch doubt. "Did we?"

Sawyer looked down at the bed. They'd just awoken in it. Clearly they'd spent at least part of the night here. But the pictures flickering into his mind were of someplace darker, like the living room, and someplace harder, like the floor. "Do you see any clothes?" he asked cautiously. He didn't. There was nothing draped over the white wicker chair in the corner, nothing thrown on the white wicker dresser, nothing dropped on the pale green carpet.

"No. I think they may be, uh, in the other room."

Sawyer's headache gave an extra-strong pulse as though in punishment for what the evidence was strongly suggesting. He raked a hand through his hair. "Were we drunk?"

"I don't know. I've never been drunk before. Do you remember much?"

"Bits and pieces."

"Did we…?"

Sawyer tuned into several of those bits and pieces. He remembered talking about Joanna but seeing Faith. He remembered touching her. He remembered that she felt very good to hold. He remembered that she was very tight inside. "I think so."

"Oh, Lord." She twisted down onto the bed, putting her back to him, which gave her a token protection from the embarrassment she felt. She rested her splitting head in her hands. "Oh, Lord. I've never, *never* done anything like this. I'm sorry, Sawyer."

"It was my fault as much as yours," he snapped.

She hunched her shoulders. "No need to be snippy about it."

He rubbed a hand over his eyes and was a while in answering. "Sorry."

"Are you always this charming when you wake up?"

"I'm not feeling great. Everything from my neck up is hurting. Even my tongue doesn't feel right."

"Maybe it overexerted itself."

"Look who's being snippy."

For a minute, she sat in quiet dejection. Then she shook her head—which was a mistake. Everything inside seemed to rattle. After another minute's recovery, she said, "I guess I was trying to be cute, only it didn't work." She closed her eyes and whispered, "I don't believe this." Her voice rose. "I don't believe I let all that happen. *Let* it happen. I did it. I goaded you on. I know I did. Why did I do that? I've never been sexually aggressive in my life!"

"You'd had too much to drink. We'd both had too much to drink. Neither of us was thinking clearly."

"But to—make—love." She tripped over the words, as though the sound of them hitting the air made the fact of what they'd done so much more real. "Making love is the most intimate thing two people can do. But we're not lovers, you and me," she cried. "We're friends!"

Sawyer winced. "You don't have to yell."

"We're friends," she repeated, but more softly.

"Some say that friends make the best lovers."

"Or that the best of friendships are ruined when friends become lovers. I don't want that to happen, Sawyer." She swore softly. "I don't believe this."

"We were tipsy."

"We were awful. Some of the things we said. What we did to Jack and Joanna. That was the *lowest*. Who are we to go on and on about them that way? To talk about the way they made love?" She buried her face in her hands and moaned. "I am so embarrassed."

"We were tipsy."

"They didn't deserve that. Do you think they're off with new lovers, talking about what *we* did in bed? I'd die if I knew Jack was doing that. Some things are sacred." She made a snorting sound. "Boy, we blew sacred, didn't we?"

"The problem is that I know Jack and you know Joanna. We used to go places, the four of us. It's almost natural that we make comparisons."

"It's terrible! How can you condone what we did?"

"I'm not condoning it. But we were tipsy."

"I *know* we were tipsy, still what we did was awful!"

"I know." He held his head. "I take that back. I don't know. Things are coming back to me, and some of them are pretty nice."

Faith whirled on him, but the sudden movement wrenched everything inside her. For a split second she feared she was going to be sick. Mercifully the feeling passed. "I think," she said with her eyes lowered, "that I'd like something for this headache and then a cup or two of very strong coffee."

Both ideas sounded good to Sawyer. He didn't move, though. He didn't want to do anything to anger Faith. She wasn't in the best of moods and neither was he. So he watched her walk from the bedroom with surprising grace, given that she was swathed in a bedsheet. He saw her go into the bathroom and shut the door. It seemed forever that she was in there. He began to wonder whether she was all right, but he didn't move. He simply stood by the side of the bed, holding the flowered quilt wrapped around his lower half.

Finally the door opened and she came out. He guessed she'd thrown water on her face and brushed her hair, because she looked a little more awake. She was also wearing a robe.

"Here," she said quietly. Keeping her eyes low—in deference to her headache rather than deference to him, he was sure—she dropped several tablets into his hand. Then she turned and, walking gingerly, headed for the kitchen.

As soon as she'd disappeared, he took his painstaking turn in the bathroom. When he joined her in the kitchen a short time later, he was wearing the sweatshirt and jeans he'd recovered, with more than a little chagrin, from the living-room floor.

The smell of perking coffee wafted about and would have been welcoming if Faith hadn't been standing so still, facing the counter, keeping her back to him. He slipped onto a bar stool. His legs weren't feeling as steady as usual. The support was welcome.

As he sat there, waiting for the pills to calm the noise in his head and take the raw edge off everything else, he wondered if Faith wanted him to leave. She had every right to be alone if she wanted. It was her house. She wasn't feeling well, and his presence was a reminder why.

But he couldn't leave. The cold water he'd doused his head with in the sink had cleared his mind that much. He and Faith had to talk.

He didn't do a thing, though, until the coffee was done and she handed him a steaming mug. He'd always thought of life as being more civilized over morning coffee, and Faith's coffee was strong. If it didn't make him more civilized, he didn't know what would. He figured it would also go a long way toward settling his stomach and dulling the ache in his head.

It did both for Faith. After a few minutes, she was able to carry her mug to the counter, take the companion stool to his and face him. "Guess we missed dinner," she said. She was relieved to see that his eyes had the same sickly red look hers did.

"Guess so."

"If we'd had something in our stomachs, the champagne wouldn't have hit so hard."

"Either that, or we'd have been bounced from the restaurant."

She started to smile at that thought, but the movement of her mouth somehow reached her eyes, which still hurt. So she made a quiet sound to acknowledge what he'd said and closed her eyes for a minute. "I feel very foolish," she whispered.

"That's two of us."

"I have never, *never* done anything like this before. I mean, even aside from what we did to Jack and Joanna, the sex was something else." She opened her eyes to his. "I don't sleep around, Sawyer. I never have. There was one guy before I met Jack, and there haven't been any since. Except you."

Sawyer thought about that for a minute. "I'm flattered."

"I didn't mean it as flattery. I meant it to tell you the way I am. I'm not loose. I'm not a frustrated divorcée. I don't go around getting drunk and begging men to make love to me."

"Is that what you thought you did?"

"Yes."

"Well, you didn't. In the first place, you didn't get drunk. If you'd done that, you'd have been incapacitated.

You'd probably have passed out. Neither of us was drunk. We were tipsy. That's all."

"Is there really a difference?" she asked.

The faint bitterness in her voice annoyed him. "Yes, there is," he insisted. "There's a big difference. If we'd been drunk we wouldn't have been so lucid."

"Lucid? You think we were lucid?"

"To some extent, yes. The things I said about Joanna were true. I probably shouldn't have said any of them. But they were true. She did a job on me sexually. There were times when I wondered whether I lacked something in that department, since I couldn't make her respond. I never would have planned what happened last night, but once we got going I must have had an inner need to keep going. You were my friend. I'd had just enough to drink. I was loose. I wanted to know if I could turn you on. So maybe I used bad judgment, and I blame that on the drink, but on some level I knew what I was doing." He paused. "My guess is you did, too."

Faith let his words sink in. Much as she tried, she couldn't completely deny them. Quietly she said, "Then we have to accept the responsibility. So that makes it worse."

"Yes and no."

She stared at him. "Explain."

"Yes, we have to accept the responsibility. We're mature adults. We can blame what we did on the wine, but that doesn't excuse it. On the other hand, maybe it wasn't so terrible."

"Are you kidding?" she cried. "Sawyer, we slept together last night! You and me. Best friends. Best buddies. We made love. We went all the way. We scr—"

He cut her off. "Don't say it, Faith. Don't even think it. You're right. We're best friends. Best buddies. We shouldn't have done what we did, but it wasn't some ugly, faceless, nameless thing, and I'm sure as hell not dropping a C-note on your counter and walking out."

Faith flinched. She bowed her head and pressed two fingers to her temple. Feeling quickly contrite, Sawyer gentled his voice. "All I'm saying is that this isn't the end of the world."

"What if I'm pregnant?"

The thought caught him off guard. He swallowed. "Is there a chance of that?"

"Yes. I don't use birth control. I haven't had any need." She grew defensive. "I don't go around doing this kind of thing."

Rattled as he was, her defensiveness hit him the wrong way. "Damn it, I know that, Faith! Will you stop saying it? I *know* you're not loose. I *know* you don't sleep around. I *know* you place value on physical intimacy. We may never have been romantically involved, but I do know you, and better than most, I'd wager."

"You must think I'm awful."

He threw his hands in the air; they came down on his hips. "It takes two to tango, y'know."

"But I kept pushing you on. I kept asking you for more." Her eyes grew moist. "I swear, Sawyer, I've never been like that before."

The tears did it. He'd had no intention of touching her, but when he saw the tears he couldn't sit by and stay physically aloof. Not after what, right or wrong, they'd done. And not when every one of his instincts as a friend and as a man directed him otherwise.

Taking a step to her stool, he wrapped his arms around her. "I want you to listen to me, Faith. You're a bright woman, probably one of the brightest I've ever met. I want you to listen and listen good. Okay?"

She nodded.

He spoke slowly, keeping his voice low and gentle. "I do not think less of you for what we did last night. If anything, the opposite is true. I'm flattered to know that there haven't been any other men but that you let me be the first since the divorce. I'm relieved to know that you're human, that deep down inside you have some of the same needs as me—even if the need is as lousy as criticizing our ex-spouses. I am not disappointed in you. I don't think I could ever be disappointed in you." He paused. "How can I be disappointed when you came so alive in my arms?"

"Sawyer," she moaned.

"Okay. We won't talk about that."

"Don't even *think* about it."

"Fine. What about your being pregnant? When will you know?"

"Two weeks, give or take."

"Then we won't think about that, either, until we know one way or another. There's no point in worrying, and there's no way we can change the chances. If it happened, it's already happened, and if that's the case, we'll sit down together and decide what to do."

Faith couldn't fault his logic. But then, she'd always found Sawyer to be logical. She'd always thought she was, too, which was why she was surprised by her own heightened emotions.

"Sound fair?" he asked, when she remained quiet in his arms.

She nodded. "What do we do in the meantime?"

It was a little while before he answered. He honestly didn't know what to do. "Maybe we ought to go on the way we always have."

"Business as usual?"

"That's right."

"There's only one problem with that. Business as usual means running into each other only by accident. But there's the little matter of the Leindecker divorce."

"The Leindecker divorce."

"Remember? The thing that brought you down to my office in the first place yesterday?"

"I remember." But he hadn't until then, and the recollection gave greater weight to what had happened in the intervening hours. "Oh boy."

Faith knew what he was thinking. "Uh-huh. If we were wondering whether there was a conflict of interest *then*, what's the story *now?*"

Reluctantly Sawyer let his arms fall from around her. He sank back onto his stool. "No different, I guess. We're still okay as long as we watch what we do."

"You can pretend last night didn't happen?"

"No. But I don't know if it'll happen again, and if it doesn't, not much has really changed." He paused. "Has it?"

"I guess not."

"Do you feel that because of last night you'll be less strong an advocate for your client?"

"I don't know. Maybe I won't be as tough a negotiator knowing I'm negotiating with you."

Sawyer narrowed his eyes, which were beginning to feel better. "You'll be tough. Probably more so than usual, if for no other reason than to make the point that you aren't biased by any relationship with me. Of course," he mused, "if you feel uncomfortable about it, you can tell Mrs. Leindecker to get another lawyer."

Faith smirked. "Would that please you?"

"No way. I said I was excited about working with you. I was simply considering your feelings."

"If you're that considerate, you could always withdraw from the case yourself. You could tell Mr. Leindecker to get another lawyer."

"But I want to work with you."

"Against me."

"Against you. It's a challenge, and in that sense both of our clients stand to benefit."

At that moment, Faith wasn't much up for challenges. But in an hour, a day, a week, things would be different. She'd been accepting challenges since she first applied to law school. Fighting prejudice, she'd had to work twice as hard because she was female, but she'd proven herself every bit as good a lawyer as any other she'd run across.

"A woman in Mrs. Leindecker's position deserves the best if she's going to get the respect she's earned," she told him.

"A man in Mr. Leindecker's position *needs* the best if he doesn't want to be taken to the cleaner's."

"They were married a long time," she warned. "She's put up with a lot."

"She's *had* a lot. She's lived like a queen."

"Which is how she deserves to be kept. You can't just expect her to go off, get a job and live hand-to-mouth all of a sudden, do you?"

"Come on, Faith. It's not like she's got little kids to take care of—or that she's doddering at the older end of the scale. She's a healthy, middle-aged woman. It wouldn't kill her to work."

"What could she do? She's not trained for anything. Any job she'd get would pay her a fraction of what your client earns. We're talking the most menial, entry-level position if she had to work. But she shouldn't have to. Not if he led her to believe that she'd always be taken care of.

There are things like service and loyalty and unspoken contracts to consider."

"Tell it to the judge."

There it was, Faith knew. The gauntlet had been thrown down. And Sawyer Bell was looking at her with a crooked half-grin on his handsome face, waiting, just waiting to see if she had the courage to pick it up.

She wasn't sure whether it was the grin, the handsome face, the need to put last night's folly behind them or the challenge itself that did it. But she rose from the stool, tipped up her chin and informed him in slow, clear words, "I intend to, thank you."

With that, she reached for the refrigerator door.

CHAPTER FOUR

FAITH MADE a huge breakfast, not so much because Sawyer might be hungry, but because she was. Then, trying to pretend that nothing out of the ordinary had happened between them, she sent him on his way.

Saturdays were workdays. On this particular one, she had to go to the grocery for food, the dry cleaner for a drop-off and pickup, the department store for stockings and a refill of mascara. Despite the aspirin, the coffee and the breakfast, she was still feeling a little logy. But she pushed herself. There were things to be done, and if she didn't grab the opportunity, she'd lose it.

She had to smile at that thought; it was the credo by which Jack lived. Over and over he'd said those words during the eight years they'd been married—usually at times when Faith was at her laziest. Since the divorce she'd been more diligent about all those non-law-related things that she would have let ride in the past. Without Jack to keep her on her toes, she had to rely on herself.

So he wasn't all bad, she told herself and knew that it was a way of compensating for how she'd belittled him with Sawyer. In honor of Jack, she even went shopping for a new suit for work, one that was conservative and practical like him, and though she'd probably have picked something more daring on another day, she knew she'd wear it well.

By the time she returned to Union Wharf it was nearly

three in the afternoon. Curled up on the sofa in deliberate defiance of what had happened behind it the night before, she spent several hours making notes on a case that would be coming up for a hearing that week. Then she slipped into a sexy black sheath, made good use of the eye makeup she'd just happened to buy along with the mascara that afternoon, and went to a harvest party at Monica's home in Concord.

The best part, she decided, was the drive to and from Concord. Faith enjoyed driving. She didn't do it often, since she usually walked to and from work, but when she had a case in one of the outlying courthouses, or when she found something to do on a weekend that took her out of the city, she drove with relish. She tuned the radio to her favorite station, the only one in Boston that played country music, and she relaxed. She beat her left foot in time to the music, clapped her hands when a traffic light freed them, hummed along from time to time, even sang aloud when a particular lyric grabbed her.

Monica's party, on the other hand, was a drag. Not that Monica hadn't warned her. Most of the guests were friends of Monica's husband, who was fifteen years older than Monica, who was ten years older than Faith. If those guests had been lawyers, Faith might have had a chance, but the men were in business, and their wives were professional wives. Faith couldn't identify with them at all.

Oh, she managed. She was adept at small talk. Sipping her customary Perrier and lime, she did her share of chatting about the weather, the turn of the leaves, the new musical that had opened at the Shubert, a recently published novel that had the city talking. She listened in on business discussions, knowing that the small bits of information she picked up would come in handy at one point or another in her life. But the talk didn't excite her.

There was nothing lively about the gathering. None of the people made her laugh in delight, and if a party wasn't for laughing in delight, Faith didn't know what it *was* for. For Monica's sake, though, she stuck it out.

She liked Monica. She also respected her. Monica had started out being like the other women at the party, but it hadn't taken her long to realize that if her marriage was to have any chance of survival, she needed something constructive to do. Fortunately her husband understood. He put her through law school and indulged her through ten years of work as a public defender. That was what she was doing when Faith met her. When Faith had decided to leave the law firm she was associated with and go out on her own, Monica was ready for a move.

For five years, they had been splitting the rent on their suite of offices and sharing Loni's salary and skills. Though they often discussed legal issues with each other, their practices were entirely independent. Outside the office, they were friends.

So when, as a friend, Monica had pleaded with Faith to come liven up her husband's party, Faith had agreed. Unfortunately the party needed a kind of livening that Faith, despite her intelligence and quick wit, couldn't begin to accomplish. Still, Faith wasn't sorry she went. The party wasn't a waste. It took up four hours. By the time she drove back into the city, parked her car and safely locked herself into her condo, she was exhausted enough to go straight to sleep.

Unfortunately she'd made a large tactical error. In keeping with the schedule she stuck to in her post-Jack life, she had done no more than make her bed that morning. Sundays were for changing the sheets.

This week, she should have changed them on Saturday. Though she'd aired the bed as always, neatly made it and fluffed the pillows, and though she was tired enough to fall asleep soon after she crawled in, she awoke at four in the morning thinking Sawyer was beside her. And no wonder. The scent of him clung to her sheets. It was so subtle that she wondered at first whether she was imagining it, but the warmth of her body had brought it to life, and she wasn't able to ignore it.

She tried. She tried doing what she'd done all of Saturday, keeping her mind busy enough so that there wasn't room for a wayward thought. But at four in the morning, she couldn't manufacture distractions. There were just the lingering lights of the harbor, the sleeping city, the night and Sawyer.

For the first time, perhaps the very first time since she'd known the man, she allowed herself to take a long, objective look at him physically. It wasn't hard. She might not have thought to heed the details before, still they'd registered. Her mind's eye held an exquisitely detailed picture of him.

He was tall, she guessed six-four or six-five. He'd played basketball in college, she knew because he'd mentioned it once, and though the injuries he sustained in Vietnam had dashed any hopes of a professional career, he still had the body of an athlete. He *was* an athlete. A runner. He'd pushed himself and pushed himself, well beyond the point his doctors had ever thought he'd be able to go, which was a testimony to his will…and to Joanna's, Faith freely admitted. Despite the scars that he'd always carry, he had full command of his body to do with as he pleased.

He was broad-shouldered and narrow-hipped, both of which she'd known forever, neither of which she'd appreciated quite as fully as she had the night before. Though she only remembered seeing his upper body naked, she remembered measuring those parts of him below the waist with her hands. Narrow-hipped, he was, indeed, with legs that could wind forever in and round her own.

Taking in a sharp breath, she put a hand to her chest to calm the wild beat of her heart. But the warmth of her palm served only to remind her of the warmth of Sawyer's hands on her skin. Oh, yes, his hands were warm. They were large and well formed, both strong and gentle.

That was pretty much the way she saw his face, too. Strong but gentle, dark but giving, sober but capable of a buoyant smile. His hair was dark brown and stylishly worn, tumbling over his brow with the least encouragement, and his skin never quite looked as pale as the rest of the world's. There was a ruddiness to it. Like a child, his color heightened with exertion or excitement—or passion, she thought, though she had no way of knowing for sure. It had been too dark in their nook behind the sofa last night to see that.

What she had seen, or felt, was the prickle of his beard. That, too, gave his face a darker, more rugged look, and though she'd never seen him with enough stubble to be called grubby, many times she'd seen a distinct five-o'clock shadow. She hadn't thought twice about it before. Now she did, and she decided that it added to the aura of masculinity that surrounded him.

Which was a whole new thought, in itself. Aura of masculinity? He did have that, and he had it in abundance. But she'd never noticed it before, and she couldn't understand why. Surely something that hit her so strongly now had to have hit her on some level before. Maybe, she mused, she'd repressed it. That was an interesting thought.

As she wrestled with it, she could almost see Sawyer standing back, finding a wry humor in her predicament. She could see his brown eyes twinkling, could see his firm mouth twitching at the corners, could even see one dark eyebrow edging upward into an arch. She tried to be annoyed with him, as he stood there in her mind, but she couldn't. He was a good man. And he was gorgeous.

Uh-huh. Gorgeous. He was. But that didn't change the fact that they were best of friends, had no intention of being involved with each other as lovers, had no *business* being intimately involved if they intended to represent the Leindeckers. And yes, if Laura Leindecker decided to go ahead with the divorce, Faith was in it on her side. In spite of what had happened the night before, she couldn't turn down the golden opportunity of seeing how Sawyer Bell worked.

FAITH STARTED SUNDAY by listing the things she wanted to do. She made it halfway down the list—changing the sheets, doing the laundry, poring through the Sunday *Globe* right down to the crossword puzzle at the back of the magazine section—before Sawyer called.

She recognized his voice at once. It might have been the deep timbre, she mused, or the faint hesitance, or she had to admit that, as much as she busied her mind, Sawyer was still a presence in it. She wasn't sure whether to be pleased he'd called or not, and for that reason she attributed the pickup of her pulse to uncertainty.

"I just wanted to make sure you were okay," he explained in a still-hesitant but gentle and sincere tone. "Somehow it didn't seem right to leave yesterday and not be in touch for days."

She agreed with him and was touched, though not entirely surprised. Sawyer was a considerate man. "Thank you. I'm doing fine." She laughed softly. "I feel a lot better today than I did yesterday. I can move my eyes."

"Mmm. Me, too. After I left you, I came home and

slept. Slept on and off for the rest of the day. I've never been hit quite like that."

"You must have been tired anyway."

"Maybe. Still, I don't think I'm ever having another drink."

"Uh-huh," she said, not believing it for a minute.

"I'm serious."

"I'm sure you are. But the holiday season is coming. There are lots of dinners and parties. One drink won't kill you."

"The second or third might."

"Mmm." She thought back to Dewey O'Day's affair. "Why did we do that, Sawyer? Why did we keep taking wine from the tray?"

"We were bored. We didn't want to be there."

"We were laughing a lot. We weren't keeping count of what we had to drink."

"We were giving each other courage. Boy, were we dumb."

"You can say that again."

"Once is enough, thanks. I usually try to be more responsible than we were that night." He paused. "At least we didn't make fools of ourselves at the party."

"The party wasn't the problem. It was all we had to drink after that."

"But if we hadn't drunk what we did at the party, we'd have been more clearheaded afterward. I'd have known not to open that bottle of wine at my place, and you'd have saved the Johnsons' champagne for a better occasion. Now it's gone."

"No loss. Besides, I wasn't about to drink that champagne all alone, and if I was going to share it with someone, who better than you? You're a friend."

"Am I still?" he asked. The hesitancy she'd heard earlier, gone for a while, was back.

"Of course you are."

"Even though I took advantage of you?"

Faith sighed indulgently. "Sawyer, you didn't take advantage of me. I asked for everything I got. And no one forced me to take out that champagne."

"But I'm bigger than you."

She didn't see the connection. He hadn't used physical force. She doubted he was capable of it where a woman was concerned. "So?"

"So I should have been able to hold my liquor better. I should have been that much more sober than you every step of the way."

"You're wallowing in guilt. Oh boy, are you wallowing."

"Damn right, I am."

"Well, don't. Because if you do, I'll have to. You say you should have been stronger physically, I say I should have been stronger mentally."

"Mentally?"

"I should have said no. Traditionally the woman is the one who has a saner head on her shoulders. I should have refused another drink the minute I knew I wasn't in total control."

"But you weren't in total control, which is why you did what you did."

"Even in *partial* control, I should have known better." She stopped for a minute to think about what they were saying. "This goes around and around, doesn't it?"

"Yeah. I thought we'd agreed—" there was a break in the transmission of his voice "—the blame—hell, my time's up. I don't have any more change."

"Change?" Apparently, he was calling from a pay phone. "Where are you?"

"The Cape. I bought a dilapidated—" there was another break "—summer—I'm fixing it up. Gotta run, Faith. Are you sure you're okay?"

"I'm fine."

"Talk with you soon, then. Bye."

He broke the connection before she could say another word. She pictured him dashing out of the phone booth before the operator could ring to tell him that he owed another quarter for the extra seconds he'd used. The image brought a smile to her face. He really was adorable. And admirable. So he'd bought a dilapidated something on the Cape and was fixing it up. Physical work on the weekends to balance the cerebral work of the week. He was a bright man, indeed.

Several hours later, she was wishing she had some physical work of her own to do. Having finished the cross-word puzzle down to the very last word, she was reading through some papers for work. But she felt restless. She wanted to be out doing something, though she didn't have any idea what that something might be. She thought of taking a walk, but the day was gray and not particularly enticing. She thought of calling a friend and going to a movie, but there wasn't one that she desperately wanted to see. She thought of calling a friend, period, but that would mean chatting about personal things, and she wasn't in the mood for that, either.

When Laura Leindecker's daughter called her on the phone, she welcomed the diversion.

"I'm sorry to bother you, Ms Barry, but Mother said you were representing her, and I had to talk with someone."

"Actually," Faith tried to explain, "your mother and I

haven't any formal agreement yet. She was going to take a few days to decide whether she really wants to go ahead with the divorce."

"I think she does," came the answering voice, soft, like her mother's, but more high-pitched. "And I think she should. Especially after what's happened this weekend."

"What is that?"

"He's been here at the house since noon yesterday, and he refuses to leave. The more Mother asks him, the more belligerent he becomes."

"Belligerent?" According to Laura, the man had been charming and humble.

"Yes, belligerent. Please. Let me talk with you. I'm taking a six-o'clock flight back to Baltimore tonight, but I could meet you at your office—or anywhere else in Boston before that. I want you to hear my side of the story."

"The divorce," Faith reminded her gently, "is between your parents. Shouldn't your mother be telling me whatever there is to tell?"

"She's too...timid sometimes. I don't know how much she'll tell. But she's suffering, and I think you should know the facts. They could come in handy when you're planning her case."

Faith couldn't deny the temptation of facts. She knew she'd have to decide whether what she was told was, indeed, factual, but she felt she owed it to her client to listen. So she gave Beth Leindecker directions to her office and agreed to meet her there at four.

BETH, IT TURNED OUT, was twenty-three, an intern at an ad agency and definitely at odds with her father. "When I arrived home on Friday night, Mother was distraught."

"Did you see or speak with your father that night?"

"No. Mother told him to sleep somewhere else. For all we know, he slept with *her*."

"Do you know who she is?"

"I didn't even know she existed until Mother called on Friday morning!"

Faith wondered whether that call had come before or after Laura's confrontation with her husband. It would be interesting to know how much Beth was egging her on. "Okay. So your father came to the house on Saturday morning."

"Around noon. We couldn't believe he dared show his face there."

"It's still his home."

"But he's not welcome there."

Faith was tempted to point out a few basic legal facts to Beth. Instead, she said, "He must have needed clothes. Grooming things."

"That was what we thought, but he wasn't back for those at all. He was back to stay, he said. He said that the whole thing had gotten out of hand, that Mother had blown it out of proportion. Can you believe that? He admits to cheating on her, then tells her she's blown it out of proportion!"

Faith held up an appeasing hand. In some ways, Beth sounded just like her mother—but with a hotter spark and a shorter fuse. "You mentioned belligerence," she prompted to keep the girl on track.

Beth nodded. "They were arguing back and forth. He was saying that what he did wasn't so awful, and Mother was saying that it was, and I agreed with her."

"You were standing right there in the middle of the fight?"

"I had to. Someone had to protect Mother."

"She couldn't protect herself?"

"Not against him. She's never been able to protect herself against him. He snaps his fingers, and she comes running. It's always been that way."

"Maybe she loves him."

Beth's only response to that was a frown. "She doesn't deserve this hurt. After all these years, she deserves some satisfaction."

"What kind of satisfaction did you have in mind?" Faith asked, genuinely curious.

"He ought to be banned from stepping foot in that house or coming near my mother. She's had a lifetime of his harassment."

"Harassment." Faith echoed the word. It didn't fit with the image Laura had painted of her husband any more than belligerence did. "Harassment by omission, as in emotional neglect?"

"For years it was that. Now it's physical. He started throwing things."

Faith grew more alert. "What kinds of things?"

"The mail, first. Letters and magazines that were on the table in the front hall. Then towels that were piled on the stairs. Then flowers that were on a table at the top of the stairs. Then books, big books from the nightstand."

"The argument worked its way to their bedroom?"

"He followed her there. She kept yelling at him, telling him to stay away, but he followed her there."

"Did he hit her at any point?"

"No."

"At any point, did he raise a hand to strike her?"

"No," Beth said, and Faith sensed a reluctance in the denial. Beth was clearly eager to think the worst of her father.

"He was just throwing things around. Anything bigger than a book?"

"He kicked the cushion off the chaise lounge. It went halfway across the room."

"Did he aim it at her?"

"No."

"Did he aim anything directly at her?"

"No. But you're missing the point," Beth insisted. "He was throwing things. She could have been hit."

Faith was quiet for several minutes, trying to put what Beth was saying in some kind of perspective, enough to decide whether there was any cause for immediate concern. "That was yesterday afternoon. I take it he's calmed down since then."

"He's still there. She wants him out."

Does she, or do you? Faith was wondering. "Has he calmed down?"

"Yes. But he's still angry. He could act up again at any time." Beth looked truly frustrated. "For the first time in her life, my mother is standing up to him. At least, she's trying to. But if someone doesn't give her a boost, she's going to fall right back on him. I think you should give her that boost, Ms. Barry."

Faith didn't like the sound of that at all, and it wasn't because she lacked the courage for it. "Morally, I'm obliged to see if the marriage can be salvaged. I can't urge your mother to push for a divorce. It has to be her decision. If she gives it fair thought, decides that there's no hope for the marriage and that divorce is the only solution, I'll help her. I'm not sure what else I can do. I'll call her, if that will make you feel better. I'll ask how she feels about his being around. There are many couples who live together right up to the point of signing a legal separation agreement. It's sometimes simpler that way.

Then again, if your mother is being physically threatened, that's another story."

"She is."

"I'll ask her about it," Faith said, and rose from her desk. "In the meantime, I think you'd be best not goading her on. Be supportive. But remember that this is between your parents. You're grown and out of the house. They have to come to terms with what they want from each other for the next however many years."

Beth took up her overnight case and started for the door. "I think mother needs a court order to keep him out of the house."

"Be supportive, Beth, not inflammatory."

"She needs someone to light a fire under her."

"Do you hate your father that much?"

"I don't hate him."

"Then why are you so eager to get him out of the house?"

"He needs to be taught a lesson. He's had everything his way for so long. It's fine and dandy for him to be delightfully pleasant when he's pulling all the strings. Let someone else pull the strings and he starts throwing things the way he did Saturday. That was an awakening, let me tell you."

"That he has a temper?"

"I'll say."

"Maybe it's a healthy outlet. After all, he was objecting to his wife's kicking him out of the house. Maybe he really wants to be there with her."

"He just wants his way."

"Maybe," Faith conceded, then smiled and squeezed the younger woman's shoulder. "Have a safe flight back to Baltimore. And remember, stay cool. Your parents are going to have to work this out themselves."

"Will you call my mother?"

"As soon as you're on your way."

But she'd barely seen Beth to the elevator and returned to her office when Laura called her. "Is Beth still there? I know she was going to meet you. Has she left?"

"Just a minute ago. Is there a problem?"

"She forgot her gray outfit, the two-piece wool she wore in on Friday. She was too warm in it then, but the weather's getting colder and she'll want it." She sighed. "It's no wonder she forgot it. She was in such a stir while she was here."

"Has she always had trouble getting along with her father?"

"Always. I've been the buffer for years. She feels that he's been unduly stingy with her."

"With money?"

"Money, time, himself. He said it would be too easy to spoil her, and he didn't want that. God forbid he should make things easy for her. When she graduated from college, she wanted to work for him, but he told her she had to work somewhere else. 'Earn her stripes' was the expression he used. What kind of father would make his daughter do that?"

"Many have."

"It was very selfish of him. But I suppose that's nothing new," Laura concluded sadly.

Faith heard the sadness. She didn't hear any sort of panic. "Beth was concerned for your physical safety. Are you all right?"

"I'm fine. Bruce is being difficult, of course. He insists on staying here. When I tell him to leave, he gets furious."

"Do you feel that you're in danger?"

"I don't know what he's going to do next. I've never seen him like this."

"Has he threatened you in any way? Forced you in any physical sense?"

"No. But one of us has to leave this house, and it isn't going to be me. *He* can leave."

"It sounds as if he won't. We can try for a restraining order, but it may be premature." While Faith was the first one to want to protect a client from physical harm, she sensed that the threat in this case was more speculative than real. Bruce had no history of violence. The court would see that. "I'd recommend that you take advantage of his presence and talk with him."

"Talk? What for? I can't trust what he says. Not anymore. Besides, it's a waste of time. I want a divorce."

"I understand that, Mrs. Leindecker, but—"

"I want a divorce. Are you going to represent me?"

"Let's discuss that on Tuesday."

"This is Sunday. My feelings won't change in two days."

"Where emotions are concerned, a lot can happen in two days."

"Not in my case. I want a divorce, and the sooner we get started, the sooner that man will see what he's done."

Divorce for the purpose of revenge was one of the things Faith least liked. It was childish, blind and often ugly. It also tended to overshadow any pluses that might have existed in a marriage. Gut instinct told her that this marriage had pluses aplenty. What she needed was time to see if those pluses could possibly reassert themselves.

"Tuesday, Laura. We'll talk again on Tuesday."

It took another minute, but she finally convinced Laura to hold off any action until then. Hanging up the phone at last, she quickly gathered her things together and left the office. She wasn't as easily able to leave behind thoughts of the case. It bothered her. Clearly, emotions were flying high in the Leindecker home. But a divorce based solely on emotional factors was the most painful for all involved, including the lawyers. Granted, any divorce stirred emotions. At some point, though, practicality and reason had to come into play. It could happen in court. Or before. Faith far preferred the latter.

Letting herself into her apartment, she had a sudden urge to phone Sawyer. She had a good excuse. Her client had called her in fear; Faith was sharing that fear with the lawyer who might, with a call to his client, be able to help.

But Sawyer wasn't home. He'd called her from the Cape—she didn't even know where on the Cape. And he'd called from a pay phone, which meant that the dilapidated something he'd bought didn't have one of its own.

Just for the hell of it, she tried his number in Boston. After ten rings without an answer, she hung up. She told herself that that was okay, that she really didn't have to speak with him, that Laura Leindecker was perfectly safe. But an hour later, she tried again, and then again an hour after that. It was ten o'clock before she finally reached him.

CHAPTER FIVE

"HI, SAWYER, it's me."

She was the last person he'd expected to hear from, still he recognized her voice at once. "Faith?"

"Uh-huh. I've been trying you. You must have just come home."

"There was an accident on the Sagamore Bridge that backed traffic up for miles. I thought it was late enough in the season for the crowds to be gone, but I sat in the middle of a jam for three hours."

She knew how frustrating that could be and would have felt sorry for him if she weren't so envious that he'd been at the Cape in the first place. "Tell me again what you were doing down there."

"I bought a place this summer. It's in East Dennis, an old broken-down thing. But it's on a lake, and it has potential. The land is gorgeous. I figured I could fix up the place myself. I'm an experienced man when it comes to repairs."

The way he drawled it made her smile. "The house in Cambridge?"

"Yeah. Then it was physical therapy more than anything. I suppose it's still that. The physical exercise is different from what I do at work all week. But it's also mentally therapeutic. Gets out the cobwebs, if you know what I mean." He wasn't sure she did. He wasn't sure she'd been thinking of him as much as he'd been thinking of her. They'd agreed to go back to business as usual. But he was having trouble doing that. Maybe the fact that she'd called him meant she was having trouble with it, too.

"Tell me about this place," she said. "How much land do you have?"

"Three acres."

"So you don't see your neighbors?"

"Nope. All I see is trees. And water. And rabbits and raccoons and geese. It's such a total change from everything I have up here—including the house. I mean, we're talking old and worn and crumbly."

"Sounds like you might want to tear it down and start over from scratch."

That thought had occurred to him. "The problem is I'm already committed. The deeper in I get, the more I find that needs to be done, but the more I've done, the less I want to ditch the whole thing." He paused. "Am I making any sense?"

"Lots of it," she said. "You've committed yourself to a course of action. You've come too far to turn back."

"Oh, I'm not sure *too* far," he drawled. "I'm still debating."

"But you keep going back, and you keep doing work, and you keep getting deeper involved."

"Like I say, it's therapeutic."

"Which means that if you finally decide to ditch the project, you'll still have gotten something out of it."

"That's one way of looking at it. You're good at rationalizing, Faith."

"Sometimes," she said. She was thinking of what they'd done with each other on Friday night. She couldn't rationalize it away so easily. Nor, much as she tried, could she forget it for long. But that was beside the point. "I have to ask your opinion on something, Sawyer."

"Shoot."

"Bruce Leindecker. Do you know him well?"

"Well enough," he answered more cautiously. "We've been passing acquaintances for several years."

"Do you think he's prone to violence?"

Sawyer didn't think so, but he wasn't about to say anything until he knew what had happened. Bruce was his client; there were certain privileges to respect. "Why do you ask?"

"I had conversations today with both his wife and his daughter. Apparently there was an ugly scene yesterday. Things were thrown around the room a little."

"By my client?" he asked, then saw no harm in rebutting it. "That surprises me. To my knowledge, he's never been a violent man."

"Are you sure?"

"I said 'to my knowledge.' Maybe the guy's been beating up women on the sly, but nothing's ever come out about it, and with a visible guy like Bruce, you'd think it would."

"Nothing ever came out about the affair he was having."

"One woman. One affair. It had been going on for two or three months. No more."

That was the first Faith had heard of Bruce's side of the story, and while it was interesting, it wasn't surprising. Bruce's story was just that—Bruce's story. And it was Sawyer's job to relate it as told. "So he says."

"I believe him. And I do believe that he wouldn't hurt a woman. Unless those two are driving him mad."

"Sawyer…"

"They may be."

That wasn't Faith's immediate worry. "Beth was concerned for her mother's safety. I take it you don't think she has cause?"

"No, I don't."

"You sound sure."

"I feel sure."

"I'm glad one of us does. I'd feel horrible if I decided to let it go and then my client was batted around. But you say you know your client fairly well. I'm trusting you on this, Sawyer."

"I'm glad you can still trust me on something."

She was a minute in responding. "What do you mean?"

"After Friday night. I'm glad you still trust me a little."

"Of course I trust you. I've always trusted you. Trust was never an issue."

But Sawyer saw it differently. "You trusted me to take care of you, and I didn't."

"Take care of me?"

"Protect you. I was thinking about this most of the day, and it's really bothering me. If you'd been with someone you trusted less on Friday night, you wouldn't have had half as much to drink. But you trusted me not to take advantage of you, so you may have been more lax than usual. Not only did I let us get carried away enough to make love, but I didn't think a thing about birth control. So now you're sitting there worrying that you're pregnant, because you have a successful career, and we all know that successful careers and babies don't mix."

Faith was astonished. "You spent most of today thinking about this?"

"While I was hammering away on the roof."

"I don't believe it, Sawyer." She took a breath. "Sawyer, do you know what year this is?"

"Of course I do."

"Then you'll know that these aren't the forties, or fifties, or even the seventies. Women have come a long way. Now, I know you don't like to think so—I know that, Sawyer, because much as I love you, you're a throwback to the heyday of male chauvinism. But really, we're not the pretty, dumb, helpless little things we used to be."

"I never said that, Faith—"

"But you imply it. I thought we agreed that on some level we both knew what we were doing Friday night. *You* were the one who said that first, and you're right. So I take at least half of the responsibility. And as far as a baby goes, I'm not sitting here worrying, because just as you said, there isn't a thing I can do until I know one way or the other, and even if I *am* pregnant, I have options! Honestly, Sawyer, these aren't the Dark Ages. I won't be sentenced to wear a scarlet letter on my breast. And I won't have to give up my practice. For your information, babies and careers are mixing better and better all the time." She stopped talking, but before he could say a word, she had another thought. This one riled her. "Ahhh. You're worried you'll have to marry me if I'm pregnant."

"That's not—"

"Save your breath, bud," she argued, suddenly and inexplicably furious. "I wasn't born yesterday, and that goes for experiencing marriage as well as understanding the male mind. I've been married once and it didn't work out. I'm not in a rush to go near it again, and I don't care if there *is* a baby involved. So you can sleep free of worry. No matter what happens, you won't be trapped." She slammed the receiver down hard.

Her hand was still pressing on the phone when it rang.

White-knuckled, she picked it up. "Leave it, Sawyer. You've said enough for one night." She hung up again.

This time when the phone rang, she lifted the handset, but dropped it right back without even putting it to her ear. Before it could ring again, she took it off the hook.

Angrily she stalked across the living room, stood for a minute at the window with her arms pressed tightly across her breasts, then stalked back and headed for the bedroom. She wasn't quite sure what had gotten out of hand, but something had. All she'd done was to call him in concern over her client. It had been a professional call, that was all.

Storming back through the apartment, she put the phone back on its hook and dialed Sawyer's number. The instant she heard his gruff hello, she said in her most confident and businesslike tone, "From what the Leindecker women have told me, we don't yet have grounds for a restraining order, but that may change. Please advise your client that if he continues to torment his wife, he'll give us those grounds." She hung up before Sawyer could get in a word.

SAWYER WAS LIVID. Sitting in the dark in his apartment that night, he couldn't remember ever being quite so angry with anyone as he was with Faith. He'd known she had an emotional bent, but he hadn't dreamed that she'd be so quick to fly off the handle at remarks as innocent as the ones he'd made.

Good Lord, she knew he was old-fashioned when it came to traditional male-female values. She'd told him so dozens of times. She'd *ribbed* him about it, which meant that she didn't think it was all bad. He certainly didn't. He liked to think he was honest and responsible. And chivalrous. Those were good things. They showed respect for a woman, and he certainly respected Faith. He might be furious with her, but he respected her—respected and trusted her, which was why he'd marry her in a minute if she was pregnant, and he'd do it happily. He wasn't committed to life as a single. Granted, it was nice to be free of Joanna's smothering, but freedom brought loneliness. Besides, Faith wasn't a smotherer.

God forbid!

She wasn't a smotherer, but she sure as hell was stubborn and hotheaded and…passionate. Ah, yes, she was that. Just as there had been fire in her voice tonight, there had been fire in her body Friday night. He couldn't forget it. His body wouldn't let him. Those same flashes of memory he'd seen through a haze on Saturday morning came to him now, only the haze had cleared.

He saw her as she'd come from the bedroom after she'd changed, wearing an oversize sweatshirt that hid her body, and slim jeans that didn't. He saw the way she'd smiled up at him, her sandy hair covering her forehead in bangs, framing her face in a gentle bob that ended an inch below her chin. He saw hazel eyes that weren't spectacular in and of themselves, but that reflected what was inside, in turn intelligence, mischief, curiosity, enthusiasm and desire. He saw a small, straight nose and lips that were as whimsical as her firm chin wasn't.

Then he saw her naked in the night light, a vision that made his body harden. Her breasts were full, larger than he'd thought, though perhaps *firm* was the word, he decided. Her waist was slim, her hips flaring just enough to brand her a woman in ways that boyishly slim models couldn't be branded. And inside—inside she was hot and moist, welcoming, generous and demanding.

He wanted her, and he wanted her badly. One night— half-zonked, but obviously not zonked enough—and he was in physical pain. Hadn't he ever seen it coming? Over and over he asked himself that question, but he wasn't able to come up with an answer. He'd known Faith for over ten years, yet things that seemed so clear to him now—such as her sex appeal and his response to it—simply hadn't occurred to him before. He'd viewed her as a friend, seeing only what was appropriate for a friend to see, overlooking the rest.

He couldn't see her that way anymore. That point of view had been lost beneath two bodies writhing on Faith's carpet Friday night. No longer could he view her only as a friend. After tonight, he wondered if she'd let him see her even as that. She was angry because she thought he was worried she'd hook him into marriage. Well, *he* was angry because she *thought* that! But she hadn't let him say a word, and that was the most infuriating part of it, as far as he was concerned. He didn't like being cut off. He didn't like being silenced when he had something to say. And he particularly didn't like being silenced by a woman.

That was why, shortly before ten the next morning, he barreled through the door of Faith's suite, tipped a finger from his forehead to Loni as he swept past, went into Faith's office and swung the door shut behind him.

She was on the phone, but the stormy look on his face wasn't to be ignored. Nor was the way he planted his hands apart on the outside edge of her desk and, leaning forward, waited. Speedily and with as much finesse as she could manage, she got off the phone. The instant the instrument was out of her hand, he opened fire.

"Don't ever do that to me again, Faith. I'm not a stupid man, and I don't say stupid things. If you have an accusation to make, make it and let me rebut it. That's the way things are done in this world. Nothing gets accomplished when a person makes an accusation and then turns and runs away."

"I didn't run away."

"Figuratively you did. You thought you knew what I was thinking and you didn't like it, so you flipped out, then you hung up on me—four times—without letting me explain myself. That was rude, Faith. *Rude*. What's the matter? Were you afraid to hear what I had to say?"

"Of course not."

"I think you were. I think you knew that I'd come out smelling like a rose, because I wasn't thinking about marriage or being trapped. I wasn't thinking about myself when I talked about the chance of a baby, only you. You're the one whose body would be affected, and you can argue until you're blue in the face, but that's a fact, Faith. As far as conception goes, my body does its thing in seconds, then it's done, while yours is just beginning, so you're the one who'll bear the brunt of a pregnancy."

"I know the facts of life."

"I'm glad to hear that, because you obviously don't know the facts of friendship. A friend doesn't desert a friend when she's in trouble. Even if there wasn't the slightest chance that I was the one who got you into trouble, I'd still be concerned. Okay, so we share the blame for what happened. I'll buy that. But I still feel guilty. I still feel I should have been more responsible." He rushed on when she opened her mouth. "And it doesn't have a goddamned thing to do with selfishness. I was thinking of you. I still am. I'm concerned for you as a friend. And lover."

"Sawyer—"

"I'm concerned, Faith. But you don't want to think that. You want to be angry with me."

"Why would I want that?"

"So that you don't have to think of being attracted to me. You want to think of last Friday night as a mistake, because maybe you've thought about it a lot, and you're feeling things you don't want to."

"Like attraction?" She tried to make light of it. "You're a *friend*, Sawyer. You've said it a million times. We were tipsy."

He leaned closer. His voice grew deeper, sounding alternately vehement and sensual. "We were aroused. We did it to each other, Faith. If you're honest with yourself, you'll admit that."

"We were tipsy."

Very slowly he straightened. The muscle in his jaw flexed. His eyes never left her face as he came around the desk.

"What are you doing, Sawyer?"

"Making my point."

"What's that supposed to mean?" She tried to sound curious rather than nervous, still she backed up a little in her chair. He was very tall, dark and imposing in his navy suit with his eyes so intent.

"I think we have a problem. I think we stumbled onto something Friday night that's not going to go away."

"Look, Sawyer, if it's the thing about a baby that's got you worried—"

"I don't give a damn about that." He bent over, putting his hands on the arms of her chair. "It's the other."

"What other?"

"The attraction."

"There *isn't* any attraction. I *told* you." She flattened a hand on his shirt to hold him off. "Don't, Sawyer. This is very unprofessional. It's criminal. It's…assault."

His face hovered over hers. "No assault."

"Please," she begged, breathing shallowly. "Leave now. Loni's sitting right out there. If I have to scream—"

"No scream. You know damn well that I won't hurt you."

"I don't want this, Sawyer. I don't want this. Please. Sawyer, this isn't *you*—"

His mouth took hers, and she was right. There was none of the teasing, none of the sampling, none of the gentleness he'd shown her on Friday night. His kiss contained the hunger that had been building since then, a hunger that he'd tried to ignore himself until he'd realized the futility of it.

Faith tried to turn her head, but he thrust a hand into her hair and held her still. When she tried to push him away, he took one of her hands, drew her right out of the chair and against him, where she was effectively immobilized. She even tried to keep her mouth closed and rigid, but she was no match for his persistence. The firm stroking of his lips was powerful; they kneaded the resistance from hers as though it had never been, then rewarded her pliancy with the kind of kiss she hadn't believed existed. It was wet and warm, unbelievably erotic. She was shaking inside, sagging weakly against him by the time he raised his head.

Unable to stand, she sank back into her chair. She knew Sawyer had allowed it, or he'd still have her clamped against him, but she wasn't about to thank him.

"Well?" he demanded. His voice was hoarse.

It was a minute before she could say anything. Then, eyes downcast, she whispered, "You've made your point."

"I didn't catch that."

"You caught it."

"Look at me and repeat it."

"What for? So your victory will be complete?"

He caught her chin and turned her face up. "No victory. I'm feeling as frustrated now as you are, but you're right, I made my point."

"And you're happy?"

"Fat chance. I have to be in court at eleven, then again at two on separate cases. I've got clients coming in at four and five-thirty. I have to prepare a motion that's due tomorrow. Somewhere in the middle, I'll have to return half a dozen phone calls and call Bruce Leindecker to discuss the issue of violence. So I'm frustrated as hell, but I can't do a thing about it. Happy? Not by a long shot."

Turning, he thundered from her office with nearly the same air of belligerence that had carried him in in the first place.

SAWYER DIDN'T LIKE starting days off that way. When he did, they invariably went downhill, and this day was no exception. The court appearance at eleven was forfeited when his client didn't show, and the one at two resulted in a continuance. He couldn't get a bead on the motion he had to prepare, because the phone kept ringing even after he'd returned the obligatory calls. The client who came in at four reported that he had inadvertently destroyed a piece of exculpatory evidence, and the client who was scheduled for five-thirty called to say he'd be an hour late.

So Sawyer called Bruce Leindecker and received an earful the likes of which he wasn't prepared for.

"The woman's crazy," Bruce claimed in a voice that lacked its customary composure. "Something's happened to her. After being utterly stoic for twenty-four years, she's suddenly turned violent."

"Violent?" That was a new twist. "Your wife?"

"Yes. I walked into the house on Saturday. I was prepared to sit down with her and try to explain why I did what I did, but she wouldn't listen. She kept cutting me off, telling me how cruel I am and how she's given me the best years of her life. I couldn't get a word in edgewise, but I kept trying, and that made her even more angry. So she started throwing things."

Sawyer knew all too well about trying to get a word in edgewise. He also knew how successfully an irate woman could prevent it. He didn't know about throwing things, though. "*She* was throwing things?"

"A cup and saucer that we'd bought in Ireland, a vase filled with flowers, the engraved picture frame that I'd given her for our twentieth anniversary. She went berserk!"

"Did she hit you?"

"No, but not for lack of trying. She's a lousy shot. Never could do anything athletic. She broke her arm when we were playing tennis in the Bahamas, fell off a donkey when we were touring the Grand Canyon, tripped and broke her ankle on the steps of the Louvre when we were in Paris. Athletic? Hah! She couldn't hit me with her eyes closed."

Bruce's irritation was real, still Sawyer sensed a ghost of indulgence beneath it. "But she kept trying?"

"Over and over, and our daughter stood there cheering her on." The indulgence vanished. "Beth is ticked off at me because I wouldn't give her a job. Well, hell, she was in the bottom third of her graduating class, not because she didn't have the brains, but because she didn't want to study. Is this a good recommendation, I ask you? And did I treat her any different from her brother? No, sir. I wouldn't give him a job, either. It's unhealthy for children to train in their father's business. Far better that they train somewhere else then come back with fresh ideas. But she wanted the easy way out. She figured she could have her cake and eat it too—have a job like a career woman, but still be able to play like her mother does."

Sawyer cleared his throat. "What does her mother—your wife—do, exactly?"

"Shop. Play cards. Meet friends for lunch."

"Has she ever done any work for you?"

"In the early days she did some typing and filing, but once the business started to grow, she retired. She comes into the office once a year to do the Christmas party, which is just fine. She doesn't have a mind for business. She does throw a good party, though. She gets the best people and she makes sure that they don't rob us blind. Caterers do that, you know. Especially with corporate clients. Laura is wise to things like that."

"It's a good quality for the wife of a man in your position."

As though only then realizing what he'd said, Bruce compensated by turning gruff. "The wife of a man in my position should know not to make a scene in the office about his indiscretions. She should know not to run to a lawyer the first chance she gets. And she should know not to bar him from his own home. I put up with that for one night, but that was it. I have never been, nor am I now, a violent man, but when my wife unfairly cuts me off, when she won't even let me explain myself, I refuse to sit idly by and take it."

Sawyer could identify with that, too. Faith had frustrated him nearly beyond belief by repeatedly hanging up on him. The frustration had built and built through the night, so that by the time he'd stormed into her office that morning, he was harboring feelings that had bordered on the violent. "What, exactly, did you do?" he asked Bruce, as curious as he was wary.

"I lost my temper, knocked a few things on the floor, but they were harmless things," he added quickly, "like letters and magazines and folded laundry. She leaves the laundry on the stairs every day. It's the most annoying thing. She finally carries it up before she goes to bed, but in the meantime it sits there staring at me."

Sawyer wouldn't mind laundry staring at him as long as it was clean and had been made so by someone other than himself. Of all the chores he'd come into since his divorce, doing laundry was the worst. "Be grateful she does it for you."

"She doesn't. The laundress does. But the laundress doesn't go upstairs. Only the cleaning girl does that, and you can't expect the cleaning girl to be putting personal things away, Laura says. I suppose she has a point. My laundry is always clean when I need it, so I really can't complain." His voice hardened. "I can complain about other things, though. The problem is that I haven't. I've kept my mouth shut too long. So now when I open it to her for the first time, she feels threatened. Well, she should!"

Sawyer would have raised an arm and shouted, "Right on!" if it hadn't been for the one point his client was conveniently forgetting. The marriage, for all its faults, had endured for twenty-four years until Bruce had cheated on his wife. Sawyer wasn't condemning him for it. That wasn't his job. His job was to best advise and represent Bruce in any divorce action that might be taken, and since misbehavior now could become a factor later, caution seemed the way to go.

"What I want you to do," he said, "is to cool it a little. If she's threatened because you're speaking up to her at home for the first time, that's one thing. But if the threat becomes physical, or she *perceives* it as being physical, that's another."

Bruce was indignant. "I wouldn't touch her. I'm not that kind of man."

"I know, but sometimes when men are provoked they do things they wouldn't normally do. It sounds to me like your wife is provoking you these days."

"That's an understatement."

"It also sounds like you've got a real communication problem."

"Maybe," Bruce admitted.

"Are you determined to stay at the house?"

"Yes. At least until she listens to my side of the story."

Sawyer paused, then asked slowly, "Do you want this divorce?" As things stood the Friday before when they'd last spoken, Bruce had been ready to file papers. He'd been angry, of course, mostly at the way his wife had confronted him, and he'd been frightened by Laura's hiring Faith, which was why he'd been so quick to put Sawyer on retainer. Apparently either the anger and fear had faded, or simply shifted in focus.

Good businessman that he was, Bruce said, "I'm making no decisions yet."

"Do you think you can salvage the marriage?"

"I don't know. She's furious. I've never seen her furious before."

"You've never cheated on her before. That does something to a woman."

"I suppose."

"Look, I'm not making judgments. I don't pretend to know what your marriage was like or what caused the affair at the Four Seasons. You should know, though, and if you don't, you'd better try to find out. Communication is the key. I can mediate things, but only to a point. Have you considered going to a counselor?"

"I haven't had time to consider much of anything. I'm too busy trying to make sure she doesn't have the locks on the house changed while I'm at work."

"Would she do that?"

"If she does, I'll put a stop on her charge cards."

"Did you tell her that?"

"Yes, sir."

"Have you told her you're not sure you want a divorce?"

"I told her I'd fight her. I didn't say whether I was talking about the divorce itself or a settlement. I just wanted her to know that I won't be a pansy anymore when it comes to her. If she wants to fight, I'll show her how it's done."

"Be cautious. I can't advise that enough. Be cautious." He hesitated. "One last thought. The affair—is it really over?"

"It's over."

"So if your wife were to hire a private investigator, he wouldn't find you anywhere you shouldn't be?"

"No, sir."

"That's good. There's no need to rile her up any more than she already is. Legally you have every right to stay at the house, but while you're doing it, try to give her some breathing space. Let her calm down a little. Maybe then you'll be able to talk."

LONG AFTER Sawyer hung up the phone he thought about that advice. It applied to Faith and him, he knew. Their relationship had taken several dramatic twists in less than three days, and in the process emotions had been stirred.

Those emotions had to simmer a bit, then settle. Maybe, he mused, he and Faith would be best not seeing each other for a few days.

It was an ironic thought. He hadn't seen Faith for *weeks* before last Friday. Their paths just hadn't crossed often lately. Yet they were best of friends. When they were together, they picked up right where they had left off. They were thoroughly compatible.

They'd always been so. He thought back to the times they'd spent together during law school, where they'd met, and then after, when they'd been establishing themselves in the legal world. They'd always been close, regardless of how frequently or infrequently they saw each other. There was one big difference between those earlier times and now, of course. They'd felt safe then, unthreatened by each other because they were married to other people.

Now they were free, which was certainly why they'd allowed Friday night to happen. But he wasn't sorry it had. He'd done his share of socializing since he and Joanna were divorced, and Faith was head and shoulders above those other women. Sure, it had been a shock waking up in her bed. It had been a shock realizing the way their making love had happened. And it was going to necessitate a rethinking of their relationship. But he wasn't convinced their becoming more than friends was so terrible.

The problem was to convince Faith of that.

CHAPTER SIX

FAITH SPENT THE WEEK trying to convince herself that Sawyer was nothing but a good friend, a fellow lawyer with whom she just happened to share a case, and a one-time lover. The last caused her the most problem, because much as she tried she couldn't forget the way he'd kissed her. Not when he was making love to her on the rug in the urban night light. But when he'd kissed her in her office in the bold light of morning.

He hadn't been drunk then, not even tipsy. There had been nothing to blur his judgment, still he'd kissed her like a lover, and she'd responded. Worse, the response hadn't ended when he'd walked out the door. It had burrowed deep inside, making her restless ever since.

He'd made his point, all right. She was attracted to him—which was just fine, she told herself. Just because a woman was attracted to a man didn't mean there had to be a heavy relationship. She didn't want a heavy relationship. She'd been through the disillusionment of one that had petered out, scattering hopes and dreams to the wind. Now she was enjoying her freedom, and if there were times when she thought of such things as having a family, she reminded herself that she had time. She was only thirty-three. Not over the hill quite yet.

Still her thoughts kept returning to Sawyer and that kiss. It had been, without a doubt, the most exciting kiss she'd ever received. As conservative as he looked on the outside, that kiss had been wild and unconstrained, and he hadn't apologized for it—not when he'd given it, nor in the hours after.

Hours stretched into days, and she didn't hear from him. She was alert when she passed through the lobby of the office building they shared, when she walked through the nearby streets, even when she was in the courthouse, but she didn't catch sight of him once.

Finally Friday morning, she had what she felt was a legitimate reason to call. She reached him at the office on the second try, just as he returned from an appointment.

"Hi, Sawyer." She sounded calm, despite the acceleration of her pulse. She wasn't sure how she'd be received.

"Faith!" He shrugged out of his trench coat, only mildly winded from the dash through the rain and up the stairs. "I just got in."

"I'm sorry to bother you."

"No bother." He was inordinately pleased that she'd called, inordinately pleased that she sounded amiable, given the way they'd last parted. "Is everything okay?"

On one hand, it was. His tone of voice, enthusiastic but with that last bit of concern, was the Sawyer she knew and loved. She felt back on stable ground, at least where he was concerned.

On the other hand, there was no stable ground at her client's house. "Laura Leindecker just called. Her husband's gone. After sticking to her like glue all week, he just…disappeared. You haven't by chance heard from him, have you?"

Sawyer frowned. "Not since Monday. When was the last time she saw him?"

"Yesterday morning. He didn't come back to the house last night."

"I'd have thought she'd be pleased. She wanted him out."

"She's worried. It may be habit, still she's worried."

Tossing his trench coat aside, he dropped into his chair. "Are you sure the word isn't *suspicious?*" he asked, but in a curious way, rather than a snide one. "Maybe she's thinking he's with another woman."

Faith had wondered about that, had even dared ask it. Laura had been uneasy with the question. "It would be impossible for her not to be suspicious. She found that note. He admitted to being unfaithful. A basic trust was destroyed then." She paused, trying to hone in on her instincts and convey them to one who might help. "Laura wants to be able to say that he's with another woman, but I think her worry goes deeper. I think she's genuinely concerned."

"Has she called the office?"

"She was embarrassed to do it herself, so she had her cleaning girl do it. He wasn't there. His secretary said he was out for the day."

"Maybe he's away on business."

"He didn't pack any things. I thought maybe he'd contacted you, but if he hasn't—"

"Let me make a few calls." Sawyer had already flipped through the pink slips that were sitting on his desk. None had to do with Bruce Leindecker. "I may be able to push the right buttons and get some information. Will you be in the office for a little while?"

"I won't go anywhere until you call back. Thanks, Sawyer."

As she quietly hung up the phone, she realized that she felt better than she had all week. She liked having Sawyer on her side. He'd been there for so many years, an able resource person, a shoulder to lean on. Strange that their doing something as intimate as making love should pit them against each other—and it had done that, more so than the Leindecker case. If she was lucky, maybe the Leindecker case would be the thing to get them back on the track of being friends. He had certainly been the old, dependable, agreeable, helpful Sawyer a minute ago.

He was all of those things when he called back half an hour later. "Bruce is fine. He's with their son, Tim, in Longmeadow."

Faith let out a soft breath. "Laura will be relieved. She'll also be furious. Why didn't he tell her where he was going?"

"He didn't know where he was going until he got there. He's pretty upset about all this. Wasn't sure Laura would give a damn."

"Of course she gives a damn. They've been married for twenty-four years."

"Apparently she's been cursing that fact in no uncertain terms all week."

"He's been in her hair all week."

"So he figured he'd give her a break. He needed one, too."

"Maybe Tim will be a calming force."

Sawyer would have liked that, but the brief time he'd spent talking with Tim on the phone wasn't reassuring. "I...wouldn't count on it."

"Uh-oh," Faith said. "What's Tim's gripe?"

"He got married last year. Laura doesn't like his wife. Doesn't think she's good enough. There are some hard feelings, I guess."

"You guess," Faith murmured. The Leindecker case, like many of the other divorces she'd handled, was beginning to sound like a soap opera. But she was being paid to consider each new plot twist. "I guess I'd better call Laura and tell her Bruce is all right. Did he say when he'll be home?"

"When I asked, he got a little annoyed. He said that he's too old to be reporting in, and anyway, she kicked him out, he says. I told him to remember that she was worried. Maybe you could tell her to bear with him."

"I think I can do that," Faith said and reflected on the discussion. Laura swore that she wanted a divorce, which was why Faith had accepted a retainer. But there were times when Faith wondered. "Are we negotiating a divorce here, or mediating a marital squabble? I mean, I'm all for encouraging reconciliation, but I'm a lawyer, not a therapist."

"Mmm. It gets tedious sometimes."

"Do you ever want out?" she asked, thinking in broader terms.

"Lots of times. That's why divorce work is only a small part of my practice. What about you? You do it more often than me."

"I don't like the tedium either. But there's probably less of it in the cases I do. Mostly I represent women, and women are the underdogs in most divorce proceedings nowadays."

"Is Laura Leindecker an underdog?"

"I'm...not quite sure. I'm not quite sure about lots of things relating to this case."

"Ditto," Sawyer said, but he was more interested in other things about which he wasn't quite sure. "I'm heading down to the Cape first thing in the morning. Want to come?"

It was a minute before Faith adjusted to the shift in gears, and even then, the invitation had popped out so suddenly that she couldn't take it seriously. "Uh, thanks, Sawyer, but I've got a million things to do tomorrow."

"Do them today."

"I'm working today."

"Tonight. Do your million things tonight. Come with me tomorrow." His voice was deep and earnest.

"You're serious," she said, realizing it just then.

"Of course I'm serious. Did you doubt it?"

"I…yes. It seemed like such an unpremeditated suggestion."

"It was, but it's a good one. I want you to see the house."

Faith wanted to see it, too. She also wanted to spend time with Sawyer, who was nicer to be with than just about anyone she knew. She'd have agreed to go in a minute—if it hadn't been for the Friday night before. Thanks to that night, something more than friendship existed between them. She'd spent far too much time thinking about that something than she cared to admit. It had haunted her—the flash of his large hand molding her breast, the wetness of his mouth on her belly, the piercing strength of him as he filled her from the inside out. The haunting made her weak in the knees, and weak in the knees translated into weak in resolve, and without resolve, she didn't trust herself.

"I don't know, Sawyer," she said so softly that her message came across loud and clear.

"Nothing has to happen," he assured her in a voice that was every bit as quiet, but far more sure. "There's nothing remotely seductive or romantic about the place. It's old and broken-down. I'm reshingling the roof. I work the whole time I'm there, and when I'm done working, I'm tired."

He was trying to paint an unappealing picture, she

knew, but he failed. The image of Sawyer Bell on the roof doing physical labor was enticing. "So if you're working all the time, what will I do?"

"Look around and decide whether you think I ought to torch the place."

"You can't torch it, Sawyer. Besides, my looking around won't take long. What do I do when I'm done with that?"

"Strip paint from the moldings around the fireplace."

"You'd put me to work?"

"If you're bored. It's good therapy. We agreed on that, remember?"

She remembered, but that didn't alter the fact that if she went to the Cape with him, they'd be together for an extended period of time. A body could only work so long. When it was done working, it could get into mischief.

"I don't know," she said again. This time her voice was softened by a blend of wistfulness and apprehension. "You'll want to stay overnight."

Sawyer hesitated for just a minute. "Yes." He knew what she was thinking. "Nothing has to happen, Faith. We can spend the day working, then go out to dinner and catch a movie or something."

"Where would we sleep?"

"Wherever you want."

"Where do you usually sleep?"

"In a sleeping bag on the floor. But that doesn't mean you have to do it. The floor is warped. It's worse than sleeping on bare ground. It's fine for me, but I wouldn't expect you to rough it that way."

"I'm not fragile."

"You're used to comfort."

"That doesn't mean I can't live without it for a night. I'm not made of fluff."

"But you're a woman."

"So?"

"So your body doesn't conform as well to the floor as mine does. You have curves, Faith. My body is straighter and harder than yours."

For the space of a breath, Faith didn't speak. Then she murmured, "That's what worries me," and it was Sawyer's turn to be silent.

Finally he said quietly, "I want to be with you this weekend, and it doesn't have to be a sexual thing. It can be purely platonic. We'll be friends like we've always been. We won't do anything you don't want to do."

"That's what worries me," she repeated, and Sawyer understood.

"You don't trust yourself?" He hoped it was true. It wasn't that he was a sadist, just that he'd been aroused and aching too often that week. He wanted to think Faith had been, too.

"I'm not sure. I keep thinking about last Friday night and asking why I didn't stop what was happening. I guess—" she rushed on before he could remind her of the wine they'd drunk "—I'm not convinced I was out of it. I remember too many things too clearly."

Sawyer had been asking himself similar questions all week, but he wasn't about to discuss them now. If he could get Faith away with him, they'd have plenty of time to talk. "We won't have anything to drink this weekend. Nothing but coffee. Come with me, Faith. It'll be good for both of us."

"I don't want to make love."

"Then we won't."

"What if I ask for it?"

"Then we will."

"But I don't want to." She straightened in her chair. "Okay, Sawyer, I'll go down to the Cape with you on one condition. You have to keep things under control. I'm telling you now that I don't want to make love. It's your responsibility to make sure we don't, regardless of what I say when we're down there."

"That's absurd."

"I won't be able to relax with you unless you agree."

Sawyer brushed at the moisture breaking out over his lip. "That's just as absurd as the other. What if you find that you do want it? What if you're relaxed but making love will relax you even more? What if the pain of *not* making love is driving you crazy? What if you're begging me for it? Christ, Faith, I'm not a saint!"

"Then I won't go."

"I'll be a saint."

She had to smile at the speed of his turnaround. But before she could comment on it, he grumbled, "I wonder if this is what Leindecker's been going through all these years. A man thinks he's in control, then a woman gives him an ultimatum and he crumbles."

"Don't crumble. I'm counting on you to be strong. That's your forte, Sawyer. You're a big, strong male. Much stronger than me—isn't that how the chauvinist credo reads?"

"Cute, Faith."

"But I'm serious, at least about your being strong. You are, and I'm trusting you." She paused. "Do you still want to go, or is the invitation rescinded?"

"We're going," he grumbled. "I'll pick you up at six tomorrow morning."

"*Six.* You didn't say anything about—"

"Six. Be ready, or I'm leaving without you."

Before Faith could argue, she was staring at the phone, which was dead in her hand. Replacing it in its cradle, she sat back in her chair, linked her fingers, pressed them to her mouth and wondered whether she was making a mistake. She'd given in to temptation, and though Sawyer had promised to save her from it—and though she trusted him to do just that—there was more to temptation than just sex.

Being with Sawyer, spending the entire weekend with him was a treat she couldn't pass up. She didn't have anything pressing to do over the weekend, and even if she had she couldn't think of anything that would appeal to her more than being with him.

Besides, she needed a weekend away.

Besides, she wouldn't mind stripping the moldings by the fireplace.

Besides, she liked the spontaneity of the whole thing.

So she was going. Feeling slightly scattered, even a little light-headed, she dropped her hands from her mouth and looked down to her desk to see what she had to do before she went home. It was a minute before she could make any sense of the papers strewn before her. They were the rough notes for a talk on family law she was delivering to a law-school class the following Wednesday night, and she wanted it to be good. She wanted to teach her own full-term course one day; for that reason alone she had to impress both her students and whatever faculty members might be listening in.

But she wasn't in the mood for concentration just then, so she gathered the papers up, thinking to work on them at home that night. Taking a file from her cabinet, she set it with the papers, then, wiping her palms on her skirt, looked around the office for anything else she'd need.

Almost absently, she glanced at her watch and realized
that it was only three o'clock. She couldn't leave for the
day. Loni hadn't left. It was far too early—unless she had
a court appearance or some other kind of appointment,
which she didn't. So she sat back down in her chair and
reached for the papers she'd so neatly piled together. She
opened to the page she'd been reading, but ten minutes
of staring at it without comprehending a word convinced
her that it was best saved for another time.

Straightening the papers again, she slid them into her
briefcase. Then she sat back, crossed her legs, took a pad
of paper onto her lap and began to make a list of calls she
wanted to make on Monday in reference to a client whose
custody hearing was approaching. She had four names
and numbers listed when, with a start, she realized that
she hadn't called Laura Leindecker back.

Cursing her distraction, she immediately phoned the
woman and passed on the information Sawyer had given
her. Laura was relieved, then annoyed.

"Where does that leave me?" she asked. "Am I supposed to sit around all weekend and wait for him to come
home?"

"What would you normally do?"

"Sit around all weekend and wait for him to come
home. But I'm tired of doing that."

"Where will you go?"

"Out."

"What will you do?"

"Shop."

"Oh. Okay." Faith took a breath. "May I make a
suggestion?"

"Please do."

"I think that perhaps you should start thinking about
what you want from this divorce in terms of the division

of property. Once we formally file papers, we'll get into those kinds of negotiations. It would help if you think about them now."

It was a new tack. Until then, Faith had focused on whether or not Laura wanted the divorce. From the start, Laura had insisted that she did, still Faith knew that the decision had been ruled by anger and hurt, far more than reason. Faith suspected that once Laura turned her thoughts to the specifics of getting divorced and *being* divorced, she might decide it wasn't what she wanted at all.

"I'll think about it," Laura said, but a bit defensively. "He'll fight me. He said he would."

"He doesn't want the divorce?"

"He *must* want it. After all, he's the one who found me so inadequate that he had to go looking for satisfaction with another woman."

Hearing Laura's hurt so bluntly expressed, Faith hurt for her in turn. "Have you asked him why he did that?" she asked gently.

Laura answered in an uneasy tone. "Went to another woman? I think it's obvious."

"Not necessarily. There are reasons why men do things, and being women, we don't always understand. It helps to ask sometimes."

"I can't. It would be too humiliating."

"It may not be as humiliating as you think. It may be that what your husband did had to do with him and something he's going through right now. It may have had little to do with you." She paused. When Laura didn't argue, she said, "Talk with him—if not about the affair, then about the divorce. And remember, stay calm. The calmer you are, the more you'll get from him. If he's determined to fight you, that's something we'll just have to face, but for now, the calmer you are, the better."

STAY CALM. STAY CALM. Those words became a litany in Faith's mind through the rest of that day. Each time she thought of going away with Sawyer, her stomach started to jump. She wasn't sure if it was excitement or nervousness, and she didn't stop to analyze which. She simply repeated the litany in her mind and went about doing everything she had to do to free herself up for Saturday and Sunday.

Actually, if it hadn't been for that jumping stomach, she'd never have made it out of bed when her alarm rang at five-thirty Saturday morning. She hadn't been able to fall asleep until after one, which meant that she was sleeping soundly when the alarm went off. It was pitch-black outside, still night in her book, but the instant she realized why she was getting up so early, her body came to life.

Quickly she showered, dried her hair and applied the lightest possible sheen of makeup. After pulling on a pair of jeans and a comfortable sweater, she put a change of clothes into an overnight bag, along with whatever else she decided she'd need for a rustic sleepover. She was zipping the bag when the doorbell rang.

Sawyer looked stern, dark and tired. She was certain something awful had happened to him, but when she asked, he merely shrugged. "I couldn't sleep." He straightened from the doorjamb which had been bearing the brunt of his weight. "Actually that's a lie. I purposely kept myself awake most of the night so that I'd be too tired to do anything tonight."

Faith closed her eyes to his self-mocking look. "Oh, Sawyer."

"You said it was my responsibility, so I'm making good on it." He reached for her bag. "Is this it?"

"We're only going overnight."

"But overnight usually means three changes of clothes, two jackets, boots, sneakers and flats, a makeup case, a hair dryer, a curling iron, a vacuum cleaner—"

Faith swept past him into the hall, tugged him out by the arm and slammed the door. She didn't say another word until he'd tucked her into the passenger's seat of his racy black Porsche. "Some car," she breathed, running a hand lightly over the butter-soft leather covering the seat. "Is it new?"

Sawyer took a deep breath. He knew he was being a pill, but he couldn't seem to help himself. He'd stayed up most of the night thinking of Faith, so not only was he tired, but his body was tight. It hadn't helped that he'd slept through his alarm. He'd had time for nothing but a record-fast shower. What he needed was coffee and fresh air.

"I got it six months ago," he said as he rolled down his window. "Usually I rent a pickup when I drive to the Cape. I need the space in back for tools and stuff."

"Why didn't you this time?"

"I wanted to impress you with the Porsche."

Studying his profile, she saw that he wasn't joking. She didn't know whether to yell at him or be pleased. In lieu of either, she said, "I'm impressed. But what are you going to do when you need the space for tools and stuff?"

"I won't this trip. Everything I need is already at the house." He shot her a quick glance, the first softened one since he'd arrived. "Did you have any trouble getting up?"

His glance warmed her. Still, she wasn't about to say

that she'd jumped right out of bed in anticipation of seeing him, so she shrugged. "It'd be nice if the sun came up."

"It's coming," he said, and once they cruised their way free of the city buildings, she could see that it was. A faint strip of lavender lay on the eastern horizon with promise of daylight. She found that reassuring. When things were dark, the confines of the car were more intimate, and intimacy wasn't something she wanted to encourage.

They headed south on the expressway. Not long after they'd left the city, Sawyer took a short exit and pulled in at a coffee shop. "Black with one sugar?"

"Good memory."

"I'll be back."

Several minutes later he returned with two large coffees, a bag of donuts and more napkins than they'd use in a year. "Are you stocking up for the house?" she teased.

Sawyer didn't answer until he'd taken several healthy swallows of coffee. The fresh air had helped when it came to mellowing his mood; he was relying on caffeine to do the rest. "They're for the car. If something spills, I want to be able to clean it up."

Faith knew how things were between a man and his car. "Ahhh," she breathed in understanding, then pulled a honey-dipped donut from the bag and took a bite.

Sawyer demolished three in the time it took her to eat one. "I'm getting a refill of coffee. Want one?"

"No, thanks. This is fine."

He left the car, returned with a fresh cup of coffee, tore the cover enough to allow him to drink, then started the engine and returned to the road.

"How long will it take to get there?" she asked.

"An hour and a half. There won't be any traffic this time of day."

"I wonder why not," she murmured, but teasingly. With

donuts filling her stomach and the warm smell of coffee filling the car, she was beginning to relax. Sawyer was a good driver. The car was a beauty. The dawning day was clear and bright. At that moment she was very glad she'd come.

The feeling was every bit as strong when Sawyer finally turned the Porsche off the main road onto the private one that wove through his property. Framed on either side by broad-leaved trees and shrubs, it narrowed, turned from hardtop to gravel and grew bumpy. He swore and slowed the Porsche to a crawl.

"Don't worry about me," Faith said, trying not to smile as she looked at him. "I don't mind the bumps." When he didn't answer, she gave in and laughed.

"What's so funny?"

"You. You look like you're in agony."

"I am."

"You're worried about the car. Don't be, Sawyer. It'll survive. What are shock absorbers for, anyway?" Returning her gaze to the front window, she couldn't contain her surprise. "Sawyer?"

He was pulling up at a most unusual structure. Turning off the engine, he curved both hands over the top of the steering wheel. "This is it."

She let out her breath in a thoroughly confused, "Ahhh."

"What do you think?"

"I think…that you're right. The setting is great. The land is gorgeous, lush even this late in the season. Are those apple trees over there? But where's the lake? You said you were on a lake." She opened the door of the car and climbed out. "Is it behind the…house?" She took off in that direction, but she hadn't gone more than three steps into the soft grass when Sawyer caught her hand.

"You don't like it," he said.

"I think it's great."

"I'm not talking about the land. We both know that's great. But what about the house?"

She forced herself to focus on the building. It was tall, round and covered with aged bricks. "It looks like a water tower."

"That's what it is."

"But you called it a house."

"If a house is defined as a place to live in, this is a house. Come on. I want you to see the inside."

Faith allowed herself to be led to a doorway that looked as though it might crumble on the spot. The doorjamb was rotted and hanging off on one side. It was a miracle that the door stayed shut.

Not only did it stay shut, but it wouldn't open—at least, not until Sawyer pushed hard.

Inside, all was dark. Sawyer seemed to know what was where, though, because within seconds he produced a hurricane lamp and lit it. Holding it aloft, he guided her into the center of the room.

Cautiously, staying close enough to him to feel the reassuring warmth of his body, Faith looked around. The room was larger than she'd expected and empty save for Sawyer's roofing material piled to one side and a network of pipes that snaked up its walls. Those walls were of the same exposed brick as the exterior, and looked nearly as weathered. The floor was concrete, dirty and cracked. There wasn't a window in sight.

"This place is spooky," she whispered.

"But it has promise." Still holding her hand, he led her forward.

They were nearly on top of the far wall before she made out a door. Pushing it open, Sawyer led her into an annex that she hadn't been able to see from outside. It was rectangular, narrower than the water tower but deeper, and had windows, wallpapered walls, planked floors and a fireplace.

While it wasn't Versailles, it was a decided improvement on the water tower. She let out a breath. "Better. Much better."

Extinguishing the hurricane lamp, Sawyer set it aside. He took a long tube from the painted mantel above the fireplace, tipped out its contents and unrolled what were clearly an architect's plans for the renovation of the place. Spreading the plans on the floor, he began to explain them to her.

By the time he was done, Faith was sitting cross-legged beside him feeling the fool for her shortsightedness. "You're right," she admitted. "It does have promise. Once windows are cut in the water tower and a sleeping loft is built above the living room, it'll be completely different."

Sawyer looked around the annex. "Once the door is widened and this place is gutted and rebuilt with modern kitchen and bathing facilities, it'll be even *more* different. I agree, it's pretty depressing right now. But there was something about it that appealed to me right away—maybe its isolation, or the woods or the lake, or the uniqueness of the whole thing. I guess that was it. The uniqueness." He gave Faith a smile that melted whatever chill may have seeped into her from the innards of the tower. "Who else do you know who can say that he lives in a converted water tower?"

"Not a soul." She looked back at the plans and grinned. "Not a soul. *Unique* is the word, all right."

"So you think I should go ahead with it?"

Her grin lingered when she raised her eyes to his. "Definitely. I think it's a super project."

"Don't think I should torch it?"

"You can't. Brick won't burn."

Other things could, though, and Faith suddenly grew aware of them—Sawyer's brown eyes darker than they'd been but warmer, heating her cheeks, her mind, her blood. She could do without that kind of burning, too.

Scrambling to her feet, she brushed off the seat of her pants. "Are we working?"

"We're working."

"Let's get to it, then. From the looks of those plans, there's plenty to do."

CHAPTER SEVEN

SAWYER DIDN'T PLAN to do all the work himself. He would have liked to, but he knew his limitations. For starters, time was a factor. At the rate of two weekends a month, it would take him years to make the place livable. He wanted to be able to enjoy it before that. And then there was the matter of skill. He was a lawyer, not a carpenter or a mason or a millworker. He knew how to reshingle a roof, how to refinish floors, how to miter moldings, even how to install cabinets, but when it came to carving windows through brick, wiring an electrical system, designing a heating system and installing new plumbing, he was willing to yield to the experts.

He told Faith as much when they took a break for lunch, which consisted of burgers at a diner on the way into town. "There's no point in doing it if it isn't done right. I don't want to end up with something that will blow apart when the first coastal storm hits."

Faith had spent a good part of the morning in and out of the water tower, first relaying shingles up to Sawyer, then trying to familiarize herself with the tower so she wouldn't shiver each time she walked in. Putting a jacket over her sweater helped beat the chill; she wasn't quite as successful fighting the heeby-jeebies.

"That water tower would withstand an assault by Attila the Hun," she maintained in a wry tone of voice.

Sawyer grinned. "Solid, huh?"

His grin was filled with pride, but it wasn't pride that suffused Faith's insides with a now familiar heat. It was the grin itself, a slash of lips and teeth that was a little curious, a little daring, a little wicked and very, very masculine. And the grin came often. With the drive behind them, with Sawyer fully awake, with the worst of his frustration expended on the roof, he was in the best of moods.

As far as Faith was concerned, that was dangerous. Each time he grinned, she felt tiny prickles of awareness march through her belly. She tried to think back to the days when he grinned and she enjoyed it in an innocent way, but those days seemed an aeon ago. She wasn't sure she was ever again going to be able to see Sawyer's grin without melting a little inside.

The water tower, she supposed, was in apt counterpoint to what she was feeling. "Very solid," she confirmed.

His grin relaxed when he took a large bite of his sandwich, but all that did was to shift her awareness from his mouth to his other features. Though he'd washed up before they left the house, he still had the rugged look of a workman. Part of it was due, she was sure, to the gray athletic T-shirt he wore under a faded flannel shirt, jeans that were old, worn and thin, and work boots. The other part was due to the muss of his dark hair, the ruddy color on his cheeks, the size and sinewed strength of his hands, and the power of his features, which seemed, here in the country, more exposed than usual.

Faith needed a diversion. "How did you find the tower? Had you been looking for land down here?"

"Not exactly," he said, but he, too, was distracted. The look in her eyes just then had been full of the kind of appreciation that men dreamed of receiving from lovely women. She fought it; he could see how she deliberately brought herself back, but for several minutes she'd been swept up by something over which she had little control.

That was a good sign, he decided. Faith had a thing about control. She was a harsh taskmaster when it came to ruling herself. It would do her good to lose control once in a while.

As long as he didn't. He'd promised her.

Clearing his throat, he finished his burger off in a bite. When it had gone the way of both its predecessor and a large order of fries, he said, "I got lost, actually. I was visiting friends who were renting a place down here, and I got the directions screwed up. I wound up at the water tower, and it intrigued me."

"Did you know it was for sale?"

"Not then. I finally managed to get where I was supposed to go, and I went back to Boston at the end of the day, but I kept thinking about the tower. It looked abandoned. So I made a few calls, found out that the whole parcel of land was for sale and came down the next weekend to look again."

Faith remembered some of the discussions she'd had with Sawyer way back when. "You always wanted a vacation place. You used to talk about finding something in northern Maine."

"Mmm. Joanna hated that idea. She may have been as maternal as they came, but Earth Mother she wasn't. The thought of being too far from civilization frightened her."

"She'd have liked it down here. You're isolated, but you're not."

"Her loss."

"Your gain. It's really a super place, Sawyer."

He raised two fingers to the waitress and called for

coffee. "It'll be even more super when it's done. It won't ever be big, but the way the architect has it planned, there'll be room for everything I want. It'll be a year-round escape." Putting his weight on his elbows, he met her gaze with a look that was frank and unguarded. "I've wanted something like this for years. I wanted it when I was a kid, only my parents couldn't afford their own house, let alone a vacation place. I wanted it when Joanna and I first married, only I didn't have the money then, either. Joanna was the one who bought the house in Cambridge. I was getting benefits from Uncle Sam, and that helped a lot when I was in school, but even when I finally graduated, it was a while before I hit the upper brackets."

The waitress came with their coffee. Sawyer handed Faith a packet of sugar, took two for himself and two thimbles of cream, and focused on the mocha-colored brew as he stirred it. "By the time I had enough in the bank to think about a second home, Joanna and I were on the skids. I felt badly about that. She deserved more of the fruits of her labor than she got. I didn't take care of her very well, at least not during our marriage."

Faith had to smile, but it was a smile made soft by understanding and admiration. Sawyer was, indeed, a throwback to the days where men took care of women. She didn't find it offensive just then, though. As he talked so quietly and honestly, she saw him for the protective and caring man that he was. Joanna, with her need to protect rather than be protected, to care for rather than be cared for, couldn't appreciate him.

Faith could. The thought surprised her, because she saw herself as a thoroughly independent woman, but at that moment, away from the city and her thoroughly independent world, she found the idea of being protected and cared for strangely appealing.

"Does Joanna know what she gave up?" she heard herself ask.

If there was a compliment inherent in the question, Sawyer missed it. He was shifting his coffee cup in its saucer, studying each turn. "She didn't give up so much. When I was in school, I studied most of the time. When I got a job, I worked most of the time. I wasn't much of a companion for her. I think she was as relieved as I was when we finally called it quits."

"Who handled the divorce?"

"Me. It was an easy thing. We agreed on the property settlement. I gave most everything and then some. She'd earned it."

"You are a good man."

He looked up at her. "I like to think I'm a fair one. The marriage wasn't going anywhere, but Joanna had invested a great deal of time and effort in me. Largely thanks to her, I was healthy and productive. She deserved a good settlement. I wasn't about to rob her of it just because I knew I could get away with it in court." He paused, frowned. "Why is it we always end up talking about the past?"

"Because it's part of us. You went through a lot with Joanna. Just because the marriage is over doesn't mean you forget her."

"Is it the same with you and Jack?"

"I don't know," Faith said. She shifted her gaze to the counter, but she was oblivious to the people perched on leather-covered stools at the bar. "Jack and I didn't go through anything like you and Joanna did. He was just there. I went about my life, he went about his. It was an increasingly uninteresting relationship."

"Was it interesting when you first met him?"

Sitting back in the booth, she looked down at her hands. "I'm not sure."

"Did you love him?"

"I guess so."

"You weren't sure?"

Faith raised her head and spoke in her own defense. "I had to do something. I was fresh out of college, just starting law school, and it seemed that everywhere I turned, someone was telling me that if I didn't marry soon, I never would. They said that once I became a career woman I wouldn't have time for anything else. They said that if I was successful, I'd become so threatening to men that none of them would come close." Her words stopped. She shrugged. The ghost of a smile touched her lips and was gone. "I guess I bought it all."

"Who was doing the selling?"

She didn't answer at first. Disloyalty wasn't something she took pride in, and this time there was no wine to blunt the effect. But Sawyer was waiting for an honest answer—Sawyer, whom she trusted. "My family."

Studying her face, he saw a vulnerability that was entirely new. Gently he said, "I've never heard you talk about your family before."

"I try not to."

"You don't get along?"

"Oh, we get along just fine, as long as we don't discuss anything more weighty than the price of eggs."

"They don't live nearby, do they?" He was sure he'd have known if they did, principally because Faith would have been more involved with them.

"They're in Oregon."

"And you're on the opposite coast. By design?"

She pursed her lips, thought for a minute, gave a single slow nod.

"Safer that way?"

"You got it. My parents are very conventional people, and I'm not criticizing that. But I'm not conventional by their standards, and they do criticize me. I go back to visit once a year. That's enough."

"They must be proud of your work."

"They know nothing about it, other than that I'm a lawyer. For all of their interest in that, I could be a toll collector on the turnpike. I've tried to tell them about what I do. I've described some of the more interesting cases I've handled, but as soon as I stop for a breath, they're asking me whether or not I'm dating."

"Did they like Jack?"

"Jack was a husband. That pleased them. But then the questions started coming about babies, and when I told them I wasn't ready to have kids, that set them off. They always found something cutting to say. I've never fit into the mold of what they think a woman should be." Faith chewed on the inside of her lip for a minute. Slowly she released it and in a small voice said, "It hurts sometimes, y'know?"

Sawyer could see that hurt clear as day on her face. It was all he could do not to take her in his arms and soothe her, but he wasn't sure she'd want that. She took pride in being independent and strong. Then again, he wondered whether it was all pride or whether there wasn't a little defensiveness involved. Was she independent and strong because she wanted to be or because that was the only way she could manage on her own? And she was alone. He saw it now as he'd never seen it before. He wanted to soothe her for that, too, but he wasn't sure she'd want that, either.

Before he had a chance to do anything, she sighed. "So, anyway, Jack wasn't the most significant part of my life. He was just a physical presence while I went ahead and did what I would have done if I'd never married him. Sad, isn't it? It was a wasted relationship. I'm glad for his sake that he got out of it. He deserves more."

Sawyer wasn't so sure about that. In his book, Jack had had a gem in his hand and had dropped it. For his lack of care, he'd gotten what he deserved. "What about you? Don't you deserve more? I knew Jack. He was a nice guy, but he wasn't right for you. You were way ahead of him in most every way. He didn't satisfy you. He didn't challenge you. He didn't do anything for you that you couldn't do for yourself. So don't *you* deserve more?"

"I have my career."

"And what else?"

"Maybe that's enough."

"Is it?"

"More coffee, folks?" the waitress asked.

They swung their heads in her direction, startled by the interruption. Sawyer was the first to recover. "Uh, no. I'm fine. Faith?"

She shook her head.

"Just the check," Sawyer quietly told the waitress. When she tore it from the pad and put it on the table, he took it up in his hand. But he didn't look at it. His thoughts were elsewhere. "You sell yourself short, Faith. Maybe we both do. I say that Joanna is better off without me. You say that Jack is better off without you. Well, what about us? Don't we deserve excitement and happiness and fulfillment?" He opened his free hand to ward off an argument. "Yes, I know we get satisfaction from our work. But is it enough?"

Faith let the peripheral conversation, the occasional

laugh or cough, the clatter of china on china fill in where she had no words. At last, she murmured, "I don't know."

He let out a breath. "It's ironic, when you think of it." Not that he had. He usually took life pretty much as it came, without deep thought to the future. "The satisfaction we get from our work was probably what did in our marriages. So now that our marriages are done in, is work enough?" He paused, held her sober-eyed gaze, shrugged. "I don't know the answer, either."

"That's a relief. It makes me feel a little less inadequate." She reached for the check.

"Don't you dare," he growled.

Carefully she retrieved her hand and tucked it in her lap. She heard the voice of command, and while there were times when she felt compelled to exert herself, this wasn't one of them. Paying for lunch at a diner wasn't going to bankrupt either one of them. Somehow it seemed foolish to argue over the bill.

Walking back to the car, he dropped an arm around her shoulder. It was a deliberately casual gesture. "You're a good girl, Faith."

She tipped her head up against his arm and gave him a pert smile, which seemed the least a good girl could do. It also told him that she wasn't grappling with heavy questions such as the one he'd posed. There was a time and a place for everything. Being away for the weekend with Sawyer had its own challenges without the pressure of intense philosophical thought. Time enough to brood about her future in the future.

They made several stops on the way back to the house—one to pick up a sleeping bag for Faith to match the one Sawyer already had, another to pick up a cooler and juice, milk and cheese for snacks, a third to pick up nails, scrapers and sandpaper. But rather than going right back to work, they took a walk. Sawyer wanted to show Faith the lay of the land, and she didn't argue. She loved the outdoors. Well beyond being a break from the city, walking through Sawyer's sun-speckled acres was a treat.

The land was beautiful. It rolled gently from one copse to the next, a world of greenery touched by the occasional crimson or gold. Though it was October, fall was reluctant in coming, as though it knew that a special something would be lost once the trees were bare. As those trees stood, a light breeze stirred their leaves. The same breeze lifted Faith's hair to her cheeks and dusted Sawyer's over his forehead. The continuity was satisfying.

The lakefront was broad and peaceful, perfect for skipping stones and imagining the delights of swimming on warmer days. There was even a dock, decaying to be sure but sturdy enough to hold Sawyer and, when she finally dared join him, Faith. For a long while they sat there, enjoying the silence of the afternoon. Neither of them thought to disturb it with words.

Faith was content. Sitting beside Sawyer on the broken-down dock, she felt she was privy to a moment out of time. She'd left her responsibilities behind in Boston. Her sole job was to…be. On impulse, she lay back on the dock with her hands as a pillow and closed her eyes to the sun. Its warmth was gentle, safe, lulling. Giving in to the soft smile that begged for release, she basked in the serenity of the day.

Looking down at her, Sawyer broke into a smile of his own. Her pleasure pleased him. He'd wanted her to like his place, and she did. She hadn't spoken as they walked, but he could tell from the look on her face that she was enjoying herself.

She might not have. He felt that he knew her well, still the focus of that knowledge was the career they shared. When it came to things beyond the law, his experience with her was more limited. For all he knew, she might have hated the house, hated the architect's plans, hated the rustic, uncultured look of the land. She might have hated the thought of sleeping in a sleeping bag on the floor in front of a fire, but when he'd pointed to a motel they'd passed, she'd given a firm shake of her head. Possibly she was out to make the point that she wasn't as soft as he thought, but if so, there wasn't a chance in hell that she'd win. Looking at her, all stretched out on the dock in her soft sweater and soft jeans, with her soft curves shaping both, he was more aware than ever of her femininity.

As was his body. The longer he looked at her, the faster his heart beat, and the faster his heart beat, the warmer his blood flowed. Somewhere in the middle of that, desire began to gather into a tight knot in his groin.

Moving to ease the knot before it grew painful, he pushed himself to his feet. The dock gave an ominous creak and an even more ominous wobble. He held his breath.

Faith raised her head to look up at him through the shade cast over her body by his. "Back to work?"

"Very carefully," he advised. He gave her a hand up, keeping the movement as smooth as possible, and waited until she'd left the dock before following her. By the time he was by her side, walking back through the tall grasses toward the house, he was in control once again.

His control lasted through the afternoon, but that was easy. He spent most of the time on the cone-shaped roof of the water tower, hammering away at the cedar shingles that had to be spaced just so, to prevent seepage of rain or snow. Yes, it was physical labor, but it demanded a certain amount of concentration from a roofer with his very limited experience. When he finally descended the ladder for the last time, it was with a sense of satisfaction in what he'd done…and a slight apprehension about the evening that lay before him.

For the first time, he wondered whether he'd been wise to invite Faith to stay overnight. Whenever he looked at her, even more when he came close, he felt the same quickening in his body. Sometimes it was in the area of the heart, sometimes in his hands, which itched to touch her, sometimes lower, where the ache was primal.

But he'd promised her that he would be the guardian of her virtue for the night, and he was determined to keep that promise.

Faith was counting on him for that, so she could relax and enjoy herself without having to exert a great deal of constraint. She worked some as Sawyer suggested, scraping and sanding chipped paint from the molding that framed the fireplace, the doors and the annex windows. But she was ready to take breaks at the slightest excuse, whether that was to convey a cold drink to the roof, to wander out in the meadow and chart the gradual descent of the sun or to sit on the grass and watch Sawyer at work.

She was impressed. He was sure-footed and able as he carefully placed and hammered down each shingle. He'd long since tossed aside his flannel shirt, leaving him in the gray T-shirt that moved more easily with his shoulders and arms. As he built up a sweat, the shirt grew darker in patches. She was impressed by that, too, but in a different way.

Sitting on the grass with her arms around her knees, she wondered once again why she'd never noticed how virile he was. It seemed hard to believe that what she could drool over now had been before her many times before, and she hadn't appreciated it. Of course, she'd never before seen Sawyer in this kind of physical context, and besides, she couldn't have exactly drooled over him with Jack and Joanna in attendance. Still, she might have privately thought certain things, yet she hadn't. In that sense, she was impressed with herself.

When she married Jack, she had vowed to be faithful. She'd kept that vow. On occasion, she wondered if Jack had. She'd found nothing incriminating—not that she'd been looking—but there had certainly been nothing comparable to the note Laura Leindecker had discovered. Indeed, there had been times toward the end when Faith had almost wished Jack *would* have an affair, if only to make something happen. As it turned out, that hadn't been necessary. Emotional attrition finally took its toll.

So now, freed of the moral obligation of being true to Jack, she was seeing Sawyer in a different light. He turned her on. She was still appalled that they'd made love the way they had that Friday night, but she'd given up denying that the attraction was there. It existed, and it was strong. If she hadn't known it before this weekend, she couldn't miss it now. The question was where it would lead. Granted there was still the possibility that she was pregnant, but she didn't put much stock in that. She wasn't sure why—maybe gut instinct, or the romantic notion that when she conceived a child she'd know at the moment it happened—but she fully expected to get her period in another week. So that left the future very much open where she and Sawyer were concerned.

Where did she want it to go? She didn't know. And she didn't want to think about it. Thinking about it made her uneasy. She wasn't sure why, but it did. So she gathered herself up and went back to work inside until Sawyer called it a day.

"Hungry?" he asked as he leaned over the large sink on the wall of the annex that served as a kitchen. The bathroom sink was miniscule, something he was going to have to remedy.

Faith leaned against the most distant wall, watching him wash up. It was torture. He'd taken off the T-shirt and was sluicing water over his head and upper body with little concern for what splashed on the floor. Wet and gleaming, the sinewed twists at his arms and shoulders stood out well.

She took a shaky breath. "Uh-huh. I'm hungry."

"We could have dinner, then see a movie. There's usually something decent playing in Hyannis."

Faith wondered whether decent meant PG. She hoped so. She wasn't sure she could make it through an R-rated film without gnawing on Sawyer's neck. "That sounds good," she said, a little breathless.

Sawyer toweled himself off, reached for a clean T-shirt and pulled it on as quickly as he could. A sweater went over that, then he turned to her. "All set?"

With a nod, she led the way out through the tower, which was faintly lit now by the deep gold of the low-lying sun. Sensing there was a danger in lingering too long there, she hurried on.

DINNER WAS AN ENJOYABLE interlude before the movie, which turned out to have nothing to do with sex, for which Sawyer was eternally grateful. He didn't need the power of suggestion. His mind was providing plenty of that, and what his mind didn't respond to, his body did.

The air had cooled by the time they left the movie, and

by the time they returned to the house, that cool air had seeped in through the uninsulated walls of the annex.

"Last chance," Sawyer warned. He was on the verge of lighting a fire, holding split logs in each hand. "I can still drive you to a motel."

Faith wore a jacket over her sweater, and though she could feel the night air through the layers, she wasn't about to seek a more cushy shelter. "Don't be silly. This is fine."

"It'll get colder before it gets warmer."

"So light the fire. If that's not enough, I'll crawl into my sleeping bag, and if that's not enough, I'll turn on your car and sleep there."

"You will not."

She laughed. "Just kidding. Go on. Light the fire." She was feeling high without having had a thing to drink. But that was Sawyer's problem. He'd agreed to see that nothing happened.

Sawyer set the logs on the grate, added a third and some kindling, then lit a match. The kindling took off instantly, the logs a few minutes later. Soon the flames were leaping high, sending off a welcome heat.

He sat back several feet from the flames and watched them in silence.

"A penny for your thoughts," Faith said softly as she scooted on her bottom across the floor until she sat at right angles to him. That way she could see both the fire and his face.

"I don't think you want to hear."

"Sure I do."

He remained quiet, though, debating the pros and cons of being honest. His decision came only after he'd dared a quick look at her. Lit by the fire, her features were warm and beckoning, making mockery of the promise he'd made. He desperately wanted to touch her, even if only in the innocent way he might have done two weeks, a month, a year ago. It occurred to him that his best hope of not touching her was to be perfectly honest about his needs.

"I'm thinking," he said in a voice that was low and a little gritty, "that I should be tired. I was up at six. I didn't get much sleep last night. I worked hard for a good part of the day. I had a huge dinner, and that movie was boring as hell. I should be ready to go to sleep. But I'm not."

"Maybe you're overtired."

"That's not the problem." Slowly and more deliberately this time, he shifted his gaze to hers. "I want you, Faith. I know I promised not to touch you, but I'm jumping around inside. Call it restlessness or whatever, but I want you."

She hadn't expected him to be so blunt. For a minute, she wondered whether he was simply trying to shock her. But he wasn't that kind of man. He didn't do things for effect unless he was in the courtroom, and he wasn't there now. The courtroom, the law, Boston were all far, far away. It was just the two of them sitting before a fire in his broken-down house on the Cape. Things were more raw here, unpadded, free of the city's gloss. That knowledge was what made the look in his eyes so stunning. It was a look of need that burned deep, and it wasn't for show.

Unable to handle the intensity of what she saw, she turned her eyes toward the fire. "I don't want that."

"I know. But I can't help it, Faith. I look at you, and it happens."

She could feel it happening to her, too. Their isolation, the fire, his physical nearness, the deep sound of his voice—those things would have done it alone, even if she hadn't seen the hunger in his eyes. "You said it wouldn't. I only came on that condition."

"And it won't. But you asked what I was thinking. So I told you."

He stopped talking, and for a time nothing broke the stillness but the crackle of the fire. Faith studied the flames, following them until they disappeared into the fireplace shaft, but if there was a pattern to their dance, she couldn't find it.

"Why is this happening, Sawyer?"

"This thing between us?" He snorted. "Because I'm a man and you're a woman."

"But we've been those things for a long time, now, and nothing happened before."

"It couldn't before."

"It could have. It's been over a year since Jack and I split and nearly as long for you and Joanna. We've seen each other several times since then, and nothing happened. Why now? Is it all because we had too much to drink last Friday night?"

"That may have started it," Sawyer conceded. He'd given the matter a lot of thought that week, mostly during the night when he'd lain awake while his body ached for what it couldn't have. "But the attraction—or the potential for it—must have been there a lot longer. We just didn't allow it to surface. That's all."

"Then you weren't aware of wanting me before that?"

"I didn't think about it. I didn't think of you in terms of sex. I thought you were pretty and sexy, but you were a friend. First you were married, and then when you were free, you were still a lawyer. A *lady* lawyer."

"Then my parents were right. I scare people away."

"That's not what I meant. I meant that you were a

colleague of mine, and I took care to view you as one. Women have worked twice as hard to establish themselves as lawyers. Men have to work twice as hard to *see* them as lawyers instead of women." He considered her concern. "I can see where you might be intimidating to some men. You're attractive, vocal and successful. But so am I. So you don't threaten me in that way."

"Maybe it would be better if I did," she mused. Her tone was bittersweet, her expression sad.

Sawyer pulled himself up straighter. "Why do you say that?" When, after a hesitation, she simply shrugged, he reached over and turned her face to his. "Tell me why. What's so awful about our being involved with each other?"

"Nothing's so awful about it," she said, raising her chin to free it from his fingers. "I'm just not sure I want to be involved with anyone right now."

"You enjoy being alone? Are you a loner at heart? Was Jack's presence that much of a strain that you don't want anyone else in your life?"

"It wasn't a strain. It was just…disappointing."

"That's an enlightening comment."

She searched his eyes for mockery and saw none. "What do you mean?"

"The only way you could have found your marriage to Jack disappointing was if you'd had hopes for something better." His voice gentled. "We hope for what we want, Faith. What was it you wanted when you got married?"

She dropped her eyes. "I don't know."

"Sure you do. You just don't want to talk about it. Maybe you don't want to *think* about it, but maybe it's time you do."

"Why?" she asked, annoyed as she raised her head.

Sawyer was putting her on the defensive, and she was prepared to fight.

He didn't blink. "Because if you're pregnant, you'll have to think about it. You'll have to think about lots of things you might not want to." He paused, watched the fight fade from her face, lifted his hand and stroked her cheek. "Have you thought about being pregnant?"

She swallowed. Still, her voice came out a shadow of itself. "I'm trying not to. I don't think I am."

"Would you want to be?"

"I don't know."

He ran his thumb along her jaw and spoke very quietly. "Yes or no. Would you want it?"

"I don't *know*," she insisted.

"Don't you want to be a mother?"

"Yes, but I'm not sure I want it *now*."

He dropped his hand to his lap. "Did you want it with Jack?"

"I used birth control when I was with Jack."

It was an evasive answer, but he let it ride. "Did Jack want it?"

"Sure." She took a breath, a lot easier now that he'd dropped his hand. She had trouble thinking when he touched her. "Babies went along with marriage, and he wanted it all. We used to argue a lot. I kept telling him the timing was wrong. It would have been hard for me to have a baby while I was in law school, and the law firm wasn't wild about the idea of maternity leaves, and then when I went out on my own, I had the full responsibility of a practice on my shoulders. I tried to explain to Jack that the timing was wrong then, too."

Sawyer wasn't buying into the bad-timing theory. "You told me there were ways to do it. When we talked about it last week, you said that a woman can have a career and a baby."

"She can."

"But you didn't have a baby with Jack."

"I didn't *want* one with Jack!" Faith cried, then stopped short and hung her head. She took one deep breath, then another. The truth hurt, still it slipped from her tongue. "It wasn't the timing. It was him. If I'd had his baby, I'd have been locked to him, and early on I knew that wasn't right. By the time I graduated from law school, I think I knew Jack and I didn't have a future. And what my own instinct didn't tell me, my exposure to family law did. Kids don't make a marriage right. They don't make a bad marriage better. They may hold two people together who'd otherwise have split, but it's doubtful whether those people are happy, and if they're not, it's tough on the kids." She studied the fire in the hopes that it might soothe her guilt. "So that's it. I didn't want a baby with Jack."

"Would you want one with me?"

Her eyes shot to his. His features were golden and strong, but his look was cautious and, in that, vulnerable. She wanted to lie. She wanted to say that she didn't want a baby with anyone, but it wasn't true. For his openness, he deserved the truth.

"If I were to have a baby," she said in a near-whisper, "I'd want it with you."

A shudder ran through him. He sucked in an audible breath, closed his eyes for a minute, tried to get a rein on the flare of desire that accompanied the shudder.

Watching him, Faith was confused. "You want a baby?" she asked in that same near-whisper, then went on in a fuller voice. "If you wanted a baby, why didn't you have one with Joanna? She would have been a wonderful mother."

It wasn't the thought of a baby that made him shudder, as much as the thought of Faith having his. But he couldn't say that. It was too soon, even for him. He took several slow, deliberately calming breaths. "I could say that the timing wasn't right for us, either. Money was an issue. I didn't want a baby until I could afford to raise it with all the things I never had." But he'd never pictured a baby with Joanna's face the way he did now with Faith's. Nor had he ever before been shot through with desire at the thought of impregnating a woman.

He didn't say a word of that, yet his expression was telling. "Don't look at me that way," she begged. She felt it, too, the desire, and it made her uneasy. "Don't hope for it, please, Sawyer? You'll be disappointed."

But he didn't think that was possible. He didn't think Faith could disappoint him even if it turned out that there was no baby. She was incredibly bright and soft and vulnerable, and she wasn't half as sure of herself as she let the world believe. *He* knew she could be the best lawyer, the best wife, the best mother in the world. He also knew she could be the best lover, and though he'd made her a promise that he intended to keep, he wasn't averse to lobbying for his cause.

Coming up on his knees, he took her face in his hands, lowered his head and began his crusade.

CHAPTER EIGHT

"No, SAWYER—" Faith whispered, but the last of the sound was taken by his mouth. She flattened a palm on his chest. Within seconds, it was clutching a handful of his sweater, because seconds were all it took for her to feel as though the earth were being swept from under her. His mouth was hot velvet, stroking hers inside and out. His silken tongue found dark, hidden depths to plunder. His large hands held her head in a vise that was gentle but unyielding.

The first touch isn't much more than a token. It's kind of like a hello. The words echoed in Sawyer's mind, but they held no relevance. He and Faith had been exchanging tokens all day, looks and glances that were as expressive as any kiss. Same for hellos. He felt as though they'd been through hours of foreplay. Light tokens and gentle hellos were beyond him now.

That didn't mean he was rough. He could never be rough with Faith. She was too much of a woman for that, and besides, a good deal of his pleasure depended on hers. If she'd been quiescent beneath his hungry mouth, he'd have pulled back. But she was responding to his kiss, opening her mouth, offering her tongue, and while she wasn't aggressive about it, he didn't want that, either. Time enough for aggression once they were familiar lovers. For now, he liked taking the lead. It fed a very masculine need, and the fact that Faith didn't cut down that need as being macho or vain or archaic turned him on all the more.

If she was dynamite professionally because she knew when to stand firm, she was dynamite personally because she knew when to give. Even now, she was offering him the slender column of her neck, the graceful curve of her shoulders, the fullness of her breasts, which continued to surprise and please him. She was offering him her breath in short, wispy gasps, and the occasional tiny sound of excitement that slipped unselfconsciously from her throat.

She was offering him herself, and she'd warned him of that. She'd made him promise to be the one in control even when she wasn't. With a low groan, he dragged his mouth from hers. Slower to follow were his hands, which were splayed just under her breasts and didn't want to leave the warmth they'd found there. He forced them to. Sitting back on his heels, he brought them to his thighs and spread them there, and while the hardness of his limbs was nowhere near as appealing as Faith's warmth, they were something solid to hold.

"Disappoint me? Ahhh, Faith." His voice was hoarse, his broad chest working hard to still the thudding of his heart. "You couldn't disappoint me. Not in a million years. It keeps getting better. Incredibly. Better."

Faith was too stunned to say much for a minute. When she came to her senses, she was aware of wanting another kiss, of wanting much more than that. Need was snaking through her, coiling at certain spots, hurting. In a self-protective gesture, she wrapped her arms tightly around her middle, and though the tightness countered the hurt some, it did nothing for the chill of being out of Sawyer's arms. Groping for the sleeping bag that lay not far away, she pulled at its strings, artlessly unrolled it and dragged it around her shoulders.

It was a shield, protecting her from the intensity of his dark brown eyes. She still felt exposed, but that was her own doing and she sensed it was inevitable. Sawyer got to her. He touched her in places no man had ever touched before, and she let him do it.

"I think," she said in a slow, wavering breath, "that we need to put up a fence between us, something we can't see through."

Sawyer's lean mouth turned at the whimsy. "It wouldn't do any good. I'd know you were there, and I'd want you just the same."

Despite the intimacies they'd shared, the words were strange coming from him, Faith thought. Over the years he'd complimented her, said she was gorgeous and sexy and that he loved her, and she'd said similar words to him, but all in the good-natured way of friends. She couldn't get used to the idea that the joking was done, that the words and thoughts and feelings were for real.

"It's so strong," she whispered mostly to herself, then raised her eyes to his. "Why is that? Is it because we've been without?" She caught herself. "I mean, I've been without. Maybe you haven't."

He twisted to reach for another log and one-handedly added it to the flames. As he watched it settle in and catch fire, he said, "It's not that. I've been with two women since Joanna, each for a night and neither one of them was particularly necessary or memorable."

"Why did you go with them? Was it just for the physical release?"

"Honestly?" He looked at her quickly, then looked back at the fire. It was easier to say something he wasn't proud of when he didn't have to risk seeing disappointment in her eyes. "I did it because I thought that was what I should be doing. I was a single man again. Right and left, friends were slapping me on the back, winking, making ribald jokes, speculating on how good I was probably getting it. It wasn't that I'd sleep with a woman because someone else expected me to, but after a little while, I guess the expectation became my own. I was beginning to think something was wrong with me because I wasn't panting after everything in skirts."

A self-deprecating smile tugged at the corners of his mouth. He drew up a knee and rested his forearm across it. "I used to do that. Way back, before Joanna, before Nam. I pretty much screwed my way through high school. I figured that I'd make up sexually for what I didn't have mentally. When it came to getting the girls, I was way ahead of the guys who drove around in their little red Corvettes." His smile vanished, his pose lost its indolence and his voice dropped into a chasm of pain. "Then came the war. Once I took that hit, I wasn't thinking of sex. I was thinking of surviving. And when I realized that I would, I began thinking about life itself and the gift that it was. I began thinking that I owed it to someone upstairs to do something more than take a cheerleader under the stands during halftime." He took a deep breath. "Just about then I met Joanna at the VA hospital. Maybe because of where and why we met, sex was never one of our big priorities."

Though he'd intimated as much before, Faith had trouble reconciling the potently masculine man before her with a relationship weak in sex. "Did you ever cheat on her?"

"No."

"Did you ever want to?"

"No. Even after I was well, I had other things on my mind besides sex. I guess that's how it's been ever since. I have a comfortable life. My work is exciting. I convinced myself that if there was a right woman for me, she'd come along and I'd want her, and until that happened, I wasn't going to spend the goods just for the sake of the spending." He thought back to all he'd said. "So yes, I've been without, but no, that's not why it's so strong between us."

Faith wanted to find a reason. She wanted to put a label on the need she felt so that it wouldn't be quite so frightening. "Maybe it's because of last Friday night. We'd been drinking. Our inhibitions were down. Maybe that set off the need for sex, and maybe it's the memory of that that's turning us on now."

He doubted that. "If it was so, why would I get horny just thinking about what's under your sweater?"

"Because you remember Friday night. You remember feeling satisfaction. It's the memory that gets you horny."

He shook his dark head slowly.

She tried again. "If it hadn't been for last Friday night, we'd still just be friends. We'd be laughing and joking the way we always have. We wouldn't be seeing each other in any kind of sexual way."

"Maybe. Maybe not."

"What is *that* supposed to mean?" she asked, irritated that he wasn't grasping on to her suggestions.

His gaze was direct. He wasn't any more eager to see something negative in her eyes now than he'd been a little while ago, but he felt strongly that she should know how serious he was. "I think last Friday night was the catalyst for something that's very right."

"You're saying that it was inevitable? Come on, Sawyer."

That wasn't what he'd been saying at all, but the fact that she'd come up with it was telling. It made a statement as to the direction of her own thoughts, and she could deny them until she was blue in the face, but he wouldn't believe her.

"I think that if last Friday night hadn't happened, we might well have gone on forever and ever not knowing any better about what could be between us. But it did happen, and I think it happened *because* there's something between us. We could have stopped, Faith. We weren't that far gone that we couldn't have stopped if there'd been something so wrong with what we were doing. If we hadn't wanted it, we would have stopped. If the potential wasn't there, if we weren't attracted to each other, if we didn't *like* each other, we'd never have made love, no matter how much wine we'd had."

She was listening. She didn't rush to argue with what he'd said. That gave him the courage to go a step further. "It's not just sex. It's a lot more than that. We share a profession. We know each other, respect each other. We have fun together—we said that a whole lot on Friday night, and it's true. We've always had fun together. So now we desire each other, too, and that takes the relationship to a different level. It's the next step in the progression." He took a slightly shaky breath. "I think we have the potential for a really deep thing here."

Faith sat very still for several minutes. With a swallow, she tore her eyes from his and focused on the fire, but that didn't seem enough of a diversion. So she took the sleeping bag from around her shoulders, unzipped the top and shimmied inside. Moments later she was sitting cross-legged inside the thing, enveloped by it, looking at the fire again.

"Faith?"

"I'm a little cold."

That wasn't what he wanted to know. "Talk to me, Faith."

But it was a minute before she did, and during that time she cursed herself as a fool for not running to the nearest motel, locking the door and burrowing in a large, lonesome bed. Then again, she wasn't a runner—at least she'd never been before—and she didn't like the way she was doing it now. She wondered if it was time she faced some of the things that had been hovering at the edges of her mind since Sawyer had made her his.

Her voice was small, muffled by the sleeping bag she hugged to her throat. "I don't want to be involved in a really deep thing."

He caught both her words and a thread of timidity so uncharacteristic that his insides clenched. Faith was a woman of strength. He couldn't fathom the cause of her timidity, didn't like it, resented it. "Why not?"

"I'm not ready for it."

"You're thirty-three."

"I'm not ready."

"Because of what you went through with Jack?"

She didn't answer.

"Faith?"

"I don't know."

"Talk to me. Tell me what you're feeling. Did your marriage to Jack leave a bad taste in your mouth?"

She thought for a minute. "Not really."

The pause worried him. He wondered whether there was more to the story of her marriage than anyone knew. "Did he hurt you?"

"Hurt me? As in beat? Of course not."

Still her voice lacked its normal zing. She sounded distant, confused, as though something had indeed happened and she was just now trying to figure it out.

"What is it?" he coaxed, letting his voice tell her that he wanted to help. He was still a friend. No matter what else ever happened, he was still a friend.

Her eyes flicked from the fire to his, and the concern she found there tore at her. "Nothing. Really. My marriage was innocuous." But she paused, disturbed, and focused blindly on the floor. "It was disappointing. I've told you that. It was just a big fat zero."

"Better a zero than hell, I'd say."

She didn't smile. "I'm not sure. It's healthier sometimes to fight than to do nothing at all. At least that shows *some* kind of feeling. But there wasn't any between Jack and me. Not for a long time."

"And that bothered you."

"Yes, it bothered me. It wasn't the way marriage was supposed to be. It wasn't the way *I* wanted marriage to be."

"How was that?"

"Close. Warm. Fun. Satisfying. Supportive. I wanted my husband to be my best friend, but he wasn't. We were roommates. Period."

Sawyer was watching her closely, but he couldn't read anything more on her face than she was saying. "So you were wrong for each other. We all make mistakes. God only knows I did. And our clients? Mistakes all the time. So your marriage didn't work out. That's no reason to punish yourself by spending the rest of your life alone."

"I'm not punishing myself."

"What would you call it?"

"Making sure I don't make the same mistake twice."

"That's crazy, Faith. I'm not like Jack."

Abundantly aware of that as she looked at him, she caught in a breath. "That's the problem."

He didn't make the connection. "What do you mean?"

"You're more vibrant than Jack. You're more fun, handsome, ambitious, interesting, sexy. You're more of just about everything. But I'm still the same."

He stared at her in confusion before muttering, "I still don't get it."

"You're *special,* Sawyer," she cried, then stopped when her throat grew tight. Dropping her eyes, she tried to regain her composure.

It was while she sat cocooned to her ears in the shiny blue sleeping bag with her eyes downcast that Sawyer began to understand.

"Babe?" When she didn't look up, he came forward, dug her chin from the slinky folds of the bag and tipped up her face. "You're afraid you can't make it in a deep relationship?"

She tried to look away, but he wouldn't allow it.

"Is that it, Faith?" He couldn't believe it. "Is *that* what you took away from your marriage to Jack?"

She swallowed the knot in her throat, but no sooner had she done that when her eyes filled with tears. Trying to maintain what little dignity she had left, she looked straight at him and said in a soft, wrenching voice, "I think the world of you, Sawyer. If I were to pick the one man I like and respect most, I'd pick you. I don't think I could bear it if we got into something deep and then it died."

What her tears started, her words finished. A tight fist closed around Sawyer's heart. "So you'd rather not try at all? Faith, that doesn't make sense!"

"It does to me. I'm the one who has to live with myself knowing that I've failed at something important."

"Is that what you've been doing for the past year? I thought you were fine after the divorce."

"I was. I was relieved to be free. But that didn't mean I didn't feel guilty about not making it work. Now, here *you* are, and suddenly the stakes are higher. You're more special than Jack any day."

Sawyer wasn't sure he believed that, but the fact that Faith did made the clenching around his heart ease into a gently kneading caress. Without another thought to what she might or might not want, he drew her, sleeping bag and all, to his chest. He pressed her cheek to his throat, where he could feel the velvet of her skin, while the long arm he coiled around her lower back anchored her to him.

"Y'know," he began softly, "for a bright lady, you can be damned dumb at times. Did it ever occur to you that I'd have an active role in whatever relationship we have? If I'm so special, would I really let it fail?"

She didn't answer. She was too comfortable being held in his arms, listening to the indulgent caress of his deep voice.

"Did it ever occur to you that you and I have a hell of a lot more going for us than you and Jack ever had? We're mature. We're established. We have money. We're both lawyers, and we're good friends. So now we're lovers. I think that sounds pretty nice."

"It sounds scary," was her muffled reply.

"Not scary, because we're not making a life-or-death commitment. We're just going with the flow."

"What flow?"

Closing his eyes, he tightened his arms around her and drew in a shuddering breath. "The one through my veins that says I need you."

"I don't want you to need me."

"Too late. It's done."

"Make it stop."

"I can't. It's too strong."

"But I want to go back to being just friends. It was more fun that way."

"How do you know? You haven't given this way a fair chance."

"I don't want to spoil what we have, Sawyer."

"How about making it better? What would you say to taking what we have and building on it?"

She'd say that it was a dream and that she'd lost dreams in the past. She'd also say that it was a risk. She could lose everything if it didn't work out. "I'm frightened."

Sawyer loosened his hold on her only enough to give him access to her mouth. He kissed her long and deep, offering her a taste of his hunger. It was his way of telling her not only how much he wanted her, but how satisfying she was. By the time he raised his head, her lips were moist and swollen.

He touched her cheek with a trembling finger. "Let's try," he whispered hoarsely. "Let's see how good it can be."

Faith wanted to do that so badly she hurt, still the fear remained. "What if it isn't?" she whispered back.

"Then we'll go back to being friends. We're both adults. We're experienced. We'll know if what we're doing isn't working." His gaze touched each of her features, pale in the fire's light and as fascinating to him as the spiraling tendrils of flame, themselves. "I'm not asking for a commitment. All I'm asking is that you give it a shot. Because I can't *not* do that, Faith. You've given me a taste, and now I want more." He paused and his voice went slack. "But maybe that's *my* problem. Maybe you don't feel the hunger."

"You know I do."

He let out a small breath. "So we share the problem. We could ignore it, but then we'll always be wanting and wondering. I don't want to live that way, Faith."

Looking up at him, Faith knew that they'd reached a crossroads. She saw it in the virile planes of his face and the quiet demand in his eyes. He'd never make a scene. He wouldn't push her to do something she didn't want to do, but he knew her well. He knew that she wanted him. What he didn't know was whether she had the courage to take him.

It hit her then, suddenly and convincingly, that there was no contest. If she refused him, she'd be disappointing him anyway, and that was the last thing she wanted. She'd take the risk. She had to. Far better to see where the wanting would lead than to live forever with the wondering.

"I don't want to live that way, Faith," he repeated in a pleading whisper.

"I don't, either."

For what seemed an eternity, they looked at each other. Only gradually did they realize that they'd reached an agreement.

"So," she whispered, feeling strangely awkward. "What do we do now?"

"Sit and talk."

His answer pleased her, enough to allow for a glimmer of her usual spunk. "You don't want to just strip and do it?"

"No. I want to sit and talk."

She glanced down at her voluminous cocoon. "Like this?"

His lips twitched. "No. Not like that."

Setting her carefully on the floor, he added another log to the fire. When it caught flame, he turned to his own sleeping bag, unzipped it, opened it wide. Seconds later he had Faith's unzipped, and while she knelt by the fire, he connected the two. Then he sat back on his heels and looked at her. "I want to hear more about your family. Will you tell me?"

She eyed him curiously. "Why?"

"Because I'm interested."

"But I'm not them."

"You were once." He sent her a lopsided grin. "You've clearly evolved into a higher form of the species, but I've always liked history. It was the one subject in school that I paid attention to."

"History was more intriguing than girls?"

"Yeah. Less fickle. More predictable. Longer lasting."

"Does that mean you'll immerse yourself in my history and forget all about me?"

"Not a chance," he said too softly.

A frisson of excitement shot up and down her spine, making her shiver.

He misinterpreted the tiny movement. "You're cold." He tugged the double sleeping bag closer to the fire and held it open. Faith crawled in. He followed and took her easily into his arms. It was a minute before they'd settled comfortably, his body supine, hers angled into it.

She was cautious at first, but her caution didn't stand much of a chance against the feel of his body. It was long and solid, still it accepted her shape with surprising malleability. He was like that, she realized. Strong, yet flexible. That made the step they were taking a little less threatening to her. Gradually, she gave him more of her weight.

Sawyer did his best not to hug her hard in thanks for her trust. And trust was what it was about just then, he knew. She was trusting him to take care with not only her body, but her mind. She'd been hurt by her marriage, and though the hurt had been by default, the pain had been real. Now, curled next to him, she was vulnerable again. He rather liked that thought. He liked feeling responsible for her. The only problem was that he wanted to make love to her there and then, only he'd told her they'd talk.

Closing his eyes, he breathed in the sweet smell of her hair. Between that and the soft feel of her body, the weight of her hand on his chest, the bend of her knee over his, he was in an agony of bliss.

Faith felt something of what he did, but for different reasons. "This is so strange," she whispered.

"How so?"

"Being with you like this. We've known each other for so long. I keep thinking we're doing something we shouldn't be doing."

"We're not."

"You sound sure."

"I am."

She sighed. "Nice, to be so sure."

"You'd be sure, too, if you stopped thinking so much. *Feel* it, Faith. It *feels* right."

It felt more than right to Faith, but what he said was true. She thought too much. She wasn't used to relying on feelings. "I analyze things to death, I guess."

"Which is great for some things. It's one of the reasons you're such a dynamite lawyer. You look at a case from every possible angle before you decide on the best course of action, and you have to, because judges and juries don't decide things by intuition. They need arguments and facts. We don't."

But there were certain facts of which she was becoming increasingly aware, such as the fact that when he spoke his deep voice rippled through her, and the fact that his shoulder was just broad enough and full enough to make a wonderful pillow, and the fact that the scent of warm male after a day's work was surprisingly exciting.

Mostly she was aware of the fact that she wanted him. She might have joked about stripping and doing it, but there must have been a little wishful thinking in the joke. The more she relaxed against him, the more she tightened up inside.

Reflecting her thoughts, Sawyer shifted his lower body.

Faith tipped back her head and looked at him. The new log had brightened the fire, still his expression wasn't easily read. His eyes were dark, his lips firm, but it was only when the flames danced up with a sudden snap and a sizzle that she was able to see tiny lines of tension.

"Don't look at me that way," he whispered, not once taking his eyes from hers. "I'm trying."

"Trying what?"

"Not to take you right now. I said we'd talk."

"Why did you say that?"

"Because I want you to know that what's between us isn't only sex."

Faith knew that. "We've been good friends for a long time. You said it yourself—we had a lot going for us before we ever tried sex."

"Still there's a lot to say. Friends say certain things, lovers say others."

She kept looking at him. She wanted to say that she'd like to experience the lover part again before they got into deep discussions, but that seemed wrong. After all, she'd been the one putting him off.

"Help me, Faith," he growled. "I'm trying, but it's not easy."

But she couldn't look away. She was intrigued by his features, so carved and commanding, so taut with desire that she had trouble believing she was the cause.

He closed his hand over hers on his chest. "Why do you look so surprised?"

"I...uh..."

He began to move her hand in widening circles. "You don't believe that I want you?"

"I don't believe how much," she said guilelessly.

"Much. Very much." The circles edged lower as a wry grin pulled at his mouth. "And more by the minute." He had her hand at the snap of his jeans, but there the circles ended. After a minute's hesitation, he moved their hands southward to cover the raised ridge of hard flesh that pushed insistently against his fly.

Faith could barely breath. Vague glimpses of that other time, made hazy by the wine she'd had, brought the recollection of heat and length. But this was different. There was no haze, and the reality straining against her palm was far more than a glimpse. Heat, length, thickness, power—she was aware of all of those things as, with agonizing slowness, Sawyer inched her hand over him. When she saw his eyelids drift shut, even more when she heard the low, guttural moan that he couldn't suppress, she realized that the power was hers, as well.

Shaping her fingers to better capture his strength in the stroking, she levered herself up and sought his mouth. He gave it to her, along with a wet, deep-seeking kiss that left her dizzy. It also left her far removed from thoughts of sensible discussions. What she was feeling, not only beneath her hand but deep inside her, was strong enough to decide the matter. She and Sawyer were making love then and there. Once they were done, they could talk.

She conveyed her decision to Sawyer by going in for

a second kiss. This one was even more involving, and by its end, she was flat on her back with him looming above her.

"Last chance," he said. His low voice vibrated with need. His dark eyes were on fire from within. "Last chance, Faith."

Again she answered without a word, this time flattening both palms on his chest, running them up to his shoulders, then reversing direction and sliding them down over his chest and belly until they met at his burgeoning sex.

He moaned again, again helpless to hold it in, but he wasn't so helpless that he didn't know the import of the moment. Making love with Faith was going to be different this time than it had been before. This time they were stone sober. They knew what they were doing and why. And Sawyer knew that it had to be better than either of them remembered it being, if they were to have a shot at the future. He had to show her that when it came to sex, she was everything he'd ever wanted.

That was actually the easy part, because it was true. He couldn't control the hunger in his mouth when he kissed her, or his need to repeat the kiss from one angle, then another. He couldn't control the depths to which his tongue plunged in its search for hidden droplets of her sweetness. He couldn't control his need to nuzzle her neck, to inhale her scent as though it were life-giving oxygen, to nudge aside the crew neck of her sweater and nibble on her collarbone.

He told her of his pleasure in a myriad of wordless ways—in the smokiness in his eyes when he cupped her breasts, the tremor of his hands when he freed her from her sweater, the eagerness of his breath when he explored her through her bra. Whispered words came when he removed that wisp of lace and nuzzled her swollen flesh. He told her how beautiful she was, how responsive, and he showed her by chafing the pad of his thumb over her nipple until it was puckered and taut, then taking the hard-ened nub into his mouth and drawing it deeply between his teeth.

By this time she was holding tight to his shoulders, arching toward him, taking short, shallow breaths, and it was easy to go on. He undid her jeans and skinned them from her legs, then smoothed his hands over her panties until they followed. As though he'd been stifled before, when she was finally fully naked he couldn't touch her enough. With broad sweeps of his hands he covered her body from top to bottom. His palms were flatter over her throat, her hips, her legs; his fingers curved around her breasts and lower, on the focus of her womanly heat.

No, showing her how precious she was was the easy part. The hard part was restraining himself. At times he shook all over with the need for penetration. At times his breathing was heavy enough to wake the dead. But he was bound and determined to bring her to a fevered pitch of arousal before offering her the satisfaction they both sought.

She complicated things by moving against him in the most provocative, if innocent, ways. With slow turns and twists, silent yearnings spoke through her body, and then, when the turns and twists grew more frenzied and still didn't give her what she craved, she reached for his clothes. He thought he was safe as long as he was dressed, but she wasn't allowing that. One minute she was writhing in response to the sensuous glide of his fingers inside her, the next she was frantically struggling with his zipper.

"*Now,* Sawyer," she whispered. "Please. Now."

Grasping her wrists, he dragged them up and pinned

them by her shoulders. His mouth closed over hers in a long, hot kiss, but if he thought that by breaking the momentum of touching he'd slow things down, it didn't work. The feel of her body beneath his was incendiary, adding the final spark to what was already glowing and ready to flame.

With a low moan, he left her long enough to grab a condom, then tear his sweater and T-shirt over his head and work his pants down. Even before he tossed his clothes aside, Faith's hands were on him.

Ironically that did slow him down. Her touch was too special to ignore, slender hands and curious fingers working their way through the hair on his chest, teasing his nipples, scoring his rib cage. He wanted to savor it, which was another way of telling her how good she made it for him, but when her hands slipped past his navel and found the grooves where his thighs connected with his torso, his resolve snapped. Coming over her, he drew her knees up to flank him and entered her with a single powerful thrust.

She gasped, stunned by the force of the filling, and for an instant Sawyer wondered if he'd hurt her. Her eyes were closed, her face shadowed. He couldn't make out her expression.

"Faith?"

But while he watched, she broke out into a slow smile, a crescent of sunlight in the midst of shadow, telling of the ecstasy she felt. "Don't stop now," came her whispered drawl. The sound was sexy to match the sultriness of her smile, both of which matched the feminine allure of her body, which was gold-tipped in the fire's dancing light.

Sawyer was driven just as much by what was going on in his head as what was happening to his body. He didn't believe that a woman could be as beautiful as Faith was and still be real. He'd set out to pleasure her as she'd never been pleasured before, but it seemed that in approaching his goal, the tables had turned. He'd never had a woman smile up at him like that, as though he were her world and she wanted no other.

He continued to bask in the heat of her smile until his body began to clamor for attention. Then he moved, slowly unsheathing himself, even more slowly and deeply returning to her heart. His breath pulsed against her lips, ragged between kisses. When soft sounds came from her throat, he increased the pressure of his mouth and stroking hands, and when she began to squirm against him, he increased the speed of his thrusts. He took pleasure in her every response, growing hotter and harder until the battle he fought against release seemed doomed. In a last-ditch effort to regain control, he paused, but in that instant, while he held himself as still as his quivering frame would allow, Faith arched into a powerful climax, and he utterly lost himself. Within seconds, bowing his back and pushing deeper than ever inside her, he vaulted into an orgasm of his own.

It was staggering, spasm after spasm of pent-up passion turned loose in her heated body, but Faith felt the powerful pulsations only as a counterpoint to her own shattering release. When the brightest of the starbursts faded, she floated for a time in the limbo between heaven and earth. Only when Sawyer's breathing evened by her ear, when he slid his sweat-slick body to the side and pulled her over to face him did she open her eyes. What she saw in his nearly sent her aloft again. Neither the night or the dying light of the fire could hide the adoration there.

"How do you feel?" he asked in a whisper. He slid one still-shaky hand into her hair and stroked her scalp through the silken strands until he'd caught the last of his racing breath.

She searched for the words to best express it, but her mind was reeling again, this time from his look. "I feel," she finally managed to whisper back, "as though I've just finished off a magnum."

He grinned at her answer. "A little drunk?"

"A lot drunk."

"A little dizzy."

"A lot dizzy."

"But you didn't have a drop. Neither of us did, and still…"

She shaped a hand to his cheek, less sure with the trailing off of his words. "Still what?"

"Still…I felt like I was taken out of myself…immersed in you…lifted…" He stopped, feeling foolish and more than a little inadequate. "I'm not good with words."

But Faith had heard him in action more than once. "You're incredible with words."

"Not when it comes to something like this. I can talk hard facts and make persuasive arguments, but I'm not a poet."

"You're on your way."

But he shook his head. "I can't describe what it was like, Faith. It would take dozens of elaborate words and silvery phrases."

"Try plain ones."

"I love you."

She hadn't expected those particular words. Her eyes went wide, and for a minute she couldn't breathe, much less speak. Finally, diffusing the moment the only way she could, she tucked a hand against his neck and said softly, casually, "We've always loved each other."

"This is different, Faith. I love you."

"Like I love you."

"Only if you're talking forever." When she didn't have a comeback for that, Sawyer drew her to him. He cradled her head against his chest and the rest of her body fell into place, as though it knew from long experience just where to go. "Too much, too fast?"

After a minute, she murmured, "Mmm."

"Scary?"

"Yes."

"I'll give you time. I won't push. All I ask is that you let me see you." He endured a minute of gut-wrenching silence before prodding. "Will you let me do that?"

It wasn't so much that she'd let him, but that she didn't think she could keep him from it. Besides, it was what she wanted. She was still frightened; she knew she'd fear disappointing him even now, and it would be worse if she agreed to forever. Selfishly, though, she couldn't bar him from her life. She wanted more of him. She wasn't so inexperienced with men that she couldn't tell a good thing when she saw it.

"Faith?"

"Yes," she said, her breath stirring the drying hairs on his chest.

"We'll see each other?"

"Yes."

His body relaxed just that tiny bit, though not completely, because her nearness was stirring his senses. He ran a hand lightly from her shoulders to the small of her back, loving the satiny feel of her skin, which, even aside from his scars, was so different from his. He half wished it were broad daylight so he could look at her. Strange, but he'd never seen her, really seen her naked.

That wasn't all that was strange. Curving a large hand

over her bottom, he drew her closer. "Funny how things turn out sometimes."

His words registered through the light-headedness she was feeling again. "Hmm?"

"Before, when we started to make love, I wanted to show you how good it could be between us. I wanted to show you that it would be better than the first time, much better. I wanted to show you that you were all I've ever wanted." He paused, buried his face against her neck, breathed in the erotic scent of woman and sex that he found there, made a low sound in his throat. "I don't know how much of that I showed you, but I sure showed myself. You're it, Faith. You're what I want."

Being held so securely in his arms, feeling the strength of his body and its masculine warmth, Faith was just high enough to believe him.

CHAPTER NINE

THAT BELIEF lasted through the weekend, and understandably so. Sawyer rarely left her side. He got her talking about all the things she didn't want to talk about and many of the things she did, and in both cases he interspersed the discussion with light touches and impulsive kisses. He wasn't fawning, though; his timing was perfect in that way. He knew when to touch, when to sit back and listen, when to ask a question, offer a comment, even tell her she was nuts. And he knew just when to take her in his arms and hold her tightly.

They made love often through Saturday night and then again on Sunday. Faith had never thought of herself as the multiorgasmic type, yet Sawyer brought her to peak after peak. His own stamina—and the multiple releases he, too, found—seemed further proof of his claim of love.

Inevitably, though, they had to return to the city. Faith put off thinking about it until the last possible moment. She felt she was living a dream and didn't want it to end.

Sawyer had no intention of letting that happen. Intent on showing her that things would be just as good between them in the city, he deliberately put off having dinner until they were back. He went with Faith to her place while she showered and changed clothes, then brought her to his while he did the same. Looking distinctly urbanized, they ate at Locke Ober's—again a deliberate move on Sawyer's part, since the restaurant, with its sense of tradition, was symbolic of the Boston they knew professionally.

Nor was he letting her slip away after that. He insisted on staying the night, and while she made token argument, sensing he was prolonging the inevitable, she let herself be convinced.

He didn't make love to her that night. "I've run out of condoms," he teased, and she almost believed him, given the number of times they'd made love. "I think I'll just hold you."

That was just what he did, and in so doing, he touched Faith more deeply than his sex ever had. Tenderly he cradled her against his large body until she'd fallen asleep, and though his hold shifted during the night with the turns both of them made in their sleep, at no point was she aware of being cold or alone.

At dawn's first light, he brought her awake with soft kisses and slow strokings, then proceeded to make love to her until she was crazy with need. No condom was necessary; he had other ways to protect her. When it was over, when she was lying utterly replete in his arms, he gave her a final hug before easing himself from the bed.

She watched him dress, feeling a loss with each part of his body that he covered. Before he left, he came to her. Planting both hands on either side of her pillow, he looked her in the eye.

"I know what you're thinking. You're thinking that we're both going back to work today and everything will be over. You're thinking that I'll sit in my office wondering what the hell the weekend was about. But you're wrong. I'll sit there thinking about you. I'll be wondering what you're doing for lunch and whether I can meet you, or whether I can manage to jimmy my schedule around so I'll bump into you in the courthouse. I'll be wondering what time you're getting home tonight and whether I can see you again." He took a breath. "I'll control myself during the day, Faith. I won't cut into your time. But I want you tonight." He stopped speaking on that declarative note.

Another time, Faith might have objected to his lack of a question—or if not objected to it, at least teased him about it. It was an extraordinarily chauvinistic thing to do, and she was a thoroughly modern woman. Just then, though, she wasn't feeling thoroughly modern. She was feeling reassured by his forcefulness, even turned on by it, though she sensed that the latter had something to do with the spark in his dark brown eyes, the random muss of his hair, the piratical shadow on his firm-drawn jaw. He was a quintessentially virile man, to which her body, still warm and tender from his loving, could attest.

Taking a slightly uneven breath, she said, "How about a study date?"

He got the message. "You have to work."

"I was planning to do lots this weekend, only a randy guy came by and swept me away."

He slanted her a grin. "Randy guy, huh? Yeah, I guess he did get carried away. But he'd do it again in a minute." He paused. "Study date? Is it that, or nothing?"

She nodded.

"Where?" he asked.

"My office. Around seven. We can bring in pizza."

Lowering his head, he fitted his face to the soft curve of her neck. He breathed in her love-warmed scent for a last minute before pulling away. "You've got yourself a date."

"HE SUGGESTED we go on a date," Laura Leindecker told her on the phone later that morning. "Can you believe it? After being gone all weekend, he wants a date. After twenty-four years of missed dinners and canceled parties and late arrivals home, he wants a date."

Faith wasn't in the mood for adversity. She'd made a successful appearance in court on behalf of a client and was back in her office feeling cautiously optimistic about life in general and Sawyer in particular. She wasn't looking for anything that might upset the moment's balance.

Nor did she think that the idea of a date was so stupid. She'd made one with Sawyer. It was standard practice for a person feeling his or her way in a relationship.

"What did he suggest?" she asked pleasantly.

"Dinner at the L'Espalier. But that's not even my favorite restaurant. He *knows* what my favorite one is—or used to be—only he didn't dare suggest it."

"He was being considerate," Faith reasoned. "He knew how you'd feel. He was respecting your right to feel that way."

Laura wasn't fully convinced. "Maybe." Her voice grew wary. "He says he wants to talk."

"Then you should go. Listen to what he has to say. You'll be safe. He wouldn't dare act up in a restaurant."

"I suppose not." She sounded nervous. "But he's so good with words. He'll convince me of something. I know he will."

Faith tried to be supportive without yielding. "You're a strong woman, Laura. Don't underestimate yourself. You don't have to forget your grievances because he's taking you to dinner. But you do need to talk about what's happened and why."

"He'll tell me about *her*. He'll probably lie."

"Will he?" She let Laura think about that for a minute. "And if you don't want to talk about what's happened, talk about what you *want* to happen. Talk about the future. Talk about getting a divorce. Talk about the division of property. But talk. You have to communicate with each other."

"I don't want to communicate," Laura argued in a soft, pleading voice. "I want to file for a divorce. I want him to know that he can't do what he did to me and get away with it."

"You want to hurt him the way he hurt you, but will that give you what you want? Think about it, Laura. I can file a Complaint for Divorce with the court tomorrow, and a copy of the complaint will be served on your husband. Once that's done, it's a matter of public record, and once that happens, even though you can withdraw the complaint, something changes. Deeper feelings get stirred up. It's harder to go back. That's why you have to be really sure of what you want." She paused. "You're paying me to guide you through a divorce, but my first priority is your well-being. If your well-being is best served by a divorce, fine. If not…"

Her words trailed off, but she'd hit the right button, because Laura did agree to have dinner with her husband. Faith felt as though she'd achieved a minor victory. She would have called Sawyer to tell him if it hadn't seemed improper. It also seemed a little contrived. When push came to shove, she just wanted to hear Sawyer's voice.

It must have been her lucky day, because her wish was granted shortly after lunch when Sawyer stopped in at her office. Wearing a charcoal-gray suit with fine pinstripes running through it, he looked very professional and devastatingly handsome.

The first thing he did was close the door to her office. The second was to come around the desk and give her a kiss that shot professionalism to bits. The third was to drop into a chair and say, "Bruce Leindecker doesn't want the divorce at all. He says he loves his wife, and he says it on no uncertain terms."

Faith was a minute coming down from his kiss and another one focusing in on what he'd said. "He loves his wife."

"That's what he says," Sawyer declared in a satisfied way.

"Interesting," she mused. Her mouth still tingled. She was feeling pleasantly warm inside and decidedly close to Sawyer, which was probably one of the reasons why she tipped her hand. "Laura is still hurt and angry. But I think she loves him, too."

"Has she said that?"

"Lord, no. She says the divorce will teach him a lesson."

"She's being vindictive."

It sounded worse coming from Sawyer. "Not vindictive. She's just venting her anger."

"Maybe she's being too emotional."

"She has a right to be emotional."

"Too emotional? Nothing is accomplished then. Bruce is still trying to talk with her, but she won't listen."

"She will," Faith said with a satisfaction of her own. "He invited her out to dinner. I got her to agree to talk with him then."

Sawyer bobbed a brow in approval. "Good work, Faith. I knew you could do it. There's nothing like a woman to calm down another woman."

"Excuse me?"

"Women understand each other. They know what it's like to be highly emotional, so they can help each other when it happens."

"Uh...Sawyer...that is a gross overgeneralization. Not

all women are emotional. Some never are. And your conclusion isn't even correct. The reason women understand each other is because they have a capacity for understanding and compassion that men just don't have. Laura Leindecker trusts me. That's why I was able to convince her to go to dinner with Bruce."

"And I think it's great. She has to listen to him for a change."

"Sawyer! She's been listening to him for twenty-four years!"

"Maybe she listens, but she sure doesn't hear."

Just as Sawyer was championing his client, so Faith championed hers. "She hears. And for twenty-four years, she's heeded. Laura has been a quiet, obedient, practically subservient wife. She has swallowed her complaints and made a comfortable life for herself. Suddenly she is betrayed. She doesn't trust Bruce the way she used to. Obedience comes harder now."

"Laura Leindecker is a highly emotional woman. She's making this whole thing far more complicated than it has to be."

"He *cheated* on her," Faith cried. "That's what started it all. How does it suddenly become Laura's fault?"

Sawyer sat forward, his eyes dark and intent. "I didn't say it was her fault. I said that she's complicating things. They might have patched up their differences without ever seeing a lawyer if she'd listened in the first place."

"Listened to what?"

"His explanations for why he had the affair."

"And why was that?"

"Because he was curious. A young, attractive woman came on to him. He's reached the age where he's flattered. He also knows dozens of men who've had affairs. He wanted to find out if it was so great."

"That's rubbish, Sawyer! Do you honestly believe him?"

"Yes, I believe him. I don't condone what he did, but I can understand how a man can be driven by curiosity that way."

Faith recalled what he'd told her about the months after his divorce from Joanna. "You weren't married then, Sawyer. You didn't hurt anyone by giving in to curiosity. Bruce did. He hurt Laura deeply. I'm not sure she can ever recover from that."

"Which is an emotional answer if I've ever heard one," he scoffed. "Of course she'll recover. She'll listen to Bruce. He'll tell her that the affair didn't mean a thing, that he only saw the woman six times and—"

"Six times! If it didn't mean a thing, why did he see her six times? Did it take him six times to satisfy his curiosity, or was it six times before his wife found out? Did he think she *wouldn't* find out? If the affair was so meaningless, why in the *hell* did he leave that note in his coat?" She raised flashing eyes to follow Sawyer, who'd risen and was coming toward her. "Bruce Leindecker was wrong, Sawyer. He betrayed a woman who'd done nothing to deserve it. If he thinks she's going to easily forgive and forget, he's crazy. And so are you if you agree with him."

Curving his hands around the arms of her chair, Sawyer bent at the waist, ducked his head and put his cheek by hers. In a deep voice that gave individual emphasis to each word, he said, "I do not agree with what he did. I think he was wrong in having that affair, and I'd think it even if his wife *had* deserved it. I believe in fidelity, Faith. I always have."

His message took the wind from her sails. Or maybe it was the deep rumble of his voice. Or the warmth of his cheek. Or his clean male scent. Or the looming presence of his body. But the fight went out of her as quickly as it had come. She grabbed his necktie just below its knot and held on.

When he spoke again, she heard a suspicious smile in his voice. "I do love it when you get emotional." He kissed the tip of her ear. "It's a definite strength. A man likes it when a woman shows some fire. It means she cares." He dragged his mouth across her cheek.

"I care about all my clients," she argued, but weakly.

"You care about me. That's what this is about."

"It is?"

"Mmm-hmm." He nibbled on her jaw. "You want to know that my judgment is sound. You want to be comfortable with the sides I take. You want to be sure that we're playing the game. You don't mind my representing the bad guy as long as I don't buy his cause, particularly in this case. Am I right?"

He was, but she didn't want to say so lest she dislodge his mouth from her lower lip.

"So," he breathed softly, "that's another way I need you in my life. You're my conscience. Without you, my chauvinism is apt to run away with itself."

Having had just about enough of his teasing, Faith tugged him down by the tie for a full-fledged kiss. When it was done, she lingered for a minute with her eyes closed and her lips a breath from his. She could stay that way forever, she knew, but if she did that, Sawyer would be onto her in more ways than one. And she had work to do.

Pushing him away the same way she'd pulled him in, she said, "Go. I have a brief to write."

He headed for the door. "Are we on for seven?"

"We're on."

THEY DIDN'T BRING in pizza after all, but imported corned-beef sandwiches from the subbasement deli in their building. By ten, Faith was nearly falling asleep at her desk.

"I can't imagine why," she quipped, yawning. "You've bored me so that I've done nothing but sleep for the past two nights."

Sawyer laughed and said nothing in his own defense, principally because he intended to keep her awake for part of a third night, as well. And she didn't fight him. When they went back to her place and he took her in his arms, she went willingly. She moaned her delight when his mouth refamiliarized itself with her body's nooks and crannies, and when her hunger took a different twist, she even became the aggressor. It was a new role for her. Passion drove her on, but during the brief instances when the newness of it stunned her, Sawyer had ready words of praise and love.

Once she fell asleep that night, Faith was completely out of it. She didn't stir when Sawyer kissed her at dawn, didn't waken when he climbed out of bed and dressed, didn't open an eye when he softly called her name.

He left her a note. It was the first thing she found after she realized she was alone, and it helped in easing her disappointment at finding him gone.

Sweetheart,
You were sleeping so soundly that nothing short of a buffalo stampede would wake you. Not having any buffalos on hand, I tried some kissing and touching, but even that didn't work. So I'm off. I have a committee meeting at six tonight that will probably drag on until nine. I'll call you then.
Love, Sawyer.

Faith lay back down and held the note to her breast for another few minutes while she slowly woke up. Then she climbed from bed and got ready for work. Just before she left, she folded the note and tucked it into a pocket of her briefcase.

That was a tactical error.

Each time she opened or closed the briefcase, which was often on a day filled with appointments outside the office, she stared at the pocket and thought of the note. By late afternoon, she'd taken it out and read it numerous times, had traced the letters of his name with her finger, had even held the folded paper to her cheek as something he'd touched. It was the last time, when she folded the note and tucked it away not in her briefcase but in her bra, that she began to realize the extent of her feelings for Sawyer.

They overwhelmed her. She didn't like that at all, because she felt she was losing control. It wasn't like her to put love letters in her bra, any more than it was like her to wait for the phone to ring, or be disappointed when she woke up alone in bed, or plan her days to free up her nights.

In an appallingly short time, she'd grown dependent on seeing Sawyer. But she'd never been dependent on a man like that before, and she didn't think it was healthy.

That was why, when Sawyer dialed her number at nine-thirty that night, the phone went unanswered. Thinking she might have run out to do a quick errand, he tried again in fifteen minutes, then in fifteen after that. So he ruled out a quick errand. On the vague chance that she was still working, he tried the office number, but the answering service ruled out her presence there.

He decided that she had to be out with friends, and while one part of him thought that was just fine, the other was furious that she hadn't bothered to tell him. A simple phone call would have done it. If he'd been out of the office, she could have left a message. That would have been the considerate thing to do, since she knew he'd be calling.

By eleven, when there was still no answer, he began to worry. So he tossed on a jacket and jogged along the waterfront until he reached Union Wharf. He rang her bell. When that produced no response, he rang it again. And again.

After the fourth or fifth stab, Faith opened the door. The relief he felt was instant, then instantly forgotten in the face of the decidedly disgruntled expression she wore. "What do you think you're doing, Sawyer?" she asked. Though her voice was imperious, her appearance was anything but. She wore a white nightgown that went from her throat to her wrists and toes, and a long white terry wrap robe over that. Her face was clear of makeup. Her hair was brushed back behind her ears.

Sawyer thought she looked tired and more than a little vulnerable. That softened his annoyance, but only a bit. "I was worried," he barked. "I've been trying to reach you for two hours. Why aren't you answering your phone?"

"I was out. I just got back."

"Where did you go?" he demanded.

"I was visiting a friend. Not that it matters. Sawyer, I don't have to report to you."

"You knew I'd be calling. I left you a note this morning and told you that. If you weren't going to be here, you could have let me know. Then I wouldn't have worried."

Her fingers whitened on the doorknob. "You shouldn't have worried anyway. I'm a big girl. I've been taking care of myself for a while now. You should have just assumed that I had other plans, instead of assuming I'd be home waiting for your call."

Sawyer put both hands on his hips and glared at her. "I never assumed you'd be waiting. I assumed you'd be around. I assumed that since it was a work night and you complained about getting no sleep, you'd be tired."

"I am," she declared. "So thank you for coming over, but you can go home now. I'm going to sleep."

She made to close the door, but a well-placed foot stopped its progress, and he slipped inside. "Not without me, you're not." He shut the door behind him.

The determination on his face was so strong that she took a step back. "What do you think you're doing? You can't just barge in here like this!" She lowered her voice to a more controlled tone. "I want you to go home. I want to be alone."

"You don't want that," he said.

"I certainly do."

He shook his head and reached for her, catching her in his arms and holding her there while she protested.

"Let me go, Sawyer."

"Not until you tell me what's bugging you. Was it the note? Was it that I didn't call you during the day? Or stop down to see you? Was it my having to work tonight?"

"No!" She pushed against his chest, but it was an unyielding wall of muscle. "I don't care whether you work or not!"

"Then it was one of the other things."

Still she squirmed. "*No!* You don't have to call me during the day, or stop down to see me. In case you hadn't noticed, I have work to do, too. I have as demanding a career as yours. I don't have time to dally between cases any more than you do. Let me *go,* Sawyer."

Ignoring her cries, he held her tightly. "I'd make the

time to dally with you if I thought you wanted it," he said in a quieter voice that flowed gently by her hair, "but I've been trying to respect your career. I know how hard you work. I know how much your work means to you. And I know how good you are at it. So I'm trying not to get in the way during the day. That was why I left the note. I figured it would carry over to tonight. I need to see you at night, Faith, and if I can't see you, I need to know why. Why didn't you call if you weren't going to be here?" He took a shuddering breath. "I love you, Faith. I know you don't want to hear those words, so I've done my best not to say them, but I do love you. Did you think I wouldn't worry when no one answered the phone after so long?"

The fight had left her with the quieting of his voice, and by the time he was done talking, its gentle, almost pleading tone had done a job on her anger. Closing her eyes, she let herself lean against him. "Oh, Sawyer."

"What?" he asked hoarsely. "What does that mean?"

"It means I don't know."

"Don't know what?"

"What I was thinking. Feeling. Doing."

He stroked her back with large, knowing hands. "Sure you know. You're just not ready to verbalize it. You're tired. You're in a lousy mood. Maybe it's that time of the month."

Tired or not, she probably would have hauled back and socked him if she hadn't heard the teasing in his voice. "That, Sawyer Bell, is the most bigoted thing you've said yet. Men have moods just like women. I have every *right* to be in a lousy mood. I'm not tired. I'm *over*tired."

Without another word, he moved her under one arm and headed for the bedroom. When she'd taken her robe off and was tucked into bed, he sat by her side. "You're right. You need sleep."

She studied his handsome face. "Are you leaving?"

"You want me to."

"You said you were staying."

"But you'd rather sleep alone."

She darted a glance at the empty side of the bed. "There's room here. I'd hate to send you out in the cold."

"It's not very cold. I can jog back the same way I came."

"Or you can jog back in the morning." She paused, then before she could ask herself what she was doing and why, whispered, "Stay, Sawyer. I want to sleep with you."

Sawyer stayed.

"THE WOMAN WON'T TALK," Bruce Leindecker complained to Sawyer when he called on Wednesday morning. "I took her to dinner, and we sat like two very civilized people. She listened to what I said, but she wouldn't talk."

"She just sat there, mute?" Sawyer asked.

"Not mute, exactly. She offered simple answers to simple questions, but when I asked her to tell me what she felt, she just stared at me. Let me tell you, that stare hurt."

"Did you tell her that?"

"No."

Sawyer rubbed the back of his neck. He was getting a little tired of hand-holding, though he was being paid well to do it. "Maybe you should have."

"Then she'd have done it more. She wants to get back at me. She wants to hurt me like I hurt her. It doesn't seem to matter how much I apologize. She's still angry. Maybe she really does want out."

"Maybe she needs more time."

"Maybe I should just give in and file for divorce myself. If I did that, she'd talk. She'd say she doesn't want the divorce after all and attack me for wanting to dump her." He paused. "Reverse psychology. It's not such a bad idea."

Reverse psychology had worked for Sawyer the night before. As soon as he'd said he was leaving, Faith had changed her mind about wanting him to. He suspected Laura might do the same—and it had nothing to do with a sexist bias, because he used the tactic repeatedly with difficult male clients. No, he suspected Laura might do the same because he was privy to information Faith had passed on. If Laura did love Bruce, she'd protest the divorce as soon as it became a serious consideration.

But gut instinct told him the timing wasn't right for that. "Wait. Just a little longer. Reverse psychology can work, or it can backfire. It would be a tactical error to threaten something and have her call your bluff. Backing down would weaken your position." He debated the alternate courses of action. "You're still living at home, aren't you?"

"Yes."

"Okay. So keep talking to her and keep after her to talk back. Don't be discouraged. She's been badly hurt, and it's the kind of hurt that won't go away with an apology or two."

"But I'm legitimately sorry. She knows that. She knows me."

Sawyer reflected on the things Faith had said. "She may have thought she did once, but she never imagined you'd go off and have an affair. So in addition to being hurt, she's probably afraid to trust you, or her own instincts where you're concerned. You have a long road ahead, Bruce. This isn't something that a woman can easily forgive and forget." He rocked back in his chair wearing a small, smug smile, thinking that Faith would be proud of him. He might be a chauvinist, but he wasn't beyond being broadened.

Bruce wasn't as pleased as he was. "From the way you talk I'd do just as well to toss in the towel now. Are you saying that I've got to *grovel?*" Sawyer could almost hear him straightening in his seat and donning his executive front. "I won't do that, Sawyer. I may love the woman, but *no* woman—or man, for that matter—runs me into the ground like that. I'm not without pride. If she pushes me too far, I'll give her a divorce with pleasure."

"I doubt it will come to that. Just give her time."

Bruce agreed to do that, and Sawyer hung up the phone. His first thought was to call Faith, but he meant what he'd said about disturbing her. It wasn't as if something momentous had happened with the case. And besides, they had a date for lunch.

That gave him the excuse he needed. Lifting the phone, he dialed her number. When she came on, he said, "Was that twelve-thirty or one? What did we finally decide?" Their plans had been a little muddled in Sawyer's dash to throw on his clothes and get out the door in time to jog home, shave, shower, dress and make an eight-o'clock breakfast meeting.

"One," she said softly.

"Ahhh. Okay. That's great." He paused. "Everything going all right?"

"Fine. Busy." But she didn't hang up.

"Great. Hey, listen, I'm sorry to bother you, but I just wasn't sure and I didn't want one of us waiting."

"You're no bother."

"Maybe I should have run downstairs, just poked my head in and asked you in person."

"*That* would have bothered me."

"Why that?"

"Because you're a distraction any way you come, but seeing you in the flesh is the worst."

"Is that a compliment or a complaint?"

"You figure it out," she said with a smile in her voice. "You can tell me what you decide at lunch. Goodbye, Sawyer."

HAVING LUNCH with Sawyer was a different experience because for the first time, eating at a local restaurant that they both frequented separately, they were seen together. The place was packed with acquaintances and colleagues, most of whom probably assumed they were discussing matters of law.

Faith knew the truth, though. This wasn't a legal lunch but a social one. She enjoyed being with Sawyer. She also enjoyed being *seen* with him, and that bothered her a little. Professionally, she had her own identity. She wasn't out to get respect riding on another lawyer's coattails. She earned her own respect.

No, the pride she felt didn't have to do with her image as a lawyer. It had to do with her image as a woman, and that was what bothered her. She felt more feminine when she was with Sawyer. She felt that people would *see* her as being more feminine, and it surprised her that she cared. But she did care, which meant that she had much more to lose if the relationship ended.

More and more, it seemed, she was growing dependent on Sawyer. He was in her mind whenever her mind wasn't occupied with work. She was quickly coming to expect that she would see him for dinner and then spend the night with him. She feared she'd be crushed if he decided he needed a night alone.

She thought of being the first to do it, of telling Sawyer herself that she couldn't see him that night and sticking to it this time. If she was the one who rejected him, it wouldn't hurt so much, she figured. The problem with the figuring was that she really wanted to see him. Making excuses would be a bit like biting off her nose to spite her face.

On and off through Wednesday afternoon, she wallowed in a state of indecision. Then Laura Leindecker called.

"My husband won't leave me alone," she cried. "We have to do something. I'm not sure how much more of this I can take."

Faith was beginning to feel like Dear Abby, and she didn't think she cared for the role. "What's he doing?"

"He is waging a campaign to win me over. First it was dinner, then breakfast. He's calling me from the office three or four times a day wanting to know how I am and what I'm doing. This is very strange for a man who absented himself from my life for so many years."

"He loves you."

"He's scared."

"Scared of losing you."

"Scared of losing the house or the Mercedes or the millions he'll have to settle on me."

"From what I understand, he's got more than enough to go around."

"But he's making me crazy with his constant attention. It's gotten so that I feel guilty going *shopping* because he can't reach me in the stores."

Taking a breath in a bid for patience, Faith said, "Maybe if you gave him a little encouragement, he wouldn't feel that he has to work so hard to convince you of his devotion."

"I don't want his devotion!"

"I thought you did. I thought that was what this was all about. You were complaining that he was never around."

"He wasn't," Laura cried, "but I got used to that. I structured my life so that I had things to do, and I have even more things to do now that the children are grown. But they're women's things, like luncheons and bridge club and garden club, and Bruce is going to be in the way."

Faith sighed. Much as she tried to respect Laura's dilemma, she was tiring of the game. "What is it you want?"

"I want things to be the way they were! I want Bruce to go his way and me go my way, and when he's not on a business trip or tied up late at the office, we can see each other. Maybe I do want him to be devoted, but I don't want to be smothered."

"And you really don't want a divorce."

"No, I don't want a divorce."

"Do you love him?"

"I've loved him for so long that I wouldn't know how *not* to love him."

"Have you told him that?"

"How can I? It's the only lever I have left."

The phone line was silent for a minute. Then, slowly and quietly, Faith said, "Please, Laura, please talk to him. Tell him what you've just told me. He doesn't want a divorce any more than you do. There's nothing wrong with your marriage that some good heart-to-hearts won't fix. Tell him how you feel. Not just the surface things, but deep down inside."

"That won't work," Laura said sadly. "We've never been able to talk that way with each other."

"Maybe it's time you started."

"But I can't trust him. I did once, and look where it got me."

"He made a mistake. He knows that and regrets it." Faith sighed. "Either you give him another chance, or we file papers tomorrow. You have to decide one way or the other, Laura. It isn't fair to you, it isn't fair to Bruce, and it isn't fair to Sawyer and me. We're lawyers. It's our job to push for reconciliation, but we can't lead you through that the way we'd be able to lead you through court. We're not trained to be marriage counselors. You have to decide which you want."

Laura made a small, bewildered sound. "Why do *I* have to make the decision?"

"Because," Faith said with sudden insight, "you're the one with the power."

CHAPTER TEN

THROUGH THE REST of the day, Faith thought a lot about women and power. They underestimated themselves, she decided. Too often they bought society's line and associated men with the power, and maybe that was true in the business sphere, but not necessarily in the personal, more emotional one. Laura Leindecker was in an enviable position. She knew what she wanted, could reach out and take it if she decided to, and in that sense she held her husband in the palm of her hand.

Sawyer wasn't one to be held in any woman's palm, and Faith wouldn't have it any other way. Still, there were times when she wished he wasn't so sure of himself and his feelings. Then she wouldn't feel so weak by comparison.

Such was her line of thinking that night at his place, which was where he took her after work, and while she watched him grill steaks and toss a salad, she felt increasingly powerless. Her relationship with him seemed to be barreling forward, and as it went, she had less and less control over it.

There were three possible reasons for that, she decided. The first was that Sawyer was right, that the relationship had lain dormant for years and now, under newly favorable circumstances, was ripe for the growing. In that case, the relationship itself, the male-female dynamics were controlling Sawyer and her.

The second possibility was that Sawyer was the one in control, that he was the force behind the onrush of their relationship. He was more aggressive than she was. He was the one making sure that they spent every free minute together, and it was at his insistence that they were sleeping together every night.

She didn't fight him very hard, which raised the third possibility. She wondered if it was simply her own *lack* of control where Sawyer was concerned that was letting things snowball. Because they were snowballing. The more she was with Sawyer, the more she enjoyed being with him, and the more she had visions—fleeting, granted, but nonetheless vivid—of being with him forever.

She might have felt a semblance of power if Sawyer was running around trying to please her. But he wasn't. He knew what he wanted, which just happened to be what she wanted. He was perfectly at ease, perfectly comfortable, perfectly happy doing things that were satisfying for them both.

He was also attuned to the tiny crease that showed up between her eyes from time to time, and whenever he saw it, he immediately and deliberately filled her mind with different thoughts. Still, the issue of who she was as a woman, whether she was an active or a passive one, whether she had any real power, shadowed her. Long after they returned to her condo, after they'd made sweet, sexy love, she lay awake thinking about it. Each time she came near to an understanding, Sawyer would do something in his sleep—tug her closer, kiss her, whisper her name— and the issues became muddied again.

She knew one thing. He did love her.

She knew another thing. She did love him.

What she didn't know was whether she was the type of woman who could sustain a relationship like that, and whether she could bear it if she wasn't.

Thursday morning came too soon. She'd found no answers to her questions and she'd had far too little sleep. It was an easy matter to keep her eyes closed while Sawyer dressed, but it was harder to ignore him when, as was becoming his habit, he came to sit beside her before he left.

"Plans for today?" he asked, smiling at her sleepy look.

"I don't know," she mumbled flatly.

"Uh-oh. You're tired."

"Mmph."

"And cranky. Should I let you get into the office and call you there?"

"Mmm."

Without another word, he bent his head and placed a chaste kiss at the corner of her mouth, then left.

Because he'd read her so well, she was in an even worse mood, and because she was in an even worse mood, she felt even weaker, which made her more angry. She stomped out of bed, went into the bathroom and slammed the door.

Then she found that she'd gotten her period.

"GOOD MORNING," came Sawyer's deep voice on the phone shortly after she'd arrived at the office.

"Hi, Sawyer," she said in a no-nonsense, businesslike way.

He got the hint. "You're busy."

"Very."

"Can I see you later?"

"Uh, I don't know." She flipped through her desk calendar—unnecessarily since the day's appointments faced her on a single page. "I have one meeting after another."

"Lunch?"

"With the mayor."

"I'm impressed."

"Don't be. It's business."

"Then I'm jealous."

"No need. It's me and six other women."

"Sounds kinky."

She sighed.

"Okay," he conceded. "I'll call you later."

HE TRIED HER at two o'clock, but she hadn't returned from lunch. He tried her again at three, but she'd returned and left again. When he tried her at five, she was with a client. So he left a message for her to call him when she was free.

She called him at six-thirty, and her tone was anything but encouraging. "Sorry I've missed you. It's been one of those days."

"You sound tired."

"I am. I think I'll go home and go to bed."

There was no mistaking the lack of an invitation. But then, Sawyer had had a premonition all day. "Is something bothering you?"

"I just said it. I'm tired."

"Beside that."

"What could be wrong?"

You could be uptight about us. You could be feeling

crowded. You could be missing your freedom. "I don't know. You tell me."

"I'm tired, Sawyer."

"But if I said that I'd go home with you and work while you sleep, you'd say no, wouldn't you?"

It was only a minute before she said, "Yes."

"You want to be alone. Why?"

"Because I want to sleep."

"You wouldn't sleep better if I was there?"

She heard his gentle teasing, but she was determined to resist its lure. "That's an egotistical question if ever there was one."

"I sleep better with you than I do alone."

"Sure. Sex is a powerful sleeping pill."

He abandoned gentle teasing. "Even when we don't make love, I sleep better when you're with me. What's wrong, Faith? What's eating you?"

"I'm tired."

"Talk to me. Tell me what it is."

"I'm tired."

"Tired of me?"

"Tired, period. I need sleep. Alone."

He listened to what she was saying and tried to read between the lines, and though he could imagine what the problem was, if she wouldn't talk, they couldn't work it out. He debated pushing her, but the idea that she might be legitimately tired kept him from it. He figured he could give her a little time.

"Okay," he said. "You go on home and get your sleep. I'll call you in the morning."

"I'll be in court in the morning."

"Then I'll call you before court."

"No. I'll be with my client before court."

"Then I'll call you after court."

"I don't know when I'll be back."

"I'll keep trying," he said, less indulgently now. "You're being crabby, Faith, and I don't think it has anything to do with being tired. It has to do with us, but unless you tell me what it is, I can't do anything about it." He was pushing her, just as he'd told himself he wouldn't do moments before, but he was helpless to stop. "There may be times when you'd like to turn back the clock and make things between us the way that they used to be, but you can't do that. I can't do it. I don't *want* to do it. So we'll talk. If not now, later." He meant every word he was saying, and then some. "You're running, Faith. But I run faster. I'll always catch up. Remember that."

He hung up the phone before Faith could tell him how dumb what he'd said was. And it was just as well. The more she thought about it, the more she realized that it hadn't been such a dumb thing to say at all. Sawyer had an advantage over her that had nothing to do with physical size or strength. It had to do with determination. He knew what he wanted, and he wasn't letting it get away.

She was flattered. More than that, she was gratified. More than that, she was touched and touched deeply— so much so that at times during Thursday night, she felt herself on the verge of tears. She was frightened. She wanted Sawyer, but didn't want to want him, and she was terrified of losing him. She was alternately confused and frustrated and angry.

By Friday morning, she was feeling totally washed out. At some point during the night, her mind had pulled a temporary blank and allowed her to sleep, but it hadn't been enough. The light of day illuminated all the things she preferred to have left hidden in the dark.

Grateful to have something to fully occupy her mind, she met with her client at eight, then went to court. By eleven-thirty she was back at her desk, and though she hadn't come up with an answer to the Sawyer dilemma, she found herself willing the phone to ring. He said he'd call. When he didn't, she felt angry—not so much at him, but at herself for being disappointed.

Being disappointed was her lot in life, she decided in a fit of self-pity as she threw papers and files into her briefcase and headed for the law library to work. If she wasn't in the office, she reasoned, she wouldn't be there to hear the phone not ring, which was some improvement on the disillusionment of waiting and wishing.

Sawyer found her at the library. It was nearly four, and neither the dimming light of day nor the heavily shaded lamp on the table could hide his irritation. Slipping into the wooden armchair beside her, one of eight at the long mahogany table, he leaned close and whispered, "Where in the hell have you been? I've been looking all over for you."

"I've been here," she whispered back. She didn't know whether to be pleased that he'd found her or not. Her heart didn't wait for her to decide; it was beating faster than it had moments before.

"Why wouldn't Loni tell me?"

"Because she didn't know. I said I was going out. I didn't want to be disturbed."

Sheltered by knitted brows, Sawyer's eyes skipped toward the two other men at the table. Though they seemed engrossed in their own work, he carefully kept his whisper low. "Well, you're going to be disturbed. We have to talk, and we have to talk now."

"I'm working now."

But he was already closing the books she'd been using. "We'll go to Timothy's. It's right around the corner. We can take a quiet booth at the back."

"Timothy's is a bar."

"So a drink might do you good."

"I don't drink."

"It might loosen up your tongue."

"I don't need a drink to loosen my tongue. I don't want to talk."

"Come on, Faith. You're pulling a Laura Leindecker, and what was it you told her? That she had to share her feelings with Bruce?"

"They're married. We're not."

"Through no fault of mine. I'd have asked you last weekend and seen the deed over and done by now if it had been up to me."

"Well, it's not." Her whisper took on a panicky edge. "Sawyer, what are you doing?"

He was gathering her papers together and stuffing them none too neatly into her briefcase. "We're getting out of here."

"I'm not leaving."

"If you don't," he said, pausing in his work to lean extra close, "I'll give you a slow...wet...deep...kiss."

Faith could hardly breathe. Sawyer's nearness was bad enough, but when his breath fanned her ear and his words heated her insides, her resolve was more fragile than ever. Still she clung to it.

Grabbing her papers from Sawyer's hands, she put them into the briefcase herself. "You'll give me no such thing. I'm going back to the office." Snapping her brief-case shut, she stood.

He was right beside her when she left the table. Before

she could go far, he closed a hand around her arm. "You're coming with me."

"No way." Her voice remained a forced whisper. "It's over, Sawyer. I've made up my mind. I apologize for having led you along, but this relationship isn't for me. It's too time-consuming. Too distracting. Too demanding. I can't possibly be what you want, and I'm exhausted trying." With the carpeted room left behind, her heels beat a rapid tattoo on the floor.

"It's the fighting that's exhausting you," Sawyer declared. Though they no longer had to whisper, he kept his voice low. That didn't blunt its urgency. "Give in. Let it happen. Say you love me."

They trotted down the broad marble stairs, nodding to a judge coming up, but not pausing. When they burst through the large double doors and hit the street, Faith tried to turn in the direction of her office. Sawyer firmly propelled her the opposite way.

"Sawyer, I can't," she cried. "I have work to do."

"Work will wait. This won't."

"What's the big rush?"

He strode on holding her arm, his dark eyes straight ahead. "Yesterday was unbearable. Last night was even worse. I won't let things go on like this. I spent years watching my marriage fizzle, and I didn't fight because I didn't care, but I care about this. You say it's over. I don't believe that. If you want to convince me, you'll have to do it now."

"I just did," she argued. "This relationship is too much for me to handle."

"Bullshit."

"Say what you want, but it's true."

"You were handling it just fine at the start of the week,"

he argued, generating anger to cover up the unsettled feeling in the pit of his stomach. "Nothing's changed since then, except that you started getting *scared* that you couldn't handle it. So you decided not to try. That is *cowardly,* Faith, *cowardly!*"

"So I'm a coward. That's as good a reason as any why it won't work."

They reached Timothy's. Sawyer kept his hand in firm possession of her arm while he drew her through the door. "Two of whatever's on tap," he called to the bartender as he swept down the long bar to a booth near the back. It was the only free one. The bar was filling up with happy-hour patrons. The noise of their chatter didn't bother him, any more than the dimness of the place did. Both provided a certain privacy.

When he'd successfully nudged Faith into the booth, he slid in opposite her. Without preamble, he pierced her with vibrant brown eyes and picked up where they'd left off. "What you're doing is totally out of character. You weren't meant to be a coward, Faith. Professionally, you're one of the bravest women I know. You've taken on cases that other lawyers have refused, and you've won. You've taken on Boston's staid legal community and done more for family law than any other lawyer in years. And you haven't done so badly personally, either. You stuck with Jack because you believed in marriage, and when it became obvious that it wouldn't work, you had the courage to let go."

She sputtered out a laugh. "That's a contrived way of looking at it. I *failed* in my marriage. I stuck with it because I *didn't* have the courage to let go. I only got out when it became obvious that there was nothing left. It didn't take courage at that point."

Sawyer wanted to scream in frustration. He didn't understand why she had to be so hard on herself. "Why do you insist on seeing the worst? Why do you choose the most pessimistic view of what happened? There were positive things in your marriage. I saw them." He gave a small, impatient shake of his head. "But I don't want to talk about your marriage to Jack. That's over and done. I want to talk about us."

Resting her head against the wood back of the booth, Faith eyed him forlornly. "Nothing's changed. Back when we were at the Cape, I told you my worries. They're the same."

"You're afraid you'll disappoint me."

"And myself."

"Monday, Tuesday and Wednesday—were you disappointed?"

She thought back to the warmth in which he'd kept her cocooned, and she couldn't lie. "No. I wasn't disappointed then."

"Because you enjoyed what we did. You enjoyed being together."

She nodded. "But I grew dependent on that, and I don't like being dependent."

"So you tried to put me off. That's why you wouldn't see me yesterday or last night."

She tried to defend herself. "Things between us have gotten too intense too fast. We need to cool off."

"But we won't. Out of sight doesn't mean out of mind." He spared only a moment's glance at the frothy steins the bartender brought. "I thought about you all last night. Can you honestly say you didn't think about me?"

"No. I thought about you."

"And you decided that since you like me so much, you

shouldn't see me so much. You don't want to become too dependent on me—or have me become too dependent on you. You don't want to be disappointed if something goes wrong." Arms on the table flanking his untouched beer, he leaned forward. "That is *convoluted logic*. It's like saying that a lamp makes reading a breeze, but you'll sit in the dark so you won't come to rely on the lamp in case the bulb blows. Well, hell, if the bulb blows, you get another. Things can be repaired. So can relationships, if they mean enough to you."

Eyes holding hers, he sat back. "The Leindeckers are together again. I got a call from Bruce after lunch telling me that they've kissed and made up."

That was news to Faith. "Really?" she asked cautiously.

He nodded.

"I haven't heard anything about it from Laura."

"Because you've been incommunicado since lunchtime. She called. Loni told me."

In the brief respite from her own troubles, Faith allowed a small smile. "They're forgetting about the divorce?"

"They're going to try to work things out. Bruce was extremely grateful to us. Especially to you. Laura told him that you kept pushing for a reconciliation. You kept telling her to talk with him and tell him how she felt." He paused, wondering if she was getting the point, deducing from the unenlightened look on her face that she wasn't, deciding to make it himself. "How can you preach that and not do it yourself?"

Her eyes widened. "I *am* talking to you. You know how I feel."

"You wouldn't talk with me yesterday, and, no, I don't

really know how you feel. You've never said whether you love me or not."

"I have, too. I've told you I love you dozens of time."

"As a friend."

She swallowed. Closing her eyes for a minute, she thought of those warm, wonderful times when she lay in his arms. "And as a lover," she said, sending him an unknowingly adoring look. "I could never respond to you the way I do, or do the things I do to you if I didn't love you."

For the first time since he'd found her at the library, Sawyer experienced a faint lightening in the area of his heart. Again, he leaned forward, this time beseechingly. "Then give it a try, Faith. Don't fight it. Don't ruin the present by worrying about the future." When he saw the skepticism on her face, he hurried on. "Listen, I don't know what the future holds. None of us do. Life doesn't come with a road map telling exactly what turn to take when in order to get to a prescribed destination." That thought gave him pause. "Where do you want to go? Do you know? Supposing you were to look ahead ten or twenty years, what do you see yourself doing, being?"

"I see myself as a successful lawyer."

"What else?"

"I don't now."

"What do you mean, you don't know? What do you *dream?*"

"I don't know."

"You do, but you won't say. You *are* as bad as Laura Leindecker."

"And you're like Bruce. You won't leave me alone. Why not, Sawyer? That's all I'm asking, just to be left alone. Is it so difficult to do?"

Straightening his shoulders, Sawyer took a different tack. Keeping his voice low, he said, "Okay. I could leave you alone. I could let you go back to the kind of life where work is basically all there is. I could let you bury yourself in the law. I could disappear from your life. Does that sound better?"

It sounded devastating, but she didn't say it.

He went on. "We could do what we did for years, bump into each other at conferences or seminars or political fundraisers. Maybe we'll even have another chance to work with each other. We could meet by accident on the street once in a while, date other people, sleep with other—"

"I don't want that."

"What?"

"To sleep with other people. I don't want it."

"You don't want to do it yourself, or you don't want *me* to do it?"

Her eyes blazed. "Both. Either."

"But you don't want to sleep with me."

She didn't answer.

Her lack of response stirred Sawyer's frustration, which in turn made his voice sound harsh. "What do you want, Faith? Beyond a career, what do you want? There must be other things. You're a woman capable of warmth and love. Don't you want an outlet for those?"

She stared at him. Oh, she knew the answer to that one, but she was afraid, so afraid to give it, and Sawyer knew that.

"Why is it so *hard?*" he asked. "You always used to talk to me. You used to tell me everything. Why can't you now?"

"Because things have changed between us!"

"We're more involved."

"Yes."

"So we should be sharing even more." He reached his limit. If she wouldn't say it, he would. "Damn it, Faith, I want it all! I want you as my law partner, my wife and the mother of my kids, and I think that if you can be honest with yourself and with me, you'd admit that you want those things, too."

Hearing him put it all into words was nearly more than she could bear. "I do," she cried softly, "but it's a dream. That's all. A dream. Life has ways of taking unwanted twists. I've seen it happen time and again. We hope for things, and when they don't happen, disillusionment sets in. I'd be devastated if that happened with us."

"It won't. We love each other. We have so much going for each other."

"But I'm a lawyer," she said, and tears began to gather on her lower lids. "I'm a lousy cook and a lousy cleaner, and I wouldn't know how to change a diaper if my life depended on it."

"So you'll learn. We'll learn."

"But I'm not even pregnant!" she cried and, feeling an awesome ache, she scrambled out of the booth and ran toward the front of the bar.

Swearing, Sawyer tossed several bills on the table to pay for the beer they hadn't touched, and took off after her. He caught up half a block from the bar. Snagging her by the wrist, he hustled her into the nearest doorway, out of the line of rush-hour foot traffic. His hands went flat against the granite on either side of her shoulders. His large body prevented her escape.

"When did you get it?" he demanded, furious enough

to momentarily overlook the tears streaking down her cheeks. "Your period. When did you get it?"

"Yesterday morning."

"And that's when the trouble started." It suddenly made sense. "You figured I'd be disappointed that you weren't pregnant."

"*I* was disappointed," she cried. "That was bad enough."

"Because you wanted to have my baby," he said. The gentleness that hit him then, the heart-wrenching care dissolved whatever anger he'd felt. His hands left the granite, slipped around her back and drew her snugly against him. "Ahhh, Faith. I do love you. You have to be one of the most bullheaded women I've ever met in my life, but I do love you."

"I wanted to be pregnant."

He recalled the way she'd talked when they'd first discussed the possibility, and knew she was telling the truth. "Why didn't you tell me? I wouldn't have had to bother with—"

"I couldn't tell you. I didn't know how you felt."

"You could have asked."

"But then I'd have *known* how you felt."

"Mmm, that makes sense."

"It does. If you hadn't wanted a baby, and it turned out I was pregnant, you'd have been disappointed. Same thing if you'd wanted a baby, and I *wasn't* pregnant. So I was better not knowing."

He tucked his head lower against hers. "You're never better not knowing, Faith. And you're never better keeping things to yourself. A relationship is about sharing. You know that. You've counseled any number of clients on it, most recently Laura Leindecker. So if you can tell them to communicate, why can't you do it yourself?"

"Because I'm emotionally involved, and when I'm emotionally involved I can't think straight!"

"You've got that right, at least. As far as the rest goes, you're out in left field."

"See? I'm a disappointment already."

"Did I say that?"

"You were thinking it."

"No, ma'am. I was thinking that I love it when you're out in left field, because it gives me a chance to play hero. It feeds the macho in me."

She groaned, but the sound was barely muffled by his coat when he pulled back, took her hand and started off. She had to trot to keep up. "Where are we going?"

"Somewhere."

"Obviously. Sawyer, I can't go anywhere," she cried as the breeze dashed the tears from her cheeks. "I have work to do."

He didn't miss a step as they turned onto Beacon Street. His hand kept hers well in its grip. "Y'know, I'll bet you didn't give Jack half this much trouble when you agreed to marry him."

"I didn't give him any trouble, and I haven't agreed to marry *you*."

"I'll bet you just smiled and said yes, when there were dozens and dozens of reasons why the marriage wouldn't work."

"I was young and stupid. So was Jack. We wanted marriage more than we wanted each other."

"And the irony of it is," Sawyer went on as though she hadn't spoken, "that here we are with dozens and dozens of reasons why a marriage between us *will* work, and you're driving both of us crazy dreaming up problems."

"I'm not dreaming them up!"

"Some people do that, y'know. They can't bear the thought of happiness so they throw stumbling blocks in their own way." Pulling Faith faster to cross Tremont Street before the light turned, he yelled, "Taxi!" The cab that had just dropped off a customer and was starting to pull away from the curb stopped. Too involved in defending herself to question him, Faith slid in at Sawyer's urging and resumed the discussion the minute he joined her.

"I *do* want to be happy. I've never deliberately thrown stumbling blocks in the way of that."

"No?" To the waiting cabbie, he said, "Copley Place."

"Copley Place?" Faith echoed. "Sawyer, I have to work." But the cab was already on its way, as were her thoughts. "I'm being cautious, that's all, and there's nothing wrong with it. I've already flunked out of one relationship. Every day I see the tattered remains of other relationships. I'm thinking of *you,* Sawyer."

"Okay," he said in a lower voice, "think of me." With the creak of aged vinyl, he shifted on the seat to face her. "Think of how much I want you, not only today and tomorrow but for all the tomorrows after that. Think of how much I want to work with you and travel with you and finish the place at the Cape with you and have kids with you—" When she looked stricken by the last, he hurried on. "Not right away. I'm glad you're not pregnant. I want you to myself for a while. Besides, if you were pregnant, you'd think that was why I wanted to get married, when it's not."

"I haven't agreed to *any*—"

The rest of her protest was lost in the kiss Sawyer gave her. It was a sweet kiss, powerful in that sweetness. It said he loved her, loved her even when she was being difficult. That was very much what he was thinking, and when—after trying the kiss from several different angles simply because her lips were so pliant—he finally lifted his mouth from hers, he felt the theme worth discussion.

"You can't disappoint me, Faith," he said. His face was inches from hers. Almost reverently he held her chin in the notch of his hand. "You can't *possibly* disappoint me. You're one of the best lawyers around. Whether you win or lose a case, you give it your all, which is more than most do and as much as any client can ask. As a wife, you'll be smashing, and I don't give a damn whether you're a lousy cook—"

"I'm lousy at it because I hate doing it," she blurted out. She was having trouble thinking with the taste of him lingering on her lips and his face so close and his voice so gentle, but she had to speak up. She feared it might be her last chance. He was so near and dear. Her resolve was slipping. "What kind of wife hates to cook?"

"The kind who has a full-time job outside the home and doesn't have the time or energy to spend working over a stove. And there's nothing wrong with that. I don't expect you to be superwoman. If we need a cook, we'll hire one. Same thing for when babies come. I may be traditional about some things, but I'll never ask you to stop working unless that's what you want. Besides, you said it yourself—babies and careers are mixing better and better these days."

"I don't know anything about parenting."

"Neither do I. So we'll learn. There are books all over

the place, and classes." He brushed the tip of his finger by the corner of her eye as he visually devoured her features, then went on in a voice that was even lower and slightly rough, "And as a lover, you're more than any man could imagine. No woman has ever turned me on like you do. No woman has ever done to me what you do." He took in a short, sharp breath. "The other night…what you did… where your mouth was and your hands…"

He didn't have to finish. Faith remembered the moment well. She'd shocked herself, not only with what she'd done but with the pleasure she'd taken in the doing. A soft, sexy smile stole over her lips. "Liked that, did ya?"

"Yeah," he whispered. "I liked it."

"I've never tried it before. So, it worked?"

"Oh, yeah." Even in memory it was working, but the jolting of the cab through the traffic was a reminder of where he was. "You're dynamite, Faith."

She liked the sound of that. "But what happens when I get older? Will I still be dynamite when my hair is gray and my breasts sag and I have cellulite on my thighs?"

"By that time, I'll be bald and paunchy and my eyesight may be so lousy that I won't be able to see the cellulite on your thighs."

"You'll never be bald and paunchy."

"How about my eyesight? Will you love me even if I can't see straight?"

"Of course I will. What kind of dumb question is that?"

"The same kind *you're* asking," he said and gave her a minute to realize it before saying, "There are two points here, m'dear. The first is that you're dynamite to me because of who you are, not what you look like. The second," and he sobered, "is that none of us knows what the future holds. We have to look at what we have now and decide whether we think it's strong enough and positive enough to make us happy today and optimistic about tomorrow." He lowered his voice again, this time in urgent coaxing. "Come on, babe. You know we can make it. Stop fighting. Give it a chance."

But before she could respond one way or the other, the cab pulled up at the Marriott Hotel. Without so much as a look at the meter, Sawyer stuffed a ten-dollar bill into the cabbie's outstretched hand, opened the door and pulled Faith out. Keeping her close by his side, he entered the hotel at a broad stride.

"What are we doing here, Sawyer?"

"You'll see."

They were passing through the lobby, and for a minute Faith thought he was going to take a room on the forty-fifth floor and make wild, passionate love to her overlooking Boston. It was a romantic idea, and it wasn't beyond him at all, she knew. When they passed the registration desk without stopping, she wondered if he'd taken a room in advance. "That was a presumptuous thing to do," she murmured, half flattered, half annoyed.

"What was?"

"Booking a room without even knowing whether I'd come. You assumed I'd cave in, didn't you? Beth Leindecker said her mother always did that. Bruce snapped his fingers, and she came running."

"I should only be so lucky," Sawyer said under his breath, then added, bemused, "I didn't book a room." Sure enough, they passed the bank of elevators and headed toward the escalator that led to the mall level.

"Oh." She frowned. "Then what are we doing here?"

"Going shopping. Watch your step. Hold on. That's it."

"Sawyer, I've been on an escalator before. But why are we going shopping? And why here? Prices are exorbitant here. I have to warn you, I'm almost as lousy a shopper as I am a cook."

"I don't believe that. You always look spectacular."

"Sure, because I'm drawn to the most expensive item on the rack. It happens every time, like there's some kind of radar flowing between the price tag and my head without my seeing a thing."

"That's fine. Price is no object. I want the best." Fingers laced through hers, he drew her off the escalator, toward the first store on the left.

"The best what?"

"Diamond ring."

Her eyes widened as they passed through Tiffany's vaulted portals. She tugged back on her hand and whispered loudly, "What are we *doing* here, Sawyer?"

Her tug didn't faze him. He strode right along. "Buying you an engagement ring. I want all the bozos in Boston to know that you're taken."

"But we're not engaged."

"We certainly are." He produced a dashing smile for the woman behind the counter. "We'd like to look at engagement rings—something substantial, maybe with a few little stones on the side—sapphires, rubies, whatever goes with diamonds—you know what I'm talking about."

The saleswoman certainly did. She had carefully removed several spectacular possibilities from the showcase and placed them on a bed of navy velvet before Faith could find her tongue.

"Sawyer," she murmured out of the side of her mouth, unable to take her eyes from the rings, "uh, Sawyer, I think we should talk."

Leaning close, he said in the same side-mouth murmur, "Definitely. What do you think? I think the blue stones look a little cold next to the diamond. I like the green, the emeralds. They go with your eyes."

"My eyes are hazel."

He looked into them. "They look green to me. Maybe it's what you're wearing." He dropped a quick glance at the long pleated skirt, sweater and blazer she wore, a blend of solids and plaids in plum and moss. "Super outfit," he mouthed. His eyes glowed in appreciation.

Cheeks growing pink, Faith tore her gaze from his and forced it back to the rings. "I can't accept one of these."

"Why not?" He put his mouth by her ear and whispered, "I love you. I'll always love you. I'll love you until the sun sets in the east, until the rivers run dry, until Santa gets stuck in a chimney in Winnemucca, Nevada—"

"They're too elaborate." She looked beseechingly at the saleswoman. "Haven't you got something a little simpler?"

Sawyer started to argue, but before he could do much more than tell her she deserved the best, the saleswoman produced two rings that stilled his tongue. Both held single stones, one round, one pear-shaped.

"Ahhh," Faith breathed in awe. Smiling, she carefully lifted the pear-shaped ring from the velvet. "This is more like it."

"Don't you want something a little more showy?"

"You're the one who wants something showy. It's the old macho pride." She continued to hold the ring, spellbound by its sparkle. "This is special. Simple but exquisite."

He had to agree that it was, still he'd envisioned something different. "Maybe we should look at something with more than one diamond." He turned to the saleswoman. "How about it? Something with one big stone and two little ones on the sides? Maybe with diamonds all the way around?"

Faith was still admiring the pear-shaped diamond when the saleswoman added two other rings to those already out. Faith didn't like either as much as the one she still held in her hand. "They're too busy. If a stone is beautiful, it should stand on its own." She took a soft breath. "I like the solitaire."

"You're worried that the others are too expensive, but I'm telling you, Faith, money isn't an object here. If I can't splurge on the woman I love, who *can* I splurge on?"

"Sir?" the saleswoman spoke up a bit nervously. "About the ring your fiancée is holding—it's the finest quality diamond we carry." She cleared her throat. "Given that and its shape and size, I'm afraid it's the most expensive one I've shown you."

Quickly but carefully, Faith set the ring down. "I should have known," she muttered. "I do it every time."

But Sawyer was lifting it, taking her left hand, slipping the ring on her third finger. It fit perfectly. "Simple and exquisite." He grinned. "We'll take it."

"We can't take it," Faith whispered, but the sharpness she'd wanted to put into the whisper fell prey to the beauty of the ring on her finger—that, and the contrast of Sawyer's long, lean hand holding hers. "We...I...can't."

"You can," he said softly, and something in his tone brought her eyes to his. They were dark and intent, filled with love and a kind of bare-hearted expectancy that made Faith tremble. "You can," he whispered. "You can do it, Faith. You have the power to reach out and try, and that's all I'll ever ask of you. Reach out and try. Give it your best shot. Nothing's a given in life, but there's so much hope in this. I want it. You want it. Together we'll make it work." Her eyes went wider, as though he'd said a magic word, but her lips remained pressed close together. "What do you say? Wanna give it a try?"

She wanted that more than anything, and in that moment she realized the extraordinary power she did have. She had the power to bring Sawyer happiness—and the power to find it herself. Yes, there was a risk. The stakes were frightfully high. But the alternative? Standing there, looking up into Sawyer's face as she could quite contentedly do for years and years, she knew that the alternative was no alternative at all.

Words eluded her, but words weren't needed. Her answer came in a short nod, a soft smile, the tears that filled her eyes and the arms that went around his neck. When he slid his own arms around her and crushed her to him, she felt a joy she'd never known. She also felt a confidence she'd never expected.

He was right. Together they'd make it work.

* * * * *

THE DREAM

CHAPTER ONE

JESSICA CROSSLYN LOWERED herself to the upholstered chair opposite the desk, smoothed the gracefully flowing challis skirt over her legs and straightened her round-rimmed spectacles. Slowly and reluctantly she met Gordon Hale's expectant gaze.

"I can't do it," she said softly. There was defeat in that softness and on her delicate features. "I've tried, Gordon. I've tried to juggle and balance. I've closed off everything but the few rooms I need. I keep the thermostat low to the point of freezing in winter. I've done only the most crucial of repairs, I've gone with the lowest bidders, and even then I've budgeted payments—" She caught in her breath. Her shoulders sagged slightly under the weight of disappointment. "But I can't do it. I just can't do it."

Gordon was quiet for a minute. He'd known Jessica from birth, had known her parents far longer than that. For better than forty years, he had been banker to the Crosslyns, which meant that he wasn't as emotionally removed as he should have been. He was deeply aware of the fight Jessica had been waging, and his heart went out to her.

"I warned Jed, you know," he said crossly. "I told him that he hadn't made adequate arrangements, but he just brushed my warnings aside. He was never the same after your mother died, never as clearheaded."

Jessica couldn't help but smile. It was an affectionate smile, a sad one as she remembered her father. "He was *never* clearheaded. Be honest, Gordon. My father wrote some brilliant scientific treatises in his day, but he was an eccentric old geezer. He never knew much about the workings of the everyday world. Mom was the one who took care of all that, and I tried to take over when she died, but things were pretty far gone by then."

"A fine woman, your mother."

"But no financial whiz, either, and so enamored with Dad that she was frightened of him. Even if she saw the financial problems, I doubt she'd have said a word to him about it. She wouldn't have wanted to upset him. She wouldn't have wanted to sully the creative mind with mention of something as mundane as money."

Gordon arched a bushy gray brow. "So now you're the one left to suffer the sullying."

"No," Jessica cautioned. She knew what he was thinking. "My mind isn't creative like Dad's was."

"I don't believe that for a minute. You have a Ph.D. in linguistics. You're fluent in Russian and German. You teach at Harvard. And you're published. You're as much of a scholar as Jed was any day."

"If I'm a scholar, it's simply because I love learning. But what I do isn't anything like what Dad did. My mind isn't like his. I can't look off into space and conjure up incredibly complex scientific theories. I can't dream up ideas. What I do is studied. It's orderly and pragmatic. I'm a foreign-language teacher. I also read literature in the languages I teach, and since I've had access to certain Russian works that no one else has had, I was a cinch to write about them. So I'm published."

"You should be proud of that."

"I am, but if my book sells a thousand copies, I'll be lucky, which means that it won't save Crosslyn Rise. Nor will my salary." She gave a rueful chuckle. "Dad and I were alike in that, I'm afraid."

"But Crosslyn Rise was his responsibility," Gordon argued. "It's been in the family for five generations. Jed spent his entire life there. He owed it to all those who came before, as much as to you, to keep it up. If he'd done that, you wouldn't be in the bind you are now. But he let it deteriorate. I told him things would be bleak if he didn't keep on top of the repairs, but he wouldn't listen."

Jessica sighed. "That's water over the dam. The thing is that on top of everything else, I'm having plumbing and electrical problems. Up to now, I've settled for patches here and there, but that won't work any longer. I've been told—and I've had second and third opinions on it—that I need new systems for both. And given the size and nature of Crosslyn Rise…"

She didn't have to finish. Gordon knew the size and nature of Crosslyn Rise all too well. When one talked about installing new plumbing and electrical systems in a home that consisted of seventeen rooms and eight bathrooms spread over nearly eighty-five hundred square feet, the prospect was daunting. The prospect was even more daunting when one considered that a myriad of unexpected woes usually popped up when renovating a house that old.

Shifting several papers that lay neatly on his desk, Gordon said in a tentative voice, "I could loan you a little."

"A little more, you mean." She gave a tiny shake of her head and chided, "I'm having trouble meeting the payments I already have. You know that."

"Yes, but I'd do it, Jessica. I knew your family, and I know you. I'm the president of this bank, humble though it may be. If I can't pull a few strings, give a little extra for special people, who can I do it for?"

She was touched, and the smile she sent him told him so. But his generosity didn't change the facts. Again she shook her head, this time slowly and with resignation. "Thanks, Gordon. I do appreciate the offer, but if I was to accept it, I'd only be getting myself in deeper. Let's face it. I love my career, but it won't ever bring me big money. I could hurry out another book or two, maybe take on another course next semester, but I'd still come up way short of what I need."

"What you need," Gordon remarked, "is to marry a wealthy old codger who'd like nothing more than to live in a place like Crosslyn Rise."

Jessica didn't flinch, but her cheeks went paler than they'd been moments before. "I did that once."

"Chandler wasn't wealthy or old."

"But he wanted the Rise," she said with a look that went from wry to pained in the matter of a blink. "I wouldn't go through that again even if Crosslyn Rise were made of solid gold."

"If it were made of solid gold, you wouldn't have to go through anything," Gordon quipped, but he regretted mentioning Tom Chandler. Jessica's memories of the brief marriage weren't happy ones. Sitting forward, he folded his hands on his desk. "So what are your options?"

"There aren't many." And she'd been agonizing about those few for months.

"Is there someone who can help you—a relative who may have even a distant stake in the Rise?"

"Stake? No. The Rise was Dad's. He outlived a brother who stood to inherit if Dad had died first, but they were never on the best of terms. Dad wasn't a great communicator, if you know what I mean."

Gordon knew what she meant and nodded.

"And, anyway, now Dad's dead. Since I'm an only child, the Rise is mine, which means that no one else in the family has what you'd call a 'stake' in it."

"How about a fascination? Are there any aunts, uncles

or cousins who've been intrigued by it over the years to the point where they'd pitch in to keep it alive?"

"No aunts or uncles, but there's a cousin. She's Dad's brother's oldest daughter, and if I called her she'd be out on the next plane from Chicago to give me advice."

Gordon studied her face. It told her thoughts with a surprising lack of guile, given that her early years had been spent, thanks to her mother, among the North Shore's well-to-do, who were anything but guileless. "I take it you know what that advice would be?"

"Oh, yes. Felicia would raze the house, divide the twenty-three acres into lots and sell each to the highest bidder. She told me that when she came for Dad's funeral, which was amusing in and of itself because she hadn't seen him since she was eighteen. Needless to say, she was here for the Rise."

"But the Rise is yours."

"And Felicia knew we were having trouble with the upkeep and that the trouble would only increase with Dad gone. She knew I'd never agree to raze the house, so her next plan was to pay me for the land around it. She figured that would give me enough money to renovate and support the house. In turn, she'd quadruple her investment by selling off small parcels of the land."

"That she would," Gordon agreed. "Crosslyn Rise stands on prime oceanfront land. Fifteen miles north of Boston, in a wealthy, well-run town with a good school system, fine municipal services, excellent public transportation... She'd quadruple her investment or better." His eyes narrowed. "Unless you were to charge her a hefty sum for the land."

"I wouldn't sell her the land for *any* sum," Jessica vowed. Rising from her seat, she moved toward the window. "I don't want to sell the land at all, but if I have to, the last person I'd sell to would be her. She's a witch."

Gordon cleared his throat. "Not quite the scholarly assessment I'd expected."

With a sheepish half smile, Jessica turned. "No. But it's hard to be scholarly when people evoke the kind of visceral response Felicia does." She slipped her hands into the pockets of her skirt, feeling more anchored that way. "Felicia and I are a year apart in age, so she used to visit when we were kids. She aspired to greatness. Being at the Rise made her feel she was on her way. She always joked that if I didn't want the Rise, she'd take it, but it was the kind of joking that wasn't really joking, if you know what I mean." When Gordon nodded, she went on. "By the time she graduated from high school, she realized that her greatness wasn't going to come from the Rise. So she went looking in other directions. I'm thirty-three now, so she's thirty-four. She's been married three times, each time to someone rich enough to settle a large lump sum on her to get out of the marriage."

"So she's a wealthy woman. But has she achieved that greatness?"

Wearing a slightly smug what-do-you-think look, Jessica gave a slow head shake. "She's got lots of money with nowhere to go."

"I'm surprised she didn't offer to buy Crosslyn Rise from you outright."

"Oh, she did. When Dad was barely in his grave." Her shoulders went straighter, giving a regal lift to her five-foot-six-inch frame. "I refused just as bluntly as she offered. There's no way I'd let her have the Rise. She'd have it sold or subdivided within a year." She paused, took a breath, turned back to the window and said in a quiet voice, "I can't let that happen."

They were back to her options. Gordon knew as well

as she did that some change in the Rise's status was necessary. "What are your thoughts, Jessica?" he asked as gently as he could.

She was very still for a time, gnawing on her lower lip as she looked out over the harbor. Its charm, part of which was visible from Crosslyn Rise, not two miles away, made the thought of leaving the Rise all the harder. But it had to be faced.

"I could sell off some of the outer acreage," she began in a dubious tone, "but that would be a stopgap measure. It would be two lots this year, two lots next year and so on. Once I sold the lots, I wouldn't have any say about what was built on them. The zoning is residential, but you know as well as I do that there are dozens of styles of homes, one tackier than the next."

"Is that snobbishness I detect?" Gordon teased.

She looked him in the eye without a dash of remorse. "Uh-huh. The Rise is Georgian colonial and gorgeous. It would be a travesty if she were surrounded by less stately homes."

"There are many stately homes that aren't Georgian colonial."

"But the Rise is. And anything around it should blend in," she argued, then darted a helpless glance toward the ceiling. "This is the last thing I want to be discussing. It's the last thing I want to be *considering*."

"You love the Rise."

She pondered the thought. "It's not the mortar and brick that I love, not the kitchen or the parlor or the library. It's the whole thing. The old-world charm. The smell of polished wood and history. It's the beauty of it—the trees and ponds, birds and chipmunks—and the peace, the serenity." But there was more. "It's the idea of Crosslyn Rise. The idea that it's been in my family for so long. The idea that it's a little world unto itself." She faltered for an instant. "Yes, I love the Rise. But I have to do something. If I don't, you'll be forced to foreclose before long."

Gordon didn't deny it. He could give her more time than another person might have. He could indeed grant her another, smaller loan in the hope that, with a twist of fortune, she'd be able to recover from her present dire straits. In the end, business was business.

"What would you like to do?" he asked.

She started to turn back to the window but realized it wouldn't make things easier. It was time to face facts. So she folded her arms around her middle and said, "If I had my druthers, I'd sell the whole thing, house and acreage as a package, to a large, lovely, devoted family, but the chances of finding one that can afford it are next to nil. I've been talking with Nina Stone for the past eight months. If I was to sell, she'd be my broker. Without formally listing the house, she'd have an eye out for buyers like that, but there hasn't been a one. The real-estate market is slow."

"That's true as far as private buyers go. Real-estate developers would snap up property like Crosslyn Rise in a minute."

"And in the next minute they'd subdivide, sell off the smallest possible lots for the biggest possible money and do everything my cousin Felicia would do with just as little care for the integrity of the Rise." Jessica stood firm, levelly eyeing Gordon through her small, round lenses. "I can't do that, Gordon. It's bad enough that I have to break apart the Rise after all these years, but I can't just toss it in the air and let it fall where it may. I want a say as to what happens to it. I want whatever is done to be done with dignity. I want the charm of the place preserved."

She finished without quite finishing. Not even her

glasses could hide the slight, anticipatory widening of her eyes.

Gordon prodded. "You have something in mind?"

"Yes. But I don't know if it's feasible."

"Tell me what it is, and I'll let you know."

She pressed her lips together, wishing she didn't have to say a word, knowing that she did. The Rise was in trouble. She was up against a wall, and this seemed the least evil of the options.

"What if we were to turn Crosslyn Rise into an exclusive condominium complex?" she asked, then hurried on before Gordon could answer. "What if there were small clusters of homes, built in styles compatible with the mansion and tucked into the woods at well-chosen spots throughout the property?" She spoke even more quickly, going with the momentum of her words. "What if the mansion itself was redone and converted into a combination health center, clubhouse, restaurant? What if we developed the harbor area into something small but classy, with boutiques and a marina?" Running out of "what ifs," she stopped abruptly.

Unfolding his hands, Gordon sat back in his chair. "You'd be willing to do all that?"

"Willing, but not able. What I'm talking about would be a phenomenally expensive project—"

He stilled her with a wave of his hand. "You'd be *willing* to have the Rise turned into a condominium complex?"

"If it was done the right way," she said. She felt suddenly on the defensive and vaguely disloyal to Crosslyn Rise. "Given any choice, I'd leave the Rise as it is, but it's deteriorating more every year. I'm long past the point of being able to put a finger in the dike. So I have to do something. This idea beats the alternatives. If it was done with forethought and care and style, we could alter the nature of Crosslyn Rise without changing its character."

"We?"

"Yes." She came away from the window to make her plea. "I need help, Gordon. I don't have any money. There would have to be loans, but once the cluster homes were built and sold, the money could be repaid, so it's not like my asking you for a loan just to fix up the Rise. Can I get a loan of the size I'd need?"

"No."

She blinked. "No? Then you don't like the idea?"

"Of the condo complex? Yes, I do. It has definite merit."

"But you won't back me."

"I can't just hand over that kind of money."

She slid into her chair and sat forward on its edge. "Why not? You were offering me money just a little while ago. Yes, this would be more, but it would be an investment that would guarantee enough profit to pay back the loan and then some."

Gordon regarded her kindly. He had endless respect for her where her work at Harvard was concerned. But she wasn't a businesswoman by any stretch of the imagination. "No financial institution will loan you that kind of money, Jessica. If you were an accredited real-estate developer, or a builder or an architect, you might have a chance. But from a banker's point of view, loaning a linguistics professor large amounts of money to build a condominium complex would be akin to loaning a librarian money to buy the Red Sox. You're not a developer. You may know what you want for the Rise, but you wouldn't know how to carry it out. Real-estate development isn't your field. You don't have the kind of credibility necessary to secure the loan."

"But I need the money," she cried. The sharp rise in

her voice was out of character, reflecting her frustration, which was growing by the minute.

"Then we'll have to find people who *do* have the necessary credibility for a project like this."

Her frustration eased. All she needed was a ray of hope. "Oh. Okay. How do we go about doing that and how does it work?"

Gordon relaxed in his chair. He enjoyed planning projects and was relieved that Jessica was open to suggestion. "We put together a consortium, a group of people, each of whom is willing to invest in the future of Crosslyn Rise. Each member has an interest in the project based on his financial contribution to it, and the amount he takes out at the end is commensurate with his input."

Jessica wasn't sure she liked the idea of a consortium, simply because it sounded so real. "A group of people? But they're strangers. They won't know the Rise. How can we be sure that they won't put their money and heads together and come up with something totally offensive?"

"We handpick them. We choose only people who would be as committed to maintaining the dignity and charm of Crosslyn Rise as you are."

"No one is as committed to that as I am."

"Perhaps not. Still, I've seen some beautiful projects, similar to what you have in mind, done in the past few years. Investors can be naturalists, too."

Jessica was only vaguely mollified, a fact to which the twisting of her stomach attested. "How many people?"

"As many as it would take to collect the necessary money. Three, six, twelve."

"Twelve people? Twelve strangers?"

"Strangers only at first. You'd get to know them, since you'd be part of the consortium. We'd have the estate appraised as to its fair market value, and that would determine your stake in the project. If you wanted, I could advance you more to broaden your stake. You'd have to decide how much profit you want."

Her eyes flashed. "I'm not in this for the profit."

"You certainly are," Gordon insisted in the tone of one who was older and wiser. "If the Rise is made into the kind of complex you mention, this is your inheritance. And it's significant, Jessica. Never forget that. You may think you have one foot in the poorhouse, but Crosslyn Rise, for all its problems, is worth a pretty penny. It'll be worth even more once it's developed."

Developed. The word made her flinch. She felt guilty for even considering it—guilty, traitorous, mercenary. In one instant she was disappointed with herself, in the next she was furious with her father.

But neither disappointment nor fury would change the facts. "Why does this have to be?" she whispered sadly.

"Because," Gordon said quietly, "life goes on. Things change." He tipped his head and eyed her askance. "It may not be all that bad. You must be lonely living at the Rise all by yourself. It's a pretty big place. You could choose one of the smaller houses and have it custom-designed for you."

She held up a cautionary hand. He was moving a little too quickly. "I haven't decided to do this."

"It's a solid idea."

"But you're making it sound as if it can really happen, and that makes me feel like I'm losing control."

"You'd be a member of the consortium," he reminded her. "You'd have a voice as to what's done."

"I'd be one out of three or six or maybe even twelve."

"But you own the Rise. In the end, you'd have final approval of any plan that is devised."

"I would?"

"Yes."

That made her feel better, but only a little. She'd always been an introverted sort. She could just imagine herself sitting at the far end of a table, listening to a group of glib investors bicker over her future. She'd be outtalked, outplanned, outwitted.

"I want more than that," she said on impulse. It was survivalism at its best. "I want to head the consortium. I want my cut to be the largest. I want to be *guaranteed* control over the end result." She straightened in her chair. "Is that possible?"

Gordon's brows rose. "Anything's possible. But advisable? I don't know, Jessica. You're a scholar. You don't know anything about real-estate development."

"So I'll listen and learn. I have common sense and an artistic eye. I know the kind of thing I want. And I love Crosslyn Rise." She was convincing herself as she talked. "It isn't enough for me to have the power to approve or disapprove. I want to be part of the project from start to finish. That's the only way I'll be able to sleep at night." She wasn't sure she liked the look on Gordon's face. "You don't think I can do it."

"It's not that." He hesitated. There were several problems that he could see, one of which was immediate. He searched for the words to tell her what he was thinking, without sounding offensive. "You have to understand, Jessica. Traditionally, men are the investors. They've been involved in other projects. They're used to working in certain ways. I'm…not sure how they'll feel about a novice telling them what to do."

"A woman, you mean," she said, and he didn't deny it. "But I'm a reasonable person. I'm not pigheaded or spiteful. I'll be open-minded about everything except compromising the dignity of Crosslyn Rise. What better a leader could they want?"

Gordon didn't want to touch that one. So he tried a different tack. "Changing the face of Crosslyn Rise is going to be painful for you. Are you sure you want to be intimately involved in the process?"

"Yes," she declared.

He pursed his lips, dropped his gaze to the desktop, tried to think of other evasive arguments, but failed. Finally he went with the truth, bluntly stating the crux of the problem. "The fact is, Jessica, that if you insist on being the active head of the consortium, I may have trouble getting investors." He held up a hand. "Nothing personal, mind you. Most of the people I have in mind don't know who or what you are, but the fact of a young, inexperienced woman having such control over the project may make them skittish. They'll fear that it will take forever to make decisions, or that once those decisions are made, you'll change your mind. It goes back to the issue of credibility."

"That's not fair!"

"Life isn't, sometimes," he murmured, but he had an idea. "There is one way we might be able to get around it."

"What?"

He was thoughtful for another minute. "A compromise, sort of. We get the entire idea down on paper first. You work with an architect, tell him what you want, let him come up with some sketches, work with him on revising them until you're completely satisfied. Then we approach potential investors with a fait accompli." He was warming to the idea as he talked. "It could work out well. With your ideas spelled out in an architect's plans, we can better calculate the costs. Being specific might help in wooing investors."

"You mean, counterbalance the handicap of working with me?" Jessica suggested dryly, but she wasn't angry.

If sexism existed, it existed. She had worked around it before. She could do it again.

"Things would be simplified all around," Gordon went on without comment. "You would have total control over the design of the project. Investors would know exactly what they were buying into. If they don't like your idea, they don't have to invest, and if we can't get enough people together, you'd only be out the architect's fee."

"How much will that be?" Jessica asked. She'd heard complaints from a colleague who had worked with an architect not long before.

"Not as much as it might be, given the man I have in mind."

Jessica wasn't sure whether to be impressed or nervous. The bravado she's felt moments before was beginning to falter with talk of specifics, like architects. "You've already thought of someone?"

"Yes," Gordon said, eyeing her directly. "He's the best, and Crosslyn Rise deserves the best."

She couldn't argue with that. "Who is he?"

"He's only been in the field for twelve years, but he's done some incredible things. He was affiliated with a New York firm for seven of those years, and during that time he worked on PUDs up and down the East Coast."

"PUDs?"

"Planned Urban Developments—in and around cities, out to suburbs. Five years ago, he established his own firm in Boston. He's done projects like the one you have in mind. I've seen them. They're breathtaking."

Her curiosity was piqued. "Who is he?"

"He's a down-to-earth guy who's had hands-on experience at the building end, which makes him an even better architect. He isn't so full of himself that he's hard to work with. And I think he'd be very interested in this project."

Jessica was trying to remember whether she'd ever read anything in the newspaper about an architect who might fit Gordon's description. But such an article would have been in the business section, and she didn't read that—which, unfortunately, underscored some of what Gordon had said earlier. Still, she had confidence in her ideas. And if she was to work with a man the likes of whom Gordon was describing, she couldn't miss.

"Who *is* he?" she asked.

"Carter Malloy."

Jessica stared at him dumbly. The name was very familiar. Carter Malloy. She frowned. Bits and snatches of memories began flitting through her mind.

"I knew a Carter Malloy once," she mused. "He was the son of the people who used to work for us at the Rise. His mom kept the house and his dad gardened." She felt a moment's wistfulness. "Boy, could I ever use Michael Malloy's green thumb now. On top of everything else, the Rise needs a landscaping overhaul. It's been nearly ten years since the Malloys retired and went south." Her wistfulness faded, giving way to a scowl. "It's been even longer since I've seen their son, thank goodness. He was obnoxious. He was older than me and never let me forget it. It used to drive him nuts that his parents were poor and mine weren't. He had a foul mouth, problems in school and a chip on his shoulder a mile wide. And he was ugly."

Gordon's expression was guarded, his voice low. "He's not ugly now."

"Excuse me?"

"I said," he repeated more clearly, "he's not ugly now. He's grown up in lots of ways, including that."

Jessica was surprised. "You've been in touch with Carter Malloy?"

"He keeps an account here. God only knows he could

easily give his business to one of the bigger banks in Boston, but he says he feels a connection with the place where he grew up."

"No doubt he does. There's a little thing about a police record here. Petty theft, wasn't it?"

"He's reformed."

Her expression said she doubted that was possible. "I was always mystified that wonderful people like Annie and Michael Malloy could spawn a son like that. The heartache he caused them." She shook her head at the shame of it. "He's not living around her, is he? Tell me, so I'll know to watch out. Carter Malloy isn't someone I'd want to bump into on the street."

"He's living in Boston."

"What is he—a used-car salesman?"

"He's an architect."

Jessica was momentarily taken aback. "Not the Carter Malloy I knew."

"Like I said, he's grown up."

The thought that popped into her head at that moment was so horrendous that she quickly dashed it from her mind. "The Carter Malloy I knew couldn't possibly have grown up to be a professional. He barely finished high school."

"He spent time in the army and went to college when he got out."

"But even if he had the gray matter for college," she argued, feeling distinctly uneasy, "he didn't have the patience or the dedication. He could never apply himself to anything for long. The only thing he succeeded at was making trouble."

"People change, Jessica. Carter Malloy is now a well-respected and successful architect."

Jessica had never known Gordon to lie to her, which was why she had to accept what he said. On a single lingering thread of hope, she gave a tight laugh. "Isn't it a coincidence? Two Carter Malloys, both architects? The one you have in mind for my project—does he live in Boston, too, or does he have a house in one of the suburbs?"

Gordon never answered. Jessica took one look at his expression, stood and began to pace the office. Her hands were tucked into the pockets of her skirt, and just as the challis fabric faithfully rendered the slenderness of her hips and legs as she paced, it showed those hands balled into fists. Her arms were straight, pressed to her sides.

"Do you know what Carter Malloy did to me when I was six? He dared me to climb to the third notch of the big elm out beyond the duck pond." She turned at the window and stared back. "Needless to say, once I got up there, I couldn't get back down. He looked up at me with that pimply face of his, gave an evil grin and walked off." She paused before a Currier and Ives print on the wall, seeing nothing of it. "I was terrified. I sat for a while thinking that he'd come back, but he didn't. I tried yelling, but I was too far from the house to be heard. One hour passed, then another, and each time I looked at the ground I got dizzy. I sat up there crying for three hours before Michael finally found me, and then he had to call the fire department to get me down." She moved on. "I had nightmares for weeks afterward. I've never climbed a tree since."

She stopped at the credenza, turned and faced Gordon, dropping her hands and hips back against the polished mahogany for support. "If the Carter Malloy I knew is the one you have in mind for this job, the answer is no. That's my very first decision as head of this consortium, and it's closed to discussion."

"Now that," Gordon said on a light note that wasn't light at all but was his best shot at an appeal, "is why I may have trouble finding backers for the project. If you're going to make major decisions without benefit of discussion with those who have more experience, there isn't much hope. I have to say that I wouldn't put my money into a venture like that. A bullheaded woman would be hell to work with."

"Gordon," she protested.

"I'm serious, Jessica. You said you'd listen and learn, but you don't seem willing to do that."

"I am. Just not where Carter Malloy is concerned. I couldn't work with him. It would be a disaster, and what would happen to the Rise, then?" Her voice grew pleading. "There must be other architects. He can't be the only one available."

"He's not, and there are others, but he's the best."

"In all of Boston?"

"Given the circumstances, yes."

"What circumstances?"

"He knows the Rise. He cares about it."

"Cares?" she echoed in dismay. "He'd as soon burn the Rise to the ground and leave it in ashes as transform it into something beautiful."

"How do you know? When was the last time you talked with him?"

"When I was sixteen." Pushing off from the credenza, she began to pace again. "It was the first I'd seen him in a while—"

"He'd been in the army," Gordon interrupted to remind her.

"Whatever. His parents didn't talk about him much, and I was the last person who'd want to ask. But he came over to get something for his dad one night. I was on the front porch waiting for a date to pick me up, and Carter said—" Her memories interrupted her this time. Their sting held her silent for a minute, finally allowing her to murmur, "He said some cruel things. Hurtful things." She stopped her pacing to look at Gordon. "Carter Malloy hates me as much as I hate him. There's no way he'd agree to do the work for me even if I wanted him to do it, which I don't."

But Gordon wasn't budging. "He'd do it. And he'd do it well. The Carter Malloy I've come to know over the past five years is a very different man from the one you remember. Didn't you ever wonder why his parents retired when they did? They were in their late fifties, not terribly old and in no way infirm. But they'd saved a little money over the years, and then Carter bought them a place in Florida with beautiful shrubbery that Michael could tend year-round. It was one of the first things Carter did when he began to earn good money. To this day he sees that they have everything they need. It's his way of making up for the trouble he caused them when he was younger. If he hurt you once, my guess is he'd welcome the chance to help out now."

"I doubt that," she scoffed, but more quietly. She was surprised by what Gordon had said. Carter Malloy had never struck her as a man with a thoughtful bone in his body. "What do you mean by help out?"

"I'd wager that he'd join the consortium."

"Out of pity for me?"

"Not at all. He's a shrewd businessman. He'd join it for the investment value. But he'd also want to be involved for old times' sake. I've heard him speak fondly of Crosslyn Rise." He paused, stroked a finger over his upper lip. "I'd go so far as to say we could get him to throw in his fee as part of his contribution. That way, he'd have a real stake in making the plans work, and if they didn't, it would be his problem. He'd swallow his own costs—which would be a far sight better than your having to come up with forty or fifty thousand if the project fizzled."

"Forty or fifty thousand?" She hadn't dreamed it would be so much. Swallowing, she sank into her chair once again, this time into the deepest corner, where the chair's back and arms could shield her. "I don't like this, Gordon."

"I know. But given that the Rise can't be saved as it is, this is an exciting option. Let me call Carter."

"No," she cried, then repeated it more quietly. "No."

"I'm talking about a simple introductory meeting. You can tell him your general thoughts about the project and listen to what he has to say in return. See how you get along. Decide for yourself whether he's the same as he used to be. There won't be an obligation. I'll be there with you if you like."

She tipped up her chin. "I was never afraid of Carter Malloy. I just disliked him."

"You won't now. He's a nice guy. Y'know, you said it yourself—it drove him nuts that he was poor and you were rich. He must have spent a lot of time wishing Crosslyn Rise was his. So let him take those wishes and your ideas and make you some sketches."

"They could be very good or very bad."

"Ah," Gordon drawled, "but remember two things. First off, Carter has a career and a reputation to protect. Second, you have final say. If you don't like what he does, you have the power of veto. In a sense that puts him under your thumb, now, doesn't it?"

Jessica thought back to the last time she'd seen Carter Malloy. In vivid detail, she recalled what he'd said to her, and though she'd blotted it from her mind over the years, the hurt and humiliation remained. Perhaps she would find a measure of satisfaction having him under her thumb.

And, yes, Crosslyn Rise was still hers. If Carter Malloy

didn't come up with plans that pleased her, she'd turn her back on him and walk away. He'd see who had the last laugh then.

CHAPTER TWO

JESSICA HAD NEVER been a social butterfly. Her mother, well aware of the Crosslyn heritage, had put her through the motions when she'd been a child. Jessica had been dressed up and taken to birthday parties, given riding lessons, sent to summer camp, enrolled in ballet. She had learned the essentials of being a properly privileged young lady. But she had never quite fit in.

She wasn't a beautiful child, for one thing. Her hair was long and unruly, her body board-straight and her features plain—none of which was helped by the fact that she rarely smiled. She was quiet, serious, shy, not terribly unlike her father. One part of her was most comfortable staying home in her room at Crosslyn Rise reading a good book. The other part dreamed of being the belle of the ball.

Having a friend over to play was both an apprehensive and exciting experience for Jessica. She liked the company and, even more, the idea of being liked, but she was forever afraid of boring her guest. At least, that was what her mother warned her against ad infinitum. As an adult, Jessica understood that though her mother worshipped her father's intellect, deep inside she found him a boring person, hence the warnings to Jessica. At the time, Jessica took those warning to heart. When she had a friend at the Rise, she was on her guard to impress.

That was why she was crushed by what Carter Malloy did to her when she was ten. Laura Hamilton, who came as close to being a best friend as any Jessica had, was over to visit. She didn't come often; the Rise wasn't thought to be a "fun" place. But Laura had come this time because she and Jessica had a project to do together for school, and the library at the Rise had the encyclopedias and *National Geographic*s that the girls needed.

When they finished their work, Jessica suggested they go out to the porch. It was a warm fall day, and the porch was one of her favorite spots. Screened in and heavily shaded by towering maples and oaks, it was the kind of quiet, private place that made Jessica feel secure.

She started out feeling secure this day, because Laura liked the porch, too. They sat close beside each other on the flowered porch sofa, pads of paper in their laps, pencils in hand. They were writing poems, which seemed to Jessica to be an exciting enough thing to do.

Carter Malloy didn't think so. Pruning sheers in hand, he materialized from behind the rhododendrons just beyond the screen, where, to Jessica's chagrin, he had apparently been sitting.

"What are you two doing?" he asked in a voice that said he knew exactly what they were doing, since he'd been listening for quite some time, and he thought it was totally dumb.

"What are *you* doing?" Jessica shot right back. She wasn't intimidated by his size or his deep voice or the fact that he was seventeen. Maybe, just a little, she was intimidated by his streetwise air, but she pushed that tiny fear aside. Given who his parents were, he wouldn't dare touch her. "What are you doing out there?" she demanded.

"Clipping the hedges," Carter answered with an insolent look.

She was used to the look. It put her on the defensive every time she saw it. "No, you weren't. You were spying on us."

He had one hip cocked, one shoulder lower than the other but both back to emphasize a developing chest. "Why in the hell would I want to do that? You're writing sissy poems."

"Who is he?" Laura whispered nervously.

"He's no one," was Jessica's clearly spoken answer. Though she'd always talked back to Carter, this time it seemed more important than ever. She had Laura to impress. "You were supposed to be cutting the shrubs, but you weren't. You never do what your father tells you to do."

"I think for myself," Carter answered. His dark eyes bore into hers. "But you don't know what that means. You're either going to tea parties like your old lady or sticking your nose in a book like your old man. You couldn't think for yourself if you tried. So whose idea was it to write poems? Your prissy little friend's?"

Jessica didn't know which to be first, angry or embarrassed. "Go away, Carter."

Lazily he raised the pruning sheers and snipped off a single shoot. "I'm working."

"Go work somewhere else," she cried with a ten-year-old's frustration. "There are lots of other bushes."

"But this one needs trimming."

She was determined to hold her ground. "We want to be alone."

"Why? What's so important about writing poems? Afraid I'll steal your rhymes?" He looked closely at Laura. "You're a Hamilton, aren't you?"

"Don't answer," Jessica told Laura.

"She is," Carter decided. "I've seen her sitting in church with the rest of her family."

"That's a lie," Jessica said. "You don't go to church."

"I go sometimes. It's fun, all those sinners begging for

forgiveness. Take old man Hamilton. He bought his way into the state legislature—"

Jessica was on her feet, her reed-slim body shaking. The only thing she knew for sure about what Carter was saying was that it was certain to offend Laura, and if that happened, Laura would never be back. "Shut up, Carter!"

"Bought his way there and does nothing but sit on his can and raise his hand once in a while. But I s'pose he doesn't have to do nothing. If I had that much money, I'd be sittin' on my can, too."

"You *don't* have that much money. You don't have *any* money."

"But I have friends. And you don't."

Jessica never knew how he'd found her Achilles' heel, but he'd hit her where it hurt. "You're a stupid jerk," she cried. "You're dumb and you have pimples. I wouldn't want to be you for anything in the world." Tears swimming in her eyes, she took Laura's hand and dragged her into the house.

Laura never did come back to Crosslyn Rise, and looking back on it so many years later, Jessica remembered the hurt she'd felt. It didn't matter that she hadn't seen Laura Hamilton for years, that by the time they'd reached high school Jessica had found her as boring as she'd feared she would be herself, that they had nothing in common now. The fact was that when she was ten, she had badly wanted to be Laura's best friend and Carter Malloy had made that harder than ever.

Such were her thoughts as the T carried her underground from one stop to the next on her way from Harvard Square to Boston. She had a two-o'clock meeting with Carter Malloy in his office. Gordon had set it up, and when he'd asked if Jessica wanted him along, she had said she'd be fine on her own.

She wasn't sure that had been the wisest decision. She was feeling nervous, feeling as though every one of the insecurities she'd suffered in childhood was back in force. She was the not-too-pretty, not-too-popular, not-too-social little girl once again. Gordon's support might have come in handy.

But she had a point to prove to him, too. She'd told him that she wanted to actively head the consortium altering Crosslyn Rise. Gordon was skeptical of her ability to do that. If he was to aggressively and enthusiastically seek out investors in Crosslyn Rise, she had to show him she was up to the job.

So she'd assured him that she could handle Carter Malloy on her own, and that, she decided in a moment's respite from doubt, was what she was going to do. But the doubts returned, and as she left the trolley, climbed the steep stairs to Park Street and headed for Winter, she hated Carter Malloy more than ever.

It wasn't the best frame of mind in which to be approaching a meeting of some importance, Jessica knew, which was why she took a slight detour on her way to Carter's office. She had extra time; punctual person that she was, she'd allowed plenty for the ride from Cambridge. So she swung over to West Street and stopped to browse at the Brattle Book Shop, and though she didn't buy anything, the sense of comfort she felt in the company of books, particularly the aged beauties George Gloss had collected, was worth the pause. It was with some reluctance that she finally dragged herself away from the shelves and set off.

Coming from school, she wore her usual teaching outfit—long skirt, soft blouse, slouchy blazer and low heels. The occasional glance in a store window as she passed told her that she looked perfectly presentable. Her hair was impossible, of course. Though not as unruly as it had once been, it was still thick and hard to handle, which was why she had it secured with a scarf at the back of her head. She wasn't trying to impress anyone, least of all Carter Malloy, but she wanted to look professional and in command of herself, if nothing else.

Carter's firm was on South Street in an area that had newly emerged as a mecca for artists and designers. The building itself was six stories tall and of an earthy brick that was pleasantly warm in contrast to the larger, more modern office tower looming nearby. The street level of the building held a chic art gallery, an equally chic architectural supply store, a not-so-chic fortune-cookie company and a perfectly dumpy-looking diner that was mobbed, even at two, with a suit-and-tie crowd.

Turning in at the building's main entrance, she couldn't help but be impressed by the newly refurbished, granite-walled lobby. She guessed that the building's rents were high, attesting to Gordon's claim that Carter was doing quite well.

As she took the elevator to the top floor, Jessica struggled, as she'd done often in the five days since Gordon had first mentioned his name, to reconcile the Carter Malloy she'd known with the Carter Malloy who was a successful architect. Try as she might, she couldn't shake the image of what he'd been as a boy and what he'd done to her then. Not even the sleekly modern reception area, with its bright walls, indirect lighting and sparse, avante-garde furnishings could displace the image of the ill-tempered, sleezy-looking juvenile delinquent.

"My name is Jessica Crosslyn," she told the receptionist in a voice that was quiet and didn't betray the unease she felt. "I have a two-o'clock appointment with Mr. Malloy."

The receptionist was an attractive woman, sleek enough to complement her surroundings, though nowhere near as new. Jessica guessed her to be in her late forties. "Won't you have a seat? Mr. Malloy was delayed at a meeting. He shouldn't be more than five or ten minutes. He's on his way now."

Jessica should have figured he'd be late. Keeping her waiting was a petty play for power. She was sure he'd planned it.

Once again she wished Gordon was with her, if for no other reason than to show him that Carter hadn't changed so much. But Gordon was up on the North Shore, and she was too uncomfortable to sit. So, nodding at the receptionist, she moved away from the desk and slowly passed one, then another of the large, dry-mounted drawings that hung on the wall. Hingham Court, Pheasant Landing, Berkshire Run—pretty names for what she had to admit were attractive complexes, if the drawings were at all true to life. If she could blot out the firm's name, Malloy and Goodwin, from the corner of each, she might feel enthusiasm. But the Malloy, in particular, kept jumping right off the paper, hitting her mockingly in the face. In self-defense, she finally turned and slipped into one of the low armchairs.

Seconds later, the door opened and her heart began to thud. Four men entered, engaged in a conversation that kept them fully occupied while her gaze went from one face to the next. Gordon had said Carter Malloy had changed a lot, but even accounting for that, not one of the men remotely resembled the man she remembered.

Feeling awkward, she took a magazine from the glass coffee table beside her and began to leaf through. She figured that if Carter was in the group, he'd know of her presence soon enough. In the meanwhile, she concentrated on keeping her glasses straight on her nose and looking calm, cool, even a bit disinterested, which was hard when the discussion among the four men began to grow heated. The matter at hand seemed to be the linkage issue, a City of Boston mandate that was apparently costing builders hundreds of thousands of dollars per project. Against her will, she found herself looking up. One of the group seemed to be with the city, another with Carter's firm and the other two with a construction company. She was thinking that the architect was the most articulate of the bunch when the door opened again. Her heart barely had time to start pounding anew when Carter Malloy came through. He took in the group before him, shook hands with the three she'd pegged as outsiders, slid a questioning gaze to the receptionist, then, in response to the woman's pointed glance, looked at Jessica.

For the space of several seconds, her heart came to a total standstill. The man was unmistakably Carter Malloy, but, yes, he'd changed. He was taller, broader. In place of a sweaty T-shirt emblazoned with something obscene, tattered old jeans and crusty work boots, he wore a tweed blazer, an oxford-cloth shirt with the neck button open, gray slacks and loafers. The dark hair that had always fallen in ungroomed spikes on his forehead was shorter, well shaped, cleaner. His skin, too, was cleaner, his features etched by time. The surly expression that even now taunted her memory had mellowed to something still intense but controlled. He had tiny lines shadowing the corners of his eyes, a small scar on his right jaw and a light tan.

Gordon was right, she realized in dismay. Carter wasn't ugly anymore. He wasn't *at all* ugly, and that complicated things. She didn't do well with men in general, but attractive ones in particular made her edgy. She wasn't sure she was going to make it.

But she couldn't run out now. That would be the greatest indignity. And besides, if she did that, what would she

tell Gordon? More aptly, what would Carter tell Gordon?
Her project would be sunk, for sure.

Mustering every last bit of composure she had stashed
away inside, she rose as Carter approached.

"Jessica?" he asked in a deep but tentative voice.

Heart thudding, she nodded. She deliberately kept her
hands in her lap. To offer a handshake seemed reckless.

Fortunately he didn't force the issue, but stood looking
down at her, not quite smiling, not quite frowning. "I'm
sorry. Were you waiting long?"

She shook her head. A little voice inside told her to
say something, but for the life of her she couldn't find
any words. She was wondering why she felt so small,
why Carter seemed so tall, how her memory could have
been so inaccurate in its rendition of as simple a matter
as relative size.

He gestured toward the inner door. "Shall we go
inside?"

She nodded. When he opened the door and held it for
her, she was surprised; the Carter she'd known would have
let it slam in her face. When she felt the light pressure of
his hand at her waist, guiding her down a corridor spattered with offices, she was doubly surprised; the Carter
she'd known knew nothing of courtly gestures, much less
gentleness. When he said, "Here we are," and showed her
into the farthest and largest office, she couldn't help but
be impressed.

That feeling lasted for only a minute, because no
sooner had she taken a chair—gratefully, since the race
of her pulse was making her legs shaky—than Carter
backed himself against the stool that stood at the nearby
drafting table, looked at her with a familiarly wicked
gleam in his eye and said, "Cat got your tongue?"

Jessica was oddly relieved. The old Carter Malloy she
could handle to some extent; sarcasm was less debilitating

than charm. Taking in a full breath for the first time since she'd laid eyes on him, she said, "My tongue's where it's always been. I don't believe in using it unless I have something to say."

"Then you're missing out on some of the finer things in life," he informed her so innocently that it was a minute before Jessica connected his words with the gleam in his eye.

Ignoring both the innuendo and the faint flush that rose on her cheeks, she vowed to state her business as quickly as possible and leave. "Did Gordon explain why I've come?"

Carter gave a leisurely nod, showing none of the discomfort she felt. But instead of picking up on his conversation with Gordon, he said, "It's been a long time. How have you been?"

"Just fine."

"You're looking well."

She wasn't sure why he'd said that, but it annoyed her. "I haven't changed," she told him as though stating the obvious, then paused. "You have."

"I should hope so." While the words settled into the stillness of the room, he continued to stare at her. His eyes were dark, touched one minute by mockery, the next by genuine curiosity. Jessica half wished for the contempt she used to find there. It wouldn't have been as unsettling.

Tearing her gaze from his, she looked down at her hands, used one to shove the nose piece of her glasses higher and cleared her throat. "I've decided to make some changes at Crosslyn Rise." She looked back up, but before she could say a thing, Carter beat her to it.

"I'm sorry about your father's death."

Uh-huh, she thought, but she simply nodded in thanks for the words. "Anyway, there's only me now, so the Rise is really going to waste." That wasn't the issue at all, but she couldn't quite get herself to tell Carter Malloy the problem was money. "I'm hoping to make something newer and more practical out of it. Gordon suggested I speak with you. Quite honestly, I wasn't wild about the idea." She watched him closely, waiting to see his reaction to her rebuff.

But he gave nothing away. In a maddeningly calm voice, he asked, "Why not?"

She didn't blink. "We never liked one another. Working together could be difficult."

"That's assuming we don't like one another now," he pointed out too reasonably.

"We don't *know* one another now."

"Which is why you're here today."

"Yes," she said, hesitated, then added, "I wasn't sure how much to believe of what Gordon told me." Her eyes roamed the room, taking in a large desk covered with rolls of blueprints, the drafting table and its tools, a corked wall that bore sketches in various stages of completion. "All this doesn't jibe with the man I remember."

"That man wasn't a man. He wasn't much more than a boy. How many years has it been since we last saw each other?"

"Seventeen," she said quickly, then wished she'd been slower or more vague when she caught a moment's satisfaction in his eye.

"You didn't know I was an architect?"

"How would I know?"

He shrugged and offered a bit too innocently, "Mutual friends?"

She did say, "Uh-huh," aloud this time, and with every bit of the sarcasm she'd put into it before. He was obviously enjoying her discomfort. *That* was more like what she'd expected. "We've never had any mutual friends."

"Spoken like the Jessica I remember, arrogant to the

core. But times have changed, sweetheart. I've come up in the world. For starters, there's Gordon. He's a mutual friend."

"And he'd have had no more reason to keep me apprised of your comings and goings than I'd have had to ask. The last I knew of you," she said, her voice hard in anger that he'd dared call her 'sweetheart,' "you were stealing cars."

Carter's indulgent expression faded, replaced by something with a sharper edge. "I made some mistakes when I was younger, and I paid the price. I had to start from the bottom and work my way up. I didn't have any help, but I made it."

"And how many people did you hurt along the way?"

"None once I got going, too many before," he admitted. His face was somber, and though his body kept the same pose, the relaxation had left it. "I burned a whole lot of bridges that I've had to rebuild. That was one of the reasons I shifted my schedule to see you when Gordon called. You were pretty bitchy when you were a kid, but I fed into it."

She stiffened. "Bitchy? Thanks a lot!"

"I said I fed into it. I'm willing to take most of the blame, but you were bitchy. Admit it. Your hackles went up whenever you saw me."

"Do you wonder why? You said and did the nastiest things to me. It got so I was conditioned to expect it. I did whatever I could to protect myself, and that meant being on my guard at the first sight of you."

Rather than argue further, he pushed off from the stool and went to the desk. He stood at its side, fingering a paper clip for a minute before meeting her gaze again. "My parents send their best."

Jessica was nearly as surprised by the gentling of his

voice as she was by what he'd said. "You told them we were meeting?"

"I talked with them last night." At the look of disbelief that remained on her face, he said, "I do that sometimes."

"You never used to. You were horrible to them, too."

Carter returned his attention to the paper clip, which he twisted and turned with the fingers of one hand. "I know."

"But why? They were wonderful people. I used to wish my parents were half as easygoing and good-natured as yours. And you treated them so badly."

He shot her a look of warning. "It's easy to think someone else's parents are wonderful when you're the one who doesn't live with them. You don't know the facts, Jessica. My relationship with my parents was very complex." He paused for a deep breath, which seemed to restore his good temper. "Anyway, they want to know everything about you—how you look, whether you're working or married or mothering, how the Rise is."

The last thing Jessica wanted to do was to discuss her personal life with Carter. He would be sure to tear it apart and make her feel more inadequate than ever. So she blurted out, "I'll tell you how the Rise is. It's big and beautiful, but it's aging. Either I pour a huge amount of money into renovations, or I make alternate plans. That's why I'm here. I want to discuss the alternate plans."

Carter made several more turns of the paper clip between his fingers before he tossed it aside. Settling his tall frame into the executive chair behind the desk, he folded his hands over his lean middle and said quietly, "I'm listening."

Business, this is business, Jessica told herself and took strength from the thought. "I don't know how much Gordon has told you, but I'm thinking of turning Crosslyn

Rise into a condominium complex, building cluster housing in the woods, turning the mansion into a common facility for the owners, putting a marina along the shore."

Gordon hadn't told Carter much of anything, judging from the look of disbelief on his face. "Why would you do that?"

"Because the Rise is too big for me."

"So find someone it isn't too big for."

"I've been trying to, but the market's terrible."

"It takes a while sometimes to find the right buyer."

I don't have a while, she thought. "It could take years, and I'd really like to do something before then."

"Is there a rush? Crosslyn Rise has been in your family for generations. A few more years is nothing in the overall scheme of things."

Jessica wished he wouldn't argue. She didn't like what she was saying much more than he did. "I think it's time to make a change."

"But condominiums?" he asked in dismay. "Why condominiums?"

"Because the alternative is a full-fledged housing development, and that would be worse. This way, at least, I'd have some control over the outcome."

"Why does that have to be the alternative?"

"Do you have any better ideas?" she asked dryly.

"Sure. If you can't find an individual, sell to an institution—a school or something like that."

"No institution, or school or something like that will take care of the Rise the right way. I can just picture large parking lots and litter all over the place."

"Then what about the town? Deed the Rise to the town for use as a museum. Just imagine the whopping-big tax deduction you'd get."

"I'm not looking for tax deductions, and besides, the town may be wealthy, but it isn't *that* wealthy. Do you have any idea what the costs are of maintaining Crosslyn Rise for a year?" Realizing she was close to giving herself away, she paused and said more calmly, "In the end, the town would have to sell it, and I'd long since have lost my say."

"But…condominiums?"

"Why not?" she sparred, hating him for putting her on the spot when, if he had any sensitivity at all, he'd know she was between a rock and a very hard place.

Carter leaned forward in his seat and pinned her with a dark-eyed stare. "Because Crosslyn Rise is magnificent. It's one of the most beautiful, most private, most special pieces of property I've ever seen, and believe me, I've seen a whole lot in the last few years. I don't even know how you can think of selling it."

"I have no choice!" she cried, and something in her eyes must have told him the truth.

"You can't keep it up?"

She dropped her gaze to the arm of her chair and rubbed her thumb back and forth against the chrome. "That's right." Her voice was quiet, imbued with the same defeat it had held in Gordon's office, and with an additional element of humiliation. Admitting the truth was bad enough; admitting it to Carter Malloy was even worse.

But she had to finish what she'd begun. "Like I said, the Rise is aging. Work that should have been done over the years wasn't, so what needs to be done now is extensive."

"Your dad let it go."

She had an easier time not looking at him. At least his voice was kind. "Not intentionally. But his mind was elsewhere, and my mother didn't want to upset him. Money was—" She stopped herself, realizing in one instant that she didn't want to make the confession, knowing in the next that she had to. "Money was tight."

"Are you kidding?"

Meeting his incredulous gaze, she said coldly, "No. I wouldn't kid about something like that."

"You don't kid about much of anything. You never did. Afraid a smile might crack your face?"

Jessica stared at him for a full second. "You haven't changed a bit," she muttered, and rose from her chair. "I shouldn't have come here. It was a mistake. I knew it would be."

She was just about at the door when it closed and Carter materialized before her. "Don't go," he said very quietly. "I'm sorry if I offended you. I sometimes say things without thinking them through. I've been working on improving that. I guess I still have a ways to go."

The thing that appalled Jessica most at that minute wasn't the embarrassment she felt regarding the Rise or her outburst or even Carter's apology. It was how handsome he was. Her eyes held his for a moment before, quite helplessly, lowering over the shadowed angle of his jaw to his chin, then his mouth. His lower lip was fuller than the top one. The two were slightly parted, touched only by the air he breathed.

Wrenching her gaze to the side, she swallowed hard and hung her head. "I do think this is a mistake," she murmured. "The whole thing is very difficult for me. Working with you won't help that."

"But I care about Crosslyn Rise."

"That was what Gordon said. But maybe you care most about getting it away from me. You always resented me for the Rise."

The denial she might have expected never came. After a short time, he said, "I resented lots of people for things that I didn't have. I was wrong. I'm not saying that I wouldn't buy the Rise from you if I had the money, because I meant what I said about it being special. But I don't have the money—any more, I guess, than you do. So that puts us in the same boat. On equal footing. Neither of us above or below the other."

He paused, giving her a chance to argue, but she didn't have anything to say. He had a right to be smug, she knew, but at that moment he wasn't. He was being completely reasonable.

"Do you have trouble with that, Jessica? Can you regard me as an equal?"

"We're not at all alike, you and I."

"I didn't say alike. I said equal. I meant financially equal."

Keeping her eyes downcast, she cocked her head toward the office behind her. "Looks to me like you're doing a sight better than I am at this point."

"But you have the Rise. That's worth a lot." When she simply shrugged, he said, "Sit down. Please. Let's talk."

Jessica wasn't quite sure why she listened to him. She figured it had something to do with the gentle way he'd asked, with the word *please,* with the fact that he was blocking the door anyway, and he wasn't a movable presence. She suspected it might have even had something to do with her own curiosity. Though she caught definite reminders of the old Carter, the changes that had taken place since she'd seen him last intrigued her.

Without a word, she returned to her seat. This time, rather than going behind his desk, Carter lowered his long frame into the matching chair next to hers. Though there was a low slate cube between them, he was closer, more visible. That made her feel self-conscious. To counter the feeling, she directed her eyes to her hands and her thoughts to the plans she wanted to make for Crosslyn Rise.

"I don't like the sound of condominiums, either, but

if the condominiums were in the form of cluster housing, if they were well-placed and limited in number, if
the renovations to the mansion were done with class and
the waterfront likewise, the final product wouldn't be so
bad. At least it would be kept up. The owners would be
paying a lot for the privilege of living there. They'd have
a stake in its future."

"Are you still teaching?"

At the abrupt change of subject, she cast him a quick
look. "I, uh, yes."

"You haven't remarried?"

When her eyes flew to his this time, they stayed. "How
did you know I'd married at all?"

"My parents. They were in touch with your mom. Once
she died, they lost contact."

"Dad isn't—wasn't very social," Jessica said by way of
explanation. But she hadn't kept in touch with the Malloys, either. "I'm not much better, I guess. How have your
parents been?"

"Very well," he said on the lightest note he'd used yet.
"They really like life under the sun. The warm weather
is good for Mom's arthritis, and Dad is thrilled with the
long growing season."

"Do you see them often?"

"Three or four times a year. I've been pretty busy."

She pressed her lips together and shook her head. "An
architect. I'm still having trouble with that."

"What would you have me be?"

"A pool shark. A gambler. An ex-con."

He had the grace to look humble. "I suppose I deserved
that."

"Yes." She was still looking at him, bound by something she couldn't quite fathom. She kept thinking that
if she pushed a certain button, said a certain word, he'd
change back into the shaggy-haired demon he'd been. But

he wasn't changing into anything. He was just sitting with one leg crossed over the other, studying her intently. It was all she could do not to squirm. She averted her eyes, then, annoyed, returned them to his. "Why are you doing that?"

"Doing what?"

"Staring at me like that."

"Because you look different. I'm trying to decide how."

"I'm older. That's all."

"Maybe," he conceded, but said no more.

The silence chipped at Jessica's already-iffy composure nearly as much as his continued scrutiny did. She wasn't sure why she was the one on the hot seat, when by rights the hot seat should have been his. In an attempt to correct the situation, she said, "Since I have an appointment back in Cambridge at four—" which she'd deliberately planned, to give her an out "—I think we should concentrate on business. Gordon said you were good." She sent a look toward the corked wall. "Are these your sketches, or were they done by an assistant?"

"They're mine."

"And the ones in the reception area?"

"Some are mine, some aren't."

"Who is Goodwin?"

"My partner. We first met in New York. He specializes in commercial work. I specialize in residential, so we complement each other."

"Was he one of the men standing out front?"

"No. The man in the tan blazer was one of three associates who work here."

"What do they do—the associates?"

"They serve as project managers."

"Are they architects?" She could have sworn the man she'd heard talking was one.

Carter nodded. "Two are registered, the third is about to be. Beneath the associates, there are four drafts-people, beneath them a secretary, a bookkeeper and a receptionist."

"Are you the leading partner?"

"You mean, of the two of us, do I bring in more money?" When she nodded, he said, "I did last year. The year before I didn't. It varies."

"Would you want to work on Crosslyn Rise?"

"Not particularly," he stated, then held up a hand in appeasement when she looked angry. "I'd rather see the Rise kept as it is. If you want honesty, there it is. But if you don't have the money to support it, something has to be done." He came forward to brace his elbows on his thighs and dangle his hands between his knees. "And if you're determined to go ahead with the condo idea, I'd rather do the work myself than have a stranger do it."

"You're a stranger," she said stiffly. "You're not the same person who grew up around Crosslyn Rise."

"I remember what I felt for the Rise then. I can even better understand those feelings now."

"I'm not sure I trust your motives."

"Would I risk all this—" he shot a glance around the room "—for the sake of a vendetta? Look, Jessica," he said with a sigh, "I don't deny who I was then and what I did. I've already said that. I was a pain in the butt."

"You were worse than that."

"Okay, I was worse than that, but I'm a different person now. I've been through a whole lot that you can't begin to imagine. I've lived through hell and come out on the other side, and because of that, I appreciate some things other people don't. Crosslyn Rise is one of those things."

Jessica wished he wasn't sitting so close or regarding her so intently or talking so sanely. Either he was being utterly sincere, or he was doing one hell of an acting job.

She wasn't sure which, but she did know that she couldn't summarily rule him off the project.

"Do you think," she asked in a tentative voice, "that my idea for Crosslyn Rise would work?"

"It could."

"Would you want to try working up some sketches?"

"We'd have to talk more about what you want. I'd need to see a plot plan. And I'd have to go out there. Even aside from the fact that I haven't been there in a while, I've never looked around with this kind of thing in mind."

Jessica nodded. What he said was fair enough. What wasn't fair was the smooth way he said it. He sounded very professional and very male. For the second time in as many minutes, she wished he wasn't sitting so close. She wished she wasn't so aware of him.

Clutching her purse, she stood. "I have to be going," she said, concentrating on the leather strap as she eased it over her shoulder.

"But we haven't settled anything."

She raised her eyes. He, too, had risen and was standing within an arm's length of her. She started toward the door. "We have. We've settled that we have to talk more, I have to get you a plot plan, you have to come out to see Crosslyn Rise." Her eyes were on the doorknob, but she felt Carter moving right along with her. "You may want to talk with Gordon, too. He'll explain the plan he has for raising the money for the project."

"Am I hired?" He reached around her to open the door.

"I don't know. We have to do all those other things first."

"When can we meet again?"

"I'll call you." She was in the corridor, moving steadily back the way she'd come, with Carter matching her step.

"Why don't we set a time now?"

"Because I don't have my schedule in front of me."

"Are you that busy?"

"Yes!" she said, and stopped in her tracks. She looked up at him, swallowed tightly, dropped her gaze again and moved on. "Yes," she echoed in a near-whisper. "It's nearly exam time. My schedule's erratic during exam time."

Her explanation seemed to appease Carter, which relieved her, as did the sight of the reception area. She was feeling overwhelmed by Carter's presence. He was a little too smooth, a little too agreeable, a little too male. Between those things and a memory that haunted her, she wanted out.

"Will you call me?" he asked as he opened the door to the reception area.

"I said I would."

"You have my number?"

"Yes."

Opening the outer door, he accompanied her right to the elevator and pushed the button. "Can I have yours?"

Grateful for something to do, she fumbled in her purse for a pen, jotted her number in a small notebook, tore out the page and handed it to him. She was restowing the pen when a bell rang announcing the elevator's arrival. Her attention was riveted to the panel on top of the doors when Carter said, "Jessica?"

She dared meet his gaze a final time. It was a mistake. A small frown touched his brow and was gone, leaving an expression that combined confusion and surprise with pleasure. When he spoke, his voice held the same three elements. "It was really good seeing you," he said as though he meant it and surprised himself in that. Then he smiled, and his smile held nothing but pleasure.

That was when Jessica knew she was in big trouble.

CHAPTER THREE

CARTER *HAD* ENJOYED seeing Jessica, though he wasn't sure why. As a kid, she'd been a snotty little thing looking down her nose at him. He had resented everything about her, which was why his greatest joy had been putting her down. In that, he had been cruel at times. He'd found her sore spots and rubbed them with salt.

Clearly she remembered. She wasn't any too happy to see him, though she'd agreed to the meeting, which said something about the bind she was in regarding Crosslyn Rise. Puzzled by that bind, Carter called Gordon shortly after Jessica left his office.

In setting up the meeting, Gordon had only told him that Jessica had wanted to discuss an architectural project relating to the Rise. Under Carter's questioning now, he admitted to the financial problems. He talked of putting together a group of investors. He touched on Jessica's insistence on being in command. He went so far as to outline the role Carter might play, as Gordon had broached it with Jessica.

Though Carter had meant what he'd said about preferring to leave Crosslyn Rise as it was, once he accepted the idea of its changing, he found satisfaction in the idea of taking part in that change. Some of his satisfaction was smug; there was an element of poetic justice in his having come far enough in the world to actively shape the Rise's future.

But the satisfaction went beyond that. Monetarily it

was a sound proposal. His gut told him that, even before he worked out the figures. Given the dollar equivalent of his professional fees added to the hundred thousand he could afford to invest, he stood to take a sizable sum out of the project in two to three years' time.

That sum would go a long way toward broadening his base of operation. Malloy and Goodwin was doing well, bringing in greater profit each year, but there were certain projects—more artistically rewarding than lucrative—that Carter would bid on given the cushion of capital funds and a larger staff.

And then, working on the alteration of Crosslyn Rise both as architect and investor, he would see more of Jessica. That thought lingered with him long after he'd hung up the phone, long after he'd set aside the other issues.

He wanted to see more of her, incredible but true. She wasn't gorgeous. She wasn't sexy or witty. She wasn't anything like the women he dated, and it certainly wasn't that he was thinking of dating *her.* But at the end of their brief meeting, he had felt something warm flowing through him. He guessed it had to do with a shared past; he didn't have that with many people, and he wouldn't have thought he'd want it with *anyone,* given the sins of his past. Still, there was that warm feeling. It fascinated him, particularly since he had felt so many conflicting things during the meeting itself.

Emotions had come in flashes—anger and resentment in an almost automatic response to any hint of arrogance on her part, embarrassment and remorse as he recalled things he'd said and done years before. She was the same as he remembered her, but different—older, though time had been kind. Her skin was unflawed, her hair more tame, her movements more coordinated, even in spite of her nervousness. And she was nervous. He made her so, he guessed, though he had tried to be amenable.

What he wanted, he realized, was for her to eye him through those granny glasses of hers and see the decent person he was now. He wanted to close the last page on the book from the past. He wanted her acceptance. Though he hadn't given two thoughts to it before their meeting, that acceptance suddenly mattered a lot. Only when he had it would he feel that he'd truly conquered the past.

JESSICA TRIED TO THINK about their meeting as little as possible in the hours subsequent to it. To that end, she kept herself busy, which wasn't difficult with exams on the horizon and the resultant rash of impromptu meetings with students and teaching assistants. If Carter's phone number seemed to burn a hole in her date book, she ignored the smoke. She had to be in command, she told herself. Carter had to know she was in command.

She wasn't terribly proud of the show she'd put on in his office. She'd been skittish in his presence, and it had showed. The most merciful thing about the meeting was that he had waited until she had a foot out the door before smiling. His smile was potent. It had confused her, excited her, frightened her. It had warned her that working with him wasn't going to be easy in any way, shape or form, and it had nearly convinced her not to try it.

Still she called him. She waited two full days to do it, then chose Thursday afternoon, when she was fresh from a buoying department meeting. She enjoyed department meetings. She liked her colleagues and was liked in return. In the academic sphere, she was fully confident of her abilities. So she let the overflow of that confidence carry her into the phone call to Carter.

"Carter? This is Jessica Crosslyn."

"It's about time you called," he scolded, and she immediately bristled—until the teasing in his voice came through. "I was beginning to think you'd changed your mind."

She didn't know what to make of the teasing. She'd never heard teasing coming from Carter Malloy before. For the sake of their working together, she took it at face value and said evenly, "It's only been two days."

"That's two days too long."

"Is there a rush?"

"There's always a rush where enthusiasm and weather are concerned."

She found that to be a curious statement. "Enthusiasm?"

"I'm really up for this now, and I have the time to get started," he explained. "It's not often that the two coincide."

She could buy that, she supposed, though she wondered if he'd purposely injected the subtle reminder that he was in demand. "And the weather?" she came back a bit skeptically. "It's not yet May. The best of the construction season is still ahead."

"Not so, once time is spent on first-draft designs then multiple rounds of revisions." Carter kept his tone easygoing. "By the time the plans are done, the investors lined up and bidding taken on contractors, it could well be September or October, unless we step on it now." Having made his point, he paused. "Gordon explained the financial setup and the fact that you want sole approval of the final plans before they're shown to potential investors."

Jessica was immediately wary. "Do you have a problem with that?"

"It depends on whether you approve what I like," he said with a grin, then tacked on a quick, "Just kidding."

"I don't think you are."

"Sure I am," he cajoled. "A client pays me for my work, I give him what he wants."

"And if you think what he wants is hideous?"

"I know not to take the job."

"So in that sense," she persisted, not sure why she was being stubborn, but driven to it nonetheless, "you ensure that the client will approve what you like."

"Not ensure—" he dug in his own heels a little "—but I maximize the likelihood of it. And there's nothing wrong with that. It's the only sensible way to operate. Besides, the assumption is that the client comes to me because he likes my style."

"I don't know whether I like your style or not," she argued. "I haven't seen much of it."

She seemed to be taking a page from the past and deliberately picking a fight. As he'd done then, so now Carter fought back. "If you'd asked the other day, I'd have shown you pictures. I've got a portfolio full of them. You might have saved us both a whole lot of time and effort. But you were in such an all-fired rush to get back to your precious ivory tower—"

He caught himself only after he realized what he was doing. Jessica remained silent. He waited for her to rail at him the way she used to, but she didn't speak. In a far quieter voice he asked, "Are you still there?"

"Yes," she murmured, "but I don't know why. This isn't going to work. We're like oil and water."

"The past is getting in the way. Old habits die hard. But I'm sorry. What I said was unnecessary."

"Part of it was right," she conceded. "I was in a rush to get back. I had another appointment." He should know that he wasn't the only one in demand. "But as far as my ivory tower is concerned, that ivory tower has produced official interpreters for assorted summit meetings as well as for embassies in Moscow, Leningrad and Bonn. My work isn't all mind-in-the-clouds."

"I know," Carter said quietly. "I'm sorry." He didn't

say anything more for a minute, hoping she'd tell him he was forgiven. But things weren't going to be so easy. "Anyway, I'd really like to talk again. Tell me when you have free time. If I have a conflict, I'll try to change it."

Short of being bitchy, which he'd accused her of being as a child, she couldn't turn her back on his willingness to accommodate her. She looked at the calendar tacked on the wall. It was filled with scrawled notations, more densely drawn for the upcoming few weeks. Given the choice, she would put off a meeting with Carter until after exams, when she'd be better able to take the disturbance in stride. But she remembered what he'd said about the weather. If she was going to do something with Crosslyn Rise, she wanted it done soon. The longer she diddled around with preliminary arrangements, the later in the season it would be and the greater the chance of winter closing in to delay the work even more. Instinctively she knew that the longer the process was drawn out, the more painful it would be.

"I'm free until noon next Tuesday morning," she said. "Do you want to come out and walk through Crosslyn Rise then?"

Carter felt a glimmer of excitement at the mention of walking through Crosslyn Rise. It had been years since he'd seen the place, and though he'd never lived there, since his parents had always rented a small house in town, returning to Crosslyn Rise would be something of a homecoming.

He had one meeting scheduled for that morning, but it was easily postponed. "Next Tuesday is fine. Time?"

"Is nine too early?"

"Nine is perfect. It might be a help if between now and then you wrote down your ideas so we can discuss them in as much detail as possible. If you've seen any pictures of things you like in newspapers or magazines you might cut them out. The more I know of what you want, the easier my job will be."

Efficient person that she was herself, she could go along with that. "You mentioned wanting to see a plot plan. I don't think I've ever seen one. Where would I get it?"

"The town should have one, but I'll take care of that. I can phone ahead and pick it up on my way. You just be there with your house and your thoughts." He paused. "Okay?"

"Okay."

"See you then."

"Uh-huh."

JESSICA COULDN'T DECIDE whether to put coffee on to brew or to assume that he'd already had a cup or two, and she spent an inordinate amount of time debating the issue. One minute she decided that the proper thing would indeed be to have it ready and offer him some; the next minute it seemed a foolish gesture. This was Carter Malloy, she told herself. He didn't expect anything from her but a hard time, which was just about all they'd ever given each other.

But that had been years ago, and Carter Malloy had changed. He'd grown up. He was an architect. A man. And though one part of her didn't want to go out of her way to make the Carter Malloy of any age feel welcome in her home, another part felt that she owed cordiality to the architect who might well play a part in her future.

As for the man in him, she pushed all awareness of that to the farthest reaches of consciousness and chose to attribute the unsettled feeling in her stomach to the nature of the meeting itself.

Carter arrived at nine on the dot. He parked his car on the pebbled driveway that circled some twenty feet in front of the ivy-draped portico. The car was dark blue and low, but Jessica wouldn't have known the make even if she'd had the presence of mind to wonder—which she didn't, since she was too busy trying to calm her nerves.

She greeted him at the front door, bracing an unsteady hand on the doorknob. Pulse racing, she watched him step inside, watched him look slowly around the rotundalike foyer, watched him raise his eyes to the top of the broadly sweeping staircase, then say in a low and surprisingly humble voice, "This is…very…weird."

"Weird?"

"Coming in the front door. Seeing this after so many years. It's incredibly impressive."

"Until you look closely."

He shot her a questioning glance.

"Things are worn," she explained, wanting to say it before he did. "The grandeur of Crosslyn Rise has faded."

"Oh, but it hasn't." He moved toward the center of the foyer. "The grandeur is in its structure. Nothing can dim that. Maybe the accessories have suffered with age, but the place is still a wonder."

"Is that your professional assessment?"

He shook his head. "Personal." His gaze was drawn toward the living room. The entrance to it was broad, the room itself huge. Knee-to-ceiling windows brought in generous helpings of daylight, saving the room from the darkness that might otherwise have come with the heavy velvet decor. Sun was streaming obliquely past the oversize fireplace, casting the intricate carving of the pine mantel in bas-relief. "Personal assessment. I always loved this place."

"I'm sure," she remarked with unplanned tartness.

He shot her a sharper look this time. "Does it gall you seeing me here? Does it prick your Victorian sensibilities?

Would you rather I stay out back near the gardener's shed?"

Jessica felt instant remorse. "Of course not. I'm sorry. I was just remembering—"

"Remembering the past is a mistake, because what you remember will be the way I acted, not the way I felt. You didn't know the way I really felt. *I* didn't know the way I really felt a lot of the time. But I knew I loved this place."

"And you hated me because I lived here and you didn't."

"That's neither here nor there. But I did love Crosslyn Rise, and I'd like to feel free to express what I'm thinking and feeling as we walk around. Can I do that, or would you rather I repress it all?"

"You?" she shot back, goaded on by the fact that he was being so reasonable. "Repress your feelings?"

"I can do it if I try. Granted, I'm not as good at it as you. But you've had years of practice. You're the expert. No doubt there's a Ph.D. in Denial mixed up with all the diplomas on your wall." His eyes narrowed, seeing far too much. "Don't you ever get tired of bottling everything up?"

Jessica's insides were beginning to shake. She wanted to think it was anger, but that was only half-true. Carter was coming close to repeating things he'd said once before. The same hurt she'd felt then was threatening to engulf her now. "I don't bottle everything up," she said, and gave a tight swallow.

"You do. You're as repressed as ever." The words were no sooner out than he regretted them. She looked fearful, and for a horrifying minute, he wondered if she was going to cry. "Don't," he whispered and approached her with his hands out to the side. "Please. I'm sorry. Damn, I'm apologizing again. I can't believe that. Why do you make me say mean things? What is it about you that brings out the bastard in me?"

Struggling against tears, she didn't speak. A small shrug was the best she could muster.

"Yell at me," Carter ordered, willing to do anything to keep those tears at bay. "Go ahead. Tell me what you think of me. Tell me that I'm a bastard and that I don't know what I'm talking about because I don't know you at all. Say it, Jessica. Tell me to keep my mouth shut. Tell me to mind my own business. Tell me to go to hell."

But she couldn't do that. Deep down inside, she knew she was the villain of the piece. She'd provoked him far more than he'd provoked her. And he was right. She was repressed. It just hurt to hear him say it. Hurt a lot. Hurt even more, at thirty-three, than it had at sixteen.

Moving to the base of the stairs, she pressed herself against the swirling newel post, keeping her back to him. "I've lived at Crosslyn Rise all my life," she began in a tremulous voice. "For as long as I can remember, it's been my haven. It's the place I come home to, the place that's quiet and peaceful, the place that accepts me as I am and doesn't make demands. I can't afford to keep it up, so I have to sell it." Her voice fell to a tormented whisper. "That hurts, Carter. It really hurts. And seeing you—" she ran out of one breath, took in another "—seeing you brings back memories. I guess I'm feeling a little raw."

The warmth Carter had experienced the last time he'd been with Jessica was back. It carried him over the short distance to where she stood, brought his hands to her shoulders and imbued his low, slow voice with something surprisingly caring. "I can understand what you're feeling about Crosslyn Rise, Jessica. Really, I can." With the smallest, most subtle of movements, his hands worked at the tightness in her shoulders. "I wish I could offer a miracle solution to keep the Rise intact, but if there was one, I'm sure either you or Gordon would have found it by now. I can promise you that I'll draw up spectacular plans for the complex you have in mind, but it doesn't matter how spectacular they are, they won't be the Crosslyn Rise you've known all your life. The thought of it hurts you now, and it'll get worse before it gets better." He kept kneading, lightly kneading, and he didn't mind it at all. Her blouse was silk and soft, her shoulders surprisingly supple beneath it. His fingers fought for and won successive bits of relaxation.

"But the hurt will only be aggravated if we keep sniping at each other," he went on to quietly make his point. "I've already said I was wrong when I was a kid. If I could turn back the clock and change things, I would." Without thinking, he gathered a stray wisp of hair from her shoulder and smoothed it toward the tortoiseshell clasp at her nape. "But I can't. I can only try to make the present better and the future better than that—and *try* is the operative word. I'll make mistakes. I'm a spontaneous person—maybe 'impulsive' is the word—but you already know that." He turned her to face him, and at the sight of her openness, gentled his voice even more. "The point is that I can be reasoned with now. I couldn't be back then, but I can be now. So if I say something that bugs you, tell me. Let's get it out in the open and be done."

Jessica heard what he was saying, but only peripherally. Between the low vibrancy of his voice and the slow, hypnotic motion of his hands, she was being warmed all over. Not even the fact that she faced him now, that she couldn't deny his identity as she might have if her back was still to him, could put a chill to that warmth.

"I'd like this job, Jessica," he went on, his dark eyes barely moving from hers yet seeming to touch on each of her features. "I'd really like this job, but I think you ought to decide whether working with me will be too painful on top of everything else. If it will be," he finished, fascinated by the softness of her cheek beneath the sweeping pad of his thumb, "I'll bow out."

His thumb stopped at the corner of her mouth, and time seemed to stop right along with it. In a flash of awareness that hit them simultaneously came the realization that they were standing a breath apart, that Carter was holding her as he would a desirable woman and Jessica was looking up at him as she would a desirable man.

She couldn't move. Her blood seemed to be thrumming through her veins in mockery of the paralysis of her legs, but she couldn't drag herself away from Carter. He gave her comfort. He made her feel not quite so alone. And he made her aware that she was a woman.

That fact took Carter by surprise. He'd always regarded Jessica as an asexual being, but something had happened when he'd put his hands on her shoulders. No, something had happened even before that, when she'd been upset and he'd wanted to help ease her through it. He felt protective. He couldn't remember feeling that for a woman before, mainly because most of the women he'd known were strong, powerful types who didn't allow for upsets. But he rather liked being needed. Not that Jessica would admit to needing him, he knew. Still, it was something to consider.

But he'd consider it another time, because she looked frightened enough at that minute to bolt, and he didn't want her to. Slowly, almost reluctantly, he dropped his hands to his sides.

A second later, Jessica dropped her chin to her chest. She raised a shaky hand to the bridge of her nose, pressed a fingertip to the nosepiece of her glasses and held it there. "I'm sorry," she whispered, sure that she'd misinterpreted what she'd seen and felt, "I don't know what came over me. I'm usually in better control of myself."

"You have a right to be upset," he said just as quietly, but he didn't step away. "It's okay to lose control once in a while."

She didn't look up. Nor did she say anything for a minute, because there was a clean, male scent in the air that held her captive. Then, cursing herself for a fool, she cleared her throat. "I, uh, I made coffee. Do you want some?"

What Carter wanted first was a little breathing space. He needed to distance himself mentally from the vulnerable Jessica, for whom he'd just felt a glimmer of desire. "Maybe we ought to walk around outside first," he suggested. "That way I'll know what you're talking about when you go through your list. You made one, didn't you?"

She met his gaze briefly. "Yes."

"Good." He remembered the feel of silk beneath his fingers. She was wearing a skirt that hit at midcalf, opaque stockings and flat shoes that would keep her warm, but her silk blouse, as gently as it fell over her breasts, wouldn't protect her from the air. "Do you want a sweater or something? It's still cool outside."

She nodded and took a blazer from the closet, quickly slipping her arms into the sleeves. Carter would have helped her with it if she hadn't been so fast. He wondered whether she wanted breathing space, too—then he chided himself for the whimsy. If Jessica had been struck in that instant with an awareness of him as a man, it was an aberration. No way was she going to allow herself to lust after Carter Malloy—*if* she knew the meaning of the word *lust,* which he doubted she did. And he certainly wasn't lusting after her. It was just that with his acceptance that she was a woman, she became a character of greater depth in his mind, someone he might like to get to know better.

They left through the front door, went down the brick

walk and crossed the pebbled driveway to the broad lawn, which leveled off for a while before slanting gracefully toward the sea. "This is the best time of year," he remarked, taking in a deep breath. "Everything is new and fresh in spring. In another week or two, the trees will have budded." He glanced at Jessica, who was looking forlornly toward the shore, and though he doubted his question would be welcome, he couldn't pass by her sadness. "What will you do—if you decide to go ahead and develop Crosslyn Rise?"

It was a minute before she answered. Her hands were tucked into the pockets of her blazer, but her head was up and her shoulders straight. The fresh air and the walking were helping her to recover the equilibrium she'd lost earlier when Carter had been so close. "I'm not sure."

"Will you stay here?"

"I don't know. That might be hard. Or it might be harder to leave. I just don't know. I haven't gotten that far yet." She came to a halt.

Carter did, too. He followed her gaze down the slope of the lawn. "Tell me what you see."

"Something small and pretty. A marina. Some shops. Do you see how the boulders go? They form a crescent. I can see boats over there—" she pointed toward the far-right curve of the crescent "—with a small beach and shops along the straightaway."

Carter wasn't sure he'd arrange the elements quite as she had, but that was a small matter. He started walking again. "And this slope?"

She came along. "I'd leave it as is, maybe add a few paths to protect the grass and some shrubbery here and there."

They descended the slope that led to the shoreline. "You used to sled down this hill. Do you remember?"

"Uh-huh. I had a Flexible Flyer," she recalled.

"New and shiny. It was always new and shiny."

"Because it wasn't used much. It was no fun sledding alone."

"I'd have shared that Flexible Flyer with you."

"Shared?" she asked too innocently.

"Uh, maybe not." He paused. "Mmm, probably not. I'd probably have chased you into the woods, buried you under a pile of snow and kept the Flyer all to myself."

Wearing a small, slightly crooked smile, she looked up at him. "I think so."

He liked the smile, small though it was, and it hadn't cracked her face after all. Rather, it made her look younger. It made him feel younger. "I was a bully."

"Uh-huh."

"You must have written scathing things about me in your diary."

"I never kept a diary."

"No? Funny, I'd have pegged you for the diary type."

"Studious?"

"Literary."

"I wrote poems."

He squinted as the memory returned. "That's…right. You did write poems."

"Not about you, though," she added quickly. "I wrote poems about pretty things, and there was absolutely nothing pretty about you that I could see back then."

"Is there now?" he asked, because he couldn't help it.

Jessica didn't know whether it was the outdoors, the gentle breeze stirring her hair or the rhythmic roll of the surf that lulled her, but her nervousness seemed on hold. She was feeling more comfortable than she had before with Carter, which was why she dared answer his question.

"You have nice skin. The acne's gone."

Carter was oddly pleased by the compliment. "I finally outgrew that at twenty-five. I had a prolonged adolescence, in *lots* of ways."

The subject of why he'd been such a troubled kid was wide open, but Jessica felt safer keeping things light. "Where did you get the tan?"

"Anguilla. I was there for a week at the beginning of March."

They'd reached the beach and were slowly crossing the rocky sand. "Was it nice?"

"Very nice. Sunny and warm. Quiet. Restful."

She wondered whether he'd gone alone. "You've never married, have you?"

"No."

On impulse, and with a touch of the old sarcasm, she said, "I'd have thought you'd have been married three times by now."

He didn't deny it. "I probably would have, if I'd let myself marry at all. Either I knew what a bad risk I was, or the women I dated did. I'd have made a lousy husband."

"Then. What about now?"

Without quite answering the question, he said, "Now it's harder to meet good women. They're all very complex by the time they reach thirty, and somehow the idea of marrying a twenty-two-year-old when I'm nearly forty doesn't appeal to me. The young ones aren't mature enough, the older ones are too mature."

"Too mature—as in complex?"

He nodded and paused, slid his hands into the pockets of his dark slacks and stood looking out over the water. "They have careers. They have established lifestyles. They're stuck in their ways and very picky about who they want and what they expect from that person. It puts a lot of pressure on a relationship."

"Aren't you picky?" she asked, feeling the need to defend members of her sex, though she'd talked to enough single friends to know that Carter was right.

"Sure I'm picky," he said with a bob of one shoulder. "I'm not getting any younger. I have a career and an established lifestyle, and I'm pretty set in my ways, too. So I'm not married." He looked around, feeling an urge to change the subject. "Were you thinking of keeping the oceanfront area restricted to people who live here?"

"I don't know. I haven't thought that out yet." She studied the crease on his brow. "Is there a problem?"

"Problem? Not if you're flexible about what you want. As I see it, either you have a simple waterfront with a beach and a pier and a boathouse or you have a marina with a dock, slips, shops and the appropriate personnel to go with them. But if you want the marina and the shops, they can't be restricted—at least, not limited to the people who live here. You could establish a private yacht club that would be joined by people from all along the North Shore, and you can keep it as exclusive as you want by regulating the cost of membership, but there's no way something as restrictive as that is going to be able to support shops, as I think of shops." As he talked, he'd been looking around, assessing the beachfront layout. Now he faced her. "What kind of shops did you have in mind?"

"The kind that would provide for the basic needs of the residents—drugstore, convenience store, bookstore, gift or crafts shop." She saw him shaking his head. "No?"

"Not unless there's public access. Shops like that couldn't survive with such a limited clientele base."

Which went to show, Jessica realized in chagrin, how little she knew about business. "But I was thinking really *small* shops. Quaint shops."

"Even the smallest, most quaint shop has to do a

certain amount of business to survive. You'd need public access."

"You mean, scads of people driving through?" But that wasn't at all what she wanted, and the look on her face made that clear.

"They wouldn't have to drive through. The waterfront area could be arranged so that cars never cross it."

"I don't know," she murmured, disturbed. Turning, she headed back up toward the house.

He joined her, walking for a time in silence before saying, "You don't have to make an immediate decision."

"But you said yourself that time was of the essence."

"Only if you want to get started this year."

"I don't *want* to get started at all," she said, and quickened her step.

Knowing the hard time she was having, he let her go. He stayed several paces behind until she reached the top of the rise, where she slowed. When he came alongside her, she raised her eyes to his and asked in a tentative voice, "Were you able to get the plot plan?"

He nodded. "It's in the car."

"Do you want to take it when we go through the woods?"

"No. I'll study it later. What I want is for you to show me the kinds of settings you had in mind for the housing. Even though ecological factors will come into play when a final decision is made, your ideas can be a starting point." He took a deep breath, hooked his hands on his hips and made a visual sweep of the front line of trees. "I used to go through these woods a lot, but that was too many years ago and never with an eye out for something like this."

She studied his expression, but it told her nothing of what he was feeling just then, and she wanted to know.

She was feeling frighteningly upended and in need of support. "You said that you really wanted this project." She started off toward a well-worn path, confident that Carter would fall into step, which he did.

"I do."

"Why?"

"Because it's an exciting one. Crosslyn Rise is part of my past. It's a beautiful place, the challenge will be to maintain its beauty. If I can do that, it will be a feather in my cap. So I'll have the professional benefit, and the personal satisfaction. And if I invest in the project the way Gordon proposed, I'll make some money. I could use the money."

That surprised her. "I thought you were doing well."

"I am. But there's a luxury that comes with having spare change. I'd like to be able to reject a lucrative job that may be unexciting and accept an exciting job that may not be lucrative."

His argument was reasonable. *He* was reasonable—far more so than she'd have expected. Gordon had said he'd changed. *Carter* had said he'd changed. For the first time, as they walked along the path side by side, with the dried leaves of winter crackling beneath their shoes, she wondered what had caused the change. Simple aging? She doubted it. There were too many disgruntled adults in the world to buy that. It might have been true if Carter had simply mellowed. But given the wretch of a teenager he'd been, mellowing was far too benign a term to describe the change. She was thinking total personality overhaul—well, not total, since he still had the occasional impulsive, sharp-tongued moment, but close.

For a time, they walked on without talking. The crackle of the leaves became interspersed with small, vague sounds that consolidated into quacks when they approached the duck pond. Emerging from the path into the open, Jessica stopped. The surface of the pond and its shores were dotted with iridescent blue, green and purple heads. The ducks were in their glory, waiting for spring to burst forth.

"There would have to be some houses here, assuming care was taken to protect the ducks. It's too special a setting to waste."

Carter agreed. "You mentioned cluster housing the other day. Do you mean houses that are physically separate from one another but clustered by twos and threes here and in other spots? Or clusters of town houses that are physically connected to one another?"

"I'm not sure." She didn't look at him. It was easier that way, she found. The bobbing heads of the ducks on the pond were a more serene sight. But her voice held the curiosity her eyes might have. "What do you think?"

"Off the top of my head, I like the town-house idea. I can picture town houses clustered together in a variation on the Georgian theme."

"Wouldn't that be easier to do with single homes?"

"Easier, but not as interesting." He flashed her a self-mocking smile, which, unwittingly looking his way, she caught. "And not as challenging for me. But I'd recommend the town-house concept for economic reasons, as well. Take this duck pond. If you build single homes into the setting, you wouldn't want to do more than two or three, and they'd have to be in the million-plus range. On the other hand, you could build three town-house clusters, each with two or three town houses, and scatter them around. Since they could be marketed for five or five-fifty, they'd be easier to sell and you'd still come out ahead."

She remembered when Gordon had spoken of profit. Her response was the same now as it was then, a sick kind of feeling at the pit of her stomach. "Money isn't the major issue."

"Maybe not to you—"

"Is it to you?" she cut in, eyeing him sharply.

He held his ground. "It's one of the issues, not necessarily the major one. But I can guarantee you that it *will* be the major issue for the people Gordon lines up to become part of his consortium. You and I have personal feelings for Crosslyn Rise. The others won't. They may be captivated by the place and committed to preserving as much of the natural contour as possible, but they won't have an emotional attachment. They'll enter into this as a financial venture. That's all."

"Must you be so blunt?" she asked, annoyed because she knew he was right, yet the words stung.

"I thought you'd want the truth."

"You don't have to be so *blunt*." She turned abruptly and, ignoring the quacks that seemed stirred by the movement, headed back toward the path.

"You want sugarcoating?" He took off after her. "Where are you going now?"

"The meadow," she called over her shoulder.

With a minimum of effort, he was by her side. "Y'know, Jessica, if you're going ahead with this project, you ought to face facts. Either you finance the whole thing yourself—"

"If I had that kind of money, there wouldn't *be* any project!"

"Okay, so you don't have the money." He paused, irked enough by the huffy manner in which she'd walked away from him to be reckless. "Why don't you have the money? I keep asking myself that. Where did it go? The Crosslyn family is loaded."

"Was loaded."

"Where did it go?"

"How do *I* know where it went?" She whirled around to face him. "I never needed it. It was something my father had that he was supposedly doing something brilliant with. I never asked about it. I never cared about it. So what do I know?" She threw up a hand. "I've got my head stuck in that ivory tower of mine. What do I know about the money that's supposed to be there but isn't?"

He caught her hand before it quite returned to her side. "I'm not blaming you. Take it easy."

"Take it easy?" she cried. "The single most stable thing in my life is on the verge of being bulldozed—by *my* decision, no less—and you tell me to take it easy? Let go of my hand."

But he didn't. His long fingers wound through hers. "Changing Crosslyn Rise may be upsetting, but it's not the end of the world. It's just a house, for heaven's sake."

"It's my family's history."

"So now it's time to write a new chapter. Crosslyn Rise will always be Crosslyn Rise. It's not going away. It's just getting a face-lift. Wouldn't you rather have it done now, when you can be there to supervise, than have it done when you die? It's not like you have a horde of children to leave the place to."

Of all the things he'd said, that hurt the most. The issue of having a family, of passing something of the Crosslyn genes to another generation had always been a sensitive issue for Jessica. Her friends didn't raise it with her. Not even Gordon had made reference to it during their discussion of Crosslyn Rise. The fact that Carter Malloy was the one to twist the knife was too much to bear.

"Let me go," she murmured, lowering both her head and her voice as she struggled to free her hand from his.

"No."

She twisted her hand, even used her other one to try

to pry his fingers free. Her teeth were clenched. "I want you to let me go."

"I won't. You're too upset."

"And you're not helping." She lifted her eyes then, uncaring that he saw the tears there. "Why do you have to say things that hurt so much?" she said softly. "Why do you do it, Carter? You could always find the one thing that would hurt me most, and that was the thing you'd harp on. You say you've changed, but you're still hurting me. Why? Why can't you just do your job and leave me alone?"

Seconds after she'd said it, Carter asked himself the same question. It should have been an easy matter to approach this job as he would another. But he was emotionally involved—as much with Jessica as with Crosslyn Rise—which was why, without pausing to analyze the details of that emotional involvement, he reached out, drew Jessica close and wrapped her in his arms.

CHAPTER FOUR

WHEN CARTER HAD been a kid, he'd imagined that Jessica Crosslyn was made of nails. He'd found a hint of give when he'd touched her earlier, but only when he held her fully against him, as he did now, did he realize that she was surprisingly soft. Just as surprising was the tenderness he felt. He guessed it had to do with the tears he'd seen in her eyes. She was fighting them still, he knew. He could feel it in her body.

Lowering his head so that his mouth wasn't far from her ear, he said in a voice only loud enough to surmount the whispering breeze, "Let it out, Jessica. It's all right. No one will think less of you, and you'll feel a whole lot better."

But she couldn't. She'd been too weak in front of Carter already. Crying would be the last straw. "I'm all right," she said, but she didn't pull away. It had been a long time since someone had held her. She wasn't yet ready to have it end, particularly since she was still in the grip of the empty feeling brought on by his words.

"I don't do it intentionally," he murmured in the same deeply male, low-to-the-ear voice. "Maybe I did when we were kids, but not now. I don't intentionally hurt you, but I blurt out things without thinking." Which totally avoided the issue of whether the things he blurted out were true, but that was for another time. For now there were more immediate explanations to be offered. "I'm sorry for that, Jessica. I'm sorry if I hurt you, and I know

I ought to be able to do my job and leave you alone, but I can't. Maybe it's because I knew you back then, so there's a bond. Maybe it's because your parents are gone and you're alone. Maybe it's because I owe you for all I put you through."

"But you're putting me through more," came the meek voice from the area of his shirt collar.

"Unintentionally," he said. His hands flexed, lightly stroking her back. "I know you're going through a hard time, and I want to help. If I could loan you the money to keep Crosslyn Rise, I'd do it, but I don't have anywhere near enough. Gordon says you've got loans on top of loans."

"See?" The reminder was an unwelcome one. "You're doing it again."

"No, I'm explaining why I can't help out more. I've come a long way, but I'm not wealthy. I couldn't afford to own a place like Crosslyn Rise myself. I have a condo in the city, and it's in a luxury building, but it's small."

"I'm not asking—"

"I know that, but I want to do something. I want to help you through this, maybe make things easier. I guess what I'm saying is that I want us to be friends."

Friends? Carter Malloy, her childhood nemesis, a friend? It sounded bizarre. But then, the fact that she was leaning against him, taking comfort from his strength was no less bizarre. She hadn't imagined she'd ever want to touch him, much less feel the strength of his body. And he was strong, she realized—physically and, to her chagrin, emotionally. She could use some of that strength.

"I'm also thinking," he went on, "that I'd like to know more about you. When we were kids, I used to say awful things to you. I assumed you were too stuck-up to be bothered by them."

"I was bothered. They hurt."

"And if I'd known it then," he acknowledged honestly, "I'd probably have done it even more. But I don't want to do that now. So if I know what you're thinking, if I know what your sore spots are, I can avoid hitting them. Maybe I can even help them heal." He liked that idea. "Sounds lofty, but if you don't aim high, you don't get nowhere."

"Anywhere," she corrected, and raised her head. There was no sarcasm, only curiosity in her voice. "When did you become a philosopher?"

He looked down into her eyes, dove-gray behind her glasses. "When I was in Vietnam. A good many of the things I am now I became then." At her startled look, he was bemused himself. "Didn't you guess? Didn't you wonder what it was that brought about the change?"

She gave a head shake so tiny it was almost imperceptible. "I was too busy trying to deny it."

"Deny it all you want, but it's true. I'll prove it to you if you let me, but I can't do it if you jump all over me every time I say something dumb." When she opened her mouth to argue, he put a finger to her lips. "I can learn, Jessica. Talk to me. Reason with me. Explain things to me. I'm not going to turn around and walk away. I'll listen."

Her fingers tightened on the crisp fabric of his shirt just above his belt, and her eyes went rounder behind her glasses. "And then what?" she asked, still without sarcasm. In place of her earlier curiosity, though, was fear. "Will you take what I've told you and turn it on me? If you wanted revenge, that would be one way to get it."

"Revenge?"

"You've always hated what I stood for."

He shook his head slowly, his eyes never once leaving hers. "I thought I hated it, but it was me I hated. That was one of the things I learned a while back. For lots of reasons, some of which became self-perpetuating, I was an unhappy kid. And I'm not saying that all changed overnight. I spent four years in the army. That gave me lots of time to think about lots of things. I was still thinking about them when I got back." His hands moved lightly just above her waist. "That last time when I saw you I was still pretty unsettled. You remember. You were sixteen."

The memory was a weight, bowing her head, and the next thing she knew she felt Carter's jaw against her crown, and he was saying very softly, "I treated you poorly then, too."

"That time was the worst. I was so unsure of myself anyway, and what you said—"

"Unsure of yourself?" His hands went still. "You weren't."

"I was."

"You didn't look it."

"I felt it. It was the second date I'd ever had." The words began to flow and wouldn't stop. "I didn't like the boy, and I didn't really want to go, but it was so important to me to be like my friends. They dated, so I wanted to date. We were going to a prom at his school, and I had to wear a formal dress. My mother had picked it out in the store, and it looked wonderful on her, but awful on me. I didn't have her face or her body or her coloring. But I put on the dress and the stockings and the matching shoes, and I let her do my hair and face. Then I stood on the front porch looking at my reflection in the window, trying to pull the dress higher and make it look better…and you came around the corner of the house. You told me that I could pull forever and it wouldn't do any good, because there was nothing there worth covering. You said—"

"Don't, Jessica—"

"You said that any man worth beans would be able to see that right off, but you told me that I probably didn't have anything to worry about, because you doubted anyone who would ask me out was worth beans. But that was no problem, either, you told me—"

"Please—"

"Because, you said, I was an uptight nobody, and the only thing I'd ever have to offer a man would be money. I could buy someone, you said. Money was power, you said, and then—"

"Jessica, don't—"

"And then you reached into your pocket, pulled out a dollar bill and stuffed it into my dress, and you said that I should try bribing my date and maybe he'd kiss me."

She went quiet, slightly appalled that she'd spilled the whole thing and more than a little humiliated even seventeen years after the fact. But she couldn't have taken back the words if she'd wanted to, and she didn't have time to consider the damage she'd done before Carter took her face in his hands and turned it up.

"Did he kiss you?"

She shook her head as much as his hold would allow.

"Then I owe you for that, too," he whispered, and before she could begin to imagine what he had in mind, his mouth touched hers. She tried to pull back, but he held her, brushing his mouth back and forth over her lips until their stiffness eased, then taking them in a light kiss.

It didn't last long, but it left her stunned. Her breath came in shallow gasps, and for a minute she couldn't think. That was the minute when she might have identified what she felt as pleasure, but when her heart began to thud again and her mind started to clear, she felt only disbelief. "Why did you do that?" she whispered, and lowered her eyes when disbelief gave way to embarrassment.

"I don't know." He certainly hadn't planned it. "I guess I wanted to. It felt right."

"You shouldn't have," she said, and exerted pressure to lever herself away. He let her go. Immediately she felt the loss of his body heat and drew her blazer closer around her. Mustering shreds of dignity, she pushed her glasses up on her nose and raised her eyes to his. "I think we'd better get going. There's a lot to cover."

She didn't wait for an answer, but moved off, walking steadily along the path that circled the rear of the house. She kept her head high and her shoulders straight, looking far more confident than she felt. Instinct told her that it was critical to pretend the kiss hadn't happened. She couldn't give it credence, couldn't let on she thought twice about it, or Carter would have a field day. She could just imagine the smug look on his face even now, which was why she didn't turn. She knew he was following, could hear the crunch of dried leaves under his shoes. No doubt he was thinking about what a lousy kisser she was.

Because he sure wasn't. He was an incredible kisser, if those few seconds were any indication of his skill. Not that she'd liked it. She couldn't possibly *like* Carter Malloy's kiss. But she'd been vulnerable at that moment. Her mind had been muddled. She was definitely going to have to get it together unless she wanted to make an utter fool of herself.

How to get it together, though, was a problem. She was walking through land that she loved and that, a year from then, wouldn't be hers, and she was being followed by a demon from her past who had materialized in the here and now as a gorgeous hunk of man. She had to think business, she decided. For all intents and purposes, in her dealings with Carter she was a businesswoman. That was all.

They walked silently on until the path opened into a clearing. Though the grass was just beginning to green up after the winter's freeze, the lushness of the spot as it would be in full spring or high summer was lost on neither of them. They had the memories to fill in where reality lay half-dormant.

Jessica stopped at the meadow's mouth. When Carter reached her side, she said, "Another grouping of homes should go here. It's so pretty, and it's already open. That means fewer trees destroyed. I want to disturb as little of the natural environment as possible."

"I understand," Carter said, and walked on past her into the meadow. He was glad he understood something. He sure didn't understand why he'd kissed her—or why he'd found it strangely sweet. Unable to analyze it just then, though, he strode along one side of the four-acre oval, stopping several times along the way to look around him from a particular spot. After standing for a time in deep concentration at the far end, he crossed back through the center.

And all the while, with nothing else to do and no excuse not to, Jessica studied him. Gorgeous hunk of man? Oh, yes. His clothes—heathery blazer, slate-colored slacks, crisp white shirt—were of fine quality and fitted to perfection, but the clothes didn't make him a gorgeous hunk. What made him that was the body beneath. He was broad shouldered, lean of hip and long limbed, but even then he wouldn't have been as spectacular if those features hadn't all worked together. His body flowed. His stride was smooth and confident, the proud set of his head perfectly comfortable on those broad shoulders, his expression male in a dark and mysterious way.

If he felt her scrutiny, it obviously didn't affect him at all. But then, she mused, he was probably used to the scrutiny of women. He was the type to turn heads.

With a sigh, she turned and started slowly back on the path. It was several minutes before Carter caught up with her. "What do you think?" she asked without looking at him.

"It would work."

"If you'd like more time there, feel free. You can meet me up at the house."

"Are you cold?" he asked, because she was still hugging the blazer around her.

"No. I'm fine."

He glanced back toward the meadow, "Well, so am I. This is just a preliminary walk-through. I've seen enough for now. What's next?"

"The pine grove."

That surprised him. "Over on the other side of the house?" When she nodded, he said, "Are you sure you want to build there?"

She looked up at him then. "I need a third spot. If you can think of someplace better, I'm open for suggestion."

Drudging up what he remembered of the south end of the property, he had to admit that the pine grove seemed the obvious choice. "But that will mean cutting. The entire area is populated with trees. There isn't any sizable clearing to speak of, not like at the duck pond or in the meadow." He shook his head. "I'd hate to have to take down a single one of those pines."

Jessica took in a deep breath and said sadly, "So now you know what I'm feeling about this project. It's a travesty, isn't it? But I have no choice." Determined to remain strong and in control, she turned her eyes forward and continued on.

For the first time, Carter did know what she felt. It was one thing when he was dealing with the idea—and his memory—of Crosslyn Rise, another when he was walking there, seeing, smelling and feeling the place, being surrounded by the natural majesty that was suddenly at the mercy of humans.

When they reached the pine grove, he was more acutely

aware of that natural majesty than ever. Trees that had been growing for scores of years stretched toward the heavens as though they had an intimate connection with the place. Lower to the ground were younger versions, even lower than that shrubs that thrived in the shade. The carpeting underfoot was a tapestry of fine moss and pine needles. The pervasive scent was distinct and divine.

I have no choice, Jessica had said on a variation of the theme she'd repeated more than once, and he believed her. That made him all the more determined to design something special.

Jessica was almost sorry when they returned to the house. Yes, she was a little chilled, though she wouldn't have said a word to Carter lest, heaven forbid, he offer her his jacket, but the wide-open spaces made his masculinity a little less commanding. Once indoors, there would be nothing to dilute it.

"You'll want to go through the house," she guessed, more nervous as they made their way across the back porch and entered the kitchen.

"I ought to," he said. "But that coffee smells good. Mind if I take a cup with me?"

She was grateful for something to do. "Cream or sugar?"

"Both."

As efficiently as possible, given the awkwardness stirring inside her, she poured him a mugful of the dark brew and prepared it as he liked it.

"You aren't having any?" he asked when she handed him the mug.

She didn't dare. Her hands were none too steady, and caffeine wouldn't help. "Maybe later," she said, and in as businesslike a manner as she could manage, led him off on a tour of the house.

The tour should have been fairly routine through the

first floor, most of which Carter had seen at one time or another. But he'd never seen it before with a knowledge of architecture, and that made all the difference. High ceilings, chair rails and door moldings, antique mantel-pieces on the three other first-floor fireplaces—he was duly impressed, and his comments to that extent came freely.

His observations were professional enough to lessen the discomfort Jessica felt when they climbed the grand stairway to the second floor. Still she felt discomfort aplenty, and she couldn't blame it on the past. Something had happened when Carter had kissed her. He'd awoken her to the man he was. Her awareness of him now wasn't of the boy she'd hated but of the man she wished she could. Because that man was calm, confident and com-manding, all the things she wanted to be just then, but wasn't. In comparison to him, she felt inadequate, and, feeling inadequate, she did what she could to blend into the woodwork.

It worked just fine as they made their way from one end of the long hall down and around a bend to the other end. Carter saw the once-glorious master bedroom that hadn't been used in years; he saw a handful of other bedrooms, some with fireplaces, and more bathrooms than he'd ever dreamed his mother had cleaned. He took everything in, sipping his coffee as he silently made notes in his mind. Only when he reached the last bedroom, the one by the back stairs, did his interest turn personal.

"This is yours," he said. He didn't have to catch her nod to know that it was, but not even the uncomfortable look on her face could have kept him from stepping inside. The room was smaller than most of the others and decorated more simply, with floral wallpaper and white furniture.

Helpless to stop himself, he scanned the paired book-shelves to find foreign volumes and literary works fully integrated with works of popular fiction. He ran a finger along the dresser, passed a mirrored tray bearing a collection of antique perfume bottles and paused at a single framed photograph. It was a portrait of Jessica with her parents when she was no more than five years old; she looked exactly as he remembered her. It was a minute before he moved on to an old trunk, painted white and covered with journals, and an easy chair upholstered in the same faded pastel pattern as the walls. Then his gaze came to rest on the bed. It was a double bed, dressed in a nubby white spread with an array of lacy white pillows of various shapes and sizes lying beneath the scrolled headboard.

The room was very much like her, Carter mused. It was clean and pure, a little welcoming, a little off-putting, a little curious. It was the kind of room that hinted at exciting things in the nooks and crannies, just beyond the pristine front.

Quietly, for quiet was what the room called for, he asked, "Was this where you grew up?"

"No," she said quickly, eager to answer and return downstairs. "I moved here to save heating the rest of the house."

The rationale was sound. "This is above the kitchen, so it stays warm."

"Yes." She took a step backward in a none-too-subtle hint, but he didn't budge. In any other area of the house, she'd have gone anyway and left him to follow. But this was her room. She couldn't leave him alone here; that would have been too much a violation of her private space.

"I like the picture," he said, tossing his head toward the dresser. A small smile played at the corner of his mouth. "It brings back memories."

She focused on the photograph so that she wouldn't

have to see his smile. "It's supposed to. That was a rare family occasion."

"What occasion?"

"Thanksgiving."

He didn't understand. "What's so rare about Thanksgiving?"

"My father joined us for dinner."

Carter studied her face, trying to decide if she was being facetious. He didn't think so. "You mean, he didn't usually do it?"

"It was hit or miss. If he was in the middle of something intense, he wouldn't take a break."

"Not even for Thanksgiving dinner?"

"No," she said evenly, and met his gaze. "Are you done here? Can we go down?"

He showed no sign of having heard her. "That's really incredible. I always pictured holidays at Crosslyn Rise as being spectacular—you know, steeped in tradition, everything warm and pretty and lavish."

"It was all that. But it was also lonely."

"Was that why you married so young?" When her eyes flew to his, he added, "My mother said you were twenty."

She wanted to know whether he'd specifically asked for the details and felt a glimmer of annoyance that he might be prying behind her back. Somehow, though, she couldn't get herself to be sharp with him. She was tired of sounding like a harpy when his interest seemed so innocent.

"Maybe I was lonely. I'm not sure. At the time I thought I was in love."

Obviously she'd changed her mind at some point, he mused. "How long did it last?"

"Didn't your mother tell you that?"

"She said it was none of my business, and it's not. If you don't want to talk about it, you don't have to.

Jessica rested against the doorjamb. She touched the wood, rubbed a bruised spot. "It's no great secret." It was, after all, a matter of public record. "We were divorced two years after we married."

"What happened?"

She frowned at the paint. "We were different people with different goals."

"Who was he?"

She paused. "Tom Chandler." Her arm stole around her middle. "You wouldn't have known him."

"Not from around here?"

She shook her head. "Saint Louis. I was a sophomore in college, he was a senior. He wanted to be a writer and figured that I'd support him. He thought we were rich." The irony of it was so strong that she was beyond embarrassment. Looking Carter in the eye, she said, "You were right. Bribery was about the only way I'd get a man. But it took me two years to realize that was what had done it."

Carter came forward, drawn by the pallor of her face and the haunted look in her eyes, either of which was preferable to the unemotional way she was telling him something that had to be horribly painful for her. "I don't understand."

"Tom fell in love with Crosslyn Rise. He liked the idea of living on an estate. He liked the idea of my father being a genius. He liked the idea of my mother devoting herself to taking care of my father, because Tom figured that was what I'd do for him. Mostly, he liked the idea of turning the attic into a garret and spending his days there reading and thinking and staring out into space."

"Then you tired of the marriage before he did?"

"I...suppose you could say that. He tired of me pretty

quickly, but he was perfectly satisfied with the marriage. That was when I realized my mistake."

There was a world of hurt that she wasn't expressing, but Carter saw it in her eyes. It was all he could do not to reach out to help, but he wasn't sure his help would be welcome. So he said simply, "I'm sorry."

"Nothing to be sorry about." She forced a brittle smile. "Two years. That was all. I was finishing my undergraduate degree, so I went right on for my Ph.D., which was what I'd been planning to do all along."

"I'm sorry it didn't work out. Maybe if you'd had someone to help with the situation here—"

"Not Tom. Forget Tom. He was about as adept with finances as my mother and twice as disinterested."

"Still, it might not have been so difficult if you hadn't been alone."

She tore her eyes from his. "Yes, well, life is never perfect." She looked at the bright side, which was what she'd tried hard to do over the years. "I have a lot to be grateful for. I have my work. I love that, and I do it well. I've made good friends. And I have Crosslyn—" she caught herself and finished in a near whisper "—Crosslyn Rise." Uncaring whether he stayed in her room or not, she turned and went quickly down the back stairs.

When Carter joined her, Jessica was standing stiffly at the counter, taking a sip of the coffee she'd poured herself. Setting the mug down, she raised her chin and asked, "So, where do we go from here as far as this project is concerned?"

Carter would have liked to talk more about the legacy of her marriage, if only to exorcise that haunted look from her eyes. His good sense told him, though, that such a discussion was better saved for another time. He was surprised that she'd confided in him as much as she had. Friends did that. It was a good sign.

"Now you talk to me some more about what you want," he said. "But first I have to get my briefcase from the car. I'll be right back."

Left alone in the kitchen for those few short moments, Jessica took several long, deep breaths. She didn't seem able to do that when Carter was around. He was a physical presence, dominating whatever room he was in. But she couldn't say that the domination was deliberate—or offensive, for that matter. He was doing his best to be agreeable. It wasn't his fault that he was so tall, or that his voice had such resonance, or that he exuded an aura of power.

"Do you have the list?" he asked, striding back into the kitchen. When she nodded and pointed to a pad of paper waiting on the round oak table nearby, he set his briefcase beside it. Then he retrieved his coffee mug. "Mind if I take a refill?"

"Of course not." She reached for the glass carafe and proceeded to fix his coffee with cream and sugar, just as he'd had it before. When he protested that he could do it, she waved him away. She was grateful to be active and efficient.

Carrying both mugs, she led him to the table, which filled a semicircular alcove off the kitchen. The walls of the alcove were windowed, offering a view of the woods that had enchanted Jessica on many a morning. On this morning, she was too aware of Carter to pay much heed to the pair of cardinals decorating the Douglas fir with twin spots of red.

"Want to start from the top?" Carter asked, eyeing her list.

She did that. Point by point, she ran through her ideas. Most were ones she'd touched on before, but there were others, smaller thoughts—ranging from facilities at the clubhouse to paint colors—that had come to her and seemed worth mentioning. She began tentatively and gained courage as she went.

Carter listened closely. He asked questions and made notes. Though he pointed out the downside of some of her ideas, not once did he make her feel as though something she said was foolish. Often he illustrated one point or another by giving examples from his own experience, and she was fascinated by those. Clearly he enjoyed his work and knew what he was talking about. By the time he rose to leave, she was feeling surprisingly comfortable with the idea of Carter designing the new Crosslyn Rise.

That comfort was from the professional standpoint.

From a personal standpoint, she was feeling no comfort at all. For no sooner had that low blue car of his purred down the driveway than she thought about his kiss. Her pulse tripped, her cheeks went pink, her lips tingled—all well after the fact. On the one hand, she was gratified that she'd had such control over herself while Carter had been there. On the other hand, she was appalled at the extent of her reaction now that he was gone.

Particularly since she hadn't liked his kiss.

But she had. She had. It had been warm, smooth, wet. And it had been short. Maybe that was why she'd liked it. It hadn't lasted long enough for her to be nervous or frightened or embarrassed. Nor had it lasted long enough to provide much more than a tempting sample of something new and different. She'd never been given a kiss like that before—not from a date, of which there hadn't been many of the kissing type, and certainly not from Tom. Tom had been as self-centered in lovemaking as he'd been in everything else. A kiss from Tom had been a boring experience.

Carter's kiss, short though it was, hadn't been boring at all. In fact, Jessica realized, she wouldn't mind experiencing it again—which was a *truly* dismaying thought.

She'd never been the physical type, and to find herself entertaining physical thoughts about Carter Malloy was too much.

Chalking those thoughts up to a momentary mental quirk, she gathered her things together and headed for Cambridge.

The diversionary tactic worked. Not once while she was at work did she think of Carter, and it wasn't simply that she kept busy. She took time out late in the afternoon for a relaxed sandwich break with two male colleagues, then did some errands in the Square and even stopped at the supermarket on her way home—none of which were intellectually demanding activities. Her mind might have easily wandered, but it didn't.

No, she didn't think about Carter until she got home, and then, as though to make up for the hours before, she couldn't escape him. Every room in the house held a memory of his presence, some more so than others. Most intensely haunted were the kitchen and her bedroom, the two rooms in which she spent the majority of her at-home hours. Standing at the bedroom door as she had done when he'd been inside, sitting once again at the kitchen table, she saw him as he'd been, remembered every word he'd said, felt his presence as though he were there still.

It was the recency of his visit, she told herself, but the rationalization did nothing to dismiss the memories. By walking through her home, by looking at all the little things that were intimate to her, he had touched her private self.

She wanted to be angry. She tried and tried to muster it, but something was missing. There was no offense. She didn't feel violated, simply touched.

And that gave her even more to consider. The Carter she'd known as a kid had been a violater from the start; the Carter who had reentered her life wasn't like that at all. When the old Carter had come near, she'd trembled in anger, indignation and, finally, humiliation; when the new Carter came near, the trembling was from something else.

She didn't want to think about it, but there seemed no escape. No sooner would she immerse herself in a diversion than the diversionary shell cracked. Such was the case when she launched into her nightly workout in front of the VCR; rather than concentrate on the routine or the aerobic benefits of the exercise, she found herself thinking about body tone and wondering whether she looked better at thirty-three for the exercise she did, than she'd looked at twenty-five. And when she wondered why she cared, she thought of Carter.

When, sweaty and tired, she sank into a hot bath, she found her body tingling long after she should have felt pleasantly drowsy, and when she stopped to analyze those tingles, she thought of Carter.

When, wearing a long white nightgown with ruffles at the bodice, she settled into the bedroom easy chair, with a lapful of reading matter that should have captured her attention, her attention wandered to those things that Carter had seen and touched. She pictured him as he had stood that morning, looking tall and dark, uncompromisingly male and curious about her. She spent a long time thinking about that curiosity, trying to focus in on its cause.

She was without conclusions when the phone rang by her bed. Startled, she picked it up after the first ring, but the sudden stretch sent the books on her lap sliding down the silky fabric of her gown to the floor. She made a feeble attempt to catch them at the same time that she offered a slightly breathless, "Hello?"

Carter heard that breathlessness and for an awful minute wondered if he'd woken her. A glance at his watch told him it was after ten. He hadn't realized it was so late. "Jessica? This is Carter." He paused. "Am I catching you at a bad time?"

Letting the books go where they would, she put a hand to her chest to still her thudding heart. "No. No. This is fine."

"I didn't wake you?"

"No. I was reading." Or trying to, she mused, but her mind didn't wander farther. It was waiting for Carter's next words. She couldn't imagine why he'd called, particularly at ten o'clock at night.

Carter wasn't sure, either. Nothing he had to say couldn't wait for another day or two, certainly for a more reasonable hour. But he'd been thinking about Jessica for most of the day. They had parted on good terms. He wanted to know whether those good terms still stood, or whether she'd been chastising herself for this, that and the other all day. And beyond that, he wanted to hear her voice.

Relieved now that he hadn't woken her, he leaned back against the strip of kitchen wall where the phone hung. "Did you get to school okay today?"

"Uh-huh."

"Everything go all right? I mean, I didn't get you going off on the wrong foot or anything, did I?"

She gave a shy smile that he couldn't possibly see, but it came though in her voice. "No. I was fine. How about you?"

"Great. It was a really good day. I think you bring me good luck."

She didn't believe that for a minute, but her smile lingered. "What happened?"

Carter was still trying to figure it out. "Nothing momentous. I spent the afternoon in the office working on other projects, and a whole bunch of little things clicked.

It was one of those days when I felt really in tune with my work."

"Inspired?"

"Yeah." He paused, worried that she'd think he was simply trying to impress her. "Does that sound pretentious?"

"Of course not. It sounds very nice. We should all have days like that."

"Yours wasn't?"

She thought back on what she'd done since she'd seen him that morning. "It was," she said, but cautiously. "It's an odd time. I gave the final lecture to my German lit class, and I was really pleased with the way it went, but the meetings I had after that were frustrating."

Carter was just getting past the point of picturing her with her nose stuck in a book all day. He wanted to know more about what she did. "In what way?"

"At the end of the term, students get nervous. They're realizing that a good part of their grade is going to depend on a final exam, a term paper or both. If they go into these last two weeks with a solid average, they're worried about keeping it up. If they go in with a low average, they're desperate to raise it. Even the most laid-back of them get a little uptight."

"Didn't you when you were in school?"

"Sure. So I try to be understanding. It's mostly a question of listening to them and giving them encouragement. That's easy to do if I know the student. I can concentrate on his strengths and relate the class material to it. If I don't know the student, it's harder, sort of like stabbing in the dark at the right button to help the student make the connection."

Carter was quiet for a minute. Then he said, "I'm impressed. You're a dedicated professor, to put that kind of thought into interactions with students. The professors

I studied under weren't like that. They were guarded, almost like they saw us as future competition, so they wanted us to learn, but not too much."

She knew some colleagues who were like that, and though she couldn't condone the behavior, she tried to explain it by saying, "You were older when you started college."

"Not that much. I was twenty-three."

"But you were wise in a worldly way that was probably intimidating."

A day or a week before, Carter might have taken the observation as an offense. That he didn't take it that way now was a comment on how far he'd come in terms of self-confidence where Jessica was concerned. It was also an indication of how far she'd come; her tone was gentle, conversational, which was how he kept his. "How did you know I was world wise at twenty-three?" She'd seen so little of him then.

"You were that way at seventeen, and you were very definitely intimidating."

He thought back to those years with an odd blend of nostalgia and self-reproach. "I tried to be. Lord, I tried. Intimidating people was about the only thing I was good at."

"You could have been good at other things. Look where you are now. That talent didn't suddenly come into being when you hit your twenties. But you let everyone think you had no brains."

"I thought it, too. I was messed up in so many other ways that no brains seemed part of the package."

Jessica wanted to ask him about being messed up. She wanted to know the why and how of it. She wanted to be able to make some sense of the person he'd been and relate it to the person he was now. Because this person was interesting. She could warm to this Carter as she would never have dreamed of doing to the one who had once been malicious.

The irony of it was that in some ways the new Carter was more dangerous.

"Are you still there?" he asked.

"Uh-huh," she answered as lightly as she could given the irregular skip of her pulse.

He figured he was either making her uncomfortable by talking about the past or boring her, and he didn't want to do either, not tonight, not when they finally seemed to be getting along. So he cleared his throat. "You're probably wondering why I called."

She was, now that he mentioned it. A man like Carter Malloy wouldn't call her just to talk. "I figured you'd get around to it in good time," she said lightly. She wanted him to know that she was taking the call in stride, just as she'd taken his kiss in stride. It wouldn't do for him to know that she was vulnerable where he was concerned.

"Well, now's the time. When I was driving back to town from Crosslyn Rise this morning, it occurred to me that it might help both of us if you were to see some of the other things I've done."

"I saw those sketches—"

"Not sketches. The real thing. I've done other projects similar in concept to the one you want done. If you were to see them in person, you might get a feeling for whether I'm the right man for this job."

Jessica felt something heavy settle around her middle. "You're having second thoughts about working here."

"It's not—"

"You can be honest," she said, tipping up her chin. "I'm not desperate. There are plenty of other architects."

"Jessica—"

"The only reason Gordon suggested you was because

you were familiar with the Rise. He figured you'd be interested."

"I *am*," Carter said loudly. "Will you please be quiet and let me speak?" When he didn't hear anything coming from the other end of the line, he breathed, "Thank you. My Lord, Jessica, when you get going, you're like a steamroller."

"I don't want to play games. That's all. If you don't want this job, I'd appreciate your coming right out and saying so, rather than beating around the bush."

"I *want* this job. I *want* this job. How many times do I have to say it?"

More quietly she said, "If you want it, why were you looking to give me an out?"

"Because I want you to *choose* me," he blurted. Standing well away from the wall now, he ran his fingers through his hair. "I'd like to feel," he said slowly, "that you honestly want me to do the work. That you're *enthusiastic* about my doing it. That it isn't just a case of Gordon foisting me on you, or your not having the time or energy to interview others."

She was thinking that he wasn't such a good businessman after all. "You're an awful salesman. You should be tooting your own horn, not warning me off. Are you this way with all your clients?"

"No. This case is different. You're special."

His words worked wonders on the heaviness inside her. She felt instantly lighter, and it didn't matter that he'd meant the words in the most superficial of ways. What he'd said made her feel good.

"Okay," she breathed. "I'm sorry I interrupted."

Stunned by the speed and grace of her capitulation, Carter drew a blank. For the life of him, he couldn't remember what had prompted the set-to. "Uh…"

"You were saying that maybe I ought to see some of the things you've done."

Gratefully he picked up the thread. "The best ones—the ones I like best—are north of you, up along the coast of Maine. The farthest is three hours away. They could all be seen in a single day." He hesitated for a second. "I was thinking that if you'd like, we could drive up together."

It was Jessica's turn to be stunned. The last thing she'd expected was that Carter would want to spend a day with her, even on business. Her words come slowly and skeptically. "Isn't that above and beyond the call of duty?"

"What do you mean?"

"You don't have to go to such extremes. I can drive north myself."

"Why should you have to go alone if I'm willing to take you?"

"Because that would be a whole day out of your time."

"So what else is my time for?"

"Working."

"I get plenty of work done during the week. So do you, and you said you were coming up on exams. I was thinking of taking a Sunday when both of us can relax."

That was even *more* incredible. "I can't ask you to take a whole Sunday to chauffeur me around!"

"Why not?"

"Because Sundays are personal, and this would be business."

"It could be fun, too. There are some good restaurants. We could stop and get something to eat along the way."

Jessica returned her hand to her chest in an attempt to slow the rapid beat of her heart.

"Or you could shop," he went on. "There are some terrific boutique areas. I wouldn't mind waiting."

She was utterly confused. "I couldn't ask you to do that."

"You don't have to ask. I'm offering." He was struck by an afterthought that hardened his voice. "Unless you'd rather not be with me for that length of time."

"That's not it."

"Then what is?"

"*Me*. Wouldn't you rather not be with *me* for that length of time? You'll be bored to tears. I'm not the most dynamic person in the world."

"Who told you that?"

"You. When I was ten, you caught me sitting on the rocks, looking out to sea. You asked what I saw, and when I wouldn't answer, you said I was dull and pathetic."

He felt like a heel. "You were only ten, and I was full of it."

"But Tom agreed. He thought I was boring, too. I've never been known as the life of the party."

"Sweetheart, a man can only take being with the life of the party for so long. Let me tell you, *that* can get boring. You, on the other hand, have a hell of a lot going for you." He let the flow of his thoughts carry him quickly on. "You read, you think, you work. Okay, so you don't open up easily. That doesn't mean you're boring. All it means is that a man has to work a little harder to find out what's going on in that pretty head of yours. I'm willing to work a little harder. I think the reward will be worth it. So you'd be doing me a favor by agreeing to spend a Sunday with me driving up the coast." He took a quick breath, not allowing himself the time to think about all he'd said. "What'll it be—yes or no?"

"Yes," Jessica said just as quickly and for the very same reason.

CHAPTER FIVE

JESSICA HAD A dream that night. It brought her awake gradually, almost reluctantly, to a dark room and a clock that read 2:24 a.m. Her skin was warm and slightly damp. Her breath was coming in short whispers. The faint quivering deep inside her was almost a memory, but not quite.

She stretched. When the quivering lingered, she curled into a ball to cradle it, because there was something very nice about the feeling. It was satisfying, soft and feminine.

Slowly, even more slowly than she'd awoken, she homed in on the subject of her dream. Her reluctance this time had nothing to do with preserving a precious feeling. As Carter Malloy's image grew clearer in her mind, the languorous smile slipped from her face. In its place came a look of dismay.

Jessica had never had an erotic dream before. Never. Not when she'd been a teenager first becoming aware of her developing body, not when she'd been dating Tom, not in the long years following the divorce. She wasn't blind to a good-looking man; she could look at male beauty, recognize it, admire it for what it was. But it had never excited her in a physical sense. It had never buried itself in her subconscious and come forward to bring her intense pleasure in the middle of the night.

Flipping to her other side, she shielded her face with

her arm, as if to hide her embarrassment from a horde of grinning voyeurs masked by the dark.

Carter Malloy. Carter Malloy, beautifully naked and splendidly built. Carter Malloy, coming to her, kissing her, stroking her. He'd been exquisitely gentle, removing her clothes piece by piece, loving her with his hands and his mouth, driving her to a fever pitch that she'd never experienced before.

With a moan, she flipped back to the other side and huddled under the covers, but the sheet that half covered her face couldn't blot out the persistent images in her mind. Carter Malloy, kissing her everywhere, *everywhere,* while he offered his own body for her eager hands and lips. In her dream, he was large and leanly muscled, textured at some spots, smooth and vulnerable at others, very, very hard and needy at still others.

Sitting bolt upright in bed, she turned on the lamp, hugged her knees to her chest and worked to ground herself among the trappings of the old and familiar. To some extent she was successful. At least the quivering inside her eased. What she was left with, though, was an undertone of frustration that was nearly as unwelcome.

She couldn't understand it. She just wasn't a passionate person. Lovemaking with Tom had been a part of marriage that she'd simply accepted. Occasionally she'd enjoyed it. Occasionally she'd even had an orgasm, though she could count the number of times that had happened on the fingers of one hand. And she hadn't minded that it was so infrequent. Sex was a highly overrated activity, she had long since decided.

That didn't explain why she'd dreamed what she did, or why the dream had brought her to a sweet, silent climax.

Mortified anew, she pressed her eyes to her knees. What if someone had seen her? What if someone had been watching her sleep? Not that anyone would have or could have seen her, still she wondered if she had made noise, or writhed about.

It was something she'd eaten, she decided. Certain foods were known to stir up the senses. Surely that was what had brought on the erotic interlude.

But she went over every morsel of food that had entered her mouth that day—easy to do, since she was neither a big eater nor an adventurous one—and she couldn't single out anything that might have inspired eroticism.

Maybe, she mused, it had to do with her own body. Maybe she was experiencing a hormonal shift, maybe even related to menopause. But she was only thirty-three! She wasn't ready for menopause!

The hormonal theory, though, had another twist. They said that women reached their peak of sexual interest at a later age than men. Women in their thirties and forties were supposed to be hot—at least, that was what the magazines said, though she'd always before wondered whether the magazines said it simply because it was what their thirty- and forty-year-old readers wanted to hear.

Maybe there was some truth to it, though. Maybe she was developing needs she'd never had before. She had been a long time without a man, better than eleven years. Maybe the dream she'd had was her body's way of saying that it was in need. Maybe that need even had to do with the biological clock. Maybe her body was telling her that it was time to have a baby.

Throwing the covers back, she scrambled from the bed, grabbed her glasses and, barefoot, half walked, half ran down the back steps to the kitchen. Soon after, she was sitting cross-legged on one of the chairs with an open tin of Poppycock nestled in her lap.

Poppycock was her panacea. When she'd been little, she had hidden it in her room, because her mother had been convinced that the caramel coating on the popcorn would rot her teeth. Now that her mother wasn't around to worry, Jessica kept the can within easy reach. It wasn't that she pigged out on a regular basis, and since she didn't have a weight problem, it probably wouldn't have mattered if she had, but Poppycock was a treat. It was light and fun, just the thing she went for when she was feeling a little down.

She wasn't feeling down now, but frustrated and confused. She was also feeling angry, angry at Carter, because no matter how long she made her list of possible excuses for what had happened, she knew it wasn't coincidence that had set Carter Malloy's face and body at the center of her dream. She cursed him for being handsome and sexy, cursed herself for being vulnerable, cursed Crosslyn Rise for aging and putting her into a precarious position.

One piece of popcorn followed another into her mouth. In time, she helped herself to a glass of milk, and by the time that was gone, it was well after three. Having set her mind to thinking about the material she had to cover in her Russian seminar that afternoon, she'd calmed down some. With a deep, steady breath, she rose from the chair, put the empty glass into the sink and the tin of Poppycock into the pantry, and went back to bed.

WHEN JESSICA HAD agreed to drive north with Carter, he had wanted to do it that Sunday for the sake of getting her feedback as soon as possible. She had put him off for a week, knowing that she had far too much work to do in preparation for exams, to take off for the whole day. In point of fact, the following Sunday wouldn't be much better; though she had teaching assistants to grade exams, she always did her share, and she liked it that way.

But Carter was eager, and she knew that she could plan

around the time. So they had settled on the day, and he had promised to call her the Saturday before to tell her when he would be picking her up. She wasn't scheduled to hear from him until then, and in the aftermath of that embarrassingly carnal dream, she was grateful for the break. Given twelve days' time, she figured she could put her relationship with him into its proper perspective.

That perspective, she decided, had to be business, which was what she thought about during those days when she had the free time to let her mind wander. She concentrated on the business of converting Crosslyn Rise into something practical and productive—and acclimating herself to that conversion.

To that end, she called Nina Stone and arranged to meet her for dinner at a local seafood restaurant, a chic establishment overlooking the water on the Crosslyn Rise end of town. The two had met the year before, browsing in a local bookstore, and several months after that, Jessica had approached her about selling Crosslyn Rise. Though Nina hadn't grown up locally, she'd been working on the North Shore for five years, and during that time she had established herself as an aggressive broker with both smarts and style. She was exactly the kind of woman Jessica had always found intimidating, but strangely, they'd hit it off. Jessica could see Nina's tough side, but there was a gentler, more approachable side, as well. That side came out when they were together and Nina let down her defenses.

Despite her reputation, despite the aggressiveness Jessica knew was there, Nina had never pressured her. She was like Carter in the sense that, having come from nothing, she was slightly in awe of Crosslyn Rise—which meant that she was in no rush to destroy it.

For that reason among others, Jessica felt comfortable sharing the latest on the Rise with her.

"A condominium community?" Nina asked warily. She was a small woman, slender and pixieish, which made her assertiveness in business somewhat unexpected and therefore all the more effective. "I don't know, Jessica. It would be a shame to do that to such a beautiful place."

"Condominium communities can be beautiful."

"But Crosslyn Rise is that much more so."

Jessica sighed. "I can't afford it, Nina. You've known that for a while. I can't afford to keep it as it is, and you haven't had any luck finding a buyer."

"The market stinks," Nina said, sounding defensive, looking apologetic. "I'm selling plenty on the low and middle end of the scale, but precious little at the top." She grew more thoughtful. "Condos are going, though, I do have to admit. Particularly in this area. There's something about the ocean. Young professionals find it romantic, older ones find it restful." She paused to sip her wine. Her fingers were slender, her nails polished red to match her suit. "Tell me more. If this was Gordon Hale's idea, I would guess that it's financially sound. The man is a rock. You say he's putting together a consortium?"

"Not yet, but he will when it's time. Right now, I'm working with someone to define exactly what it is that I want."

"Someone?"

After the slightest hesitation, she specified, "An architect."

Nina studied her for a minute. "You look uncomfortable."

Jessica pushed her glasses up on her nose. "No."

"Is this architect a toughie?"

"No. He's very nice. His name is Carter Malloy." She watched for a reaction. "Ever heard of him?"

"Sure," Nina said without blinking an eye. "He's with Malloy and Goodwin. He's good."

Jessica felt a distant pride. "You're familiar with his work, then?"

"I saw something he did in Portsmouth not long ago. Portsmouth isn't my favorite place, but this was beautiful. He had converted a textile mill into condos. Did an incredible job combining old and new." She frowned, then grinned at the same time. "If I recall correctly, the man himself is beautiful."

"I don't know as I'd call him beautiful," Jessica answered, but a little too fast, and that roused Nina's interest.

"What would you call him?"

She thought for a minute. "Pleasant looking."

"Not the man I remember. Pleasant looking is someone you'd pass by and smile at kindly. A beautiful man stirs stronger emotions. Carter Malloy was ruggedly masculine—at least, in the picture I saw."

"He is masculine looking, I suppose."

Nina came forward, voice lowered but emphatically chiding. "You suppose, my foot! I can't believe you're as immune to men as you let on. One lousy husband can't have neutered you, and you're not exactly over the hill. You have years of good fun still ahead, if you want to make something of them." She raised her chin. "Who was the last man you dated?"

Jessica shrugged.

"Who?" Nina prodded, but good-naturedly as she settled back in her seat. "You must remember."

"It's a difficult question. How do you define a date? If it's going somewhere with a man, I do that all the time with colleagues."

"That's not what I mean, and you know it. I'm talking about the kind of date who picks you up at your house, takes you out for the evening, kisses you when he brings you home, maybe even stays the night."

"Uh, I'm not into that."

"Sleeping with men?"

"Are you?" Jessica shot back, in part because she was uncomfortable doing the answering and in part because she wanted to know. She and Nina had become friends in the past year, but the only thing Jessica knew about her social life was that she rarely spent a Saturday night at home.

Nina was more amused than anything. "I'm not into sleeping around, but I do enjoy men. There are some nice ones around who are good for an evening's entertainment. Since I'm not looking to get married, I don't threaten them."

"You don't want to get married?"

"Honey, do I have the time?"

"Sure. If you want."

"What I want," Nina said, sitting back in her chair, looking determined but vulnerable, "is to make good money for myself. I want my own business."

"I thought you were making good money now."

"Not enough."

"Are you in need?"

"I've been in need since the day I learned that my mother prostituted herself to put milk on our table."

Jessica caught in a breath. "I'm sorry, Nina. I didn't know."

"It's not something I put on the multiple-listings chart," she quipped, but her voice was low and sober. "That was in Omaha. I have a fine life for myself here, but I won't ever sell myself like my mother did. So I need money of my own. I refuse to ever ask a man for a cent, and I won't have to, if I play my cards right."

"You're doing so well."

"I could be doing even better if I went out on my own. But I'll have to hustle."

Jessica was getting a glimpse of the driven Nina, the one who was restless, whose mind was always working, whose heart was prepared to sacrifice satisfaction for the sake of security. Jessica found it sad. "But you're only thirty."

"And next year I'll be thirty-one, and thirty-two the year after that. The way I figure it, if I work my tail off now and go independent within a year, by the time I'm thirty-five, I can be the leading broker in the area, with a fully trained staff, to boot. Maybe then I'll be able to ease up a little, even think of settling down." She gave a crooked smile. "Assuming there are any worthwhile men out there then."

"If there are, you'll find them," Jessica said, and felt a shaft of the same kind of envy she'd known as a child, when all the other girls were prettier and more socially adept than she. Nina had short, shiny hair, flawless skin and delicate bones. She dressed on the cutting edge between funky and sophisticated and had a personality to match. "You draw people like honey draws bees."

"Lucky for me, or I'd be a loss at what I do." She paused to give Jessica a look that was more cautious than clever. "So I've made the ultimate confession. And you? Do you ever think of settling down?"

Jessica smiled and shook her head. "I don't attract men the way you do."

"Why not?" Nina asked, perfectly serious. "You're smart and pretty and gainfully employed. Aren't those the things men look for nowadays?

Pretty. Carter had used that word. *A man has to work a little harder to find out what's going on in that pretty head of yours.* It was an expression, of course, not to be taken seriously. "Men look for eye-catching women like you."

"And once they've done the eye-catching, they take a

closer look and see the flaws. No man would want me right now. I'm too hard. But you're softer. You're established. You're confident in ways I'm not."

"What ways?" Jessica shot back in disbelief.

"Financial. You have Crosslyn Rise."

"Not for long," came the sad reminder.

While the waiter served their lobsters, Nina considered that. As soon as he left, she began to speak again. "You're still a wealthy woman, Jessica. The problem is fluidity of funds. You don't have enough to support the Rise because your assets are tied up *in* the Rise. If you go through with the project you've mentioned, you'll emerge with a comfortable nest egg. Besides, you don't have the fear—" she paused to tie the lobster bib around her neck "—of being broke that I have. You're financially sound, and you're independent. That gives you a head start in the peace-of-mind department. So all you have to do—" she tore a bright red feeler from the steaming lobster "—is to find a terrific guy, settle down somewhere within commuting distance of Harvard and have babies."

"I don't know," Jessica murmured. She was looking at her lobster as though she weren't sure which part to tackle first. "Things are never that simple."

"You watch. Things will get easier when this business with the Rise is settled." That said, she began to suck on the feeler.

Jessica, too, paused to eat, but she kept thinking about Nina's statement. After several minutes, she asked, "Are we talking about the same 'things'?"

"Men. We're talking about men."

"But what does my settling the Rise have to do with men?"

"You'll be freer. More open to the idea of a relationship." When Jessica's expression said she still didn't make the connection, Nina said, "In some respects, you've been wedded to the Rise. No—" she held up a hand "—don't take this the wrong way. I'm not being critical. But in the time I've known you, I've formed certain impressions. Crosslyn Rise is your haven. You've lived there all your life. Even when you married, you lived there."

"Tom wanted it."

"I'm sure he did. Still, you lived there, and when the marriage fell apart, he left and you were alone there again."

"I wasn't alone. My parents were there."

"But you're alone now, and you're still there. Crosslyn Rise is like a companion."

"It's a house," Jessica protested.

But Nina had a point to make. "A house with a presence of its own. When you're there, do you feel alone?"

"No."

"But you should—not that I'm wishing loneliness on you, but man wasn't put on earth to live in solitude."

"I'm with people all day. I like being alone at night."

"Do you?" she asked, arching a delicately shaped brow. "I don't. But then, my place isn't steeped in the kind of memories that Crosslyn Rise is. If I were to come home and be enveloped by a world of memories, I probably wouldn't feel alone, either." She stopped talking, poked at the lobster with her fork for a distracted minute, then looked up at Jessica. "Once Crosslyn Rise is no longer yours in the way that it's always been, you may need something more."

Jessica shot her a despairing look. "Nothing like the encouragement of a friend."

"But it *is* encouragement. The change will be good for you. More so than any other person I know, you've had a sameness to your life. Coming out from the shadow of Crosslyn Rise will be exciting."

The image of the shadow stuck in Jessica's mind. The

more she mulled it over, the more she realized that it wasn't totally bizarre. "Do you think I hide behind the Rise?" It was a timid question, offered to a friend with the demand for an honest answer.

Nina gave it as she saw it. "To some extent. Where your work is concerned, you've been as outgoing as anyone else. Where your personal life is concerned, you've fallen back on the Rise, just because it's always been there. But you can stand on your own in any context, Jessica. If you don't know that now, you will soon enough."

SOON ENOUGH WASN'T as soon as Jessica wanted. At least, that was what she was thinking the following Sunday morning as she dressed to spend the day driving north with Carter. He'd called her the morning before to ask if eight was too early to come. It wasn't; she was an early riser. Her mind was freshest during those first postdawn hours. She did some of her most productive work then.

She didn't feel particularly productive on Sunday morning, though. Nor, after mixing, matching and discarding four different outfits did she feel particularly fresh. She couldn't decide what to wear, because the occasion was strange. She and Carter certainly weren't going on a date. This was business. Still, he'd mentioned stopping for something to eat, maybe even shopping, and those weren't strictly business ventures. A business suit was too formal, jeans too casual, and she didn't want to wear a teaching ensemble, because she was *tired* of wearing teaching ensembles.

At length, she decided on a pair of gabardine slacks and a sweater she'd bought in the Square that winter. The sweater was the height of style, the saleswoman had told her, but Jessica had bought it because it was slouchy and comfortable. For the first time, she was glad it was stylish, too. She was also glad it was a pale gray tweed, not so much because it went with her eyes but because it went with the slacks, which, being black, were more sophisticated than some of her other things.

For a time, she distracted herself wondering why she wanted to look sophisticated. She should look like herself, she decided, which was more down-to-earth than sophisticated. But that didn't stop her from matching the outfit up with shiny black flats, from dusting the creases of her eyelids with mocha shadow, from brushing her hair until it shone and then coiling it into a neat twist at the nape of her neck.

She was a bundle of nerves by the time Carter arrived, and the situation wasn't helped by his appearance. He looked wonderful—newly showered and shaved, dressed in a burgundy sweater and light gray corduroy pants.

Taking her heavy jacket from her, he stowed it in the trunk of the car with his own. He held the door while she slipped into the passenger's seat, then circled the car and slid behind the wheel.

"I should warn you," Jessica said when he started the car, "that I'm a terrible passenger. If you have any intention of speeding, you'll have a basket case on your hands."

"Me? Speed?"

Without looking at him, she sensed his grin. "I can remember a certain squealing of tires."

"Years and years ago, and if it'll put your mind at ease, the last accident I had was when I was nineteen," Carter answered with good humor, and promptly stepped on the gas. He didn't step on it far, only enough to maintain the speed limit once they'd reached the highway, and not once did he feel he was holding back. Sure, there were times when he was alone in the car and got carried away by the power of the engine, but he wasn't a reckless driver.

He certainly didn't vent his anger on the road as he used to do.

But then, he didn't feel the kind of anger at the world that he used to feel. He rarely felt anger at all—frustration, perhaps, when a project that he wanted didn't come through, or when one that did wasn't going right, or when one of the people under him messed up, or when a client was being difficult—but not anger. And he wasn't feeling any of those things at the moment. He'd been looking forward to this day. He was feeling lighthearted and refreshed, almost as though the whole world was open to him just then.

He took his eyes from the road long enough to glance at Jessica. Her image was already imprinted on his mind, put there the instant she'd opened her front door, but he wanted a moment of renewed pleasure.

She looked incredibly good, he thought, and it wasn't simply a matter of having improved with age. He'd noted that improvement on the two other occasions when he'd seen her, but seeing her today took it one step further. She was really pretty—adorable, he wanted to say, because the small, round glasses sitting on her nose had that effect on her straight features, but her outfit was a little too serious to be called adorable. He liked the outfit. It was subtle but stylish, and seemed perfectly suited to who she was. He was pleased to have her in the car with him. She added the class that he never quite believed he'd acquired.

"Comfortable?" he asked.

She darted him a quick glance. "Uh-huh."

He let that go for several minutes, then asked, "How are exams going?"

"Pretty well," she said on an up note.

"You sound surprised."

"I never know what to expect. There have been years when it's been one administrative foul-up after another—exams aren't printed on time, or they're delivered to the wrong place, that kind of thing."

"At Harvard?" he teased.

She took his teasing with a lopsided smile. "At Harvard. This year, the Crimson has done itself proud."

"I'm glad of that for your sake."

"So am I," she said with a light laugh, then sobered. "Of course, now the rush begins to get things graded and recorded. Graduation isn't far off. The paperwork has to be completed well before then."

"Do you go to graduation?"

"Uh-huh."

"Must be…uplifting."

Her laugh was more of a chuckle this time, and a facetious one at that. Carter took pleasure in the sound. It said that she didn't take herself or her position too seriously, which was something he needed to know, given all the years he'd assumed she was stuck-up. She didn't seem that way now. More, she didn't seem conscious of any social difference between them. He was convinced that the more he was with her, architect to client, the less she'd think back on the past, and that was what he wanted.

He wanted even more, though. Try as he might, he couldn't forget the time he'd kissed her. It had been an impulsive moment, but it had stuck in his mind, popping up to taunt him when he least expected it.

Jessica was, he decided during one of those times, the rosebud that hadn't quite bloomed. Having been married, she'd certainly been touched, but Carter would put money on the fact that her husband hadn't lit any fires in her. Her mouth was virginal. So was her body, the way she held it, not frightened so much as unsure, almost naive.

Carter had never been a despoiler of virgins. Even in his wildest days, he'd preferred women who knew the score. Tears over blood-stained sheets or unwanted pregnancies or imagined promises weren't his style. So he'd gone with an increasingly savvy woman—exactly the kind who now left him cold.

Kissing Jessica, albeit briefly, hadn't left him cold. He'd felt warm all over, then later, when he'd had time to remember the details of that kiss, tight all over. It amazed him still, it really did. That Jessica Crosslyn, snotty little prude that she'd been, should turn him on was mind-boggling.

But she did turn him on. Even now, with his attention on driving and the gearshift and a console between them, he was deeply aware of her—of the demure way she crossed her legs and the way that caused her slacks to outline shapely thighs, of the neat way her hands lay in her lap, fingers slender and feminine, of the loose way her sweater fell, leaving an alarmingly seductive hint of her breasts beneath. Even her hair, knotted with such polish, seemed a parody of restraint. So many things about her spoke of a promise beneath the facade. And she seemed totally unaware of it.

Maybe it was his imagination. Maybe the sexy things he was seeing were simply things that had changed in her, and it was his lecherous mind that was defining them as sexy. He saw women often, but it had been a while since he'd slept with one. Maybe he was just horny.

If that was true, of course, he could have remedied the situation through tried-and-true outlets. But he wasn't interested in those outlets. He wasn't running for any outlet at all. There was a sweetness to the arousal Jessica caused; there was something different and special about the tightness in his groin. He wasn't exactly sure where it would take him, but he wasn't willing it away just yet.

"You got a vote of confidence from a friend of mine," Jessica told him as they safely sped north. "She said she'd seen a project you did in Portsmouth."

"Harborside? I was thinking we'd hit that last, on the way home."

"She was impressed with it."

He shrugged. "It's okay, but it's not my favorite."

"What is?"

"Cadillac Cove. I hate the name, but the complex is special."

"Who decides on the name?"

"The developer. I just do the designs."

Jessica had been wondering about that. "Just the designs? Is your job done when the blueprints are complete?"

"Sometimes yes, sometimes no. It depends on the client. Some pay for the blueprints and do everything else on their own. Others pay me to serve as an advisor, in which case I'm involved during the actual building. I like it that way—" he speared her with a cautioning look "—and it has nothing to do with money. Moneywise, my time's better spent working at a drafting table. But there's satisfaction in being at the site. There's satisfaction seeing a concept take form. And there's peace of mind knowing that I'm available if something goes wrong."

"Do things go wrong often? I've heard some nightmarish stories. Are they true?"

"Sometimes." He curved his long fingers more comfortably around the wheel. "Y'see, there's a basic problem with architectural degrees. They fail to require internships in construction. Most architects and would-be architects see themselves as a step above. They're the brains behind the construction job, so they think, but they're wrong. They may be the inspiration, and the brains behind the overall plan, but the workmen themselves, the guys with the hammers and nails, are the ones with the know-how. The average architect doesn't have any idea how to build a house. So, sometimes the average architect draws things into a blueprint that can't possibly be built. Forget things that don't look good. I'm talking about sheer physical impossibilities."

A bell was ringing in Jessica's mind. "Didn't Gordon say you had hands-on building experience?"

"I spent my summers during college working on construction."

"You knew all along you wanted to be an architect?"

"No." He smirked. "I knew I needed money to live on, and construction jobs paid well." The smirk faded. "But that was how I first became interested in architecture. Blueprints intrigued me. The overall designs intrigued me. The guys who stood there in their spiffy suits, wearing hard hats, intrigued me." He chuckled. "So did the luxury cars they drove. And they all drive them. Porsches, Mercedes sportsters, BMWs—this Supra is modest compared to my colleagues' cars."

"So why don't you have a Porsche?"

"I was asking myself that same question the other day when my partner showed me his new one."

"What's the answer?"

"Money. They're damned expensive."

"You're doing as well as your partner."

He shrugged. "Maybe I don't trust myself not to scratch it up. Or it could be stolen. I don't have a secured garage space. I park in a narrow alley behind my building." He pursed his lips and thought for a minute before finally saying in a quieter voice, "I think I'm afraid that if I buy a Porsche, I'll believe that I've made it, and that's not true. I still have a ways to go."

Jessica was reminded of Nina, who defined happiness as a healthy bank account. Instinctively she knew that wasn't the case with Carter. He wasn't talking about making it economically, but professionally.

Maybe even personally. But that was a guess. She didn't know anything of his hopes and dreams.

On that thought, she lapsed into silence. Though she was curious, she didn't have the courage to suddenly start asking him about hopes and dreams, so she gave herself up to the smooth motion of the car and the blur of the passing landscape. The silence was comfortable, and surprising in that Jessica had always associated silence with solitude. Usually when she was with a man in a nonacademic setting, she felt impelled to talk, and since she wasn't the best conversationalist in the world, she wound up feeling awkward and inadequate.

She didn't feel that way now. The miles that passed beneath the wheels of the car seemed purpose enough. Moreover, if Carter wanted to talk, she knew he would. He wasn't the shy type—which was really funny, the more she thought of it. She'd always gravitated toward the shy type, because with the shy type she felt less shy herself. But in some ways it was easier being with Carter, because at any given time she knew where she stood.

At that moment in time, she knew that he was as comfortable with the silence as she was. His large hands were relaxed on the wheel, his legs sprawled as much as the car would allow. His jaw—square, she noted, like his chin—was set easily, as were his shoulders. He made no effort to speak, other than to point out something about a sign or a building they passed that had a story behind it, but when the tale was told, he was content to grow quiet again.

They drove straight for nearly four hours—with Carter's occasional apology for the lengthy drive, and a single rest stop—to arrive shortly before noon at Bar Harbor.

The drive was worth it. "I'm impressed," Jessica said sincerely when Carter had finished showing her around Cadillac Cove. Contrary to Crosslyn Rise, the housing was all oceanfront condominiums, grouped in comfortable clusters that simultaneously managed to hug the shore and echo the grace of nearby Cadillac Mountain. "Is it fully sold?"

He nodded. "Not all of the units are occupied year-round. This far north, they wouldn't necessarily be. A lot of them are owned on a time-sharing plan, and I think one or two are up for resale, but it's been a profitable venture for the developer."

"And for you."

"I was paid for my services as an architect, and I've cashed in on the praise that the complex has received, but I didn't have a financial stake in the project the way I might with Crosslyn Rise."

"Has Gordon talked with you more about that?"

"No. How about you?"

She shook her head. "I think he's starting to put feelers out, but he doesn't want to line up investors until we give him something concrete to work with."

Carter liked the "we" sound. "Does he work with a list of regular investors?"

"I don't really know." Something on his face made her say, "Why?"

"Because I know of a fellow who may be interested. His name's Gideon Lowe. I worked with him two years ago on a project in the Berkshires, and we've kept in touch. He's an honest guy, one of the best builders around, and whether or not he serves as the contractor for Crosslyn Rise, he may want to invest in it. He's been looking for something sound. Crosslyn Rise is sound."

"So you say."

"So I *know*. Hey, I wouldn't be investing my own money in it if it weren't." Without skipping a beat, he said, "I'm starved. Want to get something to eat?"

It was a minute before she made the transition from

business to pleasure, and it was just as lucky she didn't have time to think about it. The less she thought, the less nervous she was. "Uh…sure."

He took her hand. "Come on. There's a place not far from here that has the best chowder on the coast."

Chowder sounded fine to Jessica, who couldn't deny the slight chill of the ocean air. Her jacket helped, as did his hand. It encircled hers in a grip that was firm and wonderfully warm.

The chowder was as good as he'd boasted it would be, though Jessica knew that some of its appeal, at least, came from the pier-front setting and the company. Along with the chowder, they polished off spinach salads and a small loaf of homemade wheat bread. Then they headed back to the car and made for the next stop on Carter's list.

Five stops—three for business, two for pleasure—and four hours later, they reached Harborside. As he'd done at each of the other projects they'd seen, Carter showed her around, giving her a brief history of the setting and how it had come to be developed, plus mention of his feelings about the experience. And as he'd done at each of the other projects, he stopped at the end to await her judgment.

"It's interesting," she said this time. "The concept—converting a mill into condominiums—limits things a little, but you've stretched those limits with the atrium. I love the atrium."

Carter felt as though he were coming to know her through her facial expressions alone, and her facial expression now, serious and somewhat analytical, told him that while she might admire the atrium, she certainly didn't love it. "It's okay, Jessica," he teased. He felt confident enough, based on her earlier reactions, to say, "You can be blunt."

She kept her eyes on the building, which was across

the street from where they were standing. "I am being blunt. Given what you had to start with, this is really quite remarkable."

"Remarkable as in wildly exciting and dramatic?"

"Uh, not dramatic. Impressive."

"But you wouldn't want to live here."

"I didn't say that."

"Would you?"

Looking up, she caught the mischievous sparkle in his eye. It sparkled right through her in a way that something mischievous shouldn't have sparkled, but she didn't look away. She didn't want him to know how wonderfully warm he was making her feel by standing so close. "I think," she conceded a bit wryly, "that I'd rather live at Cadillac Cove."

"Or Riverside," he added, starting to grin in his own pleasure at the delightfully feminine flush on her cheeks. "Or the Sands."

"Or Walker Place," she tacked on, finishing the list of the places they'd visited. "Okay, this is my least favorite. But it's still good."

"Does that mean I have the job?"

Her brows flexed in an indulgent frown that came and went. "Of course you have the job. Why do you ask?"

"Wasn't that the point of this trip—to see if you like my work?"

In truth, Jessica had forgotten that point, which surprised her, and in the midst of that surprise, she realized two things. First, she had already come to think of Carter as the architect of record. And second, she was enjoying herself and had been doing so from the time she'd first sat back in his car and decided to trust his driving. Somewhere, there, she'd forgotten to remember what a hell-raiser he'd been once. She was thinking of him in terms of the present, and liking him. Did she like his work? "I like your work just fine."

His handsome mouth twitched in gentle amusement. "You could say it with a little enthusiasm."

Bewitched by that mouth and its small, subtle movements, she did as he asked. "I like your work just fine!"

"Really?"

"Really!"

The twitch at the corner of his mouth became a tentative grin. "Do you think I could do something good for Crosslyn Rise?"

"I think you could do something great for Crosslyn Rise!"

"You're not just saying that for old times' sake?"

Gazing up at him, she let out a laugh that was as easy as it was spontaneous. "If it were a matter of old times' sake, I'd have fired you long ago."

Behind the look in her eye, the sound of her laugh and the softness of her voice, Carter could have sworn he detected something akin to affection. Deeply touched by that thought, he took her chin in his hand. His fingers lightly caressed her skin, while his eyes searched hers for further sign of emotion. And he saw it. It was there. Yes, she liked him, and that made him feel even more victorious than when she'd said she liked his work. Unable to help himself, he moved his thumb over her mouth. When her lips parted, he ducked his head and replaced his thumb with his mouth.

His kiss was whisper light, one touch, then another, and Jessica couldn't have possibly stopped it. It felt too good, too real and far sweeter even than those heady kisses she'd dreamed about. But her body began to tremble—she didn't know whether in memory of the dream or in response to his kiss—and she was frightened.

"No," she whispered against his mouth. Her hands came up to grasp his jacket. "Please, Carter, no."

Lifting his head, Carter saw her fear. His body was telling him to kiss her again and deeper; his mind told him that he could do it and she'd capitulate. But his heart wasn't ready to push.

"I won't hurt you," he said softly.

"I know." Though her hands clutched his jacket, her eyes avoided his. "But I...don't want this."

I could make you want it, Carter thought, but he didn't say it, because it was typical of something the old Carter would say, and the last thing he wanted to do was to remind her of that. "Okay," he said softly, and took a step back, but only after he'd brushed his thumb over her cheek. Half turning from her, he took a deep breath, dug his fists into the pockets of his jacket and pursed his lips toward the mill that he'd redesigned. After a minute, when he'd regained control over his baser instincts, he sent her a sidelong glance.

"You like my work, and I like that. So a celebration's in order. What say we head back and have dinner at the Pagoda. Do you like Chinese food?"

Not trusting her voice, Jessica nodded.

"Want to try it?" he asked.

She nodded again.

Not daring to touch her, he chucked his chin in the direction of the car. "Shall we?"

To nod again would have seemed foolish even to her. So, tucking her hands into her pockets, she turned and headed for the car. By rights, she told herself, she ought to have pleaded the need to work and asked Carter to drive her home. She didn't for three reasons.

First, work could wait.

Second, she was hungry.

And third, she wasn't ready to have the day end.

CHAPTER SIX

THERE WAS A fourth reason why Jessica agreed to have dinner with Carter. She wanted to show him that she could recover from his kiss, or was it herself that she wanted to show? It didn't matter, she supposed, because the end result was the same. She couldn't figure out why Carter had kissed her again, unless he'd seen in her eyes that she'd wanted him to, which she had. Since it wasn't wise for her to reinforce that impression, she had to carry on as though the kiss didn't matter.

It was easier said than done. Not only did the Pagoda have superb Chinese food, but it was elegantly served in a setting where the chairs were high backed and romantic, the drinks were fruity and potent, and the lights were low. None of that was conducive to remembering that she was there on business, that Carter's kisses most surely stemmed from either professional elation or personal arrogance, and that she didn't want or need anything from him but spectacular designs for Crosslyn Rise.

The atmosphere had *date* written all over it, and nothing Carter did dispelled that notion. He was a relaxed conversationalist, willing to talk about anything, from work to a television documentary they'd both seen, to the upcoming gubernatorial election. He drew her out in ways that she hadn't expected, got her thinking and talking about things she'd normally have felt beyond her ken. If she had stopped to remember where he'd come from, she'd have been amazed at the breadth and depth

of his knowledge. But she didn't stop, because the man
that he was obliterated images of the past. The man that
he was held dominance over most everything, including,
increasingly, her wariness of him as a man.

So her defenses were down by the time they returned
to Crosslyn Rise. Darkness had fallen, lending an un-
reality to the scene, and while the drink had made her
mellow, Carter had her intoxicated. That, added to her
enjoyment of the evening, of the entire day, was why she
gave no resistance when he slipped an arm around her as
he walked her to the door. There, under the glow of the
antique lamps, he took her chin again and tipped up her
face.

"It's been a nice day," he told her in a voice that was low
and male. "I'm glad you agreed to come with me, and not
only to see the real estate. I've enjoyed the company."

She wanted to believe him enough to indulge in the
fantasy for a few last minutes. "It has been nice," she
agreed with a shy smile, feeling as though she could easily
drown in the depths of his charcoal-brown eyes and be
happy.

"The real estate? Or the company?"

"Both," was her soft answer.

He lowered his head and kissed her, touching her lips,
caressing them for an instant before lifting his head again.
"Was that as nice?"

It was a minute before she opened her eyes. "Mmm."

"I'd like to do it again."

"You thought it was nice, too?"

"If I didn't, I wouldn't want to do it again," he said with
the kind of logic that no mind could resist, particularly
one that was floating as lightly as Jessica's. "Okay?"

She nodded, and when he lowered his head this time,
her lips were softer, more pliant than before. He explored
their curves, opening them by small degrees until he

could run his tongue along the inside. When she gasped, he drew back.

"It's all right," he whispered. He slid his arms around her, fitting her body to his. "I won't hurt you," he said when he felt the fine tremors that shook her. "Flow with it, Jessica. Let me try again."

That was just what he did, caressing innocently at first, deepening the kiss by stages until his tongue was playing at will along the inside of her mouth. She tasted fruity sweet, reminiscent of the drinks they'd had, and twice as heady. When his arms contracted to draw her even closer, he wasn't thinking as much about her trembling body as his own. He needed to feel the pressure of her breasts, of her belly and thighs, needed to feel all those feminine things against his hard, male body.

Jessica clung to his shoulders, overwhelmed by the fire he'd started within her. It was like her dream, but so much more real, with heat rushing through her veins, licking at nerve ends, settling in ultrasensitive spots. When Carter crushed her closer, then moved her body against his, she didn't protest, because she needed the friction, too. His hardness was a foil for her softness, a salve for the ache inside her.

But the salve was only good for a minute, and when the ache increased, she remembered her dream again. She'd had a similar ache in the dream—until her mind had sparked what was necessary to bring her release.

For a horrid split second, she feared that would happen again. Then the split second passed, and she struggled to regain control of herself. "Carter," she protested, dragging her mouth from his. Her palms went flat against his shoulders and pushed.

"It's okay," he said unevenly. "I won't hurt you."

"We have to stop."

It was another minute before his dark eyes focused. "Why? I don't understand."

Freeing herself completely, Jessica moved to the front door. She grasped the doorknob and leaned against the wood, taking the support from Crosslyn Rise that she'd taken from Carter moments before. "I'm not like that."

"Like what?"

"Easy."

Carter was having trouble thinking clearly. Either the throbbing of his body was interfering with his brain, or she was talking nonsense. "No one said you were easy. I was just kissing you."

"But it's not the first time. And you wanted more."

"Didn't you?" he blurted out before he could stop himself. And then he wasn't sorry, because the ache in his groin persisted, making him want to lash out at its cause.

Her eyes shot to his. "No. I don't sleep around."

"You wanted more. You were trembling for it. Be honest, Jessica. It won't kill you to admit it."

"It's not true."

"In a pig's eye," he muttered, and took a step back. Tipping his head the slightest bit, he studied her through narrowed lids. "What is it about me that you find so frightening? The fact that I'm the guy who made fun of you when we were kids, or the fact that I'm a guy, period."

"You don't frighten me."

"I can see it. I can see it in your eyes."

"Then you see wrong. I just don't want to go to bed with you. That's all."

"Why not?"

"Because."

"Because why? Come on, Jessica. You owe me an explanation. You've been leading me a merry chase all day, being just that little bit distant but closer than ever before. You've spent the better part of the day being a consummate tease—"

"I have not! I've just been me! I thought we were having a nice time. If I'd known there was a price to pay for that—" she fumbled in her purse for her keys "—I'd have been careful not to have enjoyed myself as much. Is sex part of your professional fee?"

Carter ran a hand through his hair, then dropped it to the tight muscles at the back of his neck. With the fading of desire came greater control, and with greater control, clearer thought. They were on the old, familiar road to name-calling, he knew, and that wouldn't accomplish a thing.

He held up a hand to signal a truce, then set about explaining it. In a very quiet voice, he said, "Let's get one thing straight. I want you because you turn me on."

"That's—"

"Shh. Let me finish." When she remained silent, he said even more slowly, "You turn me on. No strings attached. No price I expect you to pay for lunch or dinner. You…just…turn me on. I didn't expect it, and I don't want it, because you *are* a client and I don't get involved with clients. It's not the way I work. Sex has nothing to do with payments of any kind. It has to do with two people liking each other, then respecting each other, then being attracted to each other. It has to do with two people being close, but needing to be even closer. It has to do with two people wanting to know each other in ways that other people don't." He paused to take a breath. "That was what I wanted just now. It was what I've been wanting all day."

Jessica didn't know what to answer. If she'd been madly in love with a man, she couldn't have hoped for a sweeter explanation. But she wasn't madly in love with Carter, which had to be why she was having trouble believing in the sincerity of his desire.

"As for sleeping around," Carter went on in that same quiet voice, "it means having indiscriminate sex with lots of different people. I'm not involved with anyone else right now. I haven't been intimately involved with anyone for a while. And I feel like I know you better than I've known any woman in years. So if I took you to bed, I wouldn't be sleeping around. And neither would you, unless you've been with others—"

She shook her head so vigorously that he dropped that particular line of inquiry. He'd known it wasn't true anyway. "Have you been with anyone since your husband?"

She shook her head more slowly this time.

"Before him?"

She shook her head a third time.

"Was it unpleasant with him?" Carter asked, but he knew that he'd made a mistake the minute the words were out. Jessica bowed her head and concentrated on fitting the key to the lock. "Don't go," he said quickly, but she opened the door and stepped inside.

"I can't talk about this," she murmured.

He took a step forward. "Then we'll talk about something else."

"No. I have to go."

"Talk of sex doesn't have to make you uncomfortable."

"It does. It's not something two strangers discuss."

"We're not strangers."

She looked up at him. "We are in some ways. You're more experienced than me. You won't be able to understand what I feel."

"Try me, and we'll see."

She shook her head, said softly, "I have to go," and slowly closed the door.

For a second before the latch clicked in place, Carter was tempted to resist. But the second passed, and the opportunity was gone. Short of banging the knocker or ringing the bell, he was cut off from her.

It was just as well. She needed time to get used to the idea of wanting him. He could give her that, he supposed.

HE GAVE HER nearly an hour, which was how long it took him to drive back to Boston, change clothes and make a pot of coffee. Then he picked up the phone and called her.

Her voice sounded calm and professional. "Hello?"

"Hi, Jessica. It's me. I just wanted to make sure you're okay."

She was silent for a minute. Then she said in the same composed voice, "I'm fine."

"You're not angry, are you?"

"No."

"Good." He paused. "I didn't mean any harm by asking what I did." He tapped a finger on the lip of his coffee cup. "I'm just curious." He looked up at the ceiling. "You're afraid of me. I keep trying to figure out why."

"I'm not afraid of you," came her quiet voice, sounding less confident than before.

"Then why won't you let yourself go when I kiss you?"

"Because I'm not the letting-go type."

"I think you could be. I think you want to be."

"I want to be exactly what I am right now. I'm not unhappy with my life, Carter. I'm doing what I like with people I like. If that wasn't so, I'd have changed things. But I like my life. I really like my life. You seem to think that I'm yearning for something else, but I'm not. I'm perfectly content."

Carter thought she was being a little too emphatic and a little too repetitive. He had the distinct feeling she was making the point to herself as much as to him, which meant that she wasn't as sure of her needs as she claimed, and that suited him just fine.

"You're not content about Crosslyn Rise," he reminded her, then hurried on, "which is another reason I'm calling. I'm going to start making some preliminary sketches, but I'll probably want to come to walk around again. I'd like to take some pictures—of the house, the land, possible building sites, the oceanfront. They're all outside pictures, so you don't have to be there, but I didn't want to go wandering around without your permission."

"You have my permission."

"Great. Why don't I give you a call when I have something to show you?"

"That sounds good." She paused. "Carter?"

He held his breath. "Yes?"

After a brief hesitation, her voice came. This time it sounded neither professional nor insecure, but sincere. "Thanks again for today. It really was nice."

He let out the breath and smiled. "My pleasure. Talk with you soon."

"Uh-huh."

WHAT TIME JESSICA spent at home that week, she spent looking out the window. Or it seemed that way. She made excuses for herself—she was restless reading term papers, she needed exercise, she could use the time to think—but she managed to wander from room to room, window to window, glancing nonchalantly out each one. Her eyes were anything but nonchalant, searching the landscape for Carter on the chance that either she'd missed his car on the driveway or he'd parked out of sight.

She saw no sign of him, which mean that either he'd come while she was in Cambridge or he hadn't come at all.

Nor did he call. She imagined that he might have tried her once or twice while she was out, and for the first time in her life she actually considered buying an answering machine. But that was in a moment of weakness. She didn't like answering machines. And besides, it would be worse to have an answering machine and not receive a message, than to not have one and wonder. Where one could wonder, one had hope.

And that thought confused her, because she wasn't sure why she wanted hope. Carter Malloy was...Carter Malloy. They were involved with each other on a professional basis, but that was all. Yes, she'd enjoyed spending Sunday with him. She'd begun to realize just how far he'd come as a person in the years she'd known him. And she did hope, she supposed, that there might be another Sunday or two like that.

But nothing sexual was ever going to happen between them. He wasn't her type—a perfect example being his failure to call. In Jessica's book, when a man was romantically interested in a woman, he didn't leave her alone for days. He called her, stopped in to see her, left messages at the office. Carter certainly could have done that, but there had been no message from him among the pink slips the department secretary had handed her that week.

He was showing his true colors, she decided. Despite all his sweet talk—sex talk—he wasn't really interested in her, which didn't surprise her in the least. He was a compelling man. Sex appeal oozed from him. She, on the other hand, had no sex appeal at all. Her genes had been generous in certain fields, but sex appeal wasn't one.

So what did Carter want with her? She didn't understand the motive behind his kisses, and the more she tried to, the more frustrated she became. The only thing she could think was that he was having a kind of perverse fun with her, and that hurt. It hurt, because one part of her liked him, respected him personally and professionally and found him sexy as all get out. It would be far easier, she realized, to admire him from a distance than to let him come close and show her just how unsatisfying she was to a man.

Knowing that the more she brooded, the worse it would be, Jessica kept herself as busy as possible. Rather than wander from window to window at home, by midweek she was spending as much time as possible at school. Work, like Poppycock, had a soothing effect on her, and there was work aplenty to do. When she wasn't grading exams, she was reading term papers or working with one of the two students for whom she was a dissertation advisor. And the work was uplifting—which didn't explain why, when she returned to Crosslyn Rise Friday evening, she felt distinctly let down. She'd never had that experience before. Work had always been a bellwether for her mood. She decided that she was simply tired.

So she slept late on Saturday morning, staying in bed until nine, dallying over breakfast, taking a leisurely shower, though she had nothing but laundry and local errands and more grading to do. She didn't pay any heed to the windows, knowing that Carter wouldn't come on a Saturday. Work was work. He'd be there during the week, preferably when she wasn't around. Which was just as well, as far as she was concerned.

It was therefore purely by accident that, with her arms loaded high with sheets to be laundered, she came down the back steps and caught a glimpse of something shiny and blue out the landing window. Heart thundering, she came to an abrupt halt, stared out at the driveway and swallowed hard.

He'd come. On a Saturday. When she was wearing jeans and a sweatshirt pushed up to the elbows, looking like one of her students playing laundress. But someone had to do the laundry, she thought a bit frantically; the days of having Annie Malloy to help with it were long gone.

Ah, the irony of it, she mused. Then the back bell rang, and she ceased all musings. Panicked, she glanced at her sweatshirt, then at the linens in her arms, then down the stairs toward the door. If she didn't answer it, he'd think she wasn't home.

That would be the best thing.

But she couldn't do it. Tucking the sheets into a haphazard ball, she ran down the stairs, crossed through the back vestibule and opened the door to Carter.

His appearance did nothing to ease her breathlessness. Wearing jeans and a plaid flannel shirt, he looked large and masculine. His clothes were comfortably worn—a far cry from the last time she'd seen him in jeans, when they'd been dirty and torn—and fit his leanly muscled legs like a glove. The shirt was rolled to the elbow, much as her sweatshirt was, only his forearms were sinewy, spattered with dark hair, striped on the inside with the occasional vein. His collar was open, showing off the strength of his neck and shoulders, and from one of those shoulders hung a camera.

"Hi," she said. In an attempt to curb her breathlessness, she put a hand to her chest. "How are you?"

He was just fine, now that he was here. All week he'd debated about when to stop by; he couldn't remember when he'd given as much thought to anything. Except her. She'd been on his mind a lot. Now he knew why. Looking at her, taking in the casual way she was dressed, the oversize pink sweatshirt and the faded blue jeans that clung to slender legs, he felt relieved. Her features, too, did that to him. She was perfectly unadorned—long hair shiny clean and drawn into a high ponytail, skin free of makeup and healthy looking, smile small but bright, glasses sliding down the bridge of her nose—but she looked wonderful. She was a breath of fresh air, he decided, finally putting his finger on one of the things he most liked about her. She was different from the women he'd known. She was natural and unpretentious. She was refreshing.

"I'm real fine," he drawled with a lazy smile. "Just stoppin' in to disturb your Saturday morning." His gaze touched on the bundle she held.

Wrapping both arms around the linens, she hugged them to her. "I, uh, always use Saturdays for this. Usually I'm up earlier. I should have had two washes done by now. I slept late."

"You must have been tired." He searched for shadows under her eyes, but either her glasses hid them, or they just weren't there. Her skin was clear, unmottled by fatigue, a smooth blend of ivory and pink. "It's been a busy week?"

"Very," she said with a sigh and a smile.

"Will you be able to relax this weekend?"

"A little. I still have more work to do, but then there are things like this—" she nodded toward the linens "—and the market and the drugstore, none of which are heavily intellectual tasks. I relax when I do those."

"No time to sit back, put your feet up and vegetate?"

She shook her head. "I'm not good at vegetating."

"I used to be good at it, back in the days when I was raising hell." His mouth took on a self-effacing twist. "Used to drive my mother wild. Whenever the police showed up at the door, she knew she'd find me sprawled out in the back room watching TV." The twist gentled. "I don't have much time for vegetating now, either—" he jabbed his chin toward the camera "—which is why I'm here. I thought I'd do that exploring. I have nothing to think about but Crosslyn Rise, and it's a gorgeous day." He made a quick decision, based on the open look on her face. "Want to come?"

Nothing seemed to be helping Jessica's breathlessness or the incessant fluttering of her insides. Suddenly she didn't seem to be able to make a decision, either. "I don't know...there's this laundry to do...and vacuuming." She could feel the warm air coming in past him, and it beckoned. "I ought to dust...and you'll probably be able to think more creatively if I'm not around."

"I'd like the company. And I won't talk if the creative mode hits. Come on. Just for a little while. It's too special a day to miss."

His eyes weren't as much charcoal-brown today, she decided, as milk-chocolatey, and their lashes seemed absurdly thick. Had she never noticed that before?

"Uh, I have so much to do," she argued, but meekly.

"Tell you what," Carter said. "I'll start out and follow the same route we took last time. You take care of what you have to, then join me."

That sounded like a fair compromise to Jessica. If he was willing to be flexible, she couldn't exactly remain rigid. Besides, Saturday or not, he was working on her project. Maybe he wanted to bounce ideas off her. "I may be a little while," she cautioned.

"No sweat. I'll be here longer than that. Take your time." With a wink, he set off.

The wink set her back a good ten minutes. Several of those were spent with her back against the wall by the door, trying to catch up with her racing pulse. Several more were spent wandering through the kitchen into

the den, before she realized that she was supposed to be
headed for the laundry, which was in the basement. The
rest were spent getting the washer settings right, normally
a simple task, now complicated by a sorely distracted
mind.

Never in her life had she done the vacuuming as
quickly as she did then. It was nervous energy, she told
herself, and that reasoning held on through a dusting job
that probably stirred more than it gathered. Fortunately,
the rooms in question were only those few she used on a
regular basis, which meant that she was done in no time.
The bed linens were in the dryer and her personal things
in the wash when she laced on a pair of sneakers, grabbed
a half-filled bag of bread and slipped out the door.

Carter was sitting cross-legged on the warm grass by
the duck pond. Though for all intents and purposes he
was concentrating on the antics of the ducks, he'd kept a
lookout for her arrival. The sight of her brought the warm
feeling it always did, plus something akin to excitement—
which was amusing, since in the old days he'd have la-
beled her the least exciting person in the world. But that
was in the old days, at a time in his life when he'd appreciated precious little, certainly nothing subtle and mature,
which were the ways in which he found Jessica exciting.
He could never have appreciated her intellect, the way she
thought through issues, the natural curiosity that had her
listening to things he said and asking questions. She was
a thoroughly stimulating companion, even in silence—
unless she felt threatened. When that happened, she was
as dogmatic and closed minded as he'd once thought her
to be.

The key, of course, was to keep her from feeling threatened. Most of the time, that was easy, particularly since
he felt increasingly protective of her. The times when it
was difficult almost always had to do with sex, which

was when he was at his least controlled both physically and emotionally.

But he'd try. He'd try, because the prize was worth it.

"Watch out for the muck!" he called, and watched her give wide berth to a spot of ground that hadn't quite dried out from the spring thaw. His eyes followed her as she approached, one hand tucked into the pocket of her jeans, her ponytail swaying gently with her step. "That was fast."

"Don't you know it," she said in a way that stunned him, then pleased him in the next breath. She'd drawled the words. Yes, there was self-mockery in them, but there was playfulness, too. Opening the bag of bread, she began breaking off chunks and tossing them toward the ducks, who quacked their appreciation. "I hate cleaning. I do it dutifully. But I hate it."

"You should hire someone—and don't tell me you can't afford it. That kind of help is cheap."

But she nixed the idea with the scrunch of her nose, which served the double purpose of hitching her glasses up. "There's really not enough to do." She tossed out another handful of bread and watched the ducks try to out-waddle each other to where it landed. "I hire a crew twice a year to do the parts of the house that I don't use, but there's no good reason why I can't do the rest myself." She turned to stare at him hard, but her voice was too gentle to be accusing. "Unless someone stands at my door tempting me with the best spring weather that's come along so far." She looked around, took a deep breath, didn't pause to wonder whether the exhilaration she felt was from the air or not. She was tired of wondering about things like that. She was too analytical. For once, she wanted to— what was it he'd said—go with the flow. "So," she said, reaching for more bread, "are you being inspired?"

"Here? Always. It's a beautiful spot." Tossing several feathers out of the way, he patted the grass by his side.

She sat down and shot a look at the camera that lay in his lap. It wasn't one of the instant models, but the real thing. "Have you used it?"

He nodded. "I've taken pictures of the house, the front lawn and the beach. Not here, yet. I'm just sitting."

She aimed a handful of bread crumbs toward the ducks. "Are you a good photographer?"

"I'm competent. I get the shots I need, but they're practical, rather than artistic." He took the camera up, made several shifts in the settings, raised it to his eye and aimed it at her.

She held up a hand to block the shot and turned her head away. "I hate having my picture taken even more than I hate cleaning!"

"Why?"

"I don't like being focused on." She dared a glance at him, relaxing once she saw that he'd put the camera back down.

"Focused on" could be interpreted both broadly and narrowly. Carter had the feeling that both applied in Jessica's case. "Why not?" he asked, bemused.

"Because it's embarrassing. I'm not photogenic."

"I don't believe that."

"It's true. The camera exaggerates every flaw. I have plenty without the exaggeration."

Looking at her, with the sun glancing off her hair and a blush of self-consciousness on her cheeks, Carter could only think of how pretty she was. "What flaws do you have?"

"Come on, Carter—"

"Tell me." The quacking of the ducks seemed to second his command.

Sure that he was ridiculing her, she studied his eyes.

She saw no teasing there, though, only challenge, and where Carter challenged her, she was conditioned to respond. "I'm plain. Totally and utterly plain. My face is too thin, my nose is too small and my eyes are boring."

He stared at her. "Boring? Are you kidding? And there's nothing wrong with the shape of your face or your nose. Do you have any idea what a pleasure it is for me to look at you after having to look at other women all week?" At her blank look, he said, "You've grown up well, Jessica. You may have felt plain as a child, but you're not a child anymore, and what you think of as plainness is straightforward, refreshing good looks."

Her blankness had yielded to incredulity. "Why do you say things like that?"

"Because they're true!"

"I don't believe it for a minute," she said. It seemed the only way to cope with the awkwardness she felt. Rising to her feet, she tossed the last of the bread from the bag and set off. "You're just trying to butter me up so I'll like your designs." Wadding up the bag, she stuffed it into a pocket.

Carter was after her in a minute, gently catching her ponytail to draw her up short as he overtook her. His body was a solid wall before her, his hand in her hair a smaller but no less impenetrable wall behind. Against her temple, his breath was a warm sough of emotion. "If I wanted to butter you up, I'd just do my work and mind my own business about the rest. But I can't do it—any more than I can sit back and listen to you denigrate yourself. I'm highly attracted to you. Why can't you believe that?"

Struck as always by his closeness, Jessica's breathing had quickened. Her eyes were lowered, focusing on his shirt, and though there was nothing particularly sensual about the plaid, there was something decidedly so about the faintly musky scent of his skin.

"I'm not the kind of women men find highly attractive," she explained in a small voice.

"Is that another gem of wisdom from your ex-husband?"

"No. It's something I've deduced after thirty-three years of observation. I don't turn heads. I never have and never will."

"The women who turn heads—the sharp lookers, the fashion plates—aren't the women men want. Call it macho, but they want softer women. You're a softer woman. And I want you."

"But you have your choice of the best women in the city."

"And I choose you. Doesn't that tell you anything?"

"It tells me that you're going through a phase. Let's call it—" she raised her eyes to his to make her point "—the give-the-little-lady-a-thrill-for-old-times'-sake phase."

Dangerously close to anger, Carter drew her closer until she was flush against him. "That's insulting, Jessica." His dark eyes blazed into hers. "Can't you give me a little credit for honesty? Have I ever lied to you?" When she didn't answer, he did it for her. "No. I may have said cruel things, or downright wrong things, but they were the things I was honestly feeling at the time. We've already established that I was a bastard. But at least give me credit for honesty."

His blood was pulsing more thickly as her curves imprinted themselves on his body. "I've been honest with words. And I've been honest with this." He captured her mouth before she could open hers to protest, and he kissed her with an ardor that could have been from hunger or anger.

Jessica didn't know which. All she knew was that her defenses fell in less time than ever before, that she couldn't have kept her mouth stiff if she'd tried, that she should have been shocked when his tongue surged into her mouth, but the only source of shock was her own enjoyment.

That thought, though, came a moment too soon, because she was in for another small shock. Well before she was ready, he ended the kiss. She hadn't even begun to gather her wits when he took her hand from its stranglehold of his shirt and lowered it to the straining fly of his jeans.

"No way," he said hoarsely, "no way could I fake that." Keeping his hand over hers, he molded her fingers to his shape, pressing her palm flat, manipulating it in a rubbing motion. A low sound slipped from his throat as he pressed his lips to her neck.

Jessica was stunned by the extent of his arousal, then stunned again when the heat of it seemed to increase. Her breathing was short and scattered, but Carter's was worse, and a fine quaking simmered in the muscles of his arms and legs.

No, he couldn't fake what she felt, and the knowledge was heady. It made her feel soft and feminine and eager to know more of the strength beneath her hand. Without conscious thought, she began to stroke him. Her eyes closed. Her head tipped to give his mouth access to her throat. Her free arm stole to the bunched muscles of his back. And when she became aware of a restlessness between her legs, she arched toward him.

Carter made a low, guttural sound. Wrenching her hand from him, he wrapped her in his arms and crushed her close, then closer still. "Don't move," he warned in a voice that was more sand than substance. "Don't move. Give me a minute. A minute."

The trembling went on as he held her tight, but Jessica wasn't sure how much of it was her own. Weak-kneed and shaky, she was grateful that his convulsive hold was keeping her upright. Without it, she'd surely have slid down to the grass and begged him to take her there, which was precisely what the tight knot at the pit of her stomach demanded.

That was probably the biggest shock of all. The dream she could reason away. She could attribute it to any number of vague things. But when she was being held in Carter's arms, when she felt every hard line of his body and not only took pleasure in the hardness but hungered to have it deeper inside her, she couldn't lie to herself any longer.

The issue, of course, was what to make of the intense desire she felt for him. The moment would pass now, she knew. Once Carter regained control of his libido, he would set her back, perhaps take her hand and lead her on through the woods. He might talk, ask her what she feared, try to get her to admit to his desire and to her own, but he wouldn't force her into anything she didn't want.

It wasn't that she didn't want sex with Carter, rather that she wasn't ready for it. She'd never been a creature of impulse. It was one thing to "go with the flow" and spurn housekeeping chores in favor of a walk in the woods, quite another to "go with the flow" and expose herself, body and soul, to a man. She'd done that once and been hurt, and though she'd never made vows of chastity, the memory of that hurt kept her shy of sex.

If she was ever to make love with Carter, she had to understand exactly what she was doing and why. She also had to decide whether the risk was worth it.

CHAPTER SEVEN

CARTER DIDN'T LEAVE right away. Nor did he allow Jessica to leave. He insisted she stay while he took the pictures he needed at the duck pond, then walked her back to the house. She had feared he'd want to talk about what had happened, but either he was as surprised by its power as she, or he sensed she wasn't ready. He said nothing about the kiss, about the way she'd touched him, or about the fact that he'd nearly lost it there and then in front of the ducks.

Instead, he sent her inside to finish her chores while he completed his own outside. Then he drove her to the supermarket and walked up and down the aisles with her, tossing the occasional unusual item into her cart. When they returned to Crosslyn Rise, he made his special tuna salad, replete with diced water chestnuts and red-pepper relish.

After lunch, he left.

HE CALLED ON Monday evening to say that the photos he'd taken had come out well and that he was getting down to some serious sketching.

He called on Thursday evening to say that he was pleased with the progress he was making and would she be free on Sunday afternoon to take a look at what he'd drawn.

She was free, of course. The semester's work was over, exams and papers graded, grades duly recorded—which was wonderful in the sense of freeing her up, lousy in the sense of giving her more time to think. The thinker in her decided that she definitely wanted to see what he'd drawn, but she didn't trust him—or herself—to have a show-and-tell meeting at Crosslyn Rise.

So they arranged to meet at Carter's office, which satisfied Jessica's need on several scores. First, she was curious to see more of him in his professional milieu. Second, even if he kissed her, and even if she responded, the setting was such that nothing could come of it.

She guessed she was curious to see him, period. It had been a long week since the Saturday before, a long week of replaying what had happened, of feeling the excitement again, of imagining an even deeper involvement. Though it still boggled her mind, she had to accept that he did want her. The evidence had been conclusive. She still didn't know *why* he wanted her, and the possibilities were diverse, running from the wildly exciting to the devastating. But that was another reason why the setting suited her purpose. It was safe. She could see him, get to know him better, but she wouldn't have to take a stand on the physical side of the issue.

And then, there was Crosslyn Rise. The part of her that had acclimated itself to the conversion of the Rise was anxious to see what he'd drawn. That part wanted to get going, to decide on an architectural plan, have it formally drawn up and give it to Gordon so that he could enlist his investors. That part of Jessica wanted to act before its counterpart backed out.

Jessica wasn't sure what she'd expected when she took a first look at Carter's drawings, but it certainly wasn't the multicolored spread before her. Yes, there were pencil sketches on various odd pieces of paper, but he'd taken the best of those ideas and converted them into something that could well have been a polished promotion for the place.

"Who drew these?" she asked, slightly awed.

"I did." There were times when he left such drawings to project managers, but he'd wanted to do this himself. When it came to Crosslyn Rise, he was the project manager, and he didn't give a damn whether his partner accused him of ill-using the resources at hand. Crosslyn Rise was his baby from start to finish, even if it meant late nights such as the ones he'd put in this week. They were worth it. Concentrating on his work was better than concentrating on his need.

"But this is art. I never pictured anything like this."

"It's called a presentation," he said dryly. "The idea is to snow the client right off the bat."

"Well, I'm snowed."

"By the presentation, maybe, but do you like what's in it?"

At first glance, she did. At his caveat, she took a closer look, moving one large sheet aside to look at the next.

"I've drawn the main house in cross sections, as I envision it looking once all the work is done," he explained, "and a head-on view of the condo cluster at the duck pond. Since the clusters will all be based on the same concept, a variation on the Georgian theme, I wanted to try out one cluster on you first."

Her eyes were glued to the drawing. "It's incredible."

"Is it what you imagined?"

"No. It looks more Cape-ish than Georgian. But it's real. More modern. Interesting."

He wasn't sure if "interesting" was good or bad, but when he asked, she held up a hand and studied the drawing in silence for several minutes. "Interesting," she repeated, but there was a warmth in the word. Then she smiled. "Nice."

Carter basked in her smile, which was some consolation for the fact that he wanted to hug her but didn't dare. Not only did he sense that she wasn't ready for more hugs, but he feared that if he touched her, office or no, he wouldn't be able to stop this time. As it was, her smile, which was so rare, did dangerous things to him.

He cleared his throat. "Obviously this is rough. But I wanted to convey the general idea." He touched a lean finger to one area, then another. "The roof angle here is what reminds you of a Cape. It can be modified, but it allows for skylights. Today's market loves skylights." His finger shifted. "I've deliberately scaled down the pillars and balconies so that they don't compete with the main house. The main house should set the tone for stateliness. The clusters can echo it, but they ought to be more subtle. I want them to nestle into their surroundings. In some ways the focus of the clusters *is* those surroundings."

Jessica cast a sideways glance at him. He had a long arm propped straight on the drafting table and was close enough to touch, close enough to smell, close enough to want. Ignoring the last and the buzzing that played havoc with her insides, she said, "I think you're hung up on those surroundings."

"Me?" His dark eyes shone with indulgence one moment, vehemence the next. "No way. At least, not enough that it would color my better judgment. And my better judgment tells me that people will buy at Crosslyn Rise for the setting, nearly as much as for the nuts and bolts of what they're getting. Which isn't to say that we can skimp on those nuts and bolts." Again he referred to the drawing, tracing sweeping lines with his finger. "I've angled each of the units differently, partly for interest, partly for privacy. Either you and Gordon—or if you want to wait, the consortium—will have to decide on the size of the units. Personally, I'd hate to do anything less than a three-bedroom setup. People usually want more space rather than less."

Jessica hadn't thought that far. "The person to speak with about that might be Nina Stone. She's a broker. She'd have a feel for what people in this area want."

"Do I know Nina Stone?" Carter asked, trying to place the name.

"She knew you," Jessica replied, wondering whether the two of them would hit it off and not sure she liked that idea. "Or rather, she knew *of* you. Your reputation precedes you."

Once he'd left New York, Carter had worked long and hard to establish himself and his name. "That's gratifying."

"Uh-huh. She already has you pegged as a ruggedly masculine individual."

Which wasn't the most professional of assessments, he mused. "You discussed me with her?"

"I mentioned we were working together."

He nodded his understanding, but, to Jessica's selfish delight, had no particular interest in knowing more about Nina. His finger was back on the drawing, this time tapping his rendition of the duck pond. "We may run into a problem with water. The land in this area is wetter than in the others. When we reach the point of having the backers lined up, I'll have a geological specialist take a look."

"Could the problem be serious?"

"Nah. It shouldn't be more than a matter of shifting the clusters to the right or the left, and I want them set back anyway so the ducks won't be disturbed. The main house draws water from its own wells. I'm assuming the condos would do the same, but an expert could tell us more on that, too."

Up to that point, Jessica had been aware of only two problems—coming to terms with the sale of Crosslyn

Rise, and dealing with Carter Malloy. Now, mention of a possible water problem brought another to mind. "What if we can't get enough backers?"

Surprised by the question, he shot her a look. Her eyes were wide with concern. "To invest in the project? We'll get enough."

"Will we? You've had more experience in this kind of thing than I have. Is there a chance we'll come up with plans that no one will support?"

"It's not probable."

"But is it possible?"

"Anything's possible. It's possible that the economy will crash at ten past ten tomorrow morning, but it's no more probable that it will happen than that Gordon won't be able to find the backers we need." He paused, sliding his gaze over her face. "You're really worried?"

"I haven't been. I haven't thought about it much at all, but suddenly here you are with exciting drawings, and the project seems very real. I'd hate to go through all this and then have the whole thing fizzle."

Throwing caution to the winds, he did put his arm around her then. "It won't. Trust me. It won't."

The confidence in his voice, even more so than the words, was what did it. That, and the support his body offered. For the first time, she truly felt as though Carter shared the responsibility of Crosslyn Rise with her, and while a week or two before, that thought would have driven her wild, she was comfortable with it now. She'd come a long way.

"I have theater tickets for Thursday night," came Carter's low voice. "Come with me."

Taken totally off guard, she didn't know what to say.

His breath was warm on her hair. "Do you have other plans?"

"No."

"They're for *Cat on a Hot Tin Roof.*"

Tipping her head, she looked up at him. "You got tickets," she breathed in awe, because she'd been trying to get them for weeks without success. But going to the theater with Carter was a *date.*

"Will you come?"

"I don't know," she said a bit helplessly. Everything physical about him lured her, as did, increasingly, everything else about him. He was so good to be with. The problem, as always, lay with her.

"If you won't, I'm giving the tickets back. There's no one else I want to take, and I don't want to go alone."

"That's blackmail," she argued.

"Not blackmail. Just a chance to see the hottest revival of the decade."

"I know, I know," she murmured, weakening. It was easy to do that when someone as strong as Carter was offering support.

"The semester's over. What better way to celebrate?"

"I have to be at school all day Thursday planning for the summer term."

"But the pressure's off. So before it's on again, have a little fun. You deserve it."

She wasn't as concerned with what she deserved as with what going on a date with Carter would mean. It would mean a shift in their relationship, a broadening of it. Going on a date with Carter would mean being with him at night in a crowded theater, perhaps alone before or after. All kinds of things could happen. She wasn't sure she was ready.

Then again, she wasn't sure she could resist.

"Come on, Jessica. I really want to go."

So do I, Jessica thought. Her eyes fell to his mouth.

She liked looking at his mouth. "I'd have to meet you there."

"Why can't I pick you up?" he asked, and the corners of that mouth turned down.

"Because I don't know exactly where I'll be."

"You could call me at the office and let me know. It's only a ten-minute drive to Cambridge."

Her eyes met his. "More in traffic. And it's silly for you to go back and forth like that."

"I want to go back and forth." If he was taking her out for the evening, he wanted to do it right. Besides, he didn't like the idea of her traveling alone.

Jessica, though, was used to traveling alone. More than that, she was determined to keep things light and casual. It was the only way she could handle the thought of a date with Carter. "Tell me where to meet you and when. I'll be there."

"Why are you being so stubborn?" he asked. In the next breath, he relented. "Sorry. Six-thirty at the Sweetwater Café."

"I thought *Cat on a Hot Tin Roof* was at the Colonial." She knew very well it was—and what he was trying to do.

His naughty eyes didn't deny it. "The Sweetwater Café is close by. We can get something to eat there before the show." When she looked momentarily skeptical, he said, "You have to eat, Jessica." When still she hesitated, he added, "Indulge me. I'm letting you meet me there, which I don't like. So at least let me feed you first."

Looking up into his dark eyes, she came to an abrupt realization. It was no longer a matter of not being sure. She *couldn't* resist—not when he had an arm draped so protectively across her shoulders, not when he was looking at her so intently, not when she wanted both to go on forever and ever. He made her feel special. Cared for.

Feminine. She doubted, at that minute, that she'd have been able to refuse him a thing.

So SHE AGREED. Naturally she had second thoughts, but after a day of suffering through those, she lost patience with herself. Since she'd agreed to go out with Carter, she told herself, she was going, and since she was going, she intended to make the most of it. She had her share of pride, and that pride dictated that she do everything in her power to make sure Carter didn't regret having asked her out.

He didn't regret it so far, at least; he called her each night just to say hello. But talking on the phone or having a business meeting or even driving north on a Sunday was different from going out at night to something that had nothing to do with work. She wanted to look good.

To that end, she arranged to finish up with work by two on Thursday. The first stop she made then was to the boutique where she'd bought the sweater she'd worn to Maine; if stylish had worked once, she figured it would work again. But stylish in that shop was funky, which wasn't her style at all. She was about to give up hope when the owner brought a dress from the back that was perfect. A lime-green sheath of silk that was self-sashed and fell to just above the knee, it was sleeveless and had a high turtleneck that draped her neck in the same graceful way that the rest of the fabric draped her body. The dress was feminine without being frilly. She felt special enough in it not to look at the price tag, and by the time she had to write out a check, she was committed enough to it not to mind the higher-than-normal cost.

Her second stop was at a shoe store, where she picked up a pair of black patent leather heels and a small bag to match.

Her third stop was at Mario's. Mario had been doing

her hair—a blunt cut to keep the ends under control—
bimonthly for several years, and for the first time she
allowed him more freedom. Enhancing her own natural
wave with rollers and a heat lamp, he gave her a look
that was softer and more stylish than anything she'd ever
worn. As the icing on the cake, he caught one side high
over her ear with a pearl clip. The look pleased Jessica so
much that she left the salon, went to the jewelry store next
door and splurged on a pair of pearl earrings to match
the clip. Then she returned to her office, where she'd left
cosmetics and stockings.

The day had been warm and humid, as late-spring days
often were, and when Jessica left Harvard, retrieved her
car and set off for Boston, dull gray clouds were dotting
the sky. She barely noticed. Her thoughts were on the
way she looked and the comments she'd drawn from the
few of her colleagues she'd happened to pass as she left.
They had done double takes, which either said she looked
really good, or so different from how she usually looked
that they couldn't believe it was her.

She couldn't quite believe it was her. For one thing,
the fact that she liked the way she looked was a first. For
another, the fact that she was heading for a date with a
man like Carter Malloy was incredible. Unable to reconcile either, given that her nerves were jangling with
excitement, she half decided that it wasn't her in the car
at all, but another woman. That thought brought a silly
grin to her face.

The grin faded, but the excitement didn't. It was over-
shadowing her nervousness by the time she parked in the
garage under the Boston Common, and by the time she
emerged onto the Common itself and realized that she
was at the corner farthest from where she was going, she
was feeling too high to mind. Her step was quick, in no
way slowed by the unfamiliarity of the new heels.

What gave her pause, though, were the drops of rain that, one by one, in slow succession, began to hit her. They were large and warm. She looked worriedly at the sky, not at all reassured by the ominous cloud overhead or the blue that surrounded it in too distant a way. Furious at herself for not having brought an umbrella, she walked faster. She could beat the rain, she decided, but she wished she'd parked closer.

To her dismay, the drops grew larger, came harder and more often. She broke into a half run, holding her handbag over her head, looking around for shelter. But there was none. Trees were scattered on either side of the paved walks, but they were of the variety whose branches were too high to provide any shelter at all.

For a split second she stopped and looked frantically back at the entrance to the parking garage, but it seemed suddenly distant, separated from her by a million thick raindrops. If she returned there, she'd be farther than ever from the Sweetwater Café—and drenched anyway.

So she ran faster, but within minutes, the rain reached downpour proportions. She was engulfed as much by it as by disbelief. Other people rushed along, trying to protect themselves as she was, but she paid them no heed. All she could think of was the beautiful green silk dress that was growing wetter by the minute, the painstakingly styled hair that was growing wilder by the minute, the shiny black shoes that were growing more speckled by the minute.

Panicked, she drew up under a large-trunked tree in the hope that something, *anything* would be better than nothing. But as though to mock her, the rain began to come sideways. When she shifted around the tree, it shifted, too. Horrified at what was happening but helpless to stop it, she looked from side to side for help but there was none. She was caught in the worst kind of nightmare.

Unable to contain it, she cried out in frustration, then cried out again when the first one didn't help. The second didn't, either, and she felt nearly as much a fool for making it as for standing there in the rain. So she started off again, running as fast as she could given that her glasses were streaked with rain, her shoes were soaked and her heart felt like lead.

It was still pouring when she finally turned down the alley that led to the Sweetwater Café. As the brick walkway widened into a courtyard, she slowed her step. Rushing was pointless. There was nothing the rain could do to her that it already hadn't. She couldn't possibly go to the theater with Carter. The evening was ruined. All that was left was to tell him, return to her car and drive home.

Shortly before she reached the café's entrance, her legs betrayed her. Stumbling to the nearby brick wall, she leaned her shoulder against it, covered her face with her hands and began to cry.

That was how Carter found her, as he came from the opposite end of the courtyard. He wasn't sure it was her at first; he hadn't expected such a deep green dress, such a wild array of hair or nearly so much leg. But as he slowed his own step, he sensed the familiar in the defeated way she stood. His insides went from hot to cold in the few seconds it took him to reach her side.

"Jessica?" he asked, his heart pounding in dread. He reached out, touched the back of her hand. "Are you all right?"

With a mournful moan, she shrank into herself.

Heedless of the rain that continued to fall, he put a hand to the wall and used his body to shield her from the curious eyes of those who passed. "Jessica?" He speared his fingers into her hair to lift it away from her face. "What happened?" When she continued to cry, he grasped her wrist. "Are you all right? Tell me what happened. Are you hurt?"

"I'm wet!" she cried from behind her hands.

He could see that, but there was still an icy-cold image of something violent hovering in his mind. "Is that all? You weren't mugged or…anything?"

"I'm just wet! I got caught in the downpour, and there wasn't anywhere to go, and I wanted to look so nice. *I'm a mess,* Carter."

Carter was so relieved that she hadn't been bodily harmed in some other, darker, narrower alley, that he gave her a tight hug. "You're not a mess—"

"I'll get you wet," she protested, struggling to free herself from his hold.

He ignored her struggles. "You're looking goddamned sexy with that dress clinging to every blessed curve." When she gave a soft wail and went limp, he said, "Come on. Let's get you dry."

The next few minutes were a blur in Jessica's mind, principally because she didn't raise her eyes once. For the first time in her life, she was grateful that her hair was wild, because it fell by her cheeks like a veil. She didn't want Carter to see her, didn't want *anyone* to see her. She felt like a drowned rat, all the more pathetic in her own mind by contrast to the way she looked when she left Cambridge.

With a strong arm around her shoulder, Carter guided her out of the alley and into a cab. He didn't let her go even then, but spoke soft words to her during the short ride to his apartment. Wallowing in misery, she heard precious few of them. She kept her head down and her shoulders hunched. If she'd been able to slide under the seat, she'd have done just that.

He lived on Commonwealth Avenue, on the third floor of a time-honored six-story building. Naturally the rain had stopped by the time they reached it. He knew not to point that out to Jessica, and ushered her into the lobby before she could figure it out for herself. Though she'd stopped crying, she was distraught. The tension in her body wasn't to be believed.

"Here we go," he said as he quickly unlocked the door to his place. He led her directly into the bathroom, pulled a huge gray bath sheet from a shelf and began to wipe her arms. When he'd done what he could, he draped it around her, took a smaller towel, removed her glasses and dried them, too. "Better?"

Jessica refused to look at him. "I'm hopeless," she whispered.

"You're only wet," he said, setting the glasses by the sink. "When I saw you crying, leaning against the wall that way in the alley, I thought you'd been attacked. I honestly thought you'd been mugged. But you're only wet."

She was beyond being grateful for small favors. Turning her face away from him, she said in a woefully small voice, "I tried so hard. I wanted to look nice for you. I can't remember the last time anything meant so much to me, and I almost did it. I was looking good, and I was looking forward to tonight, and then it started to rain. I didn't know whether to go back or go on, and the rain came down harder, and then it didn't matter either way because I was soaked." Her eyes were filled with tears when they met Carter's. "It wasn't meant to be. I'm a disaster when it comes to nice things like dinner and the theater. There was a message in what happened."

"Like hell," Carter said, blotting her face with the smaller towel. "It rained. I would have been caught in it, too, if I'd walked, but I was running late, so I took a cab." He began to gently dry her hair. "Sudden storms come on like that. If it had come fifteen minutes earlier or later, you'd have been fine."

"But it didn't, and I'm not. And now everything is ruined. My dress, my shoes, my hair—"

"Your hair is gorgeous," he said, and it was. Moving the towel through it was like trying to tame a living thing. Waving naturally, it was wild and exotic. "You should wear it down like this more often. Then again, maybe you shouldn't. It's an incredible turn-on. Let everyone else see it tied up. Wear it down for me."

"There was a clip in it. It looked so pretty."

Carter found the clip buried in the maple-hued mass. "Here. Put it back in."

"I can't. I don't know how to do it. Mario did it."

"Mario?"

"My hairdresser."

She'd gone to the hairdresser. For a dinner and theater date with him. That fact, more than anything else she'd said, touched him deeply. He doubted she went to the hairdresser often, certainly not to have something as frivolous as a clip put in. But she'd wanted to look nice for him.

"Ah, Jessica." Towels and all, he took her in his arms. "I'm sorry you got rained on. You must have looked beautiful."

"Not beautiful. But nice."

"Beautiful."

"But I'm a mess. I can't go anywhere like this, not to dinner, not to the theater. Call someone else, Carter. Get someone else to go with you."

He held her back and stared down onto her face. "Are you kidding?"

"No. Call someone."

He was about to argue with her when he caught

himself. "You're right," he said. "Stay put." He left the bathroom.

Sinking down onto the lip of the tub, Jessica hugged the towel around her. But it was no substitute for his arms. It had neither living warmth nor strength—either of which might have helped soothe the soul-deep ache of disappointment she felt.

She knew it shouldn't matter so much. What was one date? Or one dress? Or one hairdo? But she'd so wanted things to be right. She hadn't realized how *much* she'd wanted that. But it was all ruined. The dress, the hairdo, her evening with Carter.

"All set," he said, returning to the bathroom. He'd taken off his jacket and tie and was rolling up his sleeves.

"What are you doing?" she asked, staring at the finely corded forearms that were emerging.

"Getting you dry."

"But I thought you phoned—"

"The ticket agent. I did. He's calling the tickets in to the box office. They'll be resold in a minute. We've got new ones for next week. Friday night this time. Okay?"

"But I thought—"

Hunkering down before her, he said softly, "You thought I was calling someone else to go with me, when I've been telling you all along that I don't want to go with anyone else." Leaning forward, he gave her a light kiss. "You don't listen to me, Jessica."

"But I've ruined your evening."

"Not my evening. Our evening. And it's not ruined. Just changed."

"What can we possibly do?" she cried. Absurdly her eyes were tearing again. He was being so kind and good and understanding, and she hadn't been able to come through at all on her end. "I'm a mess!"

Carter grinned. It was a dangerously attractive grin.

"Any more of a mess and I'd lay you right down on the floor and take you here. You really don't know how sexy you are, do you?"

"I'm not."

"You are." His grin faded as his eyes roamed her face. "You are, and I want you."

"Carter—"

"But that's not what we're going to do," he vowed as he rose to his full height. "We're going to dry you off and then go out for dinner."

She wanted that more than anything. "But I can't go anywhere! My dress is ruined!"

"Then we'll order in dinner and wait for your dress to dry. First, you'll have to take it off."

Her cheeks went pink. "I can't. I haven't anything to put on."

Raising a promising finger, he left her alone for as long as it took him to fetch a clean shirt from his closet. Back in the bathroom, he dropped it over the towel bar, stood her up, turned her and unwound the towel enough so that he could get at the back fastening of her dress.

"I can do that," she murmured, embarrassed.

"Indulge me." Gathering her hair to one side, he carefully released the hooks holding the turtleneck together. Her hair had protected that part of her dress from the rain, so the lime color there was more vivid. Carter wished he'd seen her before the storm, wished it with all his heart. He knew how sensitive Jessica was about her looks, but she'd felt good about herself then. He would have given anything to be able to share that good feeling with her.

Not that he didn't think she looked good now. He meant it when he said she looked sexy. He was aroused, and being so close to her, gently lowering her zipper, working it more slowly as the silk grew wetter wasn't doing anything to diminish that arousal. Nor was watching as each successive inch of ivory skin was exposed. He told himself to leave the bathroom, but the heat in his body was making his limbs lethargic. He knew he'd die if he couldn't touch that smooth, soft skin just once.

His fingertips were light, tentative on her spine between the spot where her zipper ended and her bra began. He heard her catch her breath, but the sound was as feminine as the rest of her and couldn't possibly have stopped him. Leaving his thumb on her spine, he flattened his fingers, moved them back and forth over butter-softness, spread them until they disappeared under the drape of her dress.

"Carter?" she whispered.

He answered by bending forward and putting his mouth where his fingers had been. Eyes closed, he reveled in the sweet smell of her skin and the velvet smoothness beneath his lips. He kissed her at one spot, slid to the next and kissed her again.

Each kiss sent a charge of sexual energy flowing through her. She clutched the towel to her front, but it was a mindless kind of thing, a need to hold tight to something. Carter's touch sent her soaring. Her embarrassment at his helping her undress was taking a backseat to the pleasure of his caress, which went on and on. His mouth moved over her skin with slow allure, his breath warming what his tongue moistened, his hand following to soothe it all.

Her knees began to feel weak, but she wasn't the only one with the problem. Carter lowered himself to the edge of the laundry hamper. Drawing her between his thighs, he slid both hands inside her dress. His fingers spanned her waist, caressing her while his mouth moved higher. His hands followed, skipping over the slim band of her bra to her shoulders, gently nudging the silk folds of her dress forward.

Jessica tried again, though she was unable to produce more than a whisper. "Maybe this isn't such a good idea."

His breath came against the back of her neck, his voice as gritty as hers was soft. "It's the best one I've had. Tell me it doesn't feel good."

The days when she might have told him that, in pride and self-defense, were gone. "It feels good."

"Then let me do it. Just a little longer."

A small sigh slipped from her lips as she tipped her head to the side to make room for his mouth below her ear. What he was doing did feel good. His thighs flanked hers, offering support, and the whispering kisses he was pressing to her skin were seeping deep, soothing away the horror of the rain. The warmth of his hands, his mouth, his breath made her feel soft and cherished. Eyes closed, she savored the feeling as, minute by minute, she floated higher.

With the slightest pressure, Carter turned her to face him. Her eyes opened slowly to focus on his. She didn't need her glasses to see the heat that simmered amid the darkness there.

He touched her cheek with the side of his thumb, then slid his fingers to the back of her neck and brought her head forward. His mouth was waiting for hers, hot and hungry, and it wasn't alone in that. Jessica's met it with an eagerness that might have shocked her once, but seemed the most natural thing now. Because something had happened to her. She would never know whether it was the words of praise and reassurance he'd spoken, or the gentle, adoring way he touched and kissed her. But she was tired of fighting. She was tired of doubting, of taking everything he said and trying to analyze his motives. If she was being shortsighted, she didn't care. She wanted to feel and enjoy, and if there would be hell to pay in humiliation later, so be it. The risk was worth it. She wanted the pleasure now.

So she followed his lead, opening her mouth wider when he did, varying its pressure from heavy to featherlight. There were times when their lips barely touched, when a kiss was little more than the exchange of breath or the touch of tongues, other times when the exchange was a more avid mating. She found one as exciting as the next, as stimulating in a breath-stopping, knee-shaking kind of way. When the knee-shaking worsened, she braced her forearms on his shoulders and anchored her fingers in his hair. She held him closer that way, wanted him closer still. And while the old Jessica was too much with her to say the words, the new Jessica spoke with the inviting arch of her body.

Carter heard her. His hands, which had been playing havoc over the gentle curves of her hips, came forward to frame her face. After giving her a final fierce kiss, he held her back.

For a time, he said nothing, just let himself drown with pleasure in the desire he saw in her eyes. If there'd ever been a different Jessica, he couldn't remember her. The only reality for him was the exquisitely sensual creature he now held between his legs.

Something else was between his legs, though, and it wasn't putting up with prolonged silence. Its heat and hardness were sending messages through the rest of his body that couldn't be ignored. His need to possess Jessica was greater than any need he'd ever known before.

His hands dropped from her face to her shoulders, then lower, to her breasts. He touched them gently, shaping his hand to their curve, brushing their hardened tips. Jessica gave a tiny sound of need and closed her eyes for a minute. When she opened them, Carter was smiling at her. "You're so beautiful," he murmured, and rewarded her for that with another kiss. This one was slower and more gentle, and by the time their lips parted, her breathing had quickened even more.

With her forearms on his shoulders and her forehead against his, she whispered, "I didn't know a kiss could do that."

"It's more than the kiss," Carter said in a low, slightly uneven voice. "It's my looking at you and touching you. And it's everything else that we haven't dared do. We've been thinking about it. At least, I have. I want to make love to you so badly, Jessica. Do you want that?"

It was a minute before she whispered, "Yes."

"Will you let me?"

"I'm frightened."

"You weren't frightened when I kissed you or when I touched your breasts."

"I was carried away."

His eyes met hers. "I'll carry you even further, if you let me. I want to do that. Will you let me?"

"I'm not good at lovemaking."

"Could've fooled me just now. I've never been kissed like that."

"You haven't?"

"You're a bombshell of innocence and raw desire. Do you have any idea how that combination turns a man on?"

She didn't, because she wasn't a man. But she knew that she was turned on herself. She could feel the pulsing deep inside her. "Will you tell me when I do things wrong?"

"You won't—"

"Will you tell me? I don't think I could bear it if we go through the whole thing and I think it's great, and then you tell me it wasn't so hot after all."

She'd spoken with neither accusation nor sarcasm,

which was why Carter was so struck by what she said. After a moment of intense self-reproach, he murmured, "I wouldn't do that to you. I know you still don't trust me, but I swear, I wouldn't do that."

"Just tell me. If it's no good, we can stop."

He put a finger to her mouth. "I'll tell you. I promise. But that goes two ways. If I'm doing something you don't like, or something that hurts, I want you to tell me, too. Will you?" His finger brushed her lips, moving lightly, back and forth. "Will you?" he whispered.

She gave a small nod.

"Then come give me a kiss. One more kiss before we hang this dress up to dry."

CHAPTER EIGHT

JESSICA KISSED HIM with every bit of the love that had been building inside her for days. She hadn't put the correct name to it then, nor did she now, but that didn't matter. Under desire's banner, she gave her mouth to him in an offering that was as selfless as the deepest form of love. And when his kiss took her places she'd never been, she gave in to the luxury of it. And the newness. She'd never known such pleasure in a man's arms. She'd dreamed it, but to live the fantasy was something else.

Her headiness was such at the end of the kiss that she didn't demur when he drew her dress down. Leaving the damp silk gathered around her waist, he put his mouth to the soft skin that swelled above the cup of her bra. She held tight to his neck as he shifted his attention from one breast to the other, and what his mouth abandoned, his hand discovered. In no time, he had released the catch of her bra and was feasting on her bare flesh.

Jessica tried to swallow the small sounds of satisfaction that surged from inside.

"Say it," Carter urged against her heated flesh. "How does it feel?"

"Good," she gasped. She bent her head over his. "So good."

"I'm not doing it too hard?"

"Oh, no. Not too hard."

"Do you want it harder?"

"A little."

Her nipple disappeared into his mouth, drawn in by the force of his sucking, and she couldn't have swallowed her satisfaction this time if she'd tried. She choked out his name and buried her face in his hair. He was a beautiful man, making her feel beautiful. She was on top of the world.

The feeling stayed with her for a time. Gently, between long, deep kisses that set her heart to reeling, Carter eased the dress over her hips and legs. Then, keeping her mouth occupied without a break, he lifted her in his arms and carried her into the bedroom. His body followed hers down to the spread, hands gliding over her, learning the shape of her belly, her hips, her thighs. He couldn't quite believe she was there, couldn't seem to touch enough of her at once. And everywhere he touched, she responded with a sigh or a cry or the arch of her body, which excited him all the more. His breathing was ragged when he finally pulled away and began to tug at the buttons of his shirt.

Jessica missed the warmth of his touch at once. Opening her eyes to see where he'd gone, she watched him toss the shirt aside and undo his belt. Her insides were at fever pitch, needing him back with her, but her mind, in the short minute that he was gone, started to clear. She couldn't tear her eyes from him. With his hair ruffled and falling over his forehead, his chest bare and massive, and his clothes following one another to the carpet, he was more man than she had ever seen in her life.

She couldn't help but be frightened. She was too inexperienced, for one thing, to take watching him in stride. For another, she'd lived too long thinking of herself as a sexless creature to completely escape self-doubt. Inching up against the headboard, she drew in her legs and folded her arms over her breasts.

"Oh, no, you don't," Carter said, lunging after her. "No,

you don't." The mattress bounced beneath his weight, but his fierceness gave way to a gentle grin as he took her wrists and flattened them on the pillow. "Please don't get cold feet on me now, honey. Not when we're so close, when I want you so badly."

"I—"

"No." His mouth covered hers, kissing her hungrily, but if he meant to drug her, he was the one who got high. His kiss gentled, grew lazier and, in that, more seductive. With a low groan, he pulled her away from the headboard, up to her knees and against his body. She cried out when her breasts first touched his chest, but he held her there, stroking her back in such a way that not only her breasts, but her belly moved against him.

He groaned again. "That feels...so...nice."

She thought so, too. The hair on his chest was an abrasive against her sensitive breasts, chafing them in the most stimulating of ways. His stomach was lean, firm against her, and his arousal was marked, a little frightening but very exciting. Coiling her arms around his neck, she held on for dear life as the force of desire spiraled inside her.

"You were made for me," he whispered brokenly. "I swear you were made for me, Jessica. We fit together so well."

The words were nearly as pleasurable as the feel of his hard body against hers. His approval meant so much to her. She desperately wanted to please him.

"I'm not too thin?"

He ran a large hand over her bottom and hips. "Oh, no. You've got curves in all the right places."

"You didn't think so once."

"I was a jackass then. Besides, I didn't see you like this then." He dipped his fingers under the waistband of her panty hose, then withdrew them in the next breath and gently lay her back on the bed. His eyes were dark and avid as they studied her breasts, his hand worshiping as it cupped a rounded curve. Then he met her gaze. "I'm going to take off the rest. I want to see all of you."

She didn't speak over the thudding of her heart, but she gave a short nod. Though she'd never have believed it possible, she wanted him to see her. She wanted him to touch her. She wanted him to make love to her. She was living the fantasy, and in the fantasy, she was a beautiful, desirable woman. Her insides were a dark, aching vacuum needing to be filled in the way that only he could.

She lifted her hips to help him. Her panties slipped down her legs along with the nylons, and all the while she watched his eyes. They followed the stockings off, then retraced the route over her calves and thighs to the dark triangle at the notch of her thighs. There they lingered, growing darker and more smoky.

Lifting his gaze to hers, he whispered in awe, "You are so very, very lovely."

At that moment, she believed him, because that was part of the fantasy. She was trembling. Her bare breasts rose and fell with each shallow breath she took, and the knot of desire grew tighter between her legs. She wanted him to touch her, to ease the ache, but she couldn't get herself to say the words.

Carter didn't need them. He had never seen such raw desire in a woman's eyes, had never known how potent such a look could be. It was pushing him higher by the minute, making him shake beneath its force. His body clamored for release. He wasn't sure how much longer he could hold back. But he wanted it to be good, so good for her.

"So very lovely," he repeated in a throaty whisper. Tearing his eyes from hers, he lowered his gaze to her body. With an exquisitely light touch, he brushed the dark curls at the base of her belly. When she made a small sound, he looked back up in time to catch her closing her eyes, rolling her head to the side, pressing a fist to her mouth. He touched her again, more daringly this time. She made another small sound and, twisting her body in a subtly seductive way, arched up off the bed.

It was his turn to moan. He was stunned by the un-tutored sensuality he saw, couldn't quite believe that a woman with Jessica's potential for loving had lived such a chaste life. But she had. He had no doubts about it, particularly when she opened her eyes and seemed as stunned as he.

"How do you feel?" he whispered. He stroked her gently, delved more deeply into her folds with each stroke.

Raising her hands to the pillow, she curled them into fists and swallowed hard. "I need you," she whispered frantically. "Please."

Between the look in her eyes, the sound of her whisper and the intense arousal to which her straining body attested, Carter was pushed to the wall. His blood was rushing hotly through his veins. He knew he couldn't wait much longer to take the possession his throbbing body demanded.

He paused only to shuck his briefs, before coming over her. "Jessica?" Unfurling her fists, he wove his fingers through hers.

She tightened the grip. Her body rose to meet his. "Please, Carter."

Rational thought was becoming harder by the second. He fought to preserve those last threads. "Are you pro-tected, honey? Are you using something?" When she gave a frustrated cry and lifted her head to open her mouth against his jaw, he whispered, "Help me. Tell me. Should I use something?"

"No," she cried, a tight, high-pitched wail. "I want a baby."

Swearing softly—and not trusting himself to stay where he was a minute longer, because the idea of her having his baby sent a shock wave of pleasure through him—he rolled off her and crossed the room to the dresser.

"Carter," she wailed.

"It's okay, honey. Hold on a second."

"I need you."

"I know. I'll be right there." A minute later, he was back, sitting on the edge of the bed to apply a condom. A minute after that, he was back over her, his hands covering hers, his mouth capturing hers. While he took her lips with a rabid hunger, he found his place between her thighs. Slowly and gently in contrast to his ravishment of her mouth, he entered her.

Her name was a low, growling sound surging from his throat, a sound of pleasure and relief when her tightness surrounded him. He squeezed his eyes shut in a battle against coming right then, but she wasn't helping his cause. She lifted her thighs higher around his in an instinctive move to deepen his penetration.

He looked down at her. Her face was flushed, lips moist and parted, eyes half-lidded and languorous. Her hair was wild, the dark waves fanning out over the slate-gray spread.

In an attempt to slow things down, he anchored her hips to the bed with the weight of his own and held himself still inside her. "Am I hurting you?" he whispered.

"Oh, no," she whispered back. "Does it feel okay?"

"More okay than it's ever felt," he answered. His words were hoarse, his breathing ragged. "You're so small and tight. Soft. Feminine. You have an incredible body. Incredible body. Are you sure I'm not hurting you?"

She managed a nod, then closed her eyes because even without his moving, the pressure inside her was building. "Please," she breathed.

"Please what?"

"Do something. I want…I need…"

He withdrew nearly all the way, returned to bury himself to the hilt. In reward for the movement, she cried out, then caught in the same breath and strained upward. "Carter!"

"That's it, honey," he said, and began to move in earnest. "Do you feel me?"

"Yes."

"That what I want." Catching her mouth, he kissed her while the motion of his hips quickened. He pulled out and thrust in, filling her more and more, seeming to defy the laws of space. A fine sheen of sweat covered his body, blending with hers where their skin touched.

He had never known such pleasure, had never dreamed that such a physical act could touch his heart so deeply. But that was what was happening, and the heart touching was an aphrodisiac he couldn't fight. Long before he was ready to have the pleasure end, his body betrayed him by erupting into a long, powerful climax. Only when he was on the downside of that did he feel the spasms that were quaking inside Jessica.

Forcing his eyes open, he watched her face while the last of her orgasm shook her. With her head thrown back on the pillow, her eyes closed, her lips lightly parted, she was the most erotic being he'd ever seen in his life.

Her breathing was barely beginning to calm when his arms gave out. Collapsing over her, he lay with his head by hers for several minutes before rolling to the side and gathering her close. Then he watched her until she opened her eyes and looked up at him.

He smiled. "Hi."

"Hi," she said, shyly and still a bit breathlessly.

"You okay?"

She nodded, but when he expected her to look away, she didn't. Her eyes were increasingly large, expectant, trepidant.

"Having second thoughts?"

"One or two."

"Don't. Do you have any idea how good that was?" When she hesitated, then gave a short shake of her head against his arm, he brushed her eyebrow with a fingertip. "It was spectacular."

Still she hesitated. "Was it?"

"Yes." His smile faded. "You don't believe me."

She didn't say a thing for a minute, then spoke in a small voice, "I want to."

"But?"

She didn't answer at all this time, simply closed her eyes and lay her cheek on his chest. Carter would have prodded if he wasn't so enjoying lying quietly with her. But her body was warm, delicate, kittenish by his. Gently he drew her closer.

Her voice was flat, sudden in the silence. "Tom used to say things after it was over. He'd tell me how lacking I was."

Carter felt a chill, part anger, part disbelief, in the pit of his stomach. "Didn't he come?"

"Yes, but that didn't matter. He told me I wasn't much better than a sack of potatoes. I suppose I wasn't. I used to just lie there. I didn't want to touch him."

Carter remembered the way her hands had tightened around his, the way she'd arched to touch him with her body when he had restrained her hands, the way she brought her knees up to deepen his surge. She had been electric.

"That was Tom's fault," he said in a harsh voice. "It was his fault that he couldn't turn you on."

"I always felt inadequate."

"You shouldn't have. You're exquisite." Cupping her face in his hand, he kissed her lightly. "I have no complaints about what we did, except that I wanted it to last longer. But that was my fault. I couldn't hold back. I've been wanting you for days. I've been imagining incredible things, and to find out that the imagining wasn't half as incredible as the real thing—" He kissed her again, more deeply this time. His tongue lingered inside her mouth, withdrawing more slowly, reluctantly leaving her lips. "Jessica," he said in a shaky whisper and clutched her convulsively. But the feel of her body did nothing to dampen his reawakening desire.

Moaning, he released her and lay back on the bed.

Jessica came up on an elbow to eye him cautiously. "What's wrong?" she whispered.

He covered his eyes with his arm. "I want you again."

She looked at that arm, looked at the silky tufts of dark hair beneath it, looked at his chest, which was hairy in thatches, then his lean middle. By the time her eyes had lowered over his belly to the root of his passion, she was feeling tingly enough herself not to be as shocked by his erection as she might have been.

Without forethought, she touched his chest. He jumped, but when she started to snatch her hand away, he caught it, placed it back on his chest and laughed. "It's like lightning when you touch me. I wasn't prepared. That's all." Her hand was lying flat. "Go on. Touch. I like it."

Very slowly she inched her hand over the broad expanse of hair-spattered flesh and muscle. She felt those muscles tighten, felt his heartbeat accelerate, knew that her own was doing the same, but she wasn't about to stop.

"I never dreamed…" Her fingertips lightly skimmed the dark, flat nipples that were already pebble hard.

"Never dreamed what?" he asked in a strained voice.

"That I'd…that we'd…you know."

"That we'd make love?"

"Mmm." Her thumb made a slow turn around his belly button.

Clapping a hand over hers, he pinned it to his stomach. When she looked up at him in surprise, his dark eyes smoldered. "Once before you touched me. Remember? By the duck pond?" She nodded. "I was wearing jeans then, and more than anything I wanted to unzip them and put your hand inside." He swallowed, then released her hand. "Touch me, Jessica?"

She looked from his eyes to his hardness and back.

"Touch me," he repeated in a beseechful whisper. The same beseechfulness was reflected in his eyes. More than anything else, that was what gave her courage.

Slowly her hand crept the short distance down a narrow line of hair to its flaring, finally to the part of him that stood, waiting straight and tall. She touched a tentative finger to him, surprised by the heat and the silkiness she found. Gradually her other fingers followed suit.

Taking in a ragged breath, Carter pushed himself into her hand. He wanted to watch her, wanted to see the expression on her face while she stroked him, but the agony of her touch was too much. She seemed to know just what to do and how fast. Closing his eyes, he savored her ministrations as long as he could before reaching down and tugging her back up. Then, when his mouth seized hers, his hands went to work.

He touched her everywhere, taking the time to explore that which he hadn't been able to do before. Where his hands left, his mouth took over. It wasn't long before Jessica was out of her mind with need, before he was, too.

Incredibly they soared higher this time. When it was done, their bodies were slick with sweat, their hearts were hammering mercilessly, their limbs were drained of energy.

They dozed off, awakening a short time later to find the sun down and the room dark. Carter left her side only long enough to light a low lamp on the dresser and draw the bedspread back. Then he took her with him between the sheets, settled her against him and faced the fact that he wanted her there forever.

"I love you," he whispered against her forehead.

Her eyes shot to his, held them for a minute before lowering. "No." She couldn't take the fantasy that far. "You're not thinking straight."

"I am. I've never said those words to a woman. I've never felt this way, felt this need to hold and protect and be with all the time. I've never wanted to wake up next to a woman, but I want it now. I don't like the idea of your going back home."

"I have to. It's where I belong."

His arm tightened. "You belong with me." When she remained silent, he said, "Do you believe in fate?"

"Predestination?"

"Mmm."

She didn't have to think about it long. "No. I believe that we get what we do. God helps those who help themselves."

But Carter disagreed. "If that were true, I'd never have returned home from Vietnam."

His words hovered in the air while Jessica's heart skipped a beat. Sliding her head back on his arm, she looked up at him. He was regarding her warily. "What do you mean?"

"I deserved to die. I hadn't done a decent thing in my life. I deserved to die."

"No one deserves to die in war."

"But someone always does." He looked away. "Good men died there. I saw them, Jessica. I saw them take hits. Some died fast, some slow, and with each one who went, I felt more like a snake."

"But you were fighting right alongside them," she argued.

"Yes, but they were good men. They were intelligent guys, guys with degrees and families and futures. A lot of them were rich—maybe not rich, but comfortable, and here I was walking around with a chip on my shoulder because I didn't have what they did. So they died, and I lived." He made a harsh sound, half laugh, half grunt. "Which says something, I guess, about the important things in life."

Jessica was beginning to understand. "That was what turned you around."

"Yes." His eyes held the fire of vehemence when they met hers. "Someone was watching over me there. Someone didn't let me die. Someone was telling me that I had things to do in life. I knew other guys who survived, but me, I never got the smallest scratch. That was fate. So was your asking me to work on Crosslyn Rise."

"Not fate. Gordon."

"But the setting was ripe for it." He turned on his side to look her in the eye. "Don't you see? You weren't married. You had been, but you were divorced. I never married. Never even had the inclination until I met you. Never wanted to think of having babies until I met you." Hearing the catch of her breath, he lowered his voice. "You do want them."

Her cheeks went red at the memory of what she'd cried out in the heat of passion.

He stroked that flush with his thumb. "I'll give you babies, Jessica. I couldn't take the chance before, because I wasn't sure you meant it. But you do, don't you?"

Silently she nodded.

"And until now the chances of it seemed remote, so you pushed it to the back of your mind. Then I said something about having children to leave the Rise to—"

"I won't be able to do that anyway. The Rise as I knew it will be gone."

"As you knew it. But all that's good about the Rise—its beauty and dignity, strength and stability—is inside you. You'll give that to your children. You'll make a wonderful mother."

Tears came to her eyes. What he was saying was too good to be true. *He* was too good to be true.

It was the aftermath of lovemaking, she decided. She didn't believe for a minute that he'd really want to marry her. Give him a day or two and he'd realize how foolish his talk was.

"I love you," he whispered, and she didn't argue. He kissed her once, then a second time, but the stirring he felt wasn't so much in his groin as in the region of his heart. He wanted to take care of her, to give her things, to do for her. She was a gentle woman, a woman to be loved and protected. He would do that if she let him.

Rubbing her love-swollen lips with the tip of his finger, he said, "You must be hungry."

"A little."

"If I order up pizza, will you have some?"

"Sure."

He kissed her a final time, then rolled away from her and out of bed. She watched him cross the room to the closet. His hips were narrow, his buttocks tight, the backs of his thighs lean and muscled, and if she'd thought that his walk was seductive when he was dressed, naked it was something else. When he put on a short terry-cloth robe, the memory of his nudity remained. When he returned to her, carrying the shirt from the bathroom, she felt shy.

"Uh-uh," he chided when she averted her eyes. "None of that." He helped her on with the shirt. "I've seen everything. I *love* everything."

"I'm not used to this, I guess," she murmured, fumbling with the buttons.

He could buy that, and in truth, he liked her shyness. It made the emergence of her innate sensuality that much more of a gift. "I'll give you time," he said softly, and led her out of the bedroom.

He was going to have to give her plenty of that, she mused a short time later. They sat on stools at the kitchen counter, eating the pizza that had just been delivered. Though it was a mundane act, she'd never done anything so cataclysmic. She couldn't believe that she was sitting there with Carter Malloy, that she was wearing nothing under his shirt, that she'd worn even less not long before.

Carter Malloy. It boggled her mind. *Carter Malloy.*

"What is it?" he asked with a perplexed half smile.

She blushed. "Nothing."

"Tell me."

Tipping her head to the side, she studied a piece of pizza crust. "I'm very…surprised that I'm here."

"You shouldn't be. We've been building toward this for a while."

He was right, but she wasn't thinking of the recent past. "I'm thinking farther back. I really hated you when I was little." She dared him a look and was struck at once by his handsomeness. "You're so different. You look so different. You *act* so different. It's hard to believe that a person can change so much."

"We all have to grow up."

"Some people don't. Some people just get bigger. You've really changed." Studying him, she was lured on by the openness of his features. "What about before Vietnam? I can understand how your experience there could shape your future, but what about your past? Why were you the way you were? It couldn't have been the money factor alone. What was it all about?"

Thoughtfully pursing his lips, Carter looked down at his hands. His mouth relaxed, but he didn't look up. "The money thing was a scapegoat. It was a convenient one, maybe even a valid one on some levels. Since my parents worked at Crosslyn Rise, we lived in town, and that town happens to be one of the wealthiest in the state. So I went to school with kids who had ten times more than me. From the very start, I was different. They all knew each other from kindergarten. I was a social outcast from the beginning, and it was a self-perpetuating thing. I was never easy to get along with."

"But why? If you were still that way, I'd say that it was a genetic thing that you couldn't control. But you're easy enough to get along with now, and you don't seem to be suffering doing it. So if it wasn't genetic, it had to come from outside you. Some of it may have come from antagonism in school, but if you were that way when you first enrolled, it had to come from your family. That's what I don't understand. Annie and Michael were always wonderful, easygoing people."

"You weren't their son," Carter said with a sharpness reminiscent of a similar comment he'd made once before.

Not for a minute did Jessica feel that the sharpness was directed at her. He was thinking back to his childhood. She could see the discomfort in his eyes. "What was it like?" she asked, needing to understand him as intimately as possible.

"Stifling."

"With Annie and Michael?" she asked in disbelief.

"They loved me to bits," he explained. "I was their pride and joy, their hope for the future. I was going to be everything they weren't, and from the earliest they told me so. I'm not sure that I understood what it all meant at the time, but when I was slow doing things, they pushed me. I didn't like being pushed—I still don't, so maybe that's a biological trait after all. I stayed in the terrible-twos stage for lots of years, and by that time, a pattern had been set. My parents were always on top of me, so I did whatever I could to thwart them. I think I was hoping that at some point they'd just give up on me."

"But they never did."

"No," he said quietly. "They never did. They were always loyal and supportive." He looked at her then. "Do you know how much pressure that can put on a person?"

Jessica was beginning to see it. "They kept hoping for the best and you kept disappointing them."

"By the time I was a teenager, I had a reputation of being tough. That hurt my parents, too. People would look at them with pity, wondering how they ever managed to have a son like me."

She remembered thinking the same thing herself, and not too long before. "They are such quiet, gentle people."

Again Carter looked away, pursing his lips. He felt guilty criticizing his parents, yet he wanted Jessica to know the truth, at least as he saw it. "Too quiet and gentle. Especially my dad."

"You would have liked him to be stronger with you?"

"With me, with *anyone*. He wasn't strong, period."

It occurred to Jessica that she'd never thought one way

or another about Michael Malloy's strength. "In what sense?"

"As a man. My mother ran the house. She did everything. I can't remember a time when Dad doted on her, when he stood up for her, when he bought her a gift. The only thing he ever did was the gardening."

"Do you think she resented that?"

"Not really. I think it suited her purposes. She liked being the one in control." He took a minute to consider what he'd said. "So maybe when I use the word *stifling* I should be using the word *controlling*. In her own quiet way, my mother was the most controlling woman I've ever met. That was what I spent my childhood rebelling against—that, and the fact that my father never once opened his mouth to complain when, in her own gentle way, she ran roughshod over him."

He grew quiet, then looked down. "Lousy of me to be bad-mouthing them, when I treated them so poorly, huh?"

"You're not bad-mouthing them. You're just explaining what you felt when you were growing up."

He met her gaze. "Does it make any sense?"

"I think so. I always thought of Annie as, yes, gentle and quiet, but also efficient. Very efficient. She definitely took control of things in our house. I can understand how 'taking control' could become 'controlling' in her own house. And Michael was always gentle and quiet... just... gentle and quiet. That was what I liked about him. He was always pleasant, always smiled. For me, that was a treat."

"It used to drive me wild. I'd do anything just to rile him."

"Did you manage?"

Carter smirked. "Not often. And he's still like that. Still quiet and gentle. I doubt he'll ever change."

Jessica was relieved to hear the fondness in his voice. "You've accepted him, then?"

"Of course. He's my father."

"And you're close to him now?"

"Close? I don't know, close. We talk regularly on the phone, but for every five minutes Dad's on, Mom's on for ten. I suppose it's just as well. They like to hear what I'm doing, but I'm not sure they appreciate the details." He gave an ironic smile. "I've finally made it, just like they wanted me to, but that means my world is very different from theirs."

"Are they happy?"

"In Florida? Yes."

"For you?"

"Very." His smile was sheepish this time. "Of course, they don't know why I have a partner, since I can do so much better by myself. And they don't know why I'm not married."

Jessica knew they'd be pleased if Carter ever told them he loved her, but she prayed he wouldn't do that. To tie their hopes to something that would never go anywhere was a waste. Even if Carter did believe that he loved her, he'd see the truth once he got back to his normal, everyday life. The fewer people who knew of the night he'd spent playing at being in love, the better.

JESSICA RETURNED TO Crosslyn Rise on Friday, soon after Carter left for work. She wanted to immerse herself in her own world, to push the events of Thursday night to the back of her mind.

That was easier said than done, because after dinner, they'd gone back to bed. Time and again during the night, they'd made love, and while Jessica never once initiated the passion, she took an increasingly aggressive part in it. That gave her more to think about than ever.

She seemed to bloom in Carter's arms. Looking back on some of the things she'd done, she shocked herself. She, who had never hungered for another man, had lusted for his body, and she couldn't even say that he taught her what to do. Impulses had just…come. She had wanted to touch him, so she had. She had wanted to taste him, so she had.

And he hadn't complained. Every so often, when she'd caught herself doing something daring, she'd paused, but in each case he had urged her on. In each case his pleasure had been obvious, which made her feel all the freer.

Freer. Free. Yes, she had felt that, and it was the strangest thing of all. Making love to Carter, even well after that first pent-up desire had been slaked, was a relief. With each successive peak she reached, she felt more relaxed. It was almost as if she'd done just what he had once accused her of doing—spent years and years denying her instincts, so that now she felt the sheer joy of letting them out.

She fought the idea of that. Once discovered, the passion in her wouldn't be as easily tucked away again—which was just fine, as long as Carter stayed with her. But she couldn't count on that happening. In the broad light of a Crosslyn Rise day, she had too many strikes against her.

She was plain. She was boring. She was broke.

Carter was just the opposite. He was on his way up in the world, and he would make it. She knew that now. She also knew that he didn't need someone like her weighing him down.

That was one of the reasons why, when he called at four to say that he was leaving the office and would be at Crosslyn Rise within the hour, she told him not to come.

CHAPTER NINE

"WHY NOT?" CARTER asked, concerned. "Is something wrong?"

"I just think that I ought to get some work done."

"You've had all day to do that."

"Well, I slept for some of the day, and I didn't concentrate well for the rest."

He didn't have to ask why on either score. "So give it up for today. You won't get much done anyway."

"I'd like to try."

"Try tomorrow. We agreed on dinner tonight."

"I know, but I'm not very hungry."

"Not now. But it'll be an hour before I get there, another hour before we get to a restaurant and get served." He paused, then scolded, "You're avoiding the issue. Come on, Jessica. Spit it out."

"There's nothing to spit out. I'd just rather stay home tonight."

"Okay. We'll stay home."

He was being difficult, she knew, and that frustrated her. "I'd rather be alone."

"You would not. You're just scared because everything that happened last night was sudden and strong."

"I'm not scared," she protested. "But I need time, Carter."

"Like hell you do," he replied, and slammed down the phone.

FORTY MINUTES LATER, he careened up the driveway and slammed on his brakes. He was out of the car in a flash, taking the steps two at a time, and he might well have pounded the door down had not Jessica been right there to haul it open after his first fierce knock.

"You have no right to race out here this way," she cried, taking the offensive before he could. She was wearing a shirt and jeans, looking as plain as she could, and as angry. "This is my house, my life. If I say that I want to spend my evening alone, that's what I want to do!"

Hands cocked low on his hips, Carter held his ground. "Why? Give me one good reason why you want to be alone."

"I don't have to give you a reason. All I have to say is yes or no."

"This morning you said yes. What happened between now and then to make you change your mind?"

"Nothing."

"What happened, Jessica?"

"Nothing!"

His brown eyes narrowed. "You started thinking, didn't you? You started thinking about all the reasons why I can't possibly feel the way I say I do about you. You came back to this place, and suddenly last night was an aberration. A fluke. A lie. Well, it wasn't, Jessica. It isn't. I loved you then, and I love you now, and you can say whatever stupid things you want, but you can't change my mind."

"Then you're the fool, because I don't want to get involved."

"Baloney." His eyes bore into hers, alive with a fire that was only barely tempered in his voice. "You want a husband, and you want kids. You can pretend that you don't, and maybe it used to work, but it won't work now. Because, whether you like it or not, you *are* involved. You can't forget what happened last night."

"What an arrogant thing to say!"

"Not arrogant. Realistic, and mutual. I can't forget it, either. I want to do it again."

"You're a sex fiend."

His voice grew tighter, reflecting the strain on his patience. "Sex had nothing to do with what we did. That was lovemaking, Jessica. We *made* love, because we *are* in love. If you don't want to admit it, fine. I can wait. But I'm going to say it whenever I want. I love you."

"You do not," she scoffed, and pushed up her glasses.

"I love you."

"You may think you do, but give yourself a little time, and you'll come to your senses. You don't love me. You can't possibly love me."

"Why not?" He took a step toward her, and his voice was as ominous as his look. "Because you're not pretty? Because you lie like a sack of potatoes in my bed? Because you're a bookworm?"

"It's Crosslyn Rise that you love."

He eyed her as though she were crazy. "Crosslyn Rise is some land and a house. It's not warm flesh and blood like me."

"But you love it, you associate me with it, hence you think you love me."

"Brilliant deduction, Professor, but wrong. You're losing Crosslyn Rise. There's no reason why I would align myself with you if the Rise is what I want."

She took a different tack. "Then it's the money. If this project goes through, you'll be making some money. So you're confusing the issues. You feel good about the money, so you feel good about me."

"I don't want the money that bad," he said with a curt laugh. "If you were a loser, no amount of money would lure me into your bed."

"What a crass thing to say!"

"It's the truth. And it should say something about my feelings for you. We did it last night more times than I've ever done it in a single night before. My muscles are killing me. Still I want more. Every time I think of you I get hard."

She pressed her hands to her ears, because his words alone could excite her. Only when his mouth remained still did she lower her hands and say very slowly, "Revenge is a potent aphrodisiac."

"*Revenge.* What in the hell are you talking about?"

She tipped up her chin. "This is the ultimate revenge, isn't it? For all those years when I had everything you wanted?"

"Are you kidding?" he asked, and for the first time there was an element of pain in his voice. "Didn't you hear a word I said last night? Didn't any of it sink in—any of the stuff about Vietnam or my parents? I've never told anyone else about those things. Was it wasted on you?"

"Of course not."

"But I didn't get through. You wanted to know what caused me to change over the years, and I told you, but I didn't get through." He paused, and the pain was replaced by a sudden dawning. "Or was that what frightened you most, because for the first time you could believe that the change was for real?" He took a step closer. "Is that it? For the first time you had to admit that I might, just might be the kind of guy you'd want to spend the rest of your life with, and that scares you." He took another step forward. Jessica matched it with one back. "Huh?" he goaded. "Is that it?"

"No. I don't want to spend the rest of my life with *any* man."

"Because of your ex-husband? Because of what he did?"

She took another step back as he advanced. "Tom and I are divorced. What he did is over and done."

"It still haunts you."

"Not enough to shape my future." She kept moving back.

"But you don't trust me. That's the crux of the problem. You don't trust that I'm on the level and that I won't hurt you the way that selfish bastard did. Damn it, Jessica, how can I prove to you that I mean what I say if you won't see me?"

"I don't want you to prove anything," she said, but her heels had reached the first riser of the stairs. When he kept coming, she sat down on the steps.

"Okay." He put one hand flat on the tread by her hip. "I'll admit things have happened quickly. If you want time, I'll give you time. I won't rush you into anything, especially something as important as marriage." He put his other hand by her other hip. His voice lowered. His eyes dropped to her mouth. "But I won't stand off in the distance or out of sight, either. I can't do that. I need to see you. I need to be with you."

Jessica wanted to argue, but she was having trouble thinking with him so close. She could see the details of the five-o'clock shadow that he hadn't had time to shave, could feel the heat of his large body, could smell the musky scent that was his alone. He looked sincere. He sounded sincere. She wanted to believe him…so… badly.

His mouth touched hers, and she was lost. Memory of the night before returned in a storm of sensation so strong that she was swept up in it and whirled around. She had to wrap her arms around his waist to keep herself anchored to something real, and then it wasn't memory that entranced her, but the sensual devouring of his mouth.

Over and over he kissed her, dueling with her lips for

supremacy in much the same way they'd argued, though neither seemed to care who won, and, in fact, both did. When her glasses fogged up, he took them off and set them aside. Pressing her back on the stairs, he touched her breasts, then slid his fingers between the buttons of her shirt to reach bareness. When that failed to satisfy his craving, he unbuttoned the shirt and unhooked her bra, but no sooner had he exposed her flesh than she brushed the back of her hand over the rigid display on the front of his slacks.

"Oh, baby," he said, "come here." Slipping a large hand under her bottom, he lowered himself and pressed her close. In the next breath, he was kissing her again, and in the next, tugging at the fastening of her jeans.

"Carter," she whispered, breathless. "What—"

"I need you," he gasped, pushing at her zipper.

"Now?"

"Oh, yeah."

"Here?"

"Anywhere. Help me, Jess." He'd turned his attention to his belt, which was giving him trouble. Jessica did what she could, but her hands were shaky and kept tangling with his, and when it came to his zipper, his erection made things even more difficult. After a futile pass or two, the most important thing seemed to be freeing her own legs from their bonds.

She didn't quite make it. Her jeans were barely below her knees when Carter pressed her back to the steps. With a single strong stroke, he was inside her, welcomed there hotly and moistly. Then the movement of his hips drove her wild, and she didn't care that they were in the front hall, that they were half-dressed, that the ghosts of Crosslyn Rise were watching, turning pink through their pallor. All she cared about was sharing a precious oneness with Carter.

THAT WEEKEND WAS the happiest Jessica had ever spent, because Carter didn't leave her for long. He made love to her freely, wherever and whenever the mood hit. And wherever or whenever that was, she was ready. Hard as it was to believe, the more they made love, the more she wanted him.

As long as he was with her, she was fine. As long as he was with her, she believed his words of love, believed that his ardor could be sustained over the years and years he claimed, believed that his head would never be turned by another woman.

When he left her on Monday morning to go to work, though, she thought of him at the office, in restaurants, with clients, and she worried. She went to work, herself, and she was the quiet, studious woman she'd always been.

Maybe if people had looked at her strangely she would have felt somehow different. But she received the same smiles and nods from colleagues she passed. No one looked twice, as had happened when she'd dressed up the Thursday before. No one seemed remotely aware of the kind of weekend she'd spent.

She didn't know what she expected. Aside from a bundle of tender muscles, she was no different physically than she'd always been. But no one knew about the muscles. No one knew about Carter Malloy. No one knew about the library sofa, the parlor rug or the attic cot.

So she saw herself as the others saw her, and everything that was risky and frightening about her affair with Carter was magnified.

Until she saw him that night. Then the doubts seemed to waft into the background and pop like nothing more weighty than a soap bubble, and she came to life in his arms.

The pattern repeated itself over the next few weeks.

Her days were filled with doubts, her nights with delight. Graduation came and went, and the summer session began, but for the first time in her life, there was a finite end to a day's work. That end came when Carter arrived. He teased her about it, even urged her to do some reading or class preparation on those occasions when he had brought work of his own with him to do, but she couldn't concentrate when he was with her. She would sit with a book while he worked, but her eyes barely touched the page, and her mind took in nothing at all but how he looked, what he was doing, what they'd done together minutes, hours or days before.

She was in love. She admitted it, though not to him. Somehow, saying the words was the most intense form of self-exposure, and though one part of her wished she had the courage because she knew how much he wanted to hear it, she wasn't that brave. She felt as though she were driving on a narrow mountain path where one moment's inattention could tip her over the edge. She wanted to be prepared when Carter's interest waned. She wanted to have a remnant of pride left to salvage.

HIS INTEREST WANED neither in her nor in Crosslyn Rise. Sketch after sketch he made, some differing from the others in only the most minor of features, but he wanted them to be right. He and Jessica had dinner one night with Nina Stone to get her opinion on the needs of the local real estate market; as a result of that meeting, they decided to offer six different floor plans, two each in two-bedroom, three-bedroom and four-bedroom configurations.

Also as a result of that meeting, Jessica learned that Carter wasn't interested in Nina Stone. Nina was interested in him; her eyes rarely left his handsome face, and when she accompanied Jessica to the ladies' room, she made her feelings clear.

"He's quite a piece of man. If things cool between you two, will you tell me?"

Jessica was surprised that Nina had guessed there was something beyond a working relationship between her and Carter. "How did you know?" she asked, not quite daring to look Nina in the eye.

"The vibes between you. They're hot. Besides, I've been sending him every come-hither look I know, and he hasn't caught a one. Honey, he's smitten."

"Nah," Jessica said, pleased in spite of herself. "We're just getting to know each other again." Far better, she knew, to minimize things, so that it wouldn't be as humiliating if the relationship ended.

Still there was no sign of that happening. On the few occasions that Carter mentioned Nina after their meeting, it was with regard to the project and with no more than a professional interest.

"Didn't you think she was pretty?" Jessica finally asked.

"Nina?" He shrugged. "She's pretty. Not soft and gentle like you, though, or half as interesting."

As though to prove his point, he spent hours talking with her. They discussed the economy, the politics in Jessica's department, the merits of a book that he'd read and had her read. He was genuinely curious about what she was thinking, was often relieved to find that she wasn't lost on some esoteric wavelength where he couldn't possibly join her.

When it came to Crosslyn Rise, he took few steps without having her by his side, considered few ideas without trying them out on her first. Though her feedback wasn't professional from an architectural standpoint, it was down-to-earth. When she didn't like something, she usually had good reason. He listened to her, and while he didn't always agree, he yielded as many times as not.

Their personal, vested interests balanced each other out; when he was too involved in the design to think of practicality, she reminded him of it, and when she was too involved in the spirit of Crosslyn Rise to see the necessity of a particular architectural feature, he pointed it out.

By the middle of July, there was a set of plans to show Gordon. As enthusiastic about them as Carter was, Jessica set up the meeting. Then the two of them stood side by side, closely watching for Gordon's reaction as he looked over the drawings.

He liked them, though after he'd said, "You two make a good team," for the third time in ten minutes, Jessica was wondering what particular message he was trying to get across. She had tried not to look at Carter, and when he caught her hand behind her skirt and drew it to the small of his back, she was sure Gordon couldn't see.

Possibly he had sensed the same vibes Nina had, though she hadn't thought Gordon the type to sense vibes, at least not of that kind. She finally decided that it was the little things that gave them away—the light lingering of Carter's hand on her back when they first arrived, the way he attributed her ideas to her rather than taking credit for them himself, the mere fact that they weren't fighting.

The last made the most sense of all. Jessica remembered her reaction when Gordon had first mentioned Carter's name. She thought back to that day, to her horror and the hurt in those memories. At some point along the way, the hurt had faded, she realized. She had superimposed fondness and understanding on the Carter Malloy who had been so angry with the world and himself, and doing that took the sting off the things he'd once said. Not that she dwelt on those memories. He had given her new ones, ones that were lovely from start to finish.

"Jess?" Carter's low, gentle voice came through her reverie. She looked up in surprise, smiled a little shamefacedly when she realized her distraction. He motioned to the nearby chair. Blushing, she sank into it.

"Everything all right, Jessica?" Gordon asked.

"Fine. Just fine."

"You know these highbrow types," Carter teased, smiling indulgently. "Always dreaming about one thing or another."

Her cheeks went even redder, but she latched on to the excuse as a convenient out. "Did I miss anything?"

"Only Gordon's approval. I have to polish up the drawings some, but he agrees that we're ready to move ahead."

Jessica's eyes flew to Gordon. "Getting the investors together?"

Gordon nodded and opened a folder that had been lying on the corner of his desk. He removed two stapled parcels, handed one to each of them, then took up his own. "I've jumped the gun, I guess, but I figured that I'd be doing this work anyway, so it wouldn't matter. These are the names and profiles of possible investors, along with a list of their general assets and the approximate contribution they might be counted on to make. You can skip through page one—that's you, Jessica—and page two— that's you, Carter. The next three are William Nolan, Benjamin Heavey and Zachary Gould. You know Ben, don't you, Carter?"

"Sure do. I worked with him two years ago on a development in North Andover." To Jessica, he said, "He's been involved in real-estate development for fifteen years. A conservative guy, but straight. He's selective with his investments, but once he's in, he's in." He looked at Gordon. "Is he interested?"

"When I mentioned your name, he was. I didn't want to tell him much else until the plans were finalized, but he just cashed in on a small shopping mall in Lynn, so he has funds available. Same with Nolan and Gould."

Jessica was trying to read as quickly as possible, but she'd barely made it halfway down the first sheet on Benjamin Heavey when Gordon mentioned the others. "Nolan and Gould?" She had to flip back a page to reach Nolan, ahead two to reach Gould.

"Are you familiar with either name?" Gordon asked.

"Not particularly." Guardedly she looked up. "Should I be?"

Carter shot her a dry grin. "Only if you're into reading the business section of the paper," which he knew, for a fact, she was not, since they'd joked about it just the Sunday before, when she'd foisted that particular section on him in exchange for the editorials.

"Bill Nolan is from the Nolan Paper Mill family," Gordon explained. "He started in northern Maine, but has been working his way steadily southward. Even with the mills up north, he has a genuine respect for the land. A project like this would be right up his alley."

Carter agreed. "From what I hear, he's not out for a killing, which is good, since he won't get one here. What he'll get is a solid return on his investment. He'll be happy." Turning several pages in his lap, he said to Gordon, "Tell me about Gould. The name rings a bell, but I can't place it."

"Zach Gould is a competitor of mine."

"A banker?" Jessica asked.

"Retired, actually, though he's not yet sixty. He was the founder and president of Pilgrim Trust and its subsidiaries. Two years ago he had a heart attack, and since he was financially set, he took his doctor's advice and removed himself from the fray. So he dabbles in this and that. He's the type who would drop in at the site every morning to keep tabs on the progress. Nice guy. Lonely. His wife left him a few years back, and his children are grown. He'd like something like this."

Jessica nodded. Determined to read the fine print when she had time alone later, she turned to the next page. "John Sawyer?"

Gordon cleared his throat. "Now we start on what I like to call the adventurers. There are three of them. None can contribute as much money as any of these other three men, or you or Carter, but each has good reason not only to want to be involved but to be sure that the project is a success." He paused for only as long as it took Carter to flip to the right page. "John Sawyer lives here in town. He owns the small bookstore on Shore Drive. I'm sure you've been there, Jessica. It's called The Leaf Turner?"

She smiled. "Uh-huh. It's a charming place, small but quaint." Her smile wavered. "I don't remember seeing a man there, though. Whenever I've been in, Minna Larken has helped me."

Gordon nodded. "You've probably been in during the morning or early afternoon hours. That's when John is home taking care of his son. By the time two-thirty rolls around, he has high school girls come in to play with the boy while he goes to work."

"How old is the kid?" Carter asked.

"Three. He'll be entering school next year. Hopefully."

At the cautious way he'd added the last, Jessica grew cautious herself. "Something's wrong with him?"

"He has problems with his hearing and his eyesight. John had tried him in a preschool program, but he needs special attention. He'll have a tough time in the public kindergarten class. There is a school that would be perfect for him, but it's very expensive."

"So he could use a good money-making venture,"

Carter concluded. "But does he have funds for an initial investment?"

Gordon nodded. "His wife died soon after the boy was born. There was some money in life insurance. John was planning to leave it in the bank for the child's college education, but from the looks of things he won't get to college unless he gets special help sooner."

"How awful," Jessica whispered, looking helplessly from Gordon to Carter and back. "She must have been very young. How did she die?"

"I don't know. John doesn't talk about it. They were living in the Midwest when it happened. He moved here soon after. He's a quiet fellow, very bright but private. In many respects, the stakes are higher for John than for some of these others. But he's been asking me about investments, and this is the most promising to come along in months."

"But will the money come through in time for him?" Carter asked. "If all goes well, we could break ground this fall and do a fair amount of framing before winter sets in. We may be lucky enough to make some preconstruction sales, but most of the units won't be ready for aggressive marketing until next spring or summer, and then the bank loans will have to be paid off first. I can't imagine that any of us will see any raw cash for eighteen months to two years. So if he's going to need the money sooner—"

"I think he's covered for the first year or two. But when he realized that the child's education was going to be a longtime drain, he knew he had to do something else."

"By all means," Jessica said, "ask him to join us." She focused her attention on the next sheet. "Gideon Lowe." She glanced at Carter. "Didn't you mention him to me once?"

"To you and to Gordon. You did call him, then?" he asked the banker.

"By way of a general inquiry, yes. I named you as the contact. He thinks you're a very talented fellow."

"I think he's even more so. He takes pride in his work, which is more than I can say for some builders I know. Now that they're getting ridiculous fees for the simplest jobs, they've become arrogant. And lazy. Cold weather? Forget it—they can't work in cold weather. Rain? Same thing. And if the sun is out, they want to quit at twelve to play golf."

"I take it Gideon Lowe doesn't play golf?" Jessica asked.

"Not quite," Carter confirmed with a knowing grin. "Gideon would die strolling around a golf course. He's an energetic man. He needs something fast."

"Like squash?" she asked, because squash was Carter's game, precisely for its speed, as he'd pointed out to her in no uncertain terms.

"Like basketball. He was All-American in high school and would have gone to college on a basketball scholarship if he hadn't had to work to support his family."

Jessica's eyes widened. "Wife and kids?"

"Mother and sisters. His mother is gone now, and his sisters are pretty well-set, but he's too old to play college basketball. So he plays on a weekend league. Summers, he plays evenings." Recalling the few games he'd watched, Carter gave a slow head shake. "He's got incredible moves, for a big guy."

"And incredible enthusiasm," Gordon interjected. "He made me promise to call him as soon as I had something more to say about Crosslyn Rise."

"Then you should call him tomorrow," Jessica said, because Carter's recommendation was enough for her. She turned to the final page on her lap and her eyes widened. "Nina Stone?" She looked questioning at Gordon.

"Miss Stone called me," Gordon explained with a slight emphasis on the *me*. "She knows something of what you're doing since you've talked with her. She knows that I'm putting a group together. She wants to be included in that group and she has the money to do it."

Jessica sent him an apologetic look. "She was insistent?"

"You could say that."

"It's her way, Gordon. Some people see it as confidence, and it sells lots of houses. I can imagine, though, that it would be a little off-putting with someone like you, particularly on the phone. Wait until you meet her, though. She's a bundle of energy." As she said it, she had an idea. Turning to Carter, she said, "I'll bet she and Gideon would get along. You didn't say if he was married."

"He's not, but forget it. They are two very forceful personalities. They'd be at each other's throats in no time. Besides," he added, and a naughty gleam came into his eye, "they're all wrong physically. She's too little and he's too big. They'd have trouble making...it, uh, you know what I mean."

She knew exactly what he meant, but she wasn't about to elaborate in front of Gordon any more than he was. The only solace for her flaming cheeks was the rush of color to Carter's.

Fortunately, that color didn't hinder his thinking process. Recovering smoothly, he said, "If Nina has the money, I see no reason why she shouldn't invest." More serious, he turned to Jessica. "What's her motive?"

"She wants to go into business for herself. She wants the security of knowing she's her own boss. How about Gideon?"

"He wants the world to know he's his own boss. Respect is what he's after."

"Doesn't he have it now?"

"As a builder, yes. As a man who works with his hands, yes. As a man with brains as well as brawn, no. He's definitely got the brains—that's what makes him so successful as a builder. But people don't always see it that way. So he wants to be involved with the tie-and-jacket crowd this time."

Jessica could understand how Carter might understand Gideon better than some. He'd seen both sides. "If Gideon wants to invest, would that rule out his doing the building?"

"I hope not," Carter said, and looked questioningly at Gordon.

"I don't see why it would," Gordon answered. "The body of investors will be bound together by a legal agreement. If Gideon should decide to bid on the job and then lose out to another builder, his position in the consortium will remain exactly the same."

"There wouldn't be a conflict of interest?"

"Not at all. This is a private enterprise." He arched a brow toward Jessica. "Theoretically, you could pick your builder now, and make it part of the package."

"I wouldn't know who to pick," she said on impulse, then realized that she was supposed to be in charge. Recomposing herself, she said to Gordon, "You pointed out that I have to be willing to listen to people, especially when they know more about things than I do. I think that Carter will help me decide on the builder. Do you have any problem with that?"

"Me? None. None at all."

Something about the way he said it gave Jessica pause. "Are you sure?"

Gordon frowned at the papers before him for a minute

before meeting her gaze. "I may be out of line saying this—" his gaze broke off from hers for a minute to touch on Carter before returning "—but I didn't expect that you two would be so close."

"We're very close," Carter said, straightening slightly in his seat. "With a little luck we'll be married before long."

"Carter!" Jessica cried, then turned to Gordon. "Forget he said that. He gets carried away sometimes. You know how it is with men in the spring."

"It's summer," Carter reminded her, "and the only thing that's relevant about that is that you'll have a few weeks off between semesters at the end of August when we could take a honeymoon."

"Carter!" She was embarrassed. "Please, Gordon. Ignore this man."

To her chagrin, Gordon looked to be enjoying the banter. "I may be able to, but the reason I raise the issue is that other people won't." He grew more sober. "It was clear from the minute you two walked in here that something was going on. I think you ought to know just what that something is before you face the rest of this group. The last thing you want them to feel is that they're at the end of a rope, swinging forward and back as your relationship does."

"They won't," Jessica said firmly.

"Are you sure?"

"Very. This is a business matter. Whatever my relationship is or isn't with Carter, I'll be very professional. After all, the crux of the matter is Crosslyn Rise." She shot Carter a warning look. "And Crosslyn Rise is mine."

CHAPTER TEN

"YOU'RE BEING unreasonable," Carter suggested, lengthening his stride to keep up with her brisk pace as they walked along the street after leaving the bank. Jessica hadn't said more than two words to him since the exchange with Gordon. "What was so terrible about my saying I want to marry you?"

"Whether we marry is between you and me. It's none of Gordon's business."

"He had a point, though. People see us together, and they wonder. Some things you can't hide. We are close. And there was nothing wrong with your deferring to me on the matter of a builder. As your husband, I'd want you to do that."

"You're my architect," she argued crossly. "You're more experienced than I am on things like choosing a builder. My deferring to you was a business move."

"Maybe in hindsight. At the time, it was pure instinct. You deferred to me because you trust me, and it's not the first time that's happened. You've done it a lot lately. Crosslyn Rise may be yours, but you're glad to have someone to share the responsibility for it." He half turned to her as they walked. "That's what I want to do, Jess. I want to help you, and it's got nothing to do with Crosslyn Rise and everything to do with loving you. Giving and sharing are things I haven't done much of in my life, but I want to do them now."

She had trouble sustaining crossness when he said things like that. "You do. You are."

"So marriage is the next step. Why are you so dead set against it?"

"I'm not dead set against it. I'm just not ready for it."

"Do you love me?"

She swung around the corner with him a half step behind. "I've been married," she said without answering his question. "Things change once the vows are made. It's as if there's no more need to put on a show."

That stopped Carter short, but only for a minute. He trotted a pace to catch up. "You actually think I've been putting on a show? That's absurd! No man—especially not one who spent years feeling second-rate, being ashamed of who he was—is going to keep after a woman the way I have after you if he doesn't love her for sure. In case you haven't realized it, I do have my pride."

She shot him a glance and said more quietly, "I know that."

"But I'll keep asking you to marry me, because it's what I want more than anything else in my life."

"It's what you *think* you want."

"It's what I *want*." Grasping her arm, he drew her to a stop. "Why won't you believe that I love you?"

She looked up at him, swallowed hard and admitted, "I do believe it. But I don't think it will last. Maybe we should just live together. That way it won't be so painful if it ends."

"It won't end. And we're practically living together now, but that's not what I want. I want you driving my car, living under my roof, using my charge cards. And my name. I want you using my name."

She eyed him warily. "That's not a very modern wish."

"I don't give a damn. It's what I want. I want to take

care of you. I want to be strong for you. I resented my father because he rode through life on my mother's coattails. I refuse to do that."

Jessica was astonished. "You couldn't do that with me. I don't *have* any coattails. My life is totally unassuming. You're more dynamic than I could ever be. You're more active, more aggressive, more successful—"

He put a finger to her lips to stem the flow of words. "Not successful enough, if I can't convince you to marry me."

With a soft moan, she kissed the tip of his finger, then took it in her hand and wagged it, in an attempt at lightness. "Oh, Carter. The problem is with me. Not you. Me. I want to satisfy you, but I don't know if I can."

"You do."

"For now. But for how much longer? A few weeks? A month? A year?"

"Forever, if you'll give yourself the chance. Can't you try, Jessica?"

SHE COULD, SHE supposed, and each time she thought of marrying Carter, her heart took wing. Still, in the back of her mind, there was always an inkling of doubt. More so than either dating or living together, marriage made a public statement about a man and a woman. If that marriage fell apart, the statement was no less public and far more humiliating—especially when the male partner was Carter Malloy. Because Carter Malloy was liked and respected by most everyone he met. That fact became clear to Jessica over the next few weeks as they met with Gordon, with lawyers, with various investors. Despite Jessica's role as the owner of Crosslyn Rise, Carter emerged as the project's leader. He didn't ask for the position, in fact he sat back quietly during many of the discussions, but he had a straight head on his shoulders and seemed to be the one, more than any other, who had a pulse on the various elements involved—architectural plans, building prospects, environmental and marketing considerations, and Jessica.

Especially Jessica. She found that she was leaning on him more and more, relying on him for the cool, calm confidence that she too often lacked. Gone were the days when her life maintained a steady emotional keel. She seemed to be living with highs and lows. Some had to do with Crosslyn Rise—highs when she was confident it would become something worthy of its past, and lows when the commercial aspects of the project stood out. Some had to do with Carter—highs when she was in his arms and there was no doubt whatsoever about the strength of his love, and lows when she was apart from him, when she eyed him objectively, saw a vibrant and dynamic man and wondered what he ever saw in her.

As the weeks passed, she felt as though she were heading toward a pair of deadlines. One had to do with Crosslyn Rise, with the progress of the project, with the approach of the trucks and bulldozers and the knowledge that once they broke ground, there was no going back.

The other had to do with Carter. He would only wait so long. He'd been so good about not mentioning marriage, but she knew he was frustrated. When August came and it was apparent there would be no honeymoon, he planned a vacation anyway, spiriting her away for a week in the Florida Keys.

"See?" he teased when they returned. "We made it through a whole week in each other's company nonstop, and I still love you."

By late September, he was pointing out that they'd made it for five months and were going strong. Jessica didn't need that pointed out. Her life revolved around Carter. He was her first thought in the morning and her last thought at night, and though there were times when she scolded herself for being so close to him, so dependent on him, she couldn't do differently—particularly with the ground-breaking at Crosslyn Rise approaching fast. It was an emotional time for her, and Carter was her rock.

Even the most solid of rocks had its weak spot, though, and Jessica was Carter's. He adored her, couldn't imagine a life without her, but the fact that she wouldn't marry him, that she didn't even say that she loved him was eroding his self-confidence and hence, his patience. When he was with her, he was fine; he loved her, she loved him, he wasn't about to ruin their time together. Alone though, he brooded. He felt thwarted. He was tired of waiting. Enough was enough.

Such were the thoughts that he was trying unsuccessfully to bury when, late in the afternoon on the last Wednesday in September, he drove to Crosslyn Rise. Before Jessica had left him in Boston that morning, she had promised to cook him dinner. He hadn't spoken with her during the day, which annoyed him, since he wanted *her* to call *him* once in a while, rather than the other way around. He needed the reassurance. She wouldn't say she loved him, so he needed her to show she cared in other ways. A phone call would have been nice.

But there'd been no call. And when he opened the back door and came into the kitchen, there didn't look to be anything by way of pots and pans on the stove. Nothing smelled as though it were cooking. Jessica was nowhere in sight.

"Jessica?" he called, then did it again more loudly. *"Jessica?"*

He was through the kitchen and into the hall when he heard her call, "I'll be right there." He guessed she was upstairs in the bedroom—the master bedroom with its king-size bed, which she'd started using when he'd begun to sleep over regularly—and that thought did bring a small smile to his face. He was early. She always freshened up, changed clothes, combed out her hair when she knew he was coming. So she wasn't quite done. That was okay. He'd help her. He'd even help her with dinner.

Which went to show how lovesick he was. The thought of being with her, of maybe getting in a little hanky-panky before dinner was enough to wipe all the frustrating thoughts from his mind. And it wasn't just that the lovemaking could do it, but when they made love, he knew that she loved him. She came alive in his arms, showed him a side of her that the rest of the world never saw. No woman could respond to him—or give—in that way if she wasn't in love.

He took the stairs two at a time, but he hadn't reached the top when she came down the hall. One look at her face and he knew there would be no hanky-panky. Indeed, she looked as though she'd newly brushed her hair and changed her clothes, even put on a little makeup, but the dab of blusher didn't hide her pallor.

"What's wrong?" he asked, coming to an abrupt halt where he was, then taking the rest of the stairs more cautiously.

"We have a problem," she said in a tight voice.

"What kind of problem?"

"With Crosslyn Rise. With the construction."

He let out a relieved breath. "A problem with the project I can handle. A problem with us I can't." He reached for her. "Come here, baby. I need a hug." Enveloping her in his arms, he held her tightly for a minute, then relaxed his hold and kissed her lightly. She was the one who clung then, her face pressed to his neck, her arms trembling. There was something almost desperate about it, which made him a little nervous. "He-ey." He laughed softly and held her back. "It can't be all that bad."

"It is," she said. "The town zoning commission won't give us a permit. They say our plans don't conform with their regulations."

Putting both hands on her shoulders, Carter ducked his head and stared at her. "What?"

"No permit."

"But why? There's nothing unusual about what we're doing. We're following all the standard rules, and we did go through the town for the subdivision allowances. So what are they picking on?"

"The number of units. The spacing of the units." She tossed up a hand, and her voice was a little wild. "I don't know. I couldn't follow it. When I got the call, all I could think of was that here we are, ready to break ground, and now the whole thing's in danger."

"No." Slipping an arm around her shoulder, he brought her down beside him on the top step. "Not in danger. It only means a little more work. Who did you speak with?"

Jessica looked at her hands, which were knotted in her lap. "Elizabeth Abbott. She's the chairwoman of the zoning commission."

"I know Elizabeth Abbott. She's a reasonable woman."

"She wasn't particularly reasonable with me. She informed me that the decision was made this morning at a meeting, and that we could apply for a waiver, but she suggested I call back the trucks. She didn't see how we could break ground until next spring or summer at the earliest." Jessica raised agonized eyes to Carter's. "Do you know what a delay will mean? Carter, I can't afford a delay. I barely have the money to keep Crosslyn Rise going through another winter. I'm already up to my ears in loans to the bank. The longer we're held up, the longer it will be until we see money on the other end. That may be just fine for men like Nolan and Heavey and Gould, and it may be okay for you, but for me and the rest of us—it's too late!"

"Shh, honey. It's not too late." But he was frowning. "We'll work something out."

"She was vehement."

Releasing her, Carter propped his elbows on his thighs and let his hands hang between his knees. "Small towns aren't usually this rigid with one of their leading citizens."

"I'm no leading citizen."

"Crosslyn Rise is. It's the leading parcel of land here."

"That's probably why they're being so picky. They want to know exactly who's coming in and when."

Carter shook his head. "Even the snobbiest of towns don't do things like this. Something stinks."

Jessica held her breath for a minute. She looked at Carter, but his frown gave away nothing of his deeper thoughts. Finally, unable to wait any longer, she said, "It's Elizabeth Abbott. I could tell from her voice. She's the force behind this."

He eyed her cautiously. "How well do you know her?"

"Only enough to say hello on the street. We never had anything in common. I'm not saying that she's deliberately sabotaging our progress, but she's clearly against what we're doing. She seemed pleased to be making the call, and she wasn't at all willing to even *consider* accommodating us." Jessica's composure began to slip. "They could hold a special meeting, Carter. How difficult would it be for three people to meet for an hour? When I asked, she said that wasn't done. She said that they'd be more than happy to consider our waiver at their next scheduled meeting in February." Her voice went higher. "But we can't wait that long, Carter. We can't wait that long."

Carter continued to frown, but the curve of his mouth suggested disgust.

"Talk to her," Jessica said softly. "She'll listen to you."

His eyes shot to hers. "What makes you say that?"

"Because you had something going with her once. She told me."

His expression grew grim. "Did she tell you that it happened seven years ago, when I was still living in New York, and that it lasted for one night?"

"Go to her. You could soften her up."

"One night, Jessica, and do you want to know why?" His eyes held hers relentlessly. "Because she was something I had to do, something I had to get out of my system. That's all. Nothing more. We were classmates here in town way back when. She was a witness to some of my most stupid stunts. Far more than you in some ways, she was synonymous in my mind with the establishment around here. So when she came up to me that night—it was at a reception in one of the big hotels, I don't even remember which—I had this sudden need to prove to myself that I'd really made it. So I took her to bed. And it was the most unsatisfying thing I've ever done. I didn't see her again in New York, and I haven't seen her since I moved back here."

Jessica's heart was alternately clenching tightly and pounding against her ribs. She believed every word Carter said—and the truth was echoed in his eyes—still she pushed on. "But she'd like to see you again. I could tell. Maybe if you gave her a call—"

"I'll call one of the other members of the commission."

"She's the chairwoman. She's the one who can make

things happen, but only if she wants. Talk to her, Carter. Make her want to help us."

Carter was beginning to feel uneasy. Sitting back against the banister to put a little more space between them, he asked cautiously, "How would you suggest I do that?"

Jessica had been tossing possibilities around for the better part of the afternoon, which was why she hadn't called him earlier to tell him about the problem. The solution she'd found was as abhorrent as it was necessary, but she was feeling desperate on several counts. "Smile a little. Sweet-talk her. Maybe even take her to dinner."

"I don't want to take her to dinner."

"You take prospective clients to dinner."

"Prospective clients take *me* to dinner."

"Then make an exception this time. Take her to dinner. Wine and dine her. She'll listen to you, Carter."

"Okay. You and I will take her to dinner."

"You're missing the point!" Jessica cried.

"No," Carter said slowly. His eyes were chilly, reflecting the cold he felt inside. "I don't think I am. I think that the point—correct me if I'm wrong—is that I should do whatever needs to be done to get a waiver from the commission, and if that means screwing Elizabeth Abbott, so be it." While he didn't miss the way Jessica flinched at his choice of words, he was too wrapped up in his own emotions to care. The coldness inside him was fast turning to anger. "Am I right?"

The harsh look in his eyes held Jessica silent for a minute.

"Am I right?" he repeated more loudly.

"Yes," she whispered.

"I don't believe it," he murmured, and though his voice was lower, the look in his eyes didn't soften. "I don't believe it. How can you ask me to do something like that?"

"It may be the only way we can go ahead with this thing."

"Is that all that matters to you? This *thing?* Crosslyn Rise?"

"Of course not."

"Could've fooled me. But then, it's no wonder. You won't say you love me, you won't say you'll marry me, and now you come up with this idiotic scheme."

"It's not idiotic. It would work. Elizabeth Abbott has a reputation for things like this."

"Well, I don't. I wouldn't demean myself by doing something like this. I'm no goddamned gigolo!" Rising from the stairs, he stormed down three steps before turning to glare at her. "I love you, Jessica. If I've told you once, I've told you dozens of times, and I'm not just blowing off hot air. I love you. That means *you're* the woman I want. Not Elizabeth Abbott."

Jessica swallowed hard. "But you were with her once—"

"And it was a mistake. I knew it at the time, and I know it even more now. I won't go so far as to say that she's holding up things for Crosslyn Rise because of me, because even when she used to call me and I wouldn't see her, she was gracious. I never thought of her as being vindictive, and I'm not about to now, but I won't sleep with her." Agitated, he thrust a hand through his hair. "How can you ask me to do that?" he demanded, and through the anger came an incredible hurt. "Don't I mean anything to you?"

Jessica was so stunned by the emotions ranging over his face that it was a minute before she could whisper, "You know you do."

But he was shaking his head. "Maybe I was fooling

myself. Part of love is respect, and if you respected me for who and what I am, you wouldn't be asking this of me." Again he thrust a hand into his hair; this time it stopped midway, as though he were so embroiled in his thoughts that he couldn't keep track of his gestures. "Did you honestly think I'd go along? Did you think I'd seduce her? Did you think I'd really be able to get it *up?*" He swore softly, and his hand fell to his side. "I blew it somewhere, Jessica. I blew it."

In all the time she'd known him, Jessica had never seen him look defeated, but he did now. It was there in the bow of his shoulders and the laxness of his features, either of which put him a galaxy apart from the angry and vengeful boy he'd been so long ago. She knew he'd changed, but the extent of the change only then hit her. She was still reeling from it when she caught the sheen of moisture in his eyes. Her knuckles came hard to her mouth.

"I'd do most anything for you, Jessica," he said in a gut-wrenching tone. "So help me, if you asked me to lie spread-eagle on the railroad track until the train blew its whistle, I'd probably do it, but not this." Swallowing once, he tore his eyes from hers, turned and started down the stairs.

"Carter?" she whispered against her knuckles. When he didn't stop, she took her hand away. "Carter?" Still he didn't stop, but reached the bottom of the stairs and headed for the door. She rose to her feet and called him again, more loudly this time, then started down. When he opened the door and went through, she quickened her step, repeating his name softly now and with a frantic edge. By the time she reached the door, he was halfway to his car.

"Carter?" Her eyes were filled with tears. "Carter!" She was losing him. "Carter, wait!" But he was at the driver's side, reaching for the door. "Carter, stop!" He was the light of her life, leaving her. Panicked, she opened her mouth and screamed, *"Carter!"*

The heartrending sound, so unusual coming from her, stopped him. He raised his head wearing such a broken look that she couldn't move for another minute. But she had to keep him there, had to touch him, had to tell him all he meant to her. Forcing her legs into action, she ran toward the car.

Stopping directly before him, she raised a hand halfway to his face, wavered, mustered enough courage to graze his cheek with a finger before pulling back, then went with her own need and slipped her hand to the back of his neck. "I'm sorry," she tried to say, but the words were more mouthed than anything. "I'm sorry." She put her other hand flat on his chest, moved it up, finally slid it around his neck, went in close to him and managed a small sound against his throat. "I'm sorry, Carter, I'm sorry. I love you so much."

Carter stood very still for a long minute before slowly lifting his hands to her hips. "What?" he whispered hoarsely.

"I love you. Love you."

It was another long minute before he let out a breath, slid his arms around her and gathered her in.

Unable to help herself, Jessica began to cry. She could no more stop the tears than the words. "That was s-such a stupid thing for me to think of—and an insult t-to you. But something happened to me wh-when she said she'd known you before. Maybe I wanted to know what w-would happen—she's very attractive—but I l-love you so much—I don't know what I'd d-do if you ever left me."

He buried his face in her hair. Even muffled, his voice sounded rough. "You were pushing me away."

"I didn't know what else t-to do."

"You should have called me right away." He tightened his hold in a punishing way, and his voice remained gruff. "There's a solution, Jessica. There's always a solution. But you've got to keep your priorities straight. Top priority is us."

She knew that now. For as long as she lived, she'd never forget the sight of big, bad Carter Malloy with tears in his eyes. They had been tears of pain, and she'd put them there. They were humbling and horrifying. She never wanted to see them again.

Going up on tiptoe, she coiled her arms more tightly around his neck. "I love you," she whispered over and over again until finally he took her face in his hands and held her back.

"What do you want?" he whispered. His face was inches from hers, his thumbs brushing tears from under her glasses while his palms held her still. "Tell me."

"You. Just you."

"But what do you want?"

She knew that he needed to hear the words, and though they represented the ultimate exposure, she was ready for that, too. "I want to marry you. I want to take your name and use your credit cards and drive your car. I want to have your babies."

Carter didn't react, simply looked at her as though he wasn't quite sure whether to believe her. So, clutching his wrists, she added, "I mean it. All of it. I think it's what I've wanted since the first time we made love, but I've been so afraid. You're so much more than me—"

"I'm not."

"You are. You've done so much more, come so much further in life, and that makes you so much more interesting. I want to marry you. I do, Carter. But if we got married and then you wanted out, I think I'd *die,* I love you so much."

"I won't want out," he said.

"But I didn't know that for sure until just now."

"I've been telling it to you for weeks."

"But I didn't know." She closed her eyes and whispered, "Oh, Carter, I don't ever want to lose you. Not ever."

"Then marry me. That's the first way to tie a man down."

Her eyes came open. "I'll marry you."

"And give me kids. That's the second way to tie a man down."

"Okay."

"And keep on teaching, because I'm so *proud* of what you do."

"You are?" she asked with a hesitant half smile.

"Damn it, yes," he said and crushed her to him. "I've always been proud of you. I'll always *be* proud of you— whether you're a scholar, mother of my kids, my wife or my woman."

Jessica smiled against his neck, feeling lighter and happier than she'd ever felt before. "I do love you," she whispered.

"Then trust me, too," he said. Taking her by the shoulders, he put her back a step and eyed her sternly. "Trust that I mean what I say when I tell you I love you. I don't want other women. I never *have* wanted other women the way I want you. I've never asked another woman to marry me, but I've asked you a dozen times. I *choose* you. I don't *have* to marry you. I *choose* you. I *want* to marry you."

"I get the point," she murmured, feeling a little shame-faced but delighted in spite of it.

"Do you also get the point about priorities?" he went on, and though a sternness remained in his voice, there was also an exciting vibrancy. "Crosslyn Rise is beautiful. It is venerable and stately and historic. I've got a whole lot of time invested in it, and money now, too, but if I had to choose between the Rise and you, there'd be no contest. I'd turn my back on the time, the money and the Rise just to have you. And I'd do it without a single regret." His eyes grew softer. "So I don't want you worrying about the zoning commission. We'll call Gordon and Gideon and the others. We'll work something out. But all that is secondary. Do you understand?"

"I do," she whispered, and it was true. In those few horrible minutes when she had seen his tears, when he had walked away from her and she'd had the briefest glimpse of the emptiness of life without him, Crosslyn Rise had been the last thing on her mind. Yes, the Rise was in trouble, but she could handle it. With Carter by her side, she could handle anything.

* * * * *